THE CHANGING

THE CHANGING

DAVY TAYLOR

authorHOUSE®

AuthorHouse™
1663 Liberty Drive
Bloomington, IN 47403
www.authorhouse.com
Phone: 1-800-839-8640

Published by AuthorHouse   03/13/2012

ISBN: 978-1-4567-8704-2 (sc)
ISBN: 978-1-4567-8797-4 (e)

CHAPTER ONE

Looking up at the clock, he noticed that he had just over another hour to get the job done; a job that he didn't want to do in the first place, but a job that would get him the eternal gratitude of the managing director (or so the sod had said!)

He thought of the MD—the advertising company's mainman; the undisputed genius of toilet rolls, TV dinners and subconscious messages urging you to buy, buy, buy . . . . and a sweaty, balding, ignorant git, who was too wrapped up in his own self-importance to notice that his beloved workforce genuinely hated his hideous persona.

"Sod this for a game of soldiers," Mick silently said to himself, and again noticed how the clock hands were deliberately going at the speed of sound just to annoy him.

He thought of the predicament he was in. A paste-up job for a local magazine's star interview—star being a very loose term. He had personally never heard of Nellie Dewhurst, the area's 'famous soap extra', but according to Walters—the MD from Hell—it was a "rush job" and Mick had until 5 pm to get it done—only fifty minutes away.

Mick found it slightly amusing that with all the work that Walters Associates Ltd received for lavish TV and highbrow magazines, that the podgy advertising maestro should still try to curry favour with the local businesses. Still, at least he was away from the back-stabbing pit he had belonged to in the West End, and at least he was now freelance, his own boss, able to discuss his own terms—well, that was the idea anyway. However, what was it about Walters that immediately made him turn into a 'yes man'? Mind you, self-assertiveness had never been his thing. Deep down he knew that given half the chance, he could be quite a coward.

He sometimes imagined himself in a knight's shining suit of armour, racing up to the dragon's lair to rescue his damsel in distress. He would boldly approach the green, scaly skinned monster, and as the dragon breathed out its fearsome fire, Mighty Mick would scream out loud . . . . "Blimey that's hot. I must just rush off to get my factor 38—ya can't be too careful these days y'know" and he would scarper, leaving his beloved to curse him until she was blue in the face!

It was fine to joke about his lack of confidence, but the truth of the matter was that it plagued him to a horrible degree.

The psychologist he had seen at the University College Hospital—he didn't want to go, but his GP had said that there must be something behind his constant ill health—was particularly fascinated by him, and confused that despite his feelings of inadequacy he was such a hit with the opposite sex. Couldn't he just transfer those feelings of bravery when chatting up women to other areas of his life?

"You never know Mick, it might just work." the dark skinned psychologist had said and flashed his pearly whites. What was his name again? George something or other. He was definitely Greek though, or maybe Turkish.

In theory, George's advice seemed valid enough, but the truth of the matter was that Mick had never had a 'serious' girlfriend in his life, and the only time he had managed to 'get off' with any girl was with Hanna, a tall Swedish girl from Uppsala, who was only in London to work as an 'au-pair' for a couple of months. That, alas, was fourteen months ago, and at twenty-eight, Mick was starting to feel very much left on the shelf.

It could've been so much different though, and as he stared down at the black and white patchwork of the paste-up, he recalled the girl who eight years earlier had taken his heart, his spirit, his very soul and had never given them back. Why did she leave the city? Why hadn't she returned the love that he knew that she felt for him? And why did the memory of her still haunt him all these years later?

"It's nice to see that you give your work a lot of thought Micky boy, or is the stress of doing rush jobs beginning to get to you?" Walters, never a man to stand on ceremony, had slid into the studio and stood looking at Mick with an expression that mixed amusement with blatant annoyance.

Mick quickly swivelled around on his chair and gazed at the ruddy, piggish features of the MD, trying to ignore that badly fitted, grey, double breasted, polyester suit that Walters always wore. Did he really have a wardrobe full of suits exactly the same, and equally as bad fitting? At least, that's what Jackson, the artist on the next board had told him anyway . . .

"Erm . . . no" stuttered Mick. "Actually, I think that with a little luck you could have my latest masterpiece at say . . . five to five?" and with that immediately groaned inwardly. Five to five would be pushing it to say the least.

"Excellent," smiled Walters. "I knew I could count on you. I won't forget this favour as you know my policy of keeping our neighbours happy. I'll probably treat you to some of my lovely Helen's cooking as a thank you!" And feeling that he had just offered Mick the reward of a lifetime, sloped off to his garishly decorated office, which came complete with a dozen choice photographs of the 'lovely Helen', and hundreds of plastic artefacts from all over the world that Walters felt underlined his wealthy status, but which Mick felt mirrored his personality.

"Yup! There's an incentive if ever I heard one. Did you know that Mrs Pig models her rock cakes on the one at Gibraltar?" Mick, who had just taken a mouthful of lukewarm coffee, had to spit it out again as he laughed at the dry wit of Jackson, who had been watching this brief exchange with fascination. Deep down he knew that Mick was in some sort of awe regarding Walters, but was too tactful to ever mention it to his colleague.

Mick looked at his friend, and with a sudden gravity to his voice muttered "I'm getting out of here Jacko. I don't think I can take much more of his condescending crap. I don't understand why I haven't done it earlier. He can shove his grotty suits and his lovely Helen up that sweaty backside of his."

Jackson smiled, and in a taunting but joking manner replied "But where are you gonna go? After a year at chez Walters, surely the only way to go is up? Are you absolutely sure that you're up to the task? Won't you miss the humbleness of our beloved guru, and the exquiteness of Helen's fabulous, flat flans?"

"Yeah, I'll be heartbroken," Mick retorted sarcastically, "but if I'm to be honest the whole rat race is getting to me. I think I'm gonna have to leave London for a while."

"Do you think that you'll come back—I mean to this rat race of ours?"

"Maybe, maybe not. It doesn't really matter. I just know that I have to leave London for a bit. Call it a feeling in my water."

Jackson, looking serious for a change, enquired further "So where to? The countryside? The seaside? A new country altogether perhaps?"

Mick thought for a moment. "The seaside. I've always wanted to live by the seaside. Maybe I can find some work in Brighton or Margate—somewhere like that."

After a brief, untuneful burst of 'Oh I do like to be beside the seaside', Jackson, in puzzled tone, giggled "The seaside? Why on earth the seaside? You can't go swimming at one of Britain's beaches y'know, you'll just come out green—like one of Helen's potatoes. At least that's what I've heard anyway!"

"What, you've heard of the green sea or the green potatoes?"

"You know what I mean! Have you really thought this through mate? I'd hate to lose you as a friend you know."

Mick looked into space and then looked quickly at his colleague "You won't lose my friendship Jacko, together we've been through too much at this dump. I dunno what it is. It just seems like a good idea at the moment, that's all."

Jackson sighed "Well, make sure you get it clear in your head first eh? I mean, you wouldn't want to have to come back crawling to that geezer now, would you?" and he nodded towards the oncoming bulk of Walters. Mick took the hint, and realising that the Nellie Dewhurst interview had come to an abrupt halt, re-started his work at an even quicker pace than before.

As Mick walked out of the advertising company's offices and started to walk down Upper Street and towards the Angel tube station, he wondered why he had told Jacko of a plan to go to the seaside. He had never wanted to go anywhere near the seaside in his life, so why did he say such a thing now? It was almost as if somebody had taken the idea and surgically implanted it into his head.

He breathed in the evening air and looked around at the North London street which he had known all his life. As he did so, he noticed the charms of a young girl in jeans and a brown, leather jacket, her blonde hair brushed behind her ears in a manner that reminded him of a girl he loved many years ago.

As he admired her backside wandering off into the distance, he absently remarked to no-one in particular "Still, I have to admit the sights still aren't so bad around here. Shame she wouldn't fancy me though." And looking down at a dishevelled, meths carrying tramp that sat against one of the walls of the tube station's entrance said "You'd probably have more chance than me matey" and tossed the hobo a pound coin.

The tramp raised his hand to his head in a sloppy salute, and drunkenly regarded the musing graphic artist heading for the escalators.

Hmmm, maybe if I just turn my head slightly to the right, maybe push the front of my hair back a little . . . . maybe I should invest in some hair gel . . . never have been able to control this bloody mop. Yeah, I think I look quite the adonis today . . . I wonder if that rather Kylie Minogueish young lady has noticed that I'm having one of my good looking days today . . . I guess not . . . I don't think she likes the look of my boots . . . maybe I should've polished them after all . . . fuck, there's always something that makes you look like a complete and utter turd. Thank you God, you really are determined to keep me single aren't you? What about you young lady? Have you noticed how handsome I'm looking today? Nah, she knows that because I'm travelling by tube, I can't possibly have a car. Why would she want to go out with a guy who doesn't have a car? Still, maybe if I did gel this bit back . . . .

. . . . And so the man in the tube train window kept staring back at him, kept telling him that he was one of the world's greatest enigmas, and that there was no reason for this constant torture that he put himself through day after day. There was always this same old scenario for him to face but he was still perplexed and oh so alone. Is it any wonder that he wished that he could go back in time; back to when he had a chance with the most wonderful woman in the world, and when he blew it like a good one.

Kylie's lookalike had got off at King's Cross, as did Mick, and as he walked towards the entrance that would take him to the Piccadilly line, he found himself walking behind the Aussie star's twin.

'Maybe she'll notice me', he thought to himself in one of his more ridiculously optimistic moods. 'Maybe she'll appreciate that I haven't chatted her up and see me for the great guy that I am.'

He sighed a genuine sigh of disappointment as the girl headed towards the station's 'Way Out' sign, and as the dank aroma of freshly urinated upon walls insulted his nostrils, he carried on walking through the station until he was standing on the Piccadilly line platform, and gazing at the board that was informing him that the next train was terminating at Cockfosters.

He rubbed his eyes and the bridge of his nose. The tingling in his nasal passages were telling him that even though he had got through most of June without the dreaded Hay Fever, it was now going to come back with a vengeance, and more often than not, there was nothing that he could do about it. The 'cures' that he had tried had all been hopeless. Pills, sprays, injections, you name it Mick had tried it.

Last summer he had begged his GP to give him something stronger, but as usual, the doctor had put it down to Mick's imagination . . . well, he hadn't actually said that, but Mick had known what he meant.

Absently squeezing his left nostril, Mick felt a rush of wind emerge from the black tunnel on his left. It woke him from his thoughts and ruffled his hair.

'Shit! Just what I need, my bloody hair looking like a tree. Oh why don't I have the fucking lot cut off.' He cursed more bad luck and moved towards the platform's edge.

The rumbling sound of an approaching train became louder, but even though the wind had died down, Mick got as close to the platform's edge as possible, until the tips of his boots were touching just where the platform dropped off onto the electrified track.

Old newspapers blew up that same track, and there behind them were the two bright eyes of the monster that could help him so damn much. All he needs is one large dive, and even the annoyed moans of the commuters wouldn't be able to touch him as his splattered brain stops them from heading towards fucking Cockfosters. Oh surely it isn't that easy?

In a matter of seconds, Mick's life had been replayed through his mind, and now that he thought about it, there was only one person to blame for his sorry state—himself. As far as he was concerned, every woman in the universe would see him as a man without guts, without spirit, without a life, and therefore find him totally repulsive.

He closed his eyes and bowed to the oncoming train. A hundred thousand thoughts flashed through his confused and depressed mind. Thoughts of his family, in particular his mother who was so proud of her artist son without ever knowing or understanding or wanting to understand the angst and anger he felt towards the world: then his father, who he knew loved him in his own way but had never taken the time to tell him just in case he grew up a 'poofter'. Images of family, of friends, of colleagues and then of her and what she represented; her and the pain that she had inflicted and which was bound to curse him for the rest of his life, for every woman would and could see that despite the lack of the word 'loser' tattooed on his forehead, that was exactly what he was.

The wind was getting stronger in the slow motion replay of this moment, his hair ruffled again and this time he didn't care. He felt numb, confused, hurt, angry and alone. The tips of his boots slid even more slowly over the edge of the platform and the smell of urine and dust assaulted his nostrils once more as the face of a pin striped businessman opened his mouth in horror. Mick Rogers wanted to take one final journey.

CHAPTER TWO

"Ouch! Get off ya stupid girl," he said in the manner that the little girl had come to know and love. She knew that Paul enjoyed the way that she pestered him, even when she was pulling his right ear to its limits like now. With a delighted scream, the girl shot across the room to her beloved Harry—a hamster with attitude, and one that Paul had wished he had never bought her (well, what would you think if you had been bitten five times by the rat?) Still, Emily thought the world of it, and if it kept her quiet . . . .

At least he had done something right. He laid back on the suede settee and gazed at the ceiling, his well deserved nap having been shattered by his boisterous relative. The paint was peeling in the corner of the room, and the light shade had what looked like a cobweb hanging from it.

"I guess that I'll have to get rid of that," he moaned to himself.

"What Paul?" replied Emily, and ran over to the resigned twenty-something and grabbed his ear. She ran back to Harry, giggling loudly.

"Calm down Em! I've told you time and time again about running in the house." Emily looked back at him with her cool gaze and stuck out her tongue. He was used to Em and her lively ways but he still wondered how the hamster could have such a calming influence on her? It was almost as if she was mothering it.

During the first few months of her stay she had been an absolute angel; the absolute epitome of a well behaved child. She rarely cried, and seemed to talk to anyone who wanted to talk to her. Then she hit nine and Paul and Maria knew that life would never be the same again. Their angelic lodger had discovered her overdrive button and her finger was constantly on it.

He didn't really have much time for children. It was bad enough that Maria had constantly badgered him for kids, but since the sudden death of Maria's mother, there had been nowhere for Em to go, and the feelings of fatherhood were being dragged screaming from him; it was an uncomfortable feeling, but it had to be said that he had tried his best.

Five years ago, when he had first started seeing Maria, his new partner had confessed that what she was really looking forward to was having children, and as soon as possible. Looking back it could be said that shouldn't have been much of a surprise, as Maria's mum had delivered Maria to the world when she was just eighteen, just two years younger than the girl he had met in a local pub. However, Maria had become so engrossed in her nursing career that babies had become extinct from the menu—until eight months ago, when his wife of only a year had brought home a friend's bundle of joy—oh how she had simpered.

"Look Pauly, he's looking at you. Look at his tiny handies. Isn't he gorgeous? You are my liddle, booty darling. Yesh you are then."

And then the dreaded words . . . . "Doesn't it make you wish you had one? Oh wouldn't it be fantastic Paul. Paul?"

He had gone into the kitchen, but he knew that the ghost of Maria's motherhood had risen again. If only he had known what was to happen next.

Laying upon the sofa, he gazed at the long, blonde locks of the mischievous child and couldn't help but feel a small laugh emerge from his throat. She had a way about her of making you warm to her innocent charm.

She could be pinching you with a pair of sharp pliers, and yet you would still forgive that cheeky grin.

He suddenly felt a wave of panic, an irrational feeling of deep protection towards the girl that was encouraging an stubborn Harry to use his exercise wheel.

What when she gets older? What when the boys start following her? Chatting her up? She is gonna be an absolute stunner no doubt about it, so how does a guardian protect such innocence from the evil of the male urges?

Emily laughed, and for one moment he believed that she had picked up on his sudden, protective feelings. Instead, she was allowing the curious rodent to sit on her head, where it was doing an intense investigation of Em's yellow hair.

What did she look like? How could you be strict with such a child? He laughed, and in a warm voice attracted the girl's attention.

"Hey Em, I'd be careful if I were you, he seems to be heading towards the back of your dress, then you'll never . . . ."

His voice trailed off as Emily swung around and focused on Paul's grinning face. She said nothing but he felt the colour drain from his cheeks and a cool breeze blew through his soul.

He checked himself and immediately thought of Diane, Maria's mother. Yes, that was it. Diane had a way of looking like that, as if you had just said something blasphemous, but in reality, she would just be paying attention to your words.

Sometimes he saw Maria looking that way, but whereas Maria had dark hair, Em had inherited Diane's flaxen tresses and that just enhanced any similarity. It was freaky, and the night of Diane's death had flooded into his mind.

It was strange that it should have happened two days after Maria had brought the baby home. Maybe a sign of things to come? He often felt things happened for a reason. Seventy years (if you're lucky) and goodnight Vienna? No, there had to be more to it than that.

They had been sitting on the sofa, with only inches between them, but for inches read miles; another stony silence would tell you that another barney had taken place. The only person talking was a northern guy on Maria's favourite soap, and she was staring too fixedly at the screen.

He had been so within himself in that scenario, that the shrieking of the telephone had made him almost climb up the wall. He had looked at Maria, and she had looked back at him. With a furrowed brow he got up to answer the intruding noise.

He stood there, his right leg crossed in front of his left one, and with his right hand pressed against the damp wall. He strained to hear the tinny, female voice on the other end of the line, and motioned to his partner to turn the TV down.

Maria glared at him with annoyance. Why does he have to make a big deal about everything? He only wants the TV turned down just to annoy her. He never turns it down during his favourite programme! Pressing the remote's button she sunk back into the armchair and turned her head again towards the figure leaning against the wall. Her body went cold as she saw the look of horror that had crossed Paul's face.

"Paul? Paul? What is it? What's happened? Who is it?" But the nurse's questions were falling on deaf ears as Paul carefully sat on the floor, her face still carrying a look of horror.

It seemed to take years, but at last Paul gazed blankly at his wife and opened his stuttering mouth.

"Yes, she is here. Yes, I think I should tell her. Hmm, okay, we we we'll leave as soon as possible. Thank you, you are very kind. Goodbye."

He stood up, and with a shaky hand replaced the phone onto its receiver. His eyes met Maria's and she knew then that something had gone wrong. Horribly wrong.

A thousand thoughts rushed through her mind. Someone very ill? Missing? Dead? Who? An aunt? An Uncle? Mother? The last thought found an outlet, and as the word formed itself on Maria's lips Paul sensed it, and rushing over to his bride, he sat down next to her and grasped her hand . . . . oh so tightly.

"Mother?" Paul nodded and told her everything that he had been told on the phone. Diane had been at her local, celebrating a birthday for a male colleague of hers. They had been dancing all evening and having the time of their life.

"It seems," said Paul with a dry mouth, "that your mum has collapsed. We need to get to the hospital as soon as we can but it's not sounding good."

With a chilling scream, Maria raced to the bedroom and Paul looked on feeling numb. He could've broken the news more gently surely? He was never good at talking about things like this.

With feelings of anger at his tactless words and love and despair for his devastated wife, he had reached out to her and showed enough true distress for Maria to realise that he was hurting too.

Before leaving for the hospital, Maria pulled herself away again from her husband, and with new horror on her face. she spoke the thought that had only just occurred to her distraught mind.

"What about Emily? My God Paul, what's going to happen to Emily?"

A high pitched screech hit his ears, and he realised that he was back in the present again, and Emily was complaining that the disobedient Harry had scratched the back of her neck.

It had been decided that as Maria's father had gone AWOL not long after Emily's birth, and as other relative's "really didn't have the room for her, although otherwise we would love her to stay," then there was only one place for her to go—big sister's. Of course it took some getting used to, having a yellowed-haired imp around the house, but he could get used to it.

As if in a sudden, hideous feeling of deja-vu, the dammed phone started to shriek again and Paul climbed off the sofa, his legs wobbling from getting up too quickly. With a look at Emily to be quiet he greeted the caller hello.

"Yes, this is Paul Weston. Yes, she is my wife. She's what? Shit! I'll be right there. Thanks."

Slamming the phone down, he rushed off to the hallway, where his Caterpillar boots and seen better days black jacket awaited him. He snapped at the bemused child who with Harry in hand was staring at him.

"Get ya coat and shoes on Em! Hurry up! Maria's been hurt. I said hurry up, and put that bloody rat away!"

The Vauxhall Corsa that he had driven for the last four years was never going to get him fast enough to the hospital. He could swear that rust was spreading like wildfire under the bright, red bodywork as he drove. Meanwhile Emily, not appreciating the seriousness of the situation, was sliding along the back seat, first one way and then the other as Paul screeched the car around corners praying that the old Bill weren't going to appear at any minute with their plastic bags and sarcastic remarks.

The sky was the darkest royal blue, a velvet backdrop that seemed strangely tinged with haze—the only reminder of a wet afternoon. As rubber sliced through water, Paul gripped the wheel and stared straight ahead. He couldn't ascertain whether the haze was to do with the sky, the wet windscreen or the dampness in his eyes—the thoughts that had filled his head earlier had obviously taken their toll.

With a sudden lurch, the car came to a halt before red traffic lights on the Euston Road. He revved the engine as high as he could, desperate to shoot off as soon as the stupid lights went amber, then he noticed that something was different; something had passed in the last few seconds, something was unusual compared to other fast journeys—Emily was still and quiet.

If only out of curiosity, he adjusted his body slightly to the left and peered around to where Emily was crouched by the car window. Her small hands were gripping the leather bound arm rest on the door, and her pixie nose was pressed flat against the window. He could see her breath misting the glass, then disappearing, then misting the glass and so on. She was staring with awe at something outside.

He tried to follow Emily's gaze, tried to follow her line of vision to see just what was keeping her so unusually quiet. He was just about to turn away in annoyance at the lack of anything special when his tired, sore eyes caught a glimpse of something there, something behind the green and white of a Camden bin that Emily was peering past.

He thought he saw a shadow; he thought he saw something dark, and yet something that was able to stand out in the evening light; he thought he saw something that brought back memoirs of a younger age, when fleeting figures in Marvel comics ruled the roost on bored, winter evenings.

His mind went off on a tangent—Batman, Spiderman, Jack The Ripper, weirdos who stalk the streets simply because they are too 'sane' to be in prison, and he felt a brief pit of despair for the young innocents of today's society.

He felt sad and angry, he felt helpless, he felt . . . . pissed off, as the blaring horn of the car behind told him that the lights had turned green. The tosser in the Esprit behind reminded him of this capital crime as he sped past, middle finger up, but Paul's mind was miles away. The journey became a blur. Before long, he was sitting in a street a few yards from the hospital and not in the slightest bit aware of how he had driven there.

Emily sat still, curling her long hair numbly around her left forefinger. She looked so angelic sitting there, and Paul was just thinking that her hair was in need of a good wash when the feeling of fear and panic gripped him again.

"Emily out," he said, as controlled as he possibly could. Em looked back blankly for a second, before the little sparkle in her eyes momentarily came back.

"Are we there Paul? Where's Maria?" Her cute features did seem genuinely curious, but she didn't seem to be in much of a hurry too and Paul reached out for her arm, grabbing the sleeve of the small, white duffle coat, that Maria thought would make Emily resemble Paddington Bear.

But Emily was not in the mood to be dragged at that moment, and Paul sensing her reluctance gripped her sleeve harder, pulling her towards the car door.

"No Paul no!" screamed the girl, but Paul ignored her protests—she was always getting her own way these days, they should get a bloody good hiding when they cheek back their elders—not enough bloody respect.

"I said NO PAUL," and as if to underline her insistence, Emily's front teeth closed upon the straining hand of the flustered brother-in-law.

Paul shouted in pain. He could feel the child's teeth grinding against the knuckle of his little finger, and as if by instinct, he clenched his left fist, an effort to stop this little sod from assaulting his throbbing hand any longer.

He thought he could feel a slight trickle on his injured hand, as if blood was starting to slowly trickle down past his wrist and onto his taut forearm—this alone was enough to instill more anger inside of him. He grabbed the child by the hair, twisting those golden locks in a vice like grip, and pulled Emily's head backwards in an attempt to get her off his agonizing hand.

And yet despite the burning pain, Paul couldn't help think how absurd this was. Em didn't bite. She may do a lot of silly little things, but she didn't bite. What the hell was she doing to him? Couldn't even her young, immature mind appreciate how worried he was? Couldn't she not even have a little worry about her own fucking sister?

"Get off you little bastard, stop biting or I'll smack you so hard that . . . ." he didn't need to finish the sentence as Emily's vice like grip loosened, and he jerked her head back so hard that he felt it could come free from her twisting body at any moment.

The infant screeched at Paul's ashen face. "You hurt me, you hurt me. I'm telling Maria you hit me, I hate you," before dissolving into uncontrollable, heaving sobs.

What was he to do? Feel sorry for his small assailant? Shake her by the shoulders and tell her of how he was going to smack her bum red raw when they got home? No, Maria was waiting and he couldn't stand this confusion any longer.

He picked up his whimpering relative, shut and locked the door as best as he could, and pounding his legs hard against the dirty, grey concrete of the pavement, sped towards the clinical building that greeted "Emergency and Outpatients" in bold red and white writing.

Emily grasped his jacket collar hard as if she felt she would fall to the ground at any moment, her crying slowly becoming a low murmur, but Paul was only concentrating on the building ahead. Skipping over manholes, fish and chip paper and used cans of drink, he ran like a man with a mission, a knight in shining armour, and with a baby dragon in his arms.

He stumbled through the hospital's swinging doors and breathed the name of his beloved at the crusty, impassive face of the receptionist.

"Weston, no WESton, for God's sake will you listen carefully? No, and I don't appreciate such language either, especially when I am wound up by people as unbothered as you. What? Fifth floor? Where's the lift? What? Yes, her husband, I told you a hundred times already, are you deaf or what?"

He didn't hear the receptionist's warning of what happens to uncivil people as he lurched towards the lift's doors, and stared blankly at the inside's of those same doors as the life made its ascent.

As the doors opened, fresh, disinfected air rushed into the claustrophobic atmosphere of the lift. The smell inside that tiny, metal box hadn't been helped by the alcoholic, piss stained stench of a small, haggard sixty-something, who seemed in a hurry to show his audience of just how itchy his dirt encrusted testicles had become, and Paul had left the lift gagging, holding Em's face tight against his lapel.

He rushed past sitting patients reading original first editions of the TV times; he skipped past nurses holding clipboards, files or plastic pots of piss, before glimpsing the destination he had spent years getting to. Ward 5c—Trotter ward.

Seeing his wife's face felt like walking into a dream; never had he been so pleased to see the girl that had made him say I love you. Even better, his bride looked chirpy and bright and the relief that Paul felt spread through him like a wave of cool water.

"Maria what happened? For heaven's sake, are you okay, are you hurt?"

Maria looked pleased at her husband's concern.

"Oh Paul, I just slipped over in the street. I wasn't watching where I was going and fell over outside Boots. The doctor said that I'm suffering from exhaustion and so they are keeping a little eye on me, but I'm gonna be fine. Don't look so worried darling!"

"But you looked fine when you left for work. Didn't you feel well then? Why didn't you tell me?" Collapsing into a chair by the bed, Paul suddenly saw the funny side of the situation, and began to smile, but Maria's amusement was checked as she saw Paul rub his wounded left hand. There was still a small amount of blood trickling from it.

"What happened to you? You look as if you need this bed more than me?"

"Oh, me and little Em had a bit of a disagreement, didn't we trouble? Em decided to show her disagreement by taking a chunk out of my finger, but I think I'll be okay."

Maria looked concerned, "But Emily doesn't bite. What did you say to her?"

"What do you mean what did I say to her? I just asked her to get a move on when I was trying to rush here to you."

"But you must've said something to upset her, I mean, for her to actually bite?"

"Like what? Since when have I ever wanted to upset her? Listen, I just wanted to be with you. Even if I was that way inclined, I didn't have the time or frame of mind to annoy a little kid."

Maria looked down at her little sister and stroked her hair away to reveal the small face that had nestled against her chest.

"Why did you bite Pauly Em? You don't bite, just like we tell you not to spit or use bad language, so why bite Pauly?"

The fragile nine year old flashed her big, blue eyes up at her concerned sibling, then raising her head slightly she glared at Paul, before her chest heaved and tears cascaded down her face once more.

"It was Paul's fault"—the girl choked the words in-between heartfelt sobs—"He smacked me hard because I wouldn't go to bed early. He smacked me and smacked me and told me hated me. He always smacks me when you are out. He wants me to go awaaaay."

As the infant's last words came moaning from her lips, Maria's dark eyes fixed Paul with a stare that could only be synonymous with a disgusted disbelief. Paul could no longer think anything in his troubled mind. He had a bizarre feeling that his world was about to crash down about him.

CHAPTER THREE

He stared at the ceiling, and tried hard to think of something totally mundane that would make his eyelids slide down easily over his tired, muddy brown eyes, and send him off to a world where Kylie Minogue was on the verge of saying yes to a night of unbridled lust—well, before his knackered old alarm clock had woken him two hours too early as usual.

He glanced at the window. It may have been the early hours of the morning, but even now thanks to the most silvery rays of dust mite swarming moonlight, he could make out the dirt and black fingerprints that happily embossed the window's white, wooden framework. To Mick, these symbols of uncleanliness said more than just a reluctance to get out the duster and polish. They summed up his whole philosophy of his 28 years on the 'Big One' fun ride of his being, and reiterated the last few lines of his last school report—*Michael could have a bright future, as long as he doesn't allow his black moods and wandering mind stop him from doing well—could try harder.*

Oh how he had hated those spineless bastards at his now defunct secondary school. How he wished he could meet his waddling prick of a maths teacher, and ram his ever-present classroom kettle up his stinking arsehole. If anyone had ever made him feel totally stupid, then without a doubt Mr Branco had made him feel as small as the size of his disappointing dick. It was probably during those so-called maths 'lessons' that Mick started to appreciate how bitter his mind was capable of getting. Sometimes, the bitterness became so strong, that it turned into hideous thoughts that made him physically shake, but hey, it's great to be an enigma uh? Who wants to be like anybody else anyway?

He untangled his sweaty legs from the flimsy nylon top sheet, and twisted to the right to lay heavily on his shoulder—his favourite position ever since he was a boy, if only because of the full sized, practically naked poster he used to have of Cheryl Ladd on his junk filled bedroom's wall.

In the darkness, he felt the dirt from the window expand all over its surrounding area, covering all six of the perfect square panes, creeping over onto the grey, wood chipped walls, sinking down to the greyish-blue shag-pile carpet, before crawling, purposefully to his creaking bed, up past the sweat and piss stained mattress, and then onto his naked, stumpy, hairy legs, when his entire body would quickly dissolve into the ignorant forgetfulness that the dirt was analogous of—maybe people would then not notice him at all? Imagine that, doing one's work and no one noticing; collecting one's cleaning and no-one seeing; lifting the skirts of passing examples of lovely ladies, and no-one even caring!

In a way, it wasn't that different from the thoughts of the subterranean sheep of the tube station earlier this evening. How many people really knew that they were about to witness the gruesome snuffing out of a guy's unhappy life? None of course, and Ladies and Gentleman, why should they? Oh come on, do you seriously mean to tell me that seeing the living blood of a helpless, dying, agonised fellow being spurt out of any slighted artery or any orifice, is of the slightest interest to the average Mr or Ms Public? Get real, I mean, helping someone may just lead to others staring at you too, and isn't that the most important thing in life? Self-preservation? Morons, the whole fucking lot of them.

All in all, this was just another piece of brain screaming imagery from the man who seemed to spend his life complaining about missed chances, dreaming of the Utopian life-style that was always just out of reach, and thinking bitterly for the girl who had stolen his heart, his soul, and had never given them back.

But let's be absolutely honest here, when one considers the constant pressure he has felt since his university days, since his affair with the falseness of the advertising world, then one cannot blame him for the bitterness he feels towards double standard feminists, racists, and people with leather filofaxes and an open window for lunch darling on the 11th of April.

He had seen them all, met them all, pitied them all and at times even hated them all. But *she* had known how to talk to him, to tell him that that he was living in a dream world, it was just a stupid dream, "so stop being so damned uptight and give us a kiss." Now what was he going to do? The bitterness had been twisted into a new and improved shade of puce, and she wasn't there to kiss him better.

He wasn't going to do a lot lying there, when the rest of the city was resting in the arms of Morpheus. The atmosphere looked like an inkblot before him, and his thoughts of the future weren't much clearer.

He laid back, closed his eyes to the darkness, and his mind, his inner, secret world of real truth and justice, and felt something pierce the small of his back. He lay there trying to feel what it was, moving around with a strained look on his face. Maybe it was the springs finally about to give in? Oh boy, finishing one's days adhered to a bed, I bet Jackson would have a field day with that one.

What was it that his colleague had said? Apparently, he had read a pearl of wisdom from one of the ladies magazines he was prone to reading, and told a not too captivated studio of how statistics show that the majority of people born in a bed, die in a bed. In fact, Jacko must've believed that fascinating contribution to a healthy lifestyle, because he now got up as early as possible and watched breakfast TV, rather than spend "unnecessary time in bed."

What were the odds of Jacko visiting his grave and muttering to a piece of cold marble "I told you so!" before going into that inane, throaty giggle of his.

No, one must not give Jacko that honour, and Mick slid his back slightly to the edge of the bed in order to escape humiliating death. The sharpness didn't disappear though—it merely changed position.

After a few seconds of total bemusement, he remembered the packet of crisps he had consumed with a glass of warmish, slightly creamy milk, followed by an out of date mini apple pie. Ugh! Eating in bed. What a disgusting habit. *She* would've gone mad to see his laziness now. *She* would've blinked and lasered his shame with her wondrous grey-green eyes . . . . and handed him the vacuum cleaner to make an obvious point.

In a fit of sheer exasperation, he heaved and pulled himself from his warm, yet creaking bed. As he lifted his body, his right leg became entangled with the top sheet and for a moment he balanced precariously to his left, as if he would topple at any moment. But his black, Ikea bookshelf, that to be honest had seen better days, was there for his waving hand to grip, to stop any ideas his body had of falling to the unclean shag-pile.

This less than graceful exit from his bed just annoyed his tired mind all the more and he gripped the sheets from his bed and became immersed in a brief tug-of-war with his aged sleeping apparatus.

The sheet finally came away and he toppled backwards with the motion of the effort. As he used his hand to brush away the crumbs from where he had been laying, he felt a sweeping flush of desperation—was this his life? Was this what he had been born for? To spend endless lonely nights cleaning his bed of the remnants of his dodgy habits, when he should've been stroking, kissing and making love to the woman who appreciated his enigmatic self and even loved him for it.

When he was sure that his bed was now fit for sleeping in, he toppled forward and buried his head into his flimsy pillows.

As he felt his hot breath come back from the closeness of the cotton, he came to yet another of the conclusions that always made him feel better for an hour or two.

"I don't care I tell you, I really don't care. There's nothing wrong with me! One of these days she will know that she made a mistake, I'll show her that I *can* live without her. I know I can. I *know* I can."

There was a sharp tingle in the corner of his eyes and a heavy feeling around his nose, and as he looked up briefly, even the darkness seemed to blur into a cascade of colours and shapes. He knew he was going to cry.

A scream made him shift into the brightness of an icy blue morning. The high-pitched ringing continued until he felt blindly to his right and switched the offending clock off.

'What to wear, what to wear, I'd wear my Paul Smith, but it's not there!' he mused to himself, and absently scratched between his legs.

It wasn't that he was scruffy. He took a fair amount of pride in his appearance, but often these days, his bodymap didn't quite work. Did it really matter? I mean, nobody looked at him anyway—especially the women.

But later, as he walked towards the tube station, after a rushed breakfast of weetabix with more warm, creamy milk, he thought that he looked pretty cool today, even after a lousy night's sleep.

This wasn't one of his favourite walks. Every bloody day he seemed to pass the same old sights—the bridge over the Caledonian Road, the train station with the invisible ticket collectors, and not to mention the white, foreboding presence that was the Pentonville hotel, for guests of her Majesty.

He trudged with his ever seemingly present black cloud to the junction with Market Road and stood waiting for the lights to go red, so that he could sprint across and not become one of the many that had had their figures mauled by the speeding traffic at this spot.

He stared across the exhaust-fume filled crossroads and tried hard to think of what shite Walters would come out with today; or what smart remarks Jacko would spit out, to show how smart and repetitive he was.

His eyes were focused on a billboard that was advertising the very latest in men's get-pissed-fast lager, using the image of a very fanciable girl in very little clothing. Yes, drink this lager, get pissed and pull this type of girl—obvious uh? The girls just *love* men that can barely stand and ejaculate only vomit. To be honest, he didn't really notice the words of the ad, or the fact that it was an account that Walters has lost only months before, due to the fat MD promising deadlines that were well out of the reach of his disillusioned freelancers.

Instead, he was thinking again of the sea, of his remark to Jackson the day before. What on Earth had got him thinking about the sea? Childhood holidays to Margate and Clacton were pleasant enough, but he had never had the urge to revisit them.

Out of the corner of his eye, Mick just glimpsed the green then amber traffic lights turn red, and was about to do the obliged rush across the road of chance when something was there at his back and pushing him forwards. It was pushing him hard and Mick felt his feet start to point in different directions as he tried to stop himself from falling over.

He twisted his head, first to the left, and then to the right in a vague attempt to see where this sudden force was coming from, and it was only when he managed to straighten himself and look back in the direction he was walking, that he saw the man with the brown, pork-pie hat.

This unusual creature had reached the other side of the road, and was walking at such a pace that if innocent passer by wasn't on their guard, then they too would be knocked aside by this brown hatted whirlwind.

Mick looked around again and looked straight into the lined, age weary face of an old lady. The pensioner was trying desperately hard to peek past her light purple headscarf that was threatening to engulf her delicate, wrinkled features.

"He hit me too, the bloody fool. Who the hell does he think he is? Tut, such bad manners. You never would've seen the like years ago, no respect, that's the problem. What do they teach them these days?"

Mick was staring intently into the rheumy, stone blue eyes of the opinionated pensioner, but his mind was still with Mr Pork-Pie. Did that guy know that he was being pig headed? There was certainly something unknowing in his gait, but Mick, for all of his worldly wise explanations, couldn't put his finger on it.

In a vague attempt to come back to the real world, Mick shook his head and showed the lady a face full of agreement and concern, before quickly making excuses about being late for work and not letting people like that ruin your day.

"Ooh yes, me too dear. Let's see if I can get to the paper shop before some other yob knocks me down. No bloody respect, that's what it is, no bloody respect."

No, thought Mick, as he finally approached the entrance to the tube station. No bloody respect. Since when has anybody treated me with bloody respect? Not that I give a toss anymore. Why should I? Give me one good reason.

In a rush of confused energy, Mick strolled past the rusting gates of the station, and was just about to walk past the knackered 'photo-me' booth when a crowd milling around the ticket office took his attention.

He tried hard to see what the people were staring at, and was just about to ask the perspiring, fat, blue uniformed ticket collector, when a tallish guy in a demin shirt and New York Yankees baseball cap spun off the crowd, protesting in a loud screech, his yellowed, jagged teeth protruding from scabby lips in what looked like a futile attempt to escape their owner's embarrassing tones.

"Just hold him down, he has no right to do that. The cops will be here in a minute. For God's sake hold him down properly."

"What do you think we are doing man? Why don't you help instead of just standing there moaning?"

The response had come from another Underground employee. He looked in his mid-twenties, and Mick could see through the crowd that his left arm was wearing a friendship band of red, black, green and yellow and was straining with the effort of holding down a leg that was dressed in brown corduroy.

Another voice from the crowd, this time belonging to a woman, tried to stress that they must hold him tight, as he "obviously has something missing upstairs." But Mick was more interested in what lay beneath the countless buttons of the ticket machine. There, propped up in the corner by an empty chip packet, was a brown pork-pie hat, only this time the hat's crease had popped up to give it a rounded, dome like appearance.

Just as Mick managed to persuade his curious eyes to stop staring at the discarded headwear, a sound like an old dog lying in agony managed to break free of the huddle of bodies. To the ears of Mick, the tone reminded him of when he had accompanied an old school pal, Simon Saint and Simon's dad to the vet, along with Simon's old collie Patch. It turned out to be Patch's last outing as the poor thing had ulcers all along his stomach lining and one of them had burst. The sounds that had emanated from poor old Patch were not a million miles from what Mick was hearing now.

Mick's sore, tired eyes switched from the hat back to the corduroy clad leg, and with a feeling of intense curiosity that he could no longer ignore, he approached the scene from where the moan had come from.

The lady who had spoken earlier noticed the arriving artist and decided that if anybody was going to be a spokesperson for the ensuing rabble, then it might as well be her.

"You won't believe what this guy just did," stated the woman, in a tone that immediately reminded Mick of his mother's gossipy neighbour Eileen Swift, a lady of dubious virtues and even more dubious opinions.

"No," responded Mick, "I most probably won't, but I'm always game for a surprise. Do tell."

With a puzzled look at Mick's words, the lady shook her head and explained. "He only pushed those young girls out of the way so that he could get his ticket first, I mean really viciously pushed them out of the way the poor things, and when we complained he threatened to kill the girls and bite me! I swear he was going to sink his teeth into my arm."

In a flash of bizarre imagination, Mick suddenly saw the woman gossiping innocently with a friend, whilst Pork-Pie held her arm, sleeve pushed up to the elbow, and sprinkled salt and pepper onto his unusual snack.

It was the sight of the two young girls that the woman had spoken of that knocked another unreal scene from his bemused mind. Neither of them could've been more than fourteen, and were obviously stunned and upset by the actions of the mysterious Pork-Pie. One of the girls was holding a tired piece of tissue with one hand and clinging onto her friend with the other. Her friend was shaking and taking in short, intermittent breaths.

The lady, not to be put off by the distant look in Mick's face, carried on with her report of the incident.

"And if that wasn't bad enough, when that black tube guy tried to calm him down, he spat in his face and told him to go fuck himself. He told him that he could burn the station down if he wanted to and nobody would be able to blame him."

It was then that like a demented jack-in-the-box, Pork-Pie had decided that enough was enough, and breaking free from the hands that were trying to compress his writhing body shot upwards until he was sitting on the cold, tiled station floor, his legs outstretched before him, and with clawing hands trying to pull him back down to his previous position.

It was the black tube worker's cry of "No man, you ain't going anywhere bro'," that had alerted Mick to the fact that Mr Pork-Pie had no intention of staying for a chat, and he was just about to ask if they could use two more hands when a guy in overalls and a tartan cap pre-empted Mick's sudden pang of social co-operation.

"Look mate, can't you see that this guy is off his head? At least you can help us to hold him down until the police get here instead of looking like you have the world's problems to deal with."

Mick quickly glimpsed the unshaven, grey stubble of the man in the cap and bent down to help with the capture of the now hatless, frantic Mr Pork-Pie.

"Yeah sure, sorry, I was just trying to figure out what was going on. Did he just do this? I mean, I think it was him that nearly knocked me and some old girl flying a few minutes ago. It just happened yeah?"

The black tube worker wiped his forehead with the back of his hand, rubbing his colourful friendship band across his furrowed eyebrows as he did so, and looking directly at the artist breathed out a long sigh that showed that he wasn't having a good day.

"You get used to it man. There are always some weirdoes around here trying to barge their way through as if they had more right to travel than others. Especially in this area. Man, I am sick of drunken dudes breathing their dog breath in my face. If they ain't abusing me, my skin or my family they are breathing their stink into my face. I said stay down man!"

The last words of his sentence had just left the tube worker's lips when the agonised whine sounded again, only this time it was accompanied by a loud roar as the trapped man gave one more huge effort to get up. He grabbed at the hands trying to hold him down with fingers that were browned from smoking and nails that were dirty and uncut. As he slowly worked his torso upwards again, the eyes of Pork-Pie finally rested on the sight of Mick's perplexed frown and screamed.

"Hey, I'm not drunk. Who said I was drunk?" The tube worker moved his face closer to the struggling man and breathed a reply.

"Ya either drunk or drugged man. Either way, you don't go around threatening and spitting in my face."

"Drunk? Drugged? What do you know you fucking loser? What do you know about how to behave in public? You behave how you behave and we all behave differently. You don't fucking accuse me of being unclean when you know fuck all yourself."

This outburst prompted the lady into her quick action. Her well made up face appeared above the head of Mick and he could feel her breath ruffle his hair as she reminded the hostile individual of how one does not behave in a cultured society.

"You were going to bite me you bastard, and you hurt those young girls. You think you're the only one in a hurry and when you can't get your own way you try and be the hard man. Well I'm sorry, people don't like being treated like that. I think the Police should . . . ."

"Yah, yah, yah! Fuck off you fucking slapper," interrupted the maniac still twisting on the floor, "just shut up and fuck off. Don't lecture me. You think you're better than me with your posh clothes and head up your own arse. You think that just because you work for even bigger tossers and come home fucked that you are better than me. Well lady you're not. Shocked eh? Yeah, you're not better than me and I'll tell you why."

The tartan capped man grabbed hold of Pork-Pie's shoulders and pushed him down in a vain attempt to stop the man's ranting, but all he did was enforce the man to an even louder outburst."

"No, you will listen to me. I *will* be heard by you ignorant fuckers. I am capable of doing things that you morons can only dream of, and if you losers had half a brain cell you could do them too, but you are too wrapped up in your own tiny worlds where you live and die for absolutely fuck all. Yeah, I push people out of the way, and I do so because I am better than you all, you are not fit to lick the shit off my shoes."

From nowhere, the guy with yellowed teeth shot forward to air his views on the subject. "Oh yeah? What makes you so special? Personally all I can see is a desperate, stinking madman with an over inflated sense of importance. You're out of your fucking mind."

"No!" shrieked the now totally out of control Pork-Pie, and in one swift movement he moved his forehead forward in a powerful, jolting motion, connecting with the creased forehead of the tube worker who was losing his battle, along with his fellow captors, of holding the fanatical man down.

With a long yell of pain, the tube worker fell backwards, and blood spurted from his nostrils onto the floor and over the cream, high heels of the lady captor. She shrieked in disgust and lost sight of what these people were trying to achieve—to hold Pork-Pie down.

Without a single hesitation, the over excited Mr Pork-Pie grabbed the right hand of the guy in the cap, and with as much force as he could muster bit down hard, until teeth grazed bone. The capped man screamed in agony, his left arm flaying until that too was grabbed and his fingers were bent back a full one hundred and eighty degrees, until a sickening click signified that they could not go back anymore.

Mick felt the weetabix he had eaten rise back up his gullet, but felt rooted to the spot, his own hands easily brushed out of the way by the manic man's efforts. What should he do? Just kneel and watch as this lunatic showed that he really was better than the rest and later mentally kick himself in the head for not trying? Or does he dive in and give the lunatic a taste of his own medicine?

The lady, staring wildly at the blood on her shoes finally muttered something that sounded like "stop him someone," and the yellow teethed man, his baseball cap now pointing at a slightly different angle than before, shouted 'instructions' to all to stop the psychotic from getting out of their reach, his voice even more weedy and grating than before.

As if with some kind of hidden instinct, Mick sprung from his haunched position and leapt for the ankles of Pork-Pie, who by now had completely broken free of the people around him and was standing and ready to flee. He felt his arms encircle the shins of the madman and for a second, Mick saw himself as a besotted lover, begging his beloved not to go and stay, if only for the kids' sake.

But the hatless maniac was not moving, and Mick looked up from his degrading position, straight into the wild eyes of the scowling Mr Pork-Pie. Mick felt all his energy leave him as if the man's burning irises were burning into his brain, and as his arms slowly slipped from their prey, Pork-Pie spoke his first words to the despondent artist.

"I wouldn't even think about it my friend. Believe me, I wouldn't even think about it."

In Mick's mind, the words had a wise ring to them as he watched the ranting man's brown-corduroyed legs disappear out the station's exit to turn left down the main road towards Holloway.

As he lay there, unaware of how stupid he looked to anyone passing the station, he heard the voices of those that had tried in vain to clear the streets of one more piece of scum. In particular, the whiny voice of the yellowed teeth man penetrated the foggy thoughts that were now rushing into his head.

"Well, that's great innit? We couldn't even stop one unstable fuckwit from getting away. And we wonder why the streets are full of madmen."

The bloodied tube worker, with a face full of pain could just about stop himself from flying at the high voiced bystander as the police sirens gradually got closer and closer to the station.

"Yeah? Well, I didn't see you dirty your hands man. That guy weren't better than me, but he were definitely better than you. No guts man."

As he got up onto his shaking legs, Mick finally made sense of his earlier seaside fascination. 'I just need a break', he thought to himself. 'A break from the jungle law of the city. Maybe there is a healthier class of loony at the sea-side?' And leaving the injured and disgusted behind him, he left the station before the police could call him as a witness. He didn't need that hassle and he had no wish to come face to face with a guy like the mad Mr Pork-Pie for some time.

CHAPTER FOUR

The slight westerly wind blew through the tall grass and weeds, bending stalks and blades first one way and then the other. If you could have put your ear close enough to them, you would've heard a slight rustle as if nature had given a voice to its pleasant inhabitants.

But nobody was kneeling down and listening so intently, nobody was inclined to at that precise moment for the nodding greenery was beside a little known lane that took one from Colchester to Wivenhoe, or Wivenhoe to Colchester, depending on your whim at the time.

It was the type of lane that made big city dwellers sigh, and dream of an England that they saw plenty of in Jane Austin adaptations, but which they never seemed to come to know in their little world.

The road was tarmacced, at least it had been once, but the stony, dusty sides were threatening to turn it into an entire shade of light brown. There wasn't anywhere to walk for the country loving pedestrian, but it was obvious that the more adventurous had tried to make their way down the lane, for some of the blades and stalks were lying down, in protest at having their environment so maliciously invaded.

Such a sight would bring cries of outrage from those who truly lived for and loved the eye-catching surroundings, where the lane twisted and turned like an important intestine in the stomach of the country's green and pleasant land.

Such people were the Trollopes, who underneath the fast, greying skies, were making their way towards the Wivenhoe bungalow that had served them loyally for over ten years. The Trollopes were quite a unique couple. After twenty-eight years of marriage, they were still the image of a loving and devoted couple. Cross words were hardly ever uttered between them, and opposing points of view between members of the Trollope clan were dismissed easily and without fuss—Daddy was right, and you know that is how it always must be.

In fact, the people of Colchester and its surrounding areas, were quite familiar with the sight of the Trollopes making their way around the little roads—most of the immediate generations had never heard of a tandem, never mind seen one, or even better ridden one, but the Trollopes adored their rusty Raleigh two seater; it was different and yet classy in a respectful and historical way, and this was the most important factor to Stephen Trollope, and he had no doubts that his spouse could not disagree.

In her furtive thoughts, Dorothy Trollope would've loved a bigger and more spongy seat, especially when the lanes curved as tightly as this current one did, but she couldn't say anything to the olive green plastic of her husband's hunched, anoraked back; and sure as eggs are eggs, she couldn't put forward her reasonable request when looking at Stephen's educated face. He would tilt his chin downwards, and peer over his horn-rimmed specs, with a look that screamed "you *are* having a little joke, aren't you Dorothy? We both know that you are joking." She would let out a sigh from the corner of her cracked lips, and giving her shoulders a quick shrug, in imitation of a knowing laugh, would reply that yes Stephen, why change something that has been so useful for so long? Stephen disliked change and Dorothy knew better than to challenge the status quo of their stable existence.

The wheels of the tandem were skidding slightly on the dusty road, causing the water levels in their dirty white "refreshment bottles" to slop up and down like miniature waves. But Stephen was at ease with the world; he actually liked the way the tandem would threaten to slide away before correcting itself. To his mind, along with the pleasant countryside, this was what bike-riding was all about.

Dorothy, however, always held her breath as the wheels moved precariously sideways and wished that her husband would either slow down or realise that they were too old for this skylarking about. In moments of too rare fantasy, she would maintain to herself that this moment of togetherness was the only time she'd had something hard between her legs; even her repressed and lonely teenage years acknowledged that cute irony. But whether irony was a good substitution for her well being, she wasn't so sure.

As the Trollopes and their tandem moved relentlessly towards the final hundred yards of the lane, Stephen noticed that the sleeve of his anorak had moved up his arm and past his watch and the cold was making the hairs of his wrist stand to attention. But the sight of the watch's deep brown leather strap was enough to stir a curiosity in him that often occurred when he was feeling pleased with himself. He wondered how long the journey was taking?

Now he knew that the hour hand was just passing the eight when they swept past the Colchester Bus Station, so to see it now halfway between the ten and eleven was tantamount to winning the lottery for Stephen Trollope. He knew this lane so well, and he rode the tandem so expertly, that to turn his head for only a brief second, would be as easy as his sixteen year old son passing all of his GCSEs with straight As.

He gripped the front handlebars a touch tighter than usual, and with glasses gently making their way down his nose, gave a quick swivel on his seat.

"This is good, even if I say so myself. We certainly know how to move these days eh Dorothy?"

Dorothy could smell Stephen's coffee tinged breath as his head did a quarter turn and he peered at her from the corner of his straining right eye. But the smell and Stephen's words suddenly meant nothing to her as she saw the penultimate curve in the winding lane.

"Stephen, please be careful, look where you are going!" Stephen sniffed in annoyance.

"I know where I am going, we have done this journey enough times for me to know it blindfolded, so please don't be so panicky."

But as Stephen tried to reiterate what he had learnt via his watch, Dorothy suddenly felt a surge of adrenaline rush through her, a sign that she was genuinely frightened and that she must put this across to her insistent partner.

"No really Stephen, please look ahead, can't you see the curve? Tell me what you want when we have stopped."

Stephen gave a laugh that Dorothy knew was one of downright derision—it was a short expelling of air, accompanied by a brief, low snort. Dorothy had heard that noise so may times in her married life, and even though she was used to its annoying resonance, she wished that her husband would just wake up to how bloody rude it was—not that Stephen considered himself rude about anything. As far as he was concerned, it was "others" who were out of touch with acceptable manners.

Happy in the knowledge that he would, as usual, prove his wife's complaints to be totally unjustified, Stephen turned his head to face the front and got ready to turn the handlebars slightly to the right to manoeuvre the oncoming corner.

"I shall tell you something my dear," Stephen remarked to the air, "you have never been quite the same since Richard left home. In fact, I believe that you took his leaving so personally that you now feel that you have to question everything that goes on in our life."

To emphasise his point even more, Dorothy looked on in dread as her partner swivelled his smug face to gaze briefly at her wide, green eyes.

"In fact, I would even go so far to say that your paranoia is affecting Adrian. You do know that he went to bed at quarter past ten last night? Says that he can't quite get his head around Barthes' idea of myth as a semiological system! I don't think I have ever seen him so unsure of himself."

Dorothy was about to suggest that maybe their sixteen year old had other, more important things on his mind, like why he had to go to bed so early anyway, and why he didn't have any friends. But her comments were stopped abruptly by the sight of a smart, middle aged gentleman making his way up the left hand side of the verge, and walking slowly through the weeds and grass in their direction.

"Not now Stephen, be careful of that man!" Stephen's brow creased at his wife's words, and pivoting his head around in search of the mentioned figure, realised that he was leaving the manoeuvre around the oncoming curve far too late.

For a very brief moment, Stephen felt his mind completely at odds with the situation, and ignoring his wife's screams of warning felt that switching the handlebars back to their original position would enable them to turn the corner comfortably and not hit the oncoming jaywalker.

But he pulled at them too quickly, and the wheels of the tandem skidded in protest at their operator's lack of judgement, the dirt of the country lane providing ample help in the bike's sudden swaying and tilting.

Stephen Trollope was not usually a man of snap decisions, and in retrospect, his final push of the handlebars to the left was probably the action of a man out of his depth in such a quick thinking scenario. However, it was this action that finally pointed the tandem towards the line of bushes that curved around the lane's penultimate corner, and enabled it and its riders to career onto them full force.

Dorothy screamed as she felt the hapless two-seater part company with her and her husband. She screamed first in terror and then in pain as she felt twigs and rough leaves scrape her skin; her body, almost in an agonising slow motion, somehow vaulted the bushes in a messy, un-choreographed way, that left her falling with a bump onto slushy, muddy grass on the other side.

For a few long seconds, Dorothy laid on her right side, her cheek pressing against the damp grass, and for a brief moment she thought she could smell dog mess—this alone was enough to make her sit upwards like a shot and look around for the offending article. All she saw was her beloved Stephen, lying on his back, his legs up against the bush as if he had been sitting on the hedge and fell backwards onto the ground without losing his body's posture.

His eyes were wide open, but there was no sound coming from his lips. The only noise in the air was the whirring of the tandem's wheels on the other side of the bush.

Without thinking as to what had happened to the bike, Dorothy climbed to her feet quickly, ignoring the sharp pain in her backside and right hip, and rushed over to her inert spouse.

"Stephen dear, are you okay? Say something Stephen, just so I know that you are okay."

As she squeezed his right hand, the dazed glare of Stephen finally adjusted itself and met the worried features of Dorothy. He opened his mouth slightly, and after a sharp expelling of breath muttered "my dear, I don't feel in the slightest bit okay. How many times have I told you not to bother me when we are cycling? Oh God, will you never listen to me? What have you done to the tandem?"

Dorothy had spent a lifetime taking the blame for events beyond her control, so for Stephen to pass responsibility for this accident was no surprise to her. Instead, she had been searching her husband's body for signs of injury, and had noticed that he had a nasty looking scratch running down from his left ear down to the corner of his mouth.

Taking her handkerchief out of her anorak pocket, she wet the tip and attempted to clean the wound of blood that was threatening to trickle down his chin. Stephen though, was not a willing patient.

"Take that away woman! If I have an injury, I really do not need you making it worse with your spittle. Honestly Dorothy, just help me up and let me see where the tandem is."

The tired wife stood up, bent her knees, and hooked her aching arms under the armpits of her husband. She was just about to heave the anoraked one up onto this feet, when her attention was again taken by the face of the middle aged gentleman she had seen before the crash. He had messy, greying hair, and was peering intently over the bush. His face was red with the increasingly cold wind, and Dorothy could see a red, paisley tie and white shirt underneath a slightly patterned black jacket.

"Excuse me, it looks as though you could use some help. I saw what happened. Very nasty. Mind you, the roads are very dusty around here. Especially when it hasn't rained much. Here, let me help you good people up. Nobody too hurt I hope."

Dorothy looked down at her husband and told the helper of her husband's injury, but as she looked up again, the man was walking towards the troubled husband and wife.

She looked towards the man, and even though she was pleased that some people could be so thoughtful, she was strangely bothered by his demeanour. Sure, he had a friendly voice, and a pleasant face, (a *very* pleasant face in Dorothy's opinion, although her ability to judge a man's good looks were severely out of practice.) But how did he get over that bush? There wasn't any kind of fence nearby to put one's feet on, and there certainly wasn't a gate nearby.

Looking at his clothes, Dorothy noted that the approaching man was wearing black trousers that suited the jacket rather well, but he didn't have any leaves or traces of bush on his clothes. Shouldn't he be even a little bit dishevelled from getting over that bush? However, his smartness was untouched.

Stephen, feeling increasingly annoyed at his wife's reluctance to lift him, decided to arouse her from her laziness.

"Yes dear, just stay there and let me get a cold in my back. I know you aren't Mrs Universe Dorothy, but at least try to help me get up, I'm not that heavy."

The stranger was quickly at Stephen's side. "Whoa there sir, I think that I can help you a lot more than your dear wife." The man had bent down and was looking at Stephen with smiling eyes. "Excuse me madam, and let Thomas Burn enlighten your day."

Dorothy stepped back from the two men, and watched as her husband was lifted, almost effortlessly, from his bizarre lying position, onto his bicycle-clip adorned legs.

Pulling his anorak straight, Stephen regarded the man with sheepish eyes, and after a cough to clear his throat mumbled his thanks. "Yes well, very kind of you I'm sure. I am only glad that we didn't come to any serious injury. Of course if my wife here had been . . . ."

"Yes sir, you are indeed quite fortunate, if a little muddy." interrupted Thomas Burn with a glint in his eye that suggested that the couple before him should have enjoyed his little jest.

Feeling a little bit embarrassed at her husband's usual lack of humour, Dorothy gave a well rehearsed smile, ran her hands back through her recently dyed hazel hair, and spoke in what she believed was her friendly, middle-class tone.

"Oh I'm sure that it'll come off easily with a quick rinse. I don't suppose you saw what happened to our tandem did you?"

Burn smiled his enigmatic smile again. "The delightful tandem? Ah such a fine machine, and such a shame we don't see the like of them anymore. Such fun too I don't doubt. Tell me sir, would I be wrong in stating that you and your fine wife are retired, maybe with some grown up children, and yet with enough energy to enjoy these little fun rides of yours, which I don't doubt, also refresh your marital status?"

Stephen was beginning to look peeved, and pushing his glasses back up his nose, he started to strain his creased neck over the bush to try and glimpse his beloved tandem. "We don't need our marital status to be refreshed thank you very much. And yes, we are retired and with children, but then, one doesn't have to be a mind-reader to come to that conclusion."

Burn gave a hearty laugh that threatened to frighten every bird from every tree within a ten mile radius; a booming laugh that started suddenly and trailed off with a strange long gurgle. "Ah yes sir, that is true, but a good piece of conjecture I am sure you can agree. And no sir, I wouldn't try to lift your leg up that high—if you don't damage your lower half, then it is a good bet that you will ruin your trousers."

Dorothy had to admit that Stephen's respectability was being severely damaged, and she found that she had to stifle a laugh as she contemplated her husband trying desperately to mount the bush that they had been thrown over. At one point, she was sure that Stephen's lifted right leg would snag onto a twig and leave him dangling like a spider attached to its web.

"And another thing sir," continue Burn, "and if you don't mind me saying so. There is actually a gate up the road." With this information, the stranger laid his hand onto Dorothy's shoulder, and gently turned her in the direction of the field's exit.

But as she looked at the wooden access, Dorothy felt a shiver run through her. A shiver that made her whole body temporarily tremble. If she didn't know any better, she would've sworn that it was the cold wind that was getting through her woollen undergarments and making her skin grow goose-bumps like never before. But it didn't feel like her body had shaken because of the cold. Maybe it was the fact that she really hadn't noticed the gate before, and her mind was playing tricks on her.

Or was it the warmth of Mr Burn and his ability to make light of her husband's obvious rudeness.

"Yes Stephen, for heaven's sake stop trying to copy Mr Burn and let's use the gate." Dorothy felt oddly excited by this remark to her husband, so much so, that she felt it would be quite fun to add, "and you aren't as young as you used to be you know!" Oh yes, that felt even better; strange that she hadn't been so facetious to her husband before!

Feeling somewhat disconcerted that his futile attempt at climbing the bush was received so sarcastically, Stephen straightened his olive anorak for the second time, brushed down his trousers, and with a slight skip moved off to join his wife and the annoying Mr Burn, who seemed to have got halfway to the gate rather quickly.

When he had got level with them, Stephen decided that a joke was a joke, but surely one's wife did not have to be so flippant in front of a complete stranger? "No Dorothy, I promise you that I wasn't trying to copy Mr Burn, but merely showing concern for our bicycle, Unfortunately, you appear to have forgotten all about that."

Burn approached Stephen in conspiratorial fashion as they walked, and for a moment, Dorothy feared that her husband would lecture the man on the invasion of one's personal space—something he was prone to do when somebody had the nerve to approach him with something synonymous to friendship—but she didn't have much need to worry, as Thomas Burn showed, if only to the absorbed Dorothy, that there was more to his persona than just a friendly willingness to help.

"Actually sir, I think it best to leave cross words back at the scene of the accident. Being injured can often bring the worst out of people, and they say things that they don't actually mean." Burn laid his hand firmly on the shoulder of the blank faced Mr Trollope, who seemed almost childlike in his reply.

"Er, yes, I do believe you to be right Mr Burn, but I am just concerned at the cost of repairing our tandem, that's all."

Dorothy felt a surge of injustice at this remark, and felt that it would not be unfair to say so. "Well, excuse me Stephen, but I just happened to be more concerned with your well being. I just wanted to be sure that you weren't bleeding, because call me old fashioned, I just happen to care—something you fail to acknowledge at times."

"Please, please," interjected Burn, "let us not argue over something so fortunate. You have both escaped a nasty injury, and came out of it scot free. Doesn't that say anything to you?"

"Yes," replied Stephen, "by the grace of God we were fortunate to not be badly hurt. I am sorry dear, I hope you are not injured."

Dorothy was just processing the apology that her husband rarely gave, when Burn gave her shoulder a reassuring grip, and with a hushed voice that caressed her ears and soothed her mind suggested, "Whatever, we both know whose grace saved you from a nasty accident, and I'm sure that God was not around either, eh Dorothy?"

Before she had time to focus on whether they had mentioned their names to Mr Burn, Dorothy found that she didn't really have a clue as to what Burn was saying, but that it didn't really matter anyway, his voice made it comforting, and after such an awful day that was what she really needed.

As the threesome approached the gate, Stephen decided that enough was enough, and that if he didn't reassert himself quickly then Dorothy would always consider this occasion as one where he showed himself inferior to the loud mouths of the world. Who the hell did this Burn person think he was anyway?

"Yes, well Mr Burn, I thank you for your assistance, but I am sure that myself and my wife can retrieve our tandem and get on our way. You have been most kind I am sure."

Burn raised his eyebrows in slight surprise, "Well, could I be of more assistance to your transport? I was always a dab hand at fixing bicycles and the like during my younger years."

As they walked into view of the fallen tandem, Stephen was sure that if they were ever going to lose this insistent man, then this was the moment.

"No really Mr Burn, I really don't think that the damage is too bad. I can be rather good at fixing machines myself. In fact as you can see, there doesn't seem to be anything to worry about."

Burn strode purposefully up to the tandem, which had its front wheel and handlebars lodged into the bush. Bending down, he grabbed the machine's back wheel and turning it slightly, motioned to the watching Stephen Trollope,

"No my friend, as you can see, this wheel is definitely buckled—just look at the way it wobbles as it turns."

Dorothy gazed back and forth at Burn, the tandem's wheel and her irritated husband. As her glance returned to the wheel, she was sure that something was obviously not right with this embarrassing contraption, that to be honest she didn't have much time for—the wheel was becoming more and more buckled the longer that Burn spun it around.

Her mind thought of her husband's earlier comment regarding mind-readers, and then of Uri Geller, he was a mind-reader too, right? But common sense kept pushing thoughts back to the real world, after all, even if Burn did have such an unreal ability, then why would he want to ruin their day even more? No, it was obvious that the bike would've fallen to pieces had they tried to ride it again—Mr Burn had obviously saved them from another nasty accident.

Stephen bent down next to Burn and examined his beloved tandem. He looked at the dark eyes of the gentleman beside him, and after noticing the unusual thickness of his eyebrows, and the way they appeared swept forward and jagged, asked the question that was prominent in his mind.

"How did you know which wheel to turn first? From where I was standing the damned thing was perfectly okay. Look at it now, totally unusable. How could you be so sure that it was so badly damaged?"

"Just a wild guess Mr Trollope I assure you. But I think that any sane person would've made the same judgement considering how you hit the bush."

Stephen was not convinced. "But why the back wheel? Why not the first one? Why didn't you pull the bike out and look at the first one? Surely any *sane* person would've done that? Surely the position of impact would've encouraged you to do that?"

Burn stood up and approached the transfixed Dorothy. Just as before, he laid his hand on her shoulder. This time though, Dorothy caught a glimpse of something gold go past her line of vision as his hand rested on her anorak. Turning her head slightly, she noticed that it was a thick, gold ring. It was square in appearance, but with slightly rounded edges, and it had a symbol on it.

Straining her eyes, she noticed that the symbol was a simple star, but with what looked like an arrow going through it. Such a simple if uncommon design, and yet rather becoming in a way that she couldn't understand. Her eyes fixed on it for a few seconds before her ears tuned into the words of its wearer.

" . . . . and basically I think that is a rather good thing too, don't you agree Dorothy?"

"Sorry Mr Burn, I didn't quite catch what you said."

"I was just saying to your husband that one can sometimes be quite illogical when one is genuinely concerned about something, do you not agree?"

Dorothy shrugged her shoulders quickly "Er yes, I suppose one does. Tell me Mr Burn, where did you get that ring? It is an interesting design."

Burn quickly withdrew his hand from its position, and after lightly brushing his lips with the front of the ring, placed both his hands into his jacket's pockets. His eyes darted between the married couple as he spoke.

"It's an heirloom . . . of a kind. My mother gave it to me a week before she died. I don't know what it signifies, but as you say it is an interesting design. Now, why don't I finish off my good deed for the day by insisting that you ride with me back to your abode? There is more than enough room in the back of my estate car."

Stephen looked uncomfortably at his wife. "No, I don't think that is necessary Mr Burn, you have been kind enough. We shan't impose on you anymore."

Dorothy regarded the tandem, her husband and then the impressive Mr Burn, and felt that to ride the tandem was one thing. To walk it home with a wonky wheel and have to suffer the indignant moans of her husband was another. If Stephen wasn't coming with her and Mr Burn then that was his problem—she had had enough, and she wasn't going to hold back her saying so.

"Oh Stephen, I really have had a rotten day. I just want to get home as quickly as possible. Yes Mr Burn, I shall be glad to take you up on your kind offer, and may I invite you into our place for a cup of tea as well? It is the least we can do for your kindness."

Ignoring the more and more outraged look on the husband's face, Burn smiled his most charming smile and gently touched Dorothy's hand. "I would be most honoured madam, and what's more, I feel it would be my duty to bring the biscuits! Would custard creams suffice?" And with a wink, he led Dorothy away in the direction he originally came from.

With a look behind her, Dorothy smiled at her baffled husband. "Get the bike darling and do hurry up. I am dying for a cuppa and a custard cream!"

Stephen bent down and tore off his bicycle clips, and in a fit of rare rage, threw them at the tandem. "Damn rude man! What is the matter with that woman? If we wanted to pick up a stray we would've gone to the dog's home! What on earth is she doing?"

As he watched his wife's figure disappear around the corner, Stephen grabbed hold of the tandem, pulled it out of the bush, and looked once again at the damaged wheel. To his eyes the thing looked fine. Too fine in fact, and he bent down to spin it around.

The disgruntled man looked on in surprise as the back wheel spun around perfectly. No buckle, no wobble, nothing. There was a slight bend in the shape of the handlebar, but nothing that would've stopped their journey home. He stood up and turned the tandem in the direction his wife had gone and mounted his seat. So she thinks that this Burn character is a saviour does she? Well, this will surprise her. He would show her that when it comes to the crunch, he was the one with the knowledge to put things right.

He thought about the way that Burn had bent down and spun the wheel with such assurance. It was obvious that the blasted man just wanted somewhere to stay for the night. Probably some businessman trickster who couldn't be bothered to pay at a hotel. Mind you, Dorothy was not helping matters by actually issuing an invite to him. She had never done such a thing before. They would always decide together who would come and go in their house. But now, all of a sudden, she feels that it is perfectly acceptable to allow a stranger, and a deeply annoying stranger at that, to enter their home without a by or leave. Well, there was still time to do something about it. And with renewed purpose, Stephen Trollope rode off in pursuit of his wife and the damned Mr Burn.

It didn't take long for him to pull alongside the silver Astra estate, and he looked on in despair as he noticed his wife in the front seat, talking in a very animated fashion to her newly acquired friend. It suddenly occurred to Stephen that if Burn had a car, then why was he walking towards them at the time of their accident? What was the damn man up to? If he dared to question Stephen's judgement again, then boy would he ask him some awkward questions!

He pulled up to the left front window and tapped onto the glass. Dorothy turned her head quickly and noticing her husband wound down the window. As soon as the glass was half-way, Stephen started his complaint.

"Now Dorothy, there is nothing wrong with the tandem as you can see. Mr Burn was obviously mistaken in what he saw wrong with it, so please get out of the car and let us go home."

Dorothy felt surprise. Not surprise at her husband's rudeness—that was something she was used to hearing—but surprise at the indignation that she suddenly felt. Never had her husband made her feel so ashamed to be his wife and she could feel her brow start to crease as she responded to Stephen's request.

"How dare you order me to get out the car! I most certainly will not. If you want to risk your neck on that ridiculous machine then fine, go ahead and risk it. I have made an invitation to this kind gentleman and I intend to honour it. If you don't like it, then I suggest you go for a long ride somewhere. I am going home for a hot drink and a nice conversation." And with that she wound up the window.

Stephen looked on in horror as the car pulled away up the lane that he and his wife had failed to complete together. He tried to think of what to say to his wife when he got her on her own, but his mind was blank. He was not used to people disagreeing with him so vehemently, especially the woman who had said "I do" to him twenty-eight years before. Feeling stunned and weary, and with the cut on his face trickling blood down his chin, Stephen Trollope made off to follow the car that was taking his ignorant wife home.

In the driving seat of the Astra, Thomas Burn gripped the steering wheel tightly and looked straight ahead. His passenger was talking to him in a very cheerful manner about something to do with the family's bungalow, but he wasn't fully paying attention. His mind was on the evening ahead, and the work that was to be done. Work that always made him feel so good to be alive and so servile to better causes. Oh Dorothy, you are going to be happy, so, so happy.

CHAPTER FIVE

"It's all about being sensible you see. I mean, I'm not saying that I am the most gifted of people, indeed, one could say that intellectually I do leave a lot to be desired . . ."

"No sir, I think you do yourself a great injustice there."

"Well, yes, thank you, but then are you a good as judge a character as you think you are. I think not."

"I'm sorry sir. I promise you that I was merely giving you my honest opinion, as unimportant as it is, and as meaningless as you think it to be."

"I don't necessarily think your opinion meaningless young Roscoe. Just a little bit wayward at times. Best keep it to yourself eh?"

"Whatever you say sir. I shall be careful to not be so . . . er . . . . presumpting in future."

"Yes, and presumptuous too. Oh dear, you really have problems with words of more than one syllable don't you?"

And with a twitch of his generous nose, the man tapped the hat of his wide eyed companion.

Feeling his head-wear move too much to the left, courtesy of the man's efforts, Roscoe raised both hands, and gripping the sides of the trilby pulled it down and centred it as much as he could. The man gave a short laugh and tapped the hat again, this time a little harder.

"Oh for Heaven's sake, will you stop being do damn pernickety with that stupid thing! It really doesn't do anything for you, you know. Anyway, what was I saying?"

"You were saying how it is all about being sensible, sir."

"Ah yes, sensible." The man shifted his black chinos and sat down on the swivelling office chair behind his desk. "You see Roscoe, if we were to suddenly go out and convert in our thousands, then we would get ourselves a very bad name, don't you think?"

Roscoe stood up and made his way to the water dispenser. Bending down, he opened his mouth and directed a spurt of water into it, before standing upright again, and wiping his wet mouth with the sleeve of his jumper.

"I would agree sir, but I think that Mr Burn has a different opinion to that. He can't stop putting himself about and charming anyone in his path."

The man stared with annoyance at Roscoe's bad manners and reached out to the box of tissues that were threatening to fall off the desk. He thought of the irony of Roscoe's comment about how Burn would put himself about. If this character thought that his appearances in public were covert, then he was severely deluding himself. Still, these problems were there to be solved, and this character had his uses, up to a certain point that is. He gazed at the shuffling, hatted man and spoke carefully.

"I think that I can cope with Mr Burn's little indiscretions. He is like a boy with a new toy that's all. I think, no I *know* that I can get him to be somewhat more selective in his choosing. And you do know what a tissue is for don't you? Honestly Roscoe, you have the manners of a Tudor peasant. I think that we should add graceful to sensible don't you?" And with that, the man handed the chagrined Roscoe a man size tissue.

Taking off his hat, Roscoe proceeded to use the tissue to wipe not just his mouth but his damp forehead too. It was a mystery to him how this man sitting in front of him could make him feel so hot and bothered, when he couldn't give a toss about anyone else.

Ever since he was a boy, he had learnt that people were there to bug you. Bug you and patronise you and flaunt their ignorance with their own opinions, which were usually wrong. He wasn't sure why they were wrong, but wrong they were. After all, he remembered with hatred the many teachers he had the misfortune to come across. The kind but fair ones, the shouting and flash ones, the quiet but strict ones, all of whom had one thing in common—they were all living a boring, humdrum life, which amounted to fuck all in the end. He, on the other hand, knew things that could make him great. He knew what people were really like, and the man in front of him had the power to help him realise his dreams.

It was just that the man also had a constant look on his face, as if any moment he was going to tell you that he was joking and that he didn't believe you at all, and could quite easily do without your presence on this planet.

At the moment though, the man had stood up and walked to the front of the desk where he sat down on its edge, pushing away a pile of papers with his back as he made room to sit down.

"Roscoe, Roscoe, or can I call you James? How inappropriate a name your poor mother chose. You certainly don't look like a James, such a classy name for such a creature as yourself. I would never ask you to perform any sort of PR for us, but please bear in mind that your appearance and mistakes may just reflect on those that guide you—in short, me. Can you just grasp that idea, or would you like me to spell it out for you?"

Looking around the spacious but gloomy office, Roscoe noticed that the mirror that was positioned above a large, grey filing cabinet. He wandered over to it, ignoring the meaningful look on the man's face, and gazed at the hatted, haggard man that began to stare back at him.

"I suppose that I could make an effort sir. I have never been the snappiest of dressers, but then I have never felt the need to dress to please others anyway."

Roscoe had just uttered the last part of his remark when a sharp, agonising pain shot up from below his belt. A pain so beggaring description that his eyes locked downwards in search of what was causing him so much grief.

There, fastened like a clampet onto his trouser fly, was the hand of the man who had been sitting on the desk only seconds before. Roscoe, in his distress, tried to remember if he had heard the man coming up behind him? He must've been too busy listening to his own words.

With hot tears starting to spring from his narrowed, tensed up eyes, he looked into the face of the man who was breathing heavily into his face. He had just absurdly worked out that the breath smelt of Doublemint before the man told him the reason for this sudden assault on his pride.

"I don't give a fuck about your pathetic desire to please others or not, as your case may be. I only know that I have worked fucking hard to perfect the abilities and plans that one needs for such a venture. You fuck them up with your shitty opinions, and I swear that I will fuck you up. Do you understand me you ignorant prick?"

Ignoring the agonised moans emanating from Roscoe's lips, the man gripped the crotch harder, enjoying the feel of power that such an action could give someone.

"I said, do you understand Roscoe?"

Placing his own hand over the man's, Roscoe tried in vain to prise the fingers away from his hurting groin, only to realise in horror that the man's grip was getting tighter.

"Don't attempt to move me Roscoe, for neither you nor the other misguided fools have the power to do so. That includes Burn and his over-active libido. Do you know, I often think that men could do without that appendage between their legs, for I have no doubt that it has been the cause of rack an ruin throughout the world since time began, and since your ancestors were just snakes in the grass."

Roscoe's face was now blood red with the sheer agony of the pain in his groin. He tried to speak through clenched teeth. "Please sir, I didn't mean to be so stupid with my words. Oh God please sir, I'm sure that what you are gripping had nothing to do with my stupid remarks."

"Bullshit. Every man's egotism stems from the pleasure he gets at hearing his own words. Pleasure that manifests itself down there, so don't tell me that you are any different. You are as egotistic and prick directed as any other bloke. No, I retract that, you are worse, for you are so full of self-important ideas. In fact, I believe that you consider yourself more fucking aware of the world than me, don't you, you miserable little shit? How much does it turn you on to think patronisingly of me uh? How much does it make you want to beat the meat?"

Feeling that at any moment he was going to pass out with this constant torture, Roscoe could only whisper his reply to the snarling face of the man so close to him. "No sir, I assure you. I am just somebody who wishes to help you. I don't consider myself better. I promise I don't. Please sir, please let go of me."

The sensation of pleasure that came to Roscoe's mind as the man finally released his crotch was so sweet that he felt like crying. But before he could thank his attacker for his kindness, the man had made his way to the office door before turning to face the gasping Roscoe. His anger had apparently subsided, and now he was looking at the hatted servant with a smile, a smile that suggested that nothing so agonising had taken place.

"You know Roscoe, perhaps I should call you James, especially after being so personal with you. But then, you know that the next time I have to deal with you so forcefully, you may not see that certain part of your body again eh?"

Roscoe unconsciously rubbed his sore groin, and nodded his head dumbly and without a sound.

"Now, you know who I want you to speak to, so try and do that without causing any trouble eh? And for God's sake, smarten yourself up man. You may enjoy looking like a walking rubbish bin, but it makes me feel sick to the stomach.

As he watched the black chinos of the man disappear through the door, Roscoe thought of vengeance against his assailant, but jumped as the box of tissues on the desk finally tipped over and fell to the floor.

Feeling goose bumps appear on his arms, Roscoe considered that the man was probably watching him even when he was alone, and maybe even hear his thoughts.

Feeling very unsafe in the man's office, he straightened his pork-pie hat, and sauntered, albeit very carefully, out through the door and to the world outside. He had a taxi to hire.

CHAPTER SIX

Leaning on one of the promenade railings, Paul looked out into the horizon and stared at an endless carpet of dark, blue water. Just below the sounds of screaming kids and arcade music, he could hear the voice of his wife as she tried to understand what had happened between him and her sister.

He had sworn over and over again that he was totally innocent of what Emily had charged him with. For heaven's sake, he loved Em as if she were his own flesh and blood—surely she knew him well enough to know that it was just the child's wild imagination that was causing this hideous mistake.

"I still don't understand it Paul. If Emily is lying then what on earth is causing her to be so ridiculous?"

Maria's voice had just carried to Paul's ears, so even though the sounds of the seaside resort were still ringing in his head, he could just about make out what she was saying, although it was hard work. He was still dazed by what had happened, and to be honest he was traipsing around like some demented Frankenstein. Oh shit, what was going on here?

He stared at the confused eyes of his wife, the dark rings under her eyes relating the tale of a sleepless night full of thinking.

"What do you want me to say Maria? Just tell me what you want me to say, because at the moment I am starting to feel guilty of something I haven't done, and do you know how that feels? Do you know what it feels like to start believing all the lies that are told about you? You saw me trying to talk to Em, trying to get the truth out of her—did you see her face? My God, if ever Oscars were handed out for real life performances, then that little cow would scoop the lot. "And the best performance by a lying little sod goes to . . . . Emily Willows, for Let's Drop Paul in the Shit," at which point he made a noise from the back of his throat that sounded like a big audience clapping. This noise used to have Maria in fits, but she wasn't laughing this time.

"You are just being bloody stupid now. Even when something is serious you just can't resist having a little joke can you? Anyway, what do you mean you are starting to believe you are guilty? What are you trying to tell me?"

With a heartfelt sigh, Paul let go of the promenade railings and started to walk away from his wife. He had trodden three paces before he spun around, his face a mixture of anger and puzzlement. "Oh yes, twist what I say. Do something new Maria! I think you want to believe Emily. I think that you want some sort of twisted ammunition to throw at me, just so you can win the petty arguments we have been having recently. You don't believe me? Fine! I'll just go and speak to someone who knows me better than you okay? That wouldn't be fucking difficult. Who knows, I may just rob a granny while I'm at it, after all, I'm a hardened criminal now eh?" And Maria watched in dismay as her husband strode off towards the main road and the amusement arcade opposite them.

"No Paul, stop! No, you misunderstand me, I'm not accusing you of anything. Paul!"

She would have caught up with the escaping Paul if it hadn't been for the pram that was being pushed by the tired looking woman. Her dirty denims, purple and green hooped jumper and dirty white Pony trainers adding to a picture of borderline poverty. If that obstacle wasn't bad enough to get around, the woman's moaning offspring also proved to be a nuisance, with their insistence that they just *had* to play on the new Grand Prix simulation game in the arcade.

Maria moved left, swerved right, inched left again, and moved a little, tiny bit forward before the situation got to her. "For fuck's sake, will you move out the fucking way!"

The tired woman turned her head in Maria's direction like a shot. "What's your fucking problem? *You* fucking move you stroppy bitch!"

Maria had just enough time to notice the moaning children staring at her, their eyes forlorn and yet questioning (an interesting diversion this—will this help to change mum's mind and get us into the arcade?) before she threw the woman a filthy look and started towards the road again. She noticed in time Paul walking past the laughing clown in the plastic box, that was tempting passer-by to waste their hard earned dosh on trying to grab a cheap, tacky toy with an impossible to control crane. Past it he went and looking straight ahead, made his way into the arcade.

Manipulating the traffic, Maria saw just how tacky the clown's prizes were, before she entered the world of the hoping and generally unlucky.

Looking around the fruit machines, passing the gun ranges, and almost knocking over a girl lining up to take a shot at pool, she finally spotted her husband in front of a Ninja fighting machine. He was checking his pockets for change, maybe hoping that he had the necessary coins to try his hand at the colourful, probably totally violent amusement.

"Paul! Paul will you talk to me." Despite the fairly short distance, she felt exhausted, and the thought that her 'exhaustion' was getting ready to topple her again, sped through her mind like a formula one car, flying a giant banner proclaiming what it was that had put her briefly in hospital before.

"Nice to meet you. Have we met before? I'm a child abuser, hitting the crap out of them my speciality, so don't let your children near me. Careful now." and with a look out of the corner of his eye, Paul pushed fifty pence into the game's slot and started pushing the green buttons in front of him.

"What is it with you? I didn't accuse you of anything. I just want an answer that's all. Can't you see that?"

"I can see that if our marriage had problems before, then boy are we heading for a big finale now. For the past few months you have twisted everything I have said. I would've thought that this was a situation much worse than me keeping the toilet seat down whilst taking a piss, but no, you just carry on and twist, twist, twist. Well twist away woman—just don't expect me to answer your accusations until you speak my language. Fuck!"

Pushing the buttons harder than was necessary, Paul tried hard to beat the ninja that had just won round one of the animated battle before him.

"Paul, will you stop playing that stupid game and look at me?"

"Look at you? Why should I look at you? I know what you look like! And it was your idea that we got away from it all wasn't it? "Let's go to Southend" you said. "Let's go and visit my folks. I need the rest after my collapse and you need a break too. We can sort out what Emily said when we are there."

Realising that the second ninja battle was going to be over quickly as well, Paul hit the buttons with his fist and turned to face his wife. Both their faces were lit with the lights from the game, and yet even he could not mistake the look of distress on Maria's face. He had seen that look a thousand times before, and he just knew that a little nudge more, and she would be smudging her mascara with tears.

"And do you know what? I believed, I *really* believed that we could sort it out. That maybe a change of scene was just what we needed. But it's just the same old thing isn't it? I bet you were really itching to tell all this morning eh? Just couldn't wait to spill the beans over the bacon and eggs. "Pass the sauce please auntie, and oh yes, did I tell you that Paul's been viciously hitting Emily?"

"Now you're being ridiculous. Oh God I *hate* it when you talk like this", and underneath her breath remarked, "you remind me of Mick Rogers."

"Who? Mick who? Sorry Maria, I didn't quite catch that last remark. An ex maybe? Someone with more sense than me no doubt. Someone who wouldn't embarrass you with your sodding sister."

She felt at first that tears were about to flow from the corners of her eyes, but Paul's remarks stung her into a defence. She was sick of trying to talk to him when he obviously felt so sorry for himself.

She spoke calmly and assuredly. More assured than she actually felt. "Yes Paul, you are spot-on. Mick was an ex of mine. Mick Rogers was the name you didn't totally catch. I was just thinking aloud of how you sound as pompous as him. Mick was just starting out as a graphic artist when I knew him, and the more I knew him, the more I was convinced that he genuinely hated the world. He always sounded as if the world owed him a favour, and boy was he a dreamer! His head was always three feet above the clouds, and he would spout incoherent ideas about the general public and think he sounded wise. But all he did was sound confused and bitter. I liked him a lot at first, but then he frightened me. Now you are starting to sound as persecuted as him and I don't think I can handle that."

With that, she raised her hand in a goodbye gesture and turned to leave the arcade.

Paul stared at the ninja game screen, totally unaware of the young boy beside him who was on tenterhooks, as he waited to ply the game with someone else's money. He wasn't feeling persecuted was he? Hey, he *was* the one that was being accused of something serious.

"Excuse me mate, are you finished with that?" Paul looked around and noticed the boy standing there, one hand on his hip and chewing a big wad of bubble gum. "You finished or what?"

Ignoring the smell of gum that had wafted from the boy's mouth, Paul looked at the screen, at the boy and finally at the ceiling, feeling a tightness in his neck as he did so. He rubbed the soreness and glanced once more at the boy noticing his Manchester United football shirt as he did so. "Yeah mate, I'm finished. Very finished. Hope you win as much as your team eh?" Then with a slight stagger, he went in search of his angry wife, not noticing the boy giving him a look that matched Maria's earlier one at the pram pushing woman.

He seemed to have walked for miles, but in reality for about five minutes, when he realised that he wasn't looking for his wife as hard as he could be. Indeed, he had been wandering along the promenade in a complete haze. So much so, that he was quite surprised to see himself standing in a street just off the promenade, and outside a shop that sold the sort of things that tourists and holiday makers considered essential seaside purchases, e.g. rock, postcards, key-rings etc. Plain and simple artefacts that amused and enchanted the unknowing punter.

Paul was even more surprised to see the collection of adult jokes that they had. Oh yes, plop this lump of sugar into your lady's tea and wait for the laughs to come rolling by as it turns into a 'realistic' willy! Would Maria enjoy that little jape? Probably not at the moment. Probably wouldn't work anyway, and it would resemble an anorexic worm instead of something remotely phallic.

He was just about to examine the naked women playing cards, when he realised that someone was at his side. It wasn't so much the feeling of someone there, but the fact that a smell of after shave was overpowering his nostrils. It reminded him of Old Spice or even Brut—definitely an old favourite from the past.

Just as he was running through some more after-shave names in his head, the person spoke, and Paul felt that he must be speaking to him. After all, wasn't he the only pervert looking at those tacky cards? "Outrageous. Outrageous and totally unnecessary. Lord what will those diseased minds think of next? You weren't planning to buy those sinful playthings were you?"

The voice was low and somewhat musical and immediately made Paul think of an actor he had seen in a film once. Joss something. Ackling? Ackland? It had Mel Gibson in it though. Lethal Weapon 23, or something like that.

Looking at the owner of the deep voice, Paul shuddered as he saw the man seemed to stand taller than any person that ever lived before. And to top it all off, way up there on top of the guy's head, was a hat that looked as if it belonged to a Mexican bandit, such was its size. Black and wide and oddly out of sync with today's modern gear—but who was going to disagree with him? Not this citizen, no way Jose! The fact was, it made this giant look even bigger than he was—quite an achievement really.

The wind blew in from the sea and attempted to dislodge the said hat from the man's head, only to be foiled at the last moment as the man's big hands pulled it down before diving into two big pockets in the front of his long, black coat. Paul had only a second to wonder whether Marks and Sparks did such a large size garment, before the man's gaze fell upon him and the deep voice sounded again.

"Damn nuisance this wind. Can't even wear a decent hat without Mother Nature trying to whip it off!" Paul would've replied with a short laugh (a false laugh, but good manners don't hurt do they? Especially with a guy this big!) but his outgoing breath was stopped by the man's own deep, booming laugh and made a headscarf wearing pensioner turn as she passed the shop and give Paul a look that suggested that the man was quite mad. Quite, quite mad, because normal folk don't laugh like that, do they dear?

Paul felt that to stay quiet would be rather discourteous, even though he really was not in the mood to speak to the local loony, and craning his head upwards, issued his response to the stranger who had, and let's be honest here Pauly, appeared from out of the blue.

"Yeah, I guess so. One of the reasons I don't wear hats really. We don't have the climate—heh!" A nervous guffaw at the end of his sentence there, but he was no Jim Davidson, he just wanted to be polite, light-hearted and away from this shop. He had given up looking at the shop's dubious offerings as soon as that deep laugh had penetrated his eardrums.

"Don't knock it my friend. I have travelled the world and I feel that I can say, quite categorically, that nothing beats the freshness of a British sea-breeze. Always very invigorating I think, and good for the soul—unlike those disgusting, insulting items in that window. I am very tempted by only one thing here, to go into this establishment and tell the owner or whoever is behind the counter, of how they have damned themselves to the horrors of Hades. Such unnecessary items of obscenity."

"Yeaaah right," replied the slightly worried Paul, "I guess that I better leave you to it then. Get some of that sea-breeze into my lungs! Cheerio!" and feeling that a rather nasty atmosphere had been left behind, like walking out of a thick, grey fog, Paul made his way up the street, away from the sea front. He could only guess that Maria had gone back to her aunt's house and so he went in that direction, and anyway, he suddenly had a need to shower.

It was whilst he was passing a newsagents that he realised that he hadn't bought his daily does of tabloid entertainment. Not that he ever admitted to gazing lustfully at some topless girlie who was being paid far more than logic suggested, but instead he would respond that it was the paper's excellent sports coverage that always captured his attention.

Nevertheless, into the shop Paul went, paid his money, rolled the paper into a tube, and rammed into his back pocket. As he left the newsagents, he noticed that they sold sherbet spaceships. Blimey, when was the last time he had tried one of those things? Years ago, blooming years ago. In fact, he could picture himself coming out of primary school, and making his way to Jeff's sweetshop just so he could experience the sweet, tangy, melt-in-the-mouth feeling of those beauties. He could even remember how he would put one on his tongue, and then wave his tongue in the air just so he could show anyone at all interested how clever he was! The feeling of the sweet melting on his tongue was a childhood memory that surely no-one could forget. Hey, why not get some now? Why not? He needed cheering up, and if Maria was going to treat him like a kid, then why not act like one anyway?

As all these cute memories flooded Paul's head, he became briefly unaware that he was still walking out the shop, and was obviously not looking where he was going. His momentum would've taken him close to the main road too, had it not been for the figure that bumped into him. All thoughts of a perfect idyllic age disappeared abruptly, as Paul felt his body fly back towards the shop's entrance, before feeling his backside come down with a painful crunch onto the dirty, sweetie-wrapper strewn pavement.

"Jesus! What the fuck do you think . . . ." Paul's expression of pain and anger was genuine, but even he was surprised at how quickly the anger dissipated as he recognised the long, black coat that swept past the figure's knees and towards natty, black brogues—the likes of which Paul hadn't seen in many a long year.

"Language young man! Please watch your language, and if you must blaspheme in such a sordid manner, then do so in the privacy of your own bedroom—away from the ears of the good people of this town, not to mention the young ones. What sort of impression does such a vernacular make?"

Dusting down his jeans and straightening the paper that had fallen buckled to the floor, Paul looked up to the deep voice that had floated down towards him. Up to the figure's face Paul's eyes went before they rested on the dark, somewhat penetrating gaze of the man in the 'Mexican' hat. The man was looking down with a grimace that had such an effect on Paul that for one moment he felt that he was going to be knocked back again. It was only the man's sudden change in demeanour that stopped that embarrassing event from happening.

"Ah yes, I see it's you," remarked the towering stranger, as if that was a good enough reason for the smile that had spread from each of his slightly hidden ears. "Forgive my outburst, but I have never been an advocate of such language. Although, I think that I could forgive you for that slip of the tongue. I mean, it did look like a rather nasty fall. And my word, if that was not my fault either. Yes, I really must apologise to you. I must've been thinking about other things, like the filth in that shop for one thing."

"No really," retorted Paul, "I was miles away. Thoughts of childhood and sherbet spaceships if you can believe it. No need to apologise." And with that, Paul went to continue his route back to Aunt Meg's before the man's voice caught him mid-stride.

"Ah sherbet spaceships. Now I can understand why you were so preoccupied! I must say that I had a liking for them too when I was younger. Do you mean to say that they are still being made?"

"Yes, and they are selling them in that shop there. I couldn't decide whether to get some or not, heh! (another nervous laugh Paul?) Anyway, better not. I don't think the wife would appreciate me spending money like that. What can you do?"

"Well" responded the man, "you can stop buying literature like that for a start," and he pointed with one big, veiny hand towards the paper that was in Paul's back pocket. "It really isn't healthy reading you know—all conjecture and pompous opinions, not to mention the jezebels who parade its pages with such contempt for the Lord. Ah, it makes you wonder does it not, as to how people could misuse their bodies in such a corrupt manner?"

Paul raised his eyes to the sky, not because his agreed with the man, but because he felt that it made him look as if he was interested. He wasn't sure if it had worked, but the man carried on regardless.

"To be honest with you young man, I have a little theory about that type of woman. I believe, no I firmly believe, that if those young women had something more to hold onto, something more . . . . shall we dare say spiritual? Then they would not feel this urge, this Devil's urge to show off parts of their naked bodies, parts that only their one and only husband should see."

"And maybe the odd doctor too," quipped Paul.

"Yes, yes, of course. But I'm sure that you know full well what I'm talking about. I'm sure that a bright man like you is fully aware that it is only a severe lack of guidance that is forcing these poor girls to desecrate their bodies like that. I mean . . ." and with a movement that was so fast, that Paul wasn't sure that it had happened, the lofty man swiped the newspaper from Paul's pocket, before continuing.

". . . . can you, in all seriousness, say that you find this sort of titillation attractive?" Paul gazed at the half page colour photograph of the topless brunette, with long, velvet gloves on her arms and little else. He had to admit that she looked rather gorgeous, but what could he say to this bible basher in front of him?

Paul was tired, mentally and even a little bit physically, and under normal circumstances he would be snapping away at anybody that was being remotely irritating, but he was very wary of this guy, and he couldn't think why. Maybe it was the man's staring gaze; maybe it was the long, black jacket? Or folks, maybe it was that bizarre Mexican style hat? Whatever, he didn't think it was very wise to take chances with somebody so tall anyway!

"Well, once you've seen one, you've seen them all. I don't really pay much attention to those photos. I'm more interested in the . . . ."

"Sports results? Yes, I imagined that you would be." Paul looked at the stranger with his mouth slightly parted, and felt a frown starting to cross his forehead as the man continued.

"But then, I am not really a sports person either. Maybe the odd game of chess, but then is chess a sport, or just a way of life?" Paul shuddered as this last remark was followed by another of the man's deep laughs, although Paul figured it sounded more like a bellow than a laugh.

Looking towards the top of the street, Paul felt that the bellow was a good a time as any to end this conversation, and make his way back to Maria. Smiling his best (false) smile, Paul raised his hand briefly and bid his goodbye a second time.

"Yes, well I really must go. If I don't get a hurry on then my wife will kill me! I'm already late as it is."

"Oh that is a shame," responded the man, "and just as we were getting along so famously. Well, at least before you go, you should take a sherbet saucer." and with a flourish that seemed much too graceful for such a tall man, the stranger dipped into one of his large coat pockets and pulled out a crumpled bag. After opening it carefully, he thrust it towards Paul, who unthinking, helped himself to a blue sherbet saucer—his favourite colour no less. (Didn't mummy tell you to never take sweets from a stranger Paul? What the hell, he was a big boy now, and the man may be even bigger, but what damage could a bible-basher do with a sherbet spaceship?)

"Take a few more, there's plenty left, take a look." Paul glanced into the bag and wasn't entirely surprised to see the bag was full of blue sherbet spaceships.

"Er no thanks. One really is enough. I must watch the old teeth you know." and at this, the man slipped the bag back into his large coat pocket.

But as the saucer melted in his mouth, a suddenly obvious thought occurred to Paul, and he felt that at the risk of being rude, he must ask the man his question or else lose a night's sleep thinking about the answer.

"But, I didn't see you buy those. I thought you didn't even know that they were still being made?"

The man put the bag deep into his pocket and shot Paul a smile that made the 27 year old cringe deep inside. It wasn't so much a smile as a knowing grin, and reminded Paul of all the school bullies that he had encountered throughout his unremarkable school career. The pathetic specimens of boyhood, who had so much trouble liking themselves that they had to strike out at anybody smaller than them. Probably, Paul had thought, because they were too stupid to hit themselves. "Yeah, too stupid", as he had said to Chris Burrows, his childhood pal at Sir Magnus Trotters secondary school, "too stupid because if they tried to hit themselves, they'd probably miss!" Oh how Chris had rolled about the class at that one!

At the moment, though, the only thing rolling was Paul's mind, and it started to roll a lot more as the man sidled closer to Paul's shoulder.

"I must disagree young man. I had already bought the saucers this morning from another shop. I merely thought that the shop I had bought them from were selling them as a kind of special offer, a one off if you like. I wasn't truly aware that they were still being manufactured. Are you sure you wouldn't like another one?"

Feeling confused, confused and more mentally tired than ever, Paul shook himself and walked off, looking over his shoulder as he went. "Thanks, but I really am off now. Enjoy your saucers, wherever you bought them. Maybe I'll get some later—if my wife will let me, heh!"

"Yes," the man replied in a voice at least a few decibels louder than the previous one, "and maybe that delightful little girl would like some too?"

Paul stopped in his tracks and turned towards the grinning man. "What little girl? What are you talking about?"

"Your little girl. No sorry, she isn't *yours* as such, a relative though. Feels like your own though, doesn't she? Such a little sweetheart. Go on, buy her some sherbet saucers. I'm sure she will let you keep the blue ones."

Was he hearing this? Surely this guy was just guessing at him having a young relative? It would be pretty easy to do, wouldn't it? He clenched his fist as his mind battled between confronting this disturbing man, or just walking away. After all, doesn't it take a 'real' man to walk away? It was the image of Maria waving goodbye in the arcade that settled it. He walked two steps towards the man, who had removed his hat to reveal long strands of grey and white hair.

With more a sense of smugness than just naked temper, Paul offered his parting shot. "And you call yourself a Christian? Ha!" before turning and making his way back up the street. He walked so quickly that he didn't hear the man's reply.

"Christian? I didn't say that I am a Christian! Young man, you are making a grave mistake. Oh a *grave* mistake. Christian? Ha, you fool! A man in your position has no right to question my beliefs. You will repent you ignorant boy, I will *make* you repent!" He put his hands back into his pocket and pulled out the same, white crumpled bag as before.

Carefully opening it, he dipped in and pulled out a round, orange lollipop. Putting the sweet carefully into his mouth, he rolled the empty bag into a ball and threw it perfectly into a nearby bin. Pivoting on the heels of his brogues, he headed back towards the sea-front, but not without a quick glance behind him. He could just make out Paul's denim jacket as he got nearer to the top of the street.

"Christian! And I thought the boy had promise! He has guts though, I think that I can see that plain enough. Well young man, we'll see if you are as brave as you think you are. Your pain hasn't even begun boy, not even begun."

CHAPTER SEVEN

"Hmm, yes indeed, a most delicious cuppa if I may say so Dorothy. You don't mind me calling you Dorothy do you?"

"No, no of course not. That is if you don't mind me calling you Thomas?"

"The pleasure is all mine Dorothy. You wouldn't believe how the pleasure is all mine."

Dorothy, for maybe the first time in over thirty years, felt herself blush so deeply at this remark, that she felt like the proverbial belisha beacon. This man had charm and what's more he knew it. So unlike some of the youngsters that had moved into the area recently. Youngsters, who she adamantly believed, were pseudo middle-upper class types; people who had momentarily got lucky with the finances (maybe a lucky break in business, or even a lottery win) but who, eventually, and without fail, would go back down the ladder of success and back to the city streets where they undoubtedly belonged. Dorothy wasn't cold or unreasonable about such things—she was just saying what a lot of the community felt, but were too uptight to mention, right?

"Right, Dorothy!"

"I'm sorry?"

"Don't be my dear. No need to be so when you make such a lovely brew, and you have such a splendid house too."

Whatever Thomas Burn was remarking about slipped her mind as he started her on one of her favourite topics—her home. Never mind the home being every Englishman's castle, this was her domain, and for all of his huffing and puffing, Stephen was usually very aware of that.

From the pine kitchen cupboards and country-style dresser, to the green bedroom, with its green carpet, green duvet and green curtains,

Dorothy had planned the decor meticulously. And okay, it was never going to be everybody's idea of domestic heaven, but she lived here, she planned it and she enjoyed it. Other people's views were not so important.

"Exactly" said Burn,

"Pardon?"

"Exactly. The hi-fi system. It is one that I have been looking for, for quite some time—where did you buy it?"

"I really can't remember Mr Burn—sorry Thomas. My husband is the hi-fi expert around here. He won't even let our son use it without permission, and even then he will hang around just to make sure that Adrian doesn't dirty the CDs, or leave fingerprints on the glass of the record player's lid."

"It must be such a bind having a partner like that. Oh my word, what am I saying? Please forgive me madam, but sometimes my inner feelings just get the better of me. Call me an old fashioned, emotional, intuitive type if you will, but there you go. I say what I will, and I mean what I say."

Maybe it was Stephen's embarrassing behaviour earlier, but in all honesty, Dorothy did not feel in the slightest bit annoyed at Burn's remark. Maybe she would've been a few years ago, but not now. Why was that? Why had this realisation only just occurred to her? She gave Burn a brief smile and replied with a voice a lot more convivial than she realised.

"Oh no, don't apologise. Honesty can be quite refreshing at times. Stephen has some odd idiosyncrasies, but then I suppose they are all part and parcel of the man who made me say "I do" all those years ago!"

"Absolutely madam. Who knows what tricks love plays on us, and what can we do to stop it? Nothing I fear. As that fine, classic song goes, "love is a many splendoured thing," an enigmatic part of human life that is to be revered and enjoyed. But if I may say so my dear, I feel that the "usual" impression of love, the meeting someone, falling in 'love' with them, and spending most of your life together aspect, is just too simple. Love is so much more than that, don't you agree?"

Dorothy had no doubt that Thomas Burn had charm, but she had to admit that some of his ramblings were very confusing, somewhat ambiguous even, and this recent effort was no different. She tried to steer the conversation into waters that she would comprehend.

"Er yes, I think so Mr Burn. But then, what above the love between families. Mother, father, son, daughter, even your pets. Love has many qualities to it, that is what makes it so special."

"Yes my lovely, I couldn't agree more. Your argument has no holes in it I assure you. But I fear that, and with absolute respect here Dorothy, you misunderstand my angle on this matter."

"I do? Oh sorry Mr Burn, its been one of those days, you know?"

"Oh yes, I know Dorothy, I really do. Here, let me try to explain to you my theory in a bit more detail."

Dorothy smiled slightly as Thomas Burn made his way to where she was sitting, on the red and pink floral sofa that her 24 year old daughter had helped to choose. Karen was convinced that it would look perfect with the living room's pink and white curtains, and despite her earlier doubts, Dorothy concurred. Karen had a way of getting around her mother's stubborn reluctance to listen to other's ideas for home decor, probably because she had shown what a good eye for design she had herself when she and her husband Mark had decorated their own little semi just on the outskirts of Colchester. And she had to admit, the sofa looked lovely with the curtains—her daughter had obviously inherited her design flare!

Now though, ideas of home decor had dissipated into the past as she felt Burn's figure settle down next to hers. But even when the charismatic character took her right hand, Dorothy did not flinch. Instead, she felt for the first time in years an absurd sense of well-being. A knowledge that some things had been missing from her life for such a long time, but now there was this chance to get those missing pieces back.

Burn's voice was much closer now, and to her ears, much deeper too. As he gently rubbed her hand, she did not so much hear the words, but feel them wash over her entire body. He was now looking into her eyes, and muttering words that were obviously so 'right', that she didn't understand why she hadn't thought of them before.

"It's okay Dorothy, my sweet Dorothy. Just relax and I shall tell you all about my visions of love. Love is to be enjoyed, by me, by you, by anybody with an open, willing and healthy mind. It is a gift from someone special, and a gift that we should not take for granted, nor let slip by, just because of some of life's false restrictions. Look around you my dear, and by all means enjoy what you have, should you so wish.

But isn't this just another form of imprisonment? It may have a lot more charm than Pentonville or Holloway, but isn't the principal the same? A place without a freedom of love?"

She was transfixed by Burn's eyes, hooked on the sight of the man's pupils opening and closing, and the red, jagged lines on his sclera, throbbed like prominent rivers of blood. His hand moved from hers and was now making its way up her arms towards her breasts. Again, for what seemed like an age, a old sensation filled her body; a wetness between her thighs that made all the nerves in her body tingle and her heartbeat quicken. She was still letting his words flow through her, and she felt that they made a new kind of sense to her world, and that he was merely highlighting what was obviously wrong with her marriage.

She opened her mouth to try and respond to Burn's words, but had felt her lips part when his dark face grew larger and larger in her field of vision. She just caught hold of his next words, before any attempt to speak was stifled by the mouth of Thomas Burn on top of hers. She wondered at the coolness of his lips as his tongue searched for her own and moved questioningly around the insides of her mouth.

"I am merely demonstrating my theory to you Dorothy, so please relax and enjoy the knowledge I wish to impart to you. relax and learn, and when Stephen comes home, you will surely view your life in a new, exciting way. You won't be disappointed I promise you. Your dear husband won't know what has hit him."

Stephen Trollope knew exactly what had hit him. A sense of indignation and shame at his own lack of action. He was never a man to stand idly by whilst others took control. Indeed, if his father could see him now, he would give him a thrashing to within an inch of his self-important life. Oh why didn't he stop that wretched Burn person when he could? He wasn't a violent man, not physically anyway, but sometimes restraining has to be used to get a desired effect. How many times had his father grabbed him by the britches and thrown him forcefully into his room, and refused to let him out for days at a time? And had that damaged him? Tough love is a true love, but try telling youngsters and politically correct mad people that these days!

Sure, he was aware that in this day and age such discipline had to be modernised somewhat, and therefore he had never tried such action on Adrian, or any of his children for that matter. But he *had* implied to his offspring that he was capable of it, and that was usually enough to keep order in the Trollope household. Even Dorothy had become aware that he was capable of it. How many times had he told her? Countless, but he was sure that he had got his message across.

But the point was, and let's be clear here, he *would've* physically stopped Burn from being so damned cocksure of himself. He would've, if it hadn't been for the sudden rudeness of his wife. It was that, and that alone that had stunned him into non-action. This was not a case of maybes, this was a fact.

At the moment though, it was foolish to let his mind wander in such a way. He was aware that concentration was paramount if he was to control the tandem properly for the rest of his journey home. It wasn't that he hadn't controlled it solo before, but it had been quite a while as his wife was usually there to accompany him on such outings.

As he entered his little home-town, he passed the delightfully stone-clad home of dear Mrs Bettings. Now there was a lady with breeding. Seventy-four summers young, and a constant attendant at every Sunday morning sermon at St Michael's. In fact, the Reverend Eve would often comment to him that Mrs Bettings was at the church more often than him!

But the gentlewoman was not at St Michael's right now. Stephen was pleased to see the small, grey-haired figure pottering up her cottage's path, her famous dark red shopping bag hooked over one arm. He would've just smiled and politely said hello to the lady before carrying on his way, but Mrs Bettings was desperate to declare the latest, local gossip, and the way her walk went from potter to slight skip made Stephen realise that she wanted to talk to the bike riding one.

"I say, Mr Trollope! Mr Trollope, care to stop and chat a while?" Ah, thought Stephen, even the lady's language is proof of good manners and breeding. If Adrian can grow up to have a molecule of Mrs Bettings' pedigree, then he will have truly succeeded as a parent.

Karen, (although he would never echo such a thought to Dorothy), was a bit of a disappointment. She was a polite and talented enough woman, and yet there was an air of rebelliousness about her. She often disagreed with her father's views, especially regarding the way they had brought up Adrian, and she didn't even have the decency to telephone regularly, or even now and then. Sometimes, it could be months before they heard from her and she only lived a few miles away.

"I say, Mr Trollope. I was talking to the Reverend only this morning, and he was saying that the preparations for the tea dance have taken a turn for the worst."

Stephen gazed absent-mindedly at the pensioner's bag, before realising that an answer would be in order here. He guessed at an appropriate reply.

"Yes I heard something about that. What exactly have you heard?"

"Well, Mrs Adamson has had to pull out at the last moment. Something to do with her husband's bad back. Mind you, I do feel that he only has himself to blame, what with all the DIY that he does and he is no spring chicken anymore. More harm than good if you ask me, don't you think Mr Trollope, Mr Trollope?"

Stephen was still staring at Mrs Bettings' bag, and was only just aware of the lady's question. "Yes Mrs Bettings, absolutely. So, what is the good Reverend going to do about it?"

"Well, dare I say it Mr Trollope, but I got the impression that he was going to ask yourself and your good wife. How is Dorothy by the way? I haven't seen her for quite a while. A few days I believe. Thursday, yes Thursday afternoon. She did look queer though. Has she been okay? She is so full of life usually, so to see her looking pale is a surprise. Is she ill? It is unusual to see you on your tandem by yourself."

Stephen searched his mind and tried to remember if there, indeed, had been anything wrong with his wife on Thursday. The only thing that came to mind though, was Dorothy's ridiculous behaviour earlier on that day.

"No, I think that she was fine. At least I think so. Must have been tiredness, she has been working very hard lately. I try to get her to lay down and relax, but all she does is busy about. Well, you know Dorothy."

"So, what will you say to the Reverend then? Do you think that you will be able to provide the essential refreshment for our little get together?"

Stephen looked back over his shoulder, back down the road he had just come from. For a second, he visualised himself and Dorothy speeding down the lanes, wind blowing through their hair, legs whizzing around and around, and the promise of a hot, home-made tea at home. Buy *why* had she behaved so stupidly earlier on? Dorothy was a reliable woman. A bit forgetful at times, and prone to moments of stubbornness, but friendly, optimistic, excellent in the kitchen and *reliable*. Yes, he was sure that they could help the Reverend out, Dorothy loved doing that sort of thing. But as for now he had to find her and make sure that she realised that just upping and leaving him with a complete stranger was not only rude, but also not the done thing in such a respectable relationship.

"Mr Trollope, are you okay?"

"Yes Mrs Bettings. I'm sorry, I was a thousand miles away. Please forgive me, but I've had a very trying day."

"Ha-ha, no problem Mr Trollope. I know exactly what you mean. But will you and Dorothy be able to provide the refreshment for us?"

"I don't see why not my dear. Dorothy loves helping the Reverend, and if there is anybody in the world that makes a better cup of tea, then I am yet to meet them!"

"Bravo to that Mr Trollope! If I see the Reverend I will tell him the good news. And of course, should you see him before me, then I am sure that you will mention your favour to him. He will be so relieved." And with a brief wave of the hand, and a smile across her wrinkled, yet sunny face, Mrs Bettings pottered off in the direction of the few shops in their quiet village.

Stephen felt uneasy, and yet he couldn't understand why. The day had been out of the ordinary, it was true, and yet something in the way that Dorothy had spoken to him had enabled a feeling of wariness to creep into his mind. He was sure he could sort it out—it was just a silly misunderstanding, yes? Of course it was. Dorothy would see sense and understand, she always did. Now, let's see if that Burn character can be ejected with the minimum of fuss. Let's get on with out comfortable life as per usual shall we?

CHAPTER EIGHT

He looked down at the racks of CDs before him and just knew that he wasn't going to find what he wanted. Why did record companies delete only the most collectable of seventies albums? Well Michael, he thought to himself, yet another trip to a second hand store no doubt or maybe a search on the Internet is in order? Anyway, why did he think that he would stand a chance of finding his most wanted records in a store away from London? Record chains tended to stock the same albums no matter where you went. It was a bit of an insult to folk who didn't live in the capital when you thought about it.

Mind you, what chance was there of finding an obscure seventies album anyway? More to the point, how can someone who was born in the early seventies find seventies music so damn good? And even more to the point, what was he doing asking himself such stupid questions in a coastal record shop, whilst staring blankly at a James Last compilation album? If he doesn't move soon, some gorgeous example of womanhood will see him eyeing the Last disc and dismiss all thoughts of approaching him, simply because of his . . . . interesting taste in music! Yes, such is my luck eh?

He turned sharply to his left and nearly managed to get to the shop's exit head first, as he tripped over the black, leather handbag of a thoughtless customer who was scanning the DVD section. The lady in question tutted loud enough to inform the entire shop of Mick's clumsy carriage, before shooting him a look that suggested that it clearly wasn't *her* that was going to change his women luck.

With blood rushing to his face, and a sense of embarrassment causing his solar plexus to turn a triple somersault without the aid of a net, Mick rushed through the door and breathed in the salty air of the street.

After five minutes of agitated, quick march ambling, Mick found himself sitting on a graffiti curtained wooden bench. Straining his neck one hundred and eighty degrees, he eyed the newness of two, red-bricked, semi-detached houses. Their brown pointed roofs, and brass knockered front doors served to remind him of his little dreams as a bewildered teenager; the little dream that always encouraged his efforts in a cruel world, when all around were letting him down, nagging him or insulting him. The nagging and insulting he now felt he could cope with; when you lived in London town, one becomes somewhat thick-skinned to that benighted behaviour. No, it was the constant letting down that hurt. How he wished he was religious, for then he could maybe ask up above as to why he was being afflicted so.

Looking numbly in front of him, he saw a vision of a boy in a tassled cowboy jacket, walking down an Islington backstreet, following the cracks in the pavement, for fear of raising his eyes and looking at a disinterested passer by. He had loved that jacket, although it was of constant amusement to his small circle of friends. How many times had they asked him where his horse was? God, some people are so sad in their obvious one-liners—like nobody in the entire world could think of them too. How those so called quips bothered him. Why they bothered him he now couldn't think of—isn't it strange how old age mellows ones insecurities? Doesn't it?

What used to *really* bother him, though, was the track his friends were taking in life. I mean, what on earth drives people to be born, grow up, work like a slave, maybe procreate, worry, worry, worry, retire and then wait for the call from St Peter? Well matey, that certainly wasn't going to happen to this soldier, and what's more, he told that small circle of friends too. How ignorant their reactions had been; or would he now call that innocent? God knows.

All he wanted was some recognition and he really believed that he would get it. Recognised for what he wasn't sure, but it was *bound* to have something to do with his creative disposition. Therefore, considering that he couldn't sing, play an instrument, or string a decent sentence together, wasn't it always on the cards that his drawing would gain him his fifteen minutes of fame—or even better, fifteen *years* of fame. And wealth.

Oh how his parents had giggled and cajoled his drawing prowess. From the age of four he was copying from his comic books, and portraits of Korky the Cat, Tweety Pie and The Bash Street Kids adorned his bedroom walls. Yeah, well, the wallpaper was so awful that he had to cover it somehow.

How he had formulated the future ahead of him; how he just knew that before too long, he and his newly betrothed would be moving their formica and steel into a brand spanking new, red-bricked, brown pointy roofed abode in the Home Counties. Yes, that would settle him very well.

Only, life isn't like that is it? Is it Michael? Michael? Look, you are away from the embarrassment of the record shop, and it is not like people are going to stop and point at you now is it? Get up, get walking, and let's find ourselves a nice bar. A cool pint of lager would be just the thing on such a day.

However, the hazy artist had only got a few yards when his own little kingdom was jolted into the real world. At first, he thought he was imagining the shove in the back. He even initially felt that there was some connection between his constant reveries, and that incident back in Caledonian Road, when Mr Kooky had knocked him aside. Unfortunately, the twisted face below him told him something somewhat different.

"Don't fuck about, just hand over ya money and I won't stab ya. Don't fuck about, cos I *will* stab ya, won't I Trev?"

"Yeah man, don't fuck abaht. He'll fucking stab ya, and so will I ya wanker."

He thought he was seeing things. There posturing in front of him were two boys, maybe not even eleven years old. The kid that first spoke had his hand inside an Adidas track suit top, blue and baggy sleeved, as if it was two or three sizes too big for him. His wrist was pressed against a bright, red football shirt that Mick had noticed was all the rage amongst the younger element these days. One of the London teams he believed—his football knowledge never was the greatest.

Apart from a piss poor Nelson imitation, Mick immediately figured that this was where the 'knife' was going to come from. He stepped back a pace to picture the situation, only to be pushed forward again by the other boy.

This 'assailant' was puffing away on a cigarette and had narrowed his eyes in an attempt to look mean and moody. James Dean he wasn't, but then, the way he obviously tottered at the feet of the first boy, showed that having his own cause, never mind being a rebel, was somewhat out of his capabilities.

"Yeah, don't fuck abaht. Come on wanker, me mate will cut ya if ya don't had over ya wallet," and almost as an afterthought, " . . . . and any fags on ya an all."

No, Mick was no hero. Nope, this geezer was always the type to talk his way out of hassle rather than clench a fist in anger. But there was something about this scenario that tickled him. He couldn't decide whether it was the way 'Trev' kept looking forwards and backwards in obvious nervousness, the limited vocabulary of the young, or the way the football supporter's 'knife' hadn't dropped out of his hand when his fist had 'let go' of it. Honestly, did this kid really think that Mick didn't recognise an empty hand when he saw one? After all the bills he had paid recently, he was pretty well used to seeing an empty hand or two, even if they were partially hidden by a tracksuit top. "In one hand and out the other," as his father used to say. What Mick wanted to know, was when did it actually hit your hand?

Thoughts of 'Crocodile Dundee' filled his head ("no mate, *this* is a knife,") but instead his mind went onto auto-pilot, and a good thing too, as he never was one for organised speech making.

"Look guys, you obviously have me cornered. Just let me get my wallet okay, and I'll give you what you want. Just let me . . . ."

"No fucking about man, I fucking mean it, don't I Trev?"

"Yes, we had covered that before I think you'll find. But how can I give you the money if I can't get my wallet. Talking of which, promise me that you'll only take my money and not my wallet uh?"

"Might do. Just give me the money wanker."

'Trev' stamped out his fag and mumbled his latest contribution. "Why, what's so special about the wallet? From ya mother is it? I bet she's an old slapper anyway."

"Ha, yeah right Trev, I bet she's even uglier than you ya fucking wanker."

Swallowing with difficulty this insult to his mum, he glared at the 'knife' carrier, and spoke slowly and with restrained menace.

"No muppet, no uglier than a brain dead slug on the sole of a diseased trog from Hell like you." The 'knifer' immediately grabbed Mick's jacket just above his pocket and screamed "You wanker!", but Mick was not to be deterred.

"The wallet just happens to be a rather sweet sentiment from the boys. Always been grateful to me the boys have, especially when I didn't grass them up for the Southfields murders. Always said they owed me one or four for saving them from Pentonville, but then, I suppose guys like you are well clued up as to the latest stockade news. In fact, they should be catching me up any minute, why don't you ask Bones where he bought it?"

"You think I'm stupid man? You wanker."

"I dunno Mike, I heard of the Southfields murders, didn't you?"

Mick smiled at fag smoker's remark. "Oh, you're a Michael too? Pleased to meet you Michael, and you too Trev."

"Shut up wanker. Don't be a prat Trev . . . . Steve!"

"A bit late for the pseudonyms, don't you think boys?"

"What? For fuck's sake Trev! Honest you wanker, I'm gonna stab ya, I fucking mean it."

He didn't know whether it was the sudden appearance of the brunette rushing across the other side of the road, or the shout of "No, for God's sake no!" from up the road that did it, but as quick as when they arrived, the two wannabe jailbirds suddenly flew away and started towards where the deep voice had come from.

Mick looked up to where the boys had gone and his eyes briefly caught hold of the image of the delinquents looking up at a tall man, a very tall man, and one that was wearing an unusually long coat. From a distance it looked black, but who knows, dark blue looks black from a distance doesn't it? As if anyone cared about such details.

He may have looked at what the boys had been up to for a moment longer had his attentions not been taken by the disappearing brunette that was walking up the street. There was something about her that rang a bell, and what's more this bell was Big Ben size and was making his brain shake in alarm. What was it about her? Hadn't he seen that shapely rear before? The style of jacket certainly said something to him. What about that forceful walk? No, it was the hair. The lady's hair was neatly cut into a bob, and was gently moving to and fro as the woman walked.

As if he was in some kind of movie flashback, Mick abruptly saw that hair next to him on a pillow. He smelt its fragrance from a henna conditioner bottle, and felt its silky touch slip through his fingers. There was only one woman with tresses like that and he wanted to see them just one more time. If only to say hello and how are you, he had to see the way that hair shone as its owner spoke in her soft voice once more.

Not giving a damn anymore about the two half-wits that had tried their pathetic best to mug him, and certainly not giving a toss about his troubles and the over evaluated opinions of others, Mick started off up the street to where the woman was walking. A sense of urgency overtook him; adrenaline rushed through every pore in his body and sweat started to break out on his frowning, concentrated forehead.

His thoughts were focused on only one thing, and he even pushed away the last thing he had noticed about the boys before he started walking—the fact that they looked frightened; not slightly freaked out, not upset that they had done something wrong and were being told off, but genuinely, completely and totally frightened. Well, he figured, play with fire and expect to get burnt. If only he knew how close to the truth his vague sentiments were.

CHAPTER NINE

"Ninety pence a pound and I'm not joking missus! Ninety pence a pound and I promise to not even tell ya husband! You know that it makes sense missus, you *know* you want these luvverly plums of mine! Come on girls, a once in a lifetime offer this is, a bargain, a giveaway, ninety pence a pound and ya husband needn't even know how you got this luvverly bargain!"

"Here mate, give us a pound then," spoke a lady in a pleasant blue, paisley patterned scarf.

"Oh you luvverly, luvverly lady! You are a true connoisseur of the plum kind. Here ya go, take these home and give Barry's plums a good suck! You'll know what pleasure is all about I promise ya!"

"Ooh get away you sod! If my old man 'eard you speak like that he'd box your ears he would."

"And bleedin' right an all I reckon! If you were my woman I'd wine ya, dine ya and even sixty . . ."

"Don't you dare you cheeky sod!"

"Ha, only joking darlin! Can't help my natural impulses ya see! All this testosterone ya know!"

"What am I gonna do with you Barry! Ya gonna find yourself in real trouble one day!"

"I know, but I can't help it. I'm surrounded by all these luvverly ladies. What sane man could resist you luvverly lot!"

And so it went on. If life on the fruit and veg stall was as pleasurable as Barry Bowker made out, then it was a wonder that the job centres were still packed, and yet, Barry couldn't find a reliable helper for love nor money. But Barry had what is more commonly known as the 'gift of the gab', and what other guys would probably label 'bullshit'. He had a touch of style, and a whole lot of ego, and whether you believed in that sort of person or not it certainly sold a lot of fruit and veg.

The thing that did often bother Barry though was the hours. Up at the crack of dawn and normally finishing around sixish wasn't his idea of fun. But still, it paid the mortgage and made him a hell of a lot of friends. Everybody liked Barry Bowker—what was there to dislike about him? Just a harmless Cockney in his harmless Cockney world.

But today was a hot day. Today was a sunshiney bright, pheromone filled day, and to be quite honest he felt like having a short day. He was going on the pull tonight so why not treat himself to a half(ish) day, so that he can get home, pull on his snazzy gear and spray on a whole lot of Lynx. Ah yes, being one's own boss certainly had its perks.

As he threw in the last of the pallets into the back of his red Ford Transit van, Barry was startled by the short, intermittent burst of "Land Of Hope and Glory" from his newly acquired toy—the very latest in iPhone mobile technology, with vibrating alert and numerous apps for when he was bored.

Plucking it gracefully from the inside of his lightweight bomber jacket, he flipped open the case and muttered the immortal words "Hello, Barry Bowker. Fruit, Veg and a little something extra if ya think ya can handle it."

"Yes, hello Barry. Look, do you *have* to speak like that every time you answer the bloody phone. It sounds so unprofessional and childish."

"Sorry love, can't teach an old dog and all that. Ya know what I'm like!"

"What are you like Bowker?"

"What *am* I like!"

"Hmm, I know you too bloody well Bowker, that's what I don't like. Anyway, when you gonna pick me up?"

"Pick you up?"

For a second or two, Barry had forgotten all about Tina and her need to have dinner at 'Mario's' every month. What on earth had possessed him to forget all about this month's little treat? He *never* forgot it usually! It must be the air—there is definitely something around that smells of sex and he sure is not in the mood to be slushy to the bird he married only seven months before.

He would always maintain that it really wasn't his idea to marry at the age of 27, in fact, right up to the day itself he had been playing the field like a good 'un. But, as his friend and confidant Stan Mills had said: "marriage gives you that little bit of stability that every man needs in his life. You know, freshly done washing, dinner on the table, that kinda thing." Not one of your PC brigade was Stan, but he had a point.

"You there Barry? When ya picking me up? Blimey, don't tell me you've bloody forgotten again? You bloody men are all the bloody same."

"Us bloody men? What are you like Tine, what are you *like*? You assume everything don'tcha? Yeah, just assume that I have had a bloody awkward morning, not a single punter interested in me plums and now me missus nagging me an all. Stick that in ya assuming pipe and smoke it. I tell ya what girl, what are you gonna be like in ten years time? Blimey, tell me it don't get worse!"

"I'm not nagging you Barry, but I know how you forget things. Sorry lover, I just need a night out. Doreen at the salon has been a right old cow this morning. Talk about nagging, she blames me for bloody everything. Even blamed me for not putting enough sugar in some old bag's coffee this morning. Who does she think she is?"

"Yeah Tine, what is she like?"

"What is she *like* you mean!"

"Ha, tell me about it! I tell ya what, if you can get off early, I'll take you shopping before we go for our nosh. I've had enough for one day and it sounds like you have too. About fiveish?"

"Lovely lover! See ya later then. Love you!"

"Yeah, you know it girl. Bye!"

Fuck it, thought the very annoyed stall holder. Still, there is always tomorrow. He supposed that deep down he did love Tina more than he would really admit. She was a good girl and deserves someone a lot better than him. But Stan's words were always there in his head, and when it came down to it, wasn't it all about security? She'd do, there was no doubt about that.

He slammed the doors of the Transit shut and felt in his jeans pocket for his wallet. All in all, it had been a good month for money, and he had shifted more stock than he let on. Still, no point in telling the world and its neighbour about how much money you really had, was there? Especially when Tina was snooping around his wallet.

He checked to see how much he had, and double checked to make sure that his credit cards were there. He was then about to take off his jacket to throw it on the van's passenger seat when the lady in the patterned scarf approached him with an odd look on her world wearied face. If Barry didn't know better, he would've joked that the poor girl needed the toilet pretty quick, but there was something in her demeanour that checked his words before they leapt from his mouth.

"Yes love. Enjoyed the plums already have ya? Can't give ya anymore I'm afraid. Just going off to get a cuppa. Hot day innit?"

"No Barry, I didn't want anymore of your stinking plums. As for whether I enjoyed them—were you having a laugh with me or what?"

"I don't understand missus. They were fresh in this morning. What was wrong with 'em?"

"Oh Barry, let's not play games. Let's have an adult conversation shall we? None of the drivel you normally come out with on your bloody stall."

This wasn't right. Barry Bowker was more used to making friends than getting into petty arguments. Okay, so you would get the odd geezer who thought that he was talking a load of rubbish and that he was one step away from a right old pasting, but they were really few and far between.

Anyway, he really wasn't in the mood for this old cow. He bought his stock, took it to market, and tried to sell it for a profit. That was all he wanted to do. If some people had a problem with that, then tough. He had a missus to keep happy now.

"I mean Barry, I'm not saying that people in general find you a complete prat, but you do have a habit of going a bit too far and it is when you do that, that people get offended, and people can't get offended, not if we are to have a more pleasant world, don't you see?"

Barry let out a long sigh, and with his back to the scarfed one, opened the driver's door of the van.

"Love, I really don't have a clue what you are wittering on about, and to be blunt, I couldn't give a toss anyway. Just get off my back and we will all be happier. If you don't like me or my stuff then go somewhere else. No problem."

"No Barry, it isn't as simple as that. It really isn't, but if *you* want to go somewhere else, somewhere nowhere near as nice as this world, then that can be arranged."

He was just about to let out another sigh and tell the woman where he felt she could stick her nice world, when the sharp pain in the small of his back started. The pain got worse, hotter and somehow more wetter, until it felt like someone had hooked him up to a wire and was trying to wriggle it about. Heavier and more sickening the pain got, until it reached his chest, and he couldn't help but scream out louder than he ever had in his short life.

The woman had taken off her scarf and had wrapped it around the biggest kitchen knife she could find in her knife drawer. She used to use it to cut her freshly baked bread, its violent serrated edges slicing easily through the loaf, but right now, as she wiggled it back and forth in Barry's back, she found that it sliced human tissue just as beautifully.

The effort she put into manoeuvring soon had its desired effect, and hot blood started to flow from the ever widening wound. As she withdrew the knife, Barry, with a look on his face that suggested that *he* now needed the toilet, slipped to the dirty, roadside floor. He gripped the Transit door's handle and his falling weight helped him to open it, before he hung there, holding onto the handle as if it were the only answer to the fate he now suffered.

The woman took out the knife from the dying man's back, and feeling pity for the man, feeling that dogs like that had to be put out of their misery, she plunged it through his chest, Barry's shirt providing a useless barrier, and into his barely beating heart before looking around her and rushing back up the street she had come from.

Not a good end to the day, thought Barry, as his last gasps escaped from his mouth. Just as well that he couldn't make the date with his missus now, as she would go spare what with all the blood stains on his shirt. But Christ, how he loved that woman. He *really* loved her.

As darkness closed in, Barry Bowker felt his eyelids drag down and down. He couldn't stop himself from falling into the black abyss upon him, and yet he somehow no longer cared. Everything was going to be alright, just let it all go, and let's see where it takes us.

As soon as the woman had departed, a shuffling figure turned the corner to see what was going on. He smoothed down the legs of his new, brown, corduroy trousers, and tried to pick off a tiny strip of cotton that had stuck to his left calf.

Noticing the inert body of the stall holder, he went over to the Transit's drivers door, and prised what remained of Barry's grip from the handle. The arm of the Cockney fell to the floor and lay awkwardly, with the hand twisted between the body and the road.

Looking down, the figure giggled and muttered "and what are you *like* eh?" and straightened his hat, making sure it was as central to his head as possible, before he too made his exit—his lolloping gait at odds with the grace he was trying so hard to maintain.

Jackson strolled down Upper Street, and tried hard not to laugh as he walked. A good day he thought, and definitely more profitable than in recent times, if only Mick had been around to enjoy the day's events. He'd have loved them!

He pushed his blonde hair away from his eyes and wondered about his friend. Funny, but now he came to think about it there was more to young Michael than met the eye. He knew that he was very insecure about a lot of things, and he often had the urge to grab him by the shoulders and tell him to wake up. He also had the urge to tell him that it was okay to be a little bit aware of one's boss—just don't overdo the reverence that's all. At the end of the day, they were just as human as you.

Still, after his little chat with Walters that morning, he didn't think that Mick would feel quite so unsure about his work anymore. He had done his friend a huge favour, and he was sure that a thousand thanks were forthcoming. The look on Walters' face had been an absolute picture!

He looked into the window of a rather bohemian clothes shop and examined a rather obscene looking waistcoat that was resting on the shoulders of a dummy that had obviously seen better days. A mixture of reds, blues and yellows, and with tiny mirrors dotted down by its reddish buttons, Jackson felt that if anything was in a time warp then that article was. Honestly, what kind of dude feels the need to buy something like that? Probably one of those guys that buys an Islington cupboard for £550,000, and tells his young business associates of how perfect it is for a single man.

Oh yes, he bet that that dude would strip off his pin-stripe suit at the end of the day in a City office, and after a quick, cramped shower, pull on this fashionable piece of sixties history.

Ah well, each to his own! He, in the meantime, had some work of his own to do, and by looking in the windows of this ever more cosmopolitan street's shops, he was just wasting valuable time.

Heading towards the Islington High Street, a high pitched voice calling his name made him turn around quickly until he was looking in the direction he had just come from.

"Hey Jacko! Jacko hold up! God's sake, don't you bloody listen?"

Jackson's smile froze on his lips as he noticed the form of Helen Walters rushing towards him. Her beige slacks flowing around her plump figure, and her heavily bangled arms jangling against her silk, expensive blouse. He knew that this was a new acquisition for Mrs Walters, as Mr Walters had been going on about how expensive it was only that morning.

"Still Jacko," the irritating, self-confessed power-lover had babbled, "if you have a big wad, then why not spend ya wad eh? Eh Jacko? Helen just loves me to spend my wads, in the shops *and* up her Jack and Danny! Geddit son? Wads? Money? Shagging?"

What Jackson didn't get, was how people like Walters considered their sexist double-entendres remotely amusing, but then, maybe that came with the territory? Power over others and a crap sense of humour?

"Hey Helen, I was just thinking of you and your old man! I just *love* that blouse. I bet it's new ain't it? Go on, tell me it's new. And it suits ya a treat! Where d'ya get it?"

Mrs Walters blushed so deeply, in such a ruddy manner, that her cheeks glowed an unhealthy, raspberry colour, and Jackson suddenly had the nauseating vision of Walters huffing and puffing his little prick in and out of her obese body, and her going that ruddy colour with the joy of it all. The thought was galling, yet strangely provoking.

"Oh Jacko, it was just something that he picked up down Knightsbridge way. You know what he's like—generous to a fault, even if I do tell him off for wasting hard earned cash like that. But what can you do?"

"Yes, hard earned cash. Hard earned wads eh Helen? Likes to spend his wads don't he? He tells us all about his wads Hel. Don't mind if I call you Hel do you?"

The flush dropped abruptly from Helen Walters' face, and a perplexed look crossed her puffy, over made-up features. Twisting her bangles, forcing them up her fleshy forearm, she spoke in a way that reminded Jacko of his first primary school teacher—gently, but with a touch of authority. Or pseudo authority in Helen Walters' case.

"Actually Jacko, only Henry calls me Hel, and I'm sure that I don't know what you mean by . . . . wads. Would you care to explain?"

"It was just a joke that me, Henry and the boys were having this morning. A stupid double meaning jape that's all—sorry, I guess I get carried away sometimes."

"Yeah, well, I suppose that he can be a little risqué when he wants to be. Ha, he's a one ain't he?" and with a smile returning to her mouth, and her previous joviality returning, she grabbed Jackson's arm and marched him towards Chapel Market.

"Anyway Jacko, I'm going to take you to the pub, cos I'm gasping for a G and T, and then you're going to tell me about all these rumours of you and a certain lady? And don't give me any excuses, cos I'm not listening. Helen always knows best right?"

And before he could blink, he was sitting in a dark green and gold public bar, perched on a fairly uncomfortable suede bench and gazing across the table at the animated figure of Helen Walters. She was telling with enthusiasm the story of how she and Henry went on their first shopping spree together. Of how Henry couldn't believe how anybody could keep on their feet for so long, and find every single shop a challenge to explore.

"But then, he has always been generous Jacko, not just in money but in nature too, and he has never grumbled once. Honestly, you guys see him at work and I suppose that you view him like any other boss, only I'm sure you agree that he treats his staff well."

"Yes, he can be quite a . . . ."

"He has always come home and told me of how he sees the staff as extended family, and you know what, I believe him! He makes such a lovely father figure, and has never taken his role as a boss too seriously, and I try to follow his example. I mean, could you ever see me as the boss's wife? Have I ever been stuck-up with you guys?"

"Well, there was a time when . . . ."

"Exactly! And that's where other companies go wrong. They don't treat their staff right. How happy are you at work Jacko?"

A little bit sidetracked by the sudden question, Jackson grinned with tight lips and drained half a pint of Fosters. He felt the liquid slide down his throat before burping under his breath and wiping his mouth with the cuff of his shirt.

"Actually Helen, it may serve you well to know, that most of us are freelance. So in a way, Henry isn't our 'boss'. I mean, he may like to think so, but really, if Mick for example, was to suddenly walk out, then poor old Henry wouldn't have a fat leg to stand on. Wads an all!"

For the second time in fifteen minutes, Helen's skin defied the thick foundation on her cheeks, and paled abruptly. Only this time, it wasn't indignation that was causing her to look at Jackson in shock, but the look in the artist's glare. Jacko was well known as a cheeky and quirky man, as well as being a damned good graphic artist, but something was wrong, something was horribly wrong, and when Jackson grabbed Helen Walters' bangled wrist, holding it up in front of her podgy nose, she knew that she was in a little bit of trouble. Jackson spoke in low, menacing tones.

"Don't even think about patronising me Helen. Look at this tacky shit on your arms and listen to what I am going to tell you. Listen carefully, because I'm not going to tell you again without having to resort to the medically incorrect placing of gold up your fat arse."

Helen's mouth opened, but only spittle came bubbling from the corners of her lips—her sudden fear causing her to lose all power of speech.

"You see Helen, Henry wasn't a 'boss' at all. He certainly wasn't *my* boss. In fact most of us thought of him as a fat bastard who got lucky, and felt that he could speak loudly in his common accent at Ascot, simply because he had money. The fact that he spent his money on crap like cack models of the tourist attractions, and tacky jewellery to squeeze onto your hammy arms, never really mattered did it? He wasted money like he wasted good manners. For your information missus, he treated us like shit, and considering that he was an example of the shittiest in the world, that is not surprising."

"Jacko please, what are you saying? Why the past tense? Where is my Henry? What are you so angry darling?"

"Who the fuck are you calling darling? Fancy me do you? Want me to have some fun with these?"

Looking down in terror and pain, Helen Walters could only scream as Jackson grabbed her plentiful breasts and squeezed them with all the force he could muster. She felt hot tears run down her face, making tracks through the make-up and blurring her vision. It was only by quickly turning her head that she noticed the two men making their way towards Jacko, who as quickly as he had let go of her breasts, was making his exit out of the pub.

"You little bastard! Come here and do that again and we'll kick your head in you dirty little git." Then more calmly. "Are you alright love?"

Shivering in shock, Helen Walters' words tumbled out of her mouth. Her bangles were covered in sweat as she twisted them nervously to and fro.

"I'm fine loves. It was just a misunderstanding that's all."

"Misunderstanding? Well, misunderstanding or not, you don't treat a lady like that. The little shit deserves a good slap!"

Looking out of a window, she glanced past the dark figure looking in, and at what she thought was the retreating figure of Jackson. Her breasts hurting, and her make-up running in thick rivulets, a sudden (irrational?) thought occurred to her? Where exactly was Henry? He was supposed to have phoned her that morning as they were going to pick up some flowers for her mother's graveside. Why was Jacko so angry with her? What would Henry say about this? How could she tell him about such a thing. No, best kept to herself—Jacko just wasn't that sort of guy. She glanced up at the men looking down at her.

"No really, he's a good man usually. He is just upset at the moment. He'll be alright. I'll be alright too. Everything is alright."

CHAPTER TEN

She gazed somewhat blankly as her husband stood with his back to the fireplace, and with a hot mug of tea in his hand started the questions. She was used to seeing Stephen moaning about something, indeed Karen was often referring to him as the county's "very own Victor Meldrew", but this moan was slightly different. Honestly Stephen, she thought, don't fanny about, just tell me what I've done wrong this time, and let's get the whole, nasty business over and done with. Stephen sipped some tea, scratched his nose, coughed and began.

"What I fail to understand Dorothy, is why you were so indifferent as to this Burn character's introduction into our home? I mean, I would like to think that we are a welcoming family but . . . ."

Dorothy gave a short laugh which he made a point of ignoring.

". . . . but this man was obviously of a very unhealthy disposition. What I would . . . ."

"Unhealthy disposition? Who are you Stephen to categorise people in such a negative manner? Why do you always see the worst in people? Why can't you be a real man and show a bit of gratitude at times? God, you can be so bloody graceless!"

Stephen was stunned by this retort, but sipping more tea to wet his suddenly dry throat, he became more determined to show his wife that she was wrong.

"Dorothy. How would you feel if Adrian was to suddenly bring home to tea a woman of disturbing appearance, who he had just happened to have picked up off the street?"

"How dare you make such an insulting analogy Stephen Trollope! First of all, what you are suggesting in your usual clumsy, unthinking way, is that I am prone to picking up men to take home, like I am some sort of cheap tart . . . ."

"No, no, you have my words all wrong . . ."

". . . . and secondly, I very much doubt that Adrian would even pick up a brick from the street and bring it home, never mind another person, no, never mind a *woman*, simply because of the fear that you have instilled into him!"

Stephen had put down his tea and taken off his glasses. This conversation was proving to be more challenging than he ever considered before. And as for this slight about Adrian.

"What on earth do you mean fear? I have always wanted the best for our son, and even you can't say that his education has been a disappointment—top grades in everything that he has undertaken. He could've become another Robert or Karen, but no, this time I was determined to make sure that he would mature with the right manners and the right skills for a successful future. He has become a . . . ."

"He has become a little, grey town mouse. A sixteen year old who is too frightened to fart in case you send him to his room. And anyway, what is wrong with Robert and Karen? Others wouldn't know that you are talking about your children. Just because they escaped to live lives that were fairer, freer and more fucking fun, you have to condemn them as fucking undesirables. Adrian has done remarkably well at school, I agree, and for what? I would rather have a moron for a son if it meant him having a free spirit and a sense of humour."

Stephen spat out his reply to his tirade, knowing that all hopes of him being the head of the household were slipping away fast. But one thing was certain, nobody spoke in such filthy terms to him.

"How dare you use such disgusting language of the gutter to me—I suppose you picked that up from Burn eh? A gentleman is he? Yet, after only a short time with him, you seem to be speaking like scum from the street."

"Oh dear, did I say 'fucking' Stephen? Have your sensitive ears been offended by a word that the vast majority of the English speaking public utter almost every day? Well, guess what husband of mine, I'm going to use it again, and do you know why? Because while you were pissing about with your bloody tandem, me and Thomas were 'fucking' right here on the carpet. In fact, my knickers were lying right where your feet are now as Thomas gave me a right good seeing to. Pleased are you? You should be, because if you hadn't been such a prat for the past ten years of our marriage, if you had been a *real* man and seen me as a woman and not as your verbal punch-bag, housemaid and cook, then maybe I wouldn't have felt the need to 'pick up' Thomas from 'the street', as you like to refer to it.

If ever a human being had such a pole-axed look on their face, a look of sheer disbelief and dumbness, then Stephen Trollope did at that moment. Physically trembling, he tried hard to control the words coming from his lips, trying desperately to sound calm and assured.

"You're lying Dorothy. Not only have you picked up disgusting language, and very quickly too I might add, but obviously some disgusting ideas too. I forbid you to ever go near that man again."

"Oh forbid me do you? I'm sitting here, feeling more free and more satisfied than I can ever remember, and you *forbid* me to not see the person responsible again? Sorry dearest, but I have found some happiness, some excitement, for God's sake some *sex* and I want more!"

"If what you say is true Dorothy, then I am not sure that I want to be in the same house as you. If you really have been indulging in such perverted actions then I don't recognise you and I don't wish to be attached to a wife that I no longer recognise."

Dorothy laughed and walked up to her outraged spouse. With her face inches from the wide eyes of Stephen Trollope, Dorothy gave another snigger, only this one seemed to have more meaning to it. To an innocent bystander, the laugh that came from her lips was tantamount to wicked derision, Yes derision, just like the attitude shown to her for nearly all of her married life by her husband, but derision tinged with malice. Purposefully, she grabbed two of Stephen's belt hoops, and in a bizarre sight tried to drag him down to her level. Apart from a slight bending in his knees, the act hadn't worked in its strangeness, but to Dorothy, it was making a statement—a kind of transferring of power: a personal invasion of the personal space of Stephen Percival Trollope, and a liberty that she never would've dreamt of before. Eyes flashing, she hissed her words slowly and deliberately.

"No Stephen, you don't recognise me, because you don't recognise that I now feel love and passion. Oh yes, for the first time in God knows how long, I feel an overwhelming love that you could never feel, never mind give to me or our children."

"Love? No, if what you has said is true, then all you feel is lust and I think it's rather pathetic. A woman of your years acting like some randy teenager, the sight—if it happened—must have been absolutely preposterous, not to mention degrading."

"Oh but it *did* happen, oh ye of little faith and brain. What do I have to do to convince you? Show you the stains in my knickers? I think you better wake up and realise that things are going to change around here . . ."

"No, I think you better . . . ."

"Shut up Stephen! God, you just don't get it do you? You, for sick reasons best known to yourself, see any kind of carnal intercourse as a cause for reproach. You won't let yourself, *can't* let yourself become more contemporary, full of contempt, but lacking in a contemporary way of life. You are behind the times dearest, can't you see that? You just can't, you just *refuse* to channel your snobbish views into a more worthwhile cause, because believe it or not, it can be done, even with an old fart like you!"

"I'm sure that I've never been . . . ."

"Yes, and I'm sure that you've never been so wrong in your life too Stephen. Sex *can* be dangerous, and filthy and all the other negative adjectives you have for it, but a lot of the time that is what makes it so much fun! And with the right person, at the right time, and with a common purpose in mind it is beautiful, and forges unions that can only be for the good of the world. It is when people become selfish, out to enjoy life for their own gains, or when people become too critical almost to the point of overbearing self-importance, that they become dangerous and have to be stopped."

"And how do you, in all your new found wisdom, think that people like that should be stopped?"

"It's different horses for different course. As Thomas says, not everybody is beyond redemption, people *can* change. Thomas actually admired your stance against him, and says that you have qualities that can be developed for real goodness. But as we both agreed, as long as you fight your lonesome fight against those you feel are below you, then you too will have nothing to show for it. Look at me Stephen, look at how a few moments with Thomas have made everything clear to me. Why don't you talk to him too? He is prepared to give you a chance, take it and let's make the world a better place together—not hide in our own little world like we have for so long, being nasty to each other, resenting each other.

During Dorothy's speech, Stephen had been inching slowly away to the kitchen. However, she had kept with him with every move he had made, and therefore made his escape to the back door more awkward. It wasn't that he was frightened of this change in his wife, although there was a glint in her eye that did trouble him somewhat. Instead, it was obvious to him that Dorothy had finally flipped, and that only a second opinion could make her see sense; see that she was talking nonsense, and that he would forgive her if she just calmed down and made them the hot dinner that he had been looking forward to all day. Janet and Doug next door would help.

In Stephen's opinion, Janet and Doug were not the greatest neighbours in the world, simply because their TV was always too loud, their children always too rowdy, and their dogs always too messy, but they were down to earth folk and knew common sense fairly well when they saw it. However, as he finally reached the lemon and white scenario of the kitchen, with its disinfected worktops and impressive collection of international cookbooks, he found that the back door was locked and the key was nowhere to be seen.

"No Stephen, Thomas thought that you may try to wriggle out of this, so we took precautions. Very thoughtful man isn't he? No, we have to talk about this, you, me and Thomas. He'll be back in a moment. Had to see a man about a girl or something! Just hold onto your strides and let's be friends. We used to be friends Stephen, a long time ago.

From feeling some sort of vague control of the situation, Stephen now felt the ground moving beneath his feet. What that damned Burn man had been saying to his wife, he wouldn't like to subject to conjecture, but it was now clear to him that something *had* taken place between them. He supposed that he should feel anger, and threaten to kill Burn for having his evil way with his Dorothy, but now all he could feel was an increasing sense of apprehension and even the seedlings of fear beginning to sprout in his mind.

He had never seen her so sure of herself and he had to admit that she looked very well on it, much more of a contented look on her face. But all she had to do was tell him that she hadn't been happy with their life and he was sure that they could've worked something out. Maybe a bicycle tour of the south-west? She had always enjoyed the fresh air and the togetherness of the tandem—despite her earlier comments against it. He was sure that those were just words of frustration. Why hadn't she spoken of her frustration before? Was he really so unapproachable? Now it looked like things were going to change for the worst. This lifestyle of his was all he had ever known, and the fear of massive change and of Dorothy's absurd change in attitude, was growing.

But it needn't have to be like that. Things could still change for the better and they weren't going to improve with him standing there, waiting for the animal Burn to return. No, he had to get his neighbour's help and get it now. He turned and ran back through the living room and towards the front door.

Dorothy had been so sure that her charm would make her husband see her point of view, despite his stubbornness, that she was knocked off guard by her husband's escape. She had sat down at the kitchen table while Stephen had stood so obviously deep in thought, and read the front page of yesterday's Daily Mail, only to look up a moment later and see him gone.

She jumped up, calling his name in a distant and humorous fashion, as if she considered this a game that is played with a child and followed his footsteps, only to stop at the open front door. She looked down at the figure lying prone on the doorstep across the bristled welcome mate. Gazing at her husband's face it was initially hard to see why his features were all screwed up in obvious agony, until she focused on the line across his neck. It was bright red and getting wider. Wider and bloodier. He was trying to reach up to it with his hands, but they only seemed to reach his chest before the effort became too much.

From out of nowhere, the figure of Thomas Burn came to lift up Stephen's head, before tugging at something behind his neck. The wound became so wide and so full of blood that Dorothy felt vomit creep up her chest towards her mouth, and she watched in wide eyed wonder as her beloved husband's head tilted abnormally at ninety degrees from the slice in his neck. Blood poured in torrents down Stephen's shirt, and his open mouth made no sound, just a brief outpouring of wet, rasping breath.

She had a brief moment to consider that Stephen's head and neck looked like something out of a Monty Python animation, where the cartoon character's mouth was so exaggerated that you felt that the top half of its head would come off. But her thoughts were quickly pushed aside as Burn got up and approached her, carrying something thin, wiry and coated in blood.

"Chicken wire. Very dangerous in the wrong hands, But in the right, careful hands, something that can cause quite a desired effect, and you have to admit, he didn't have a chance to complain about that! Anyway, I didn't want to go too far—I understand he never was one to lose his head, so why start now eh?"

Dorothy Trollope, nee Chatsworth, watched Burn move her Stephen's body inside the house with his foot, and close the front door shut with a gentle click before letting herself be walked up the garden path and towards the Astra estate of her new male companion.

"Won't the police find his body?" she asked, almost as an afterthought. Burn turned his charismatic smile to her face and replied.

"No, I know people that can sort that out for you. I can bring you your son too, if you like. Improving the number of youth in our task is always a good thing."

She didn't even allow herself a look behind her, but instead concentrated on what lay ahead of her. Adrian would have to be told about his father's terrible accident, but knowing the way that his mind had been moulded from such an early age, she didn't think that he would take much convincing. In fact, he may even be grateful for some freedom. As for Karen and Robert, well, what they didn't know wouldn't hurt them and she was sure that their time would come, whatever route they decided to take.

As she settled into the Astra's front seat, thoughts of earlier days appeared in her mind and she felt almost sorry that things had ended in this manner. Stephen hadn't been a bad man, just ignorant of the world around him. Her thoughts became louder and escaped as whispers from her lips.

"Don't be angry Stephen, just be grateful that you won't be around to let your stubbornness drive you insane, because with everything that's going to happen, it would've. I know you too well. God bless you."

"And God bless us all," responded Thomas Burn. "God bless us all, for we will surely be blessed beyond even His expectations."

Dorothy nodded, closed her eyes, and after a few minutes fell headlong into a restless sleep.

CHAPTER ELEVEN

The room was dark. Dark apart from the dull periphery of light that surrounded a barely alive candle.

It was surroundings like this that brought out the best in him. It was his world, where ideas and theories and plans could be mulled over in silence and where nobody could interfere with their wretched points of view. Blackness is good, blackness is so tangible that one can almost feel it seep into one's ears and immerse the brain in a relaxing, soothing balm, from which thoughts of such brilliance cannot but fail to be produced.

He stared at the candle. It wasn't really strong enough for the room, but bright enough to provide the only doorway from an inky, charged atmosphere should one require it. But he didn't really require it. Only the weak require it. The building he was in had seen so many people and seen such tragedies. He felt the souls of the dead still wandering around, some laughing at him, some crying at him. But he dismissed their words and their actions. They had lost direction in life and were directionless in death. That was their problem—he knew how to help living people gain the true direction. He could stop sorry souls from ending up in the place that some people called limbo.

Eyes flickering to the left, to the right, and there near the corner of the room he could just make out the corner of a table. Only just. A vain attempt by an inanimate object to pierce this curtain of gloom.

However, it was this mere corner that was all he needed to focus on, and his eyes rested on it and stuck like the proverbial glue. They weren't going to be moved. He wasn't going to be moved. He just fixed his steadfast gaze on the corner, without blinking, without the slightest itch.

The room around him started to change. The darkness all but dissipated to be replaced by the vaguest light that was neither white nor yellow, but some kind of shade in between. To the everyday mortal, this would be a cause for concern, a worry that the mind was about to be lost. But he could feel this light come from within. It built up through every nerve in his body and burst forth from the power source in the middle of his forehead.

He felt his cerebrum become hotter and hotter, and imagined the folds and creases of his cerebral cortex being mere channels for the flow of energy, but even the old grey matter wouldn't be able to hold back what was happening to him now. It was strange how this concentrated effort seemed to make his personality so much more powerful and those around him revered his presence all the more. It was so obvious to him and so damn pleasing.

His eyes started to water such was the intensity of his stare, but his concentration did not waver; still he locked onto the corner of the table, deep in the darkness of the room.

With tears starting to roll down his cheeks and his eyes bulging, he saw the yellowy light from his forehead start to narrow, until eventually all he could perceive was a funnel of brightness issuing from his forehead and onto the corner of the table. Then this passage of light abruptly changed direction, as if it had bounced off the table and found its way back towards him where it spread, opened up and enveloped his entire body.

The feeling was exquisite. Yellowy-white ripples covered his entirety, creating a feeling of gentle water splashing over his skin. And yet, the impression was also one of intense power. With every ripple, there was an injection of strength: strength of body, strength of mind and most importantly to him, strength of morals.

If even he could feel cleansed and excited by such efforts, then what he could do for those unfortunates outside was surely only for the good of mankind? It wasn't by accident that he had been given this gift and surely he and only he knew how to employ it wisely?

Unfortunately, his chosen associates had taken his help to a few extremes. They were excitable and foolish at times, and therefore putting his work at risk, but they were expendable. They would do for now. People were being turned, being brought into the cause, there was no sudden need for change. It was Roscoe he was most worried about. That man was going to have to go pretty soon, before he made everything backfire. But then he was so loyal . . . .

With the light flowing around him, he thought back to times when he himself had been loyal. Loyal to his parents, loyal to his work, loyal to his principals, loyal to his faith. But what had that loyalty done for him? His parents had decided when he was born what faith he would follow. They also decided what clothes suited him best and what food was good for him. They decided what career would most suit his talents, and he had plenty—you didn't get four A levels (with top grades) and a first class BA without being multi-faceted.

Yes he was academically intelligent. He didn't need to be told that. What he did need to be told though was that his efforts were going to be appreciated. After all, everybody likes to have their work praised, and just like if you tell someone enough times they are stupid they start to believe it, then tell somebody enough times they are brilliant and it makes them become more confident—logical enough surely? He didn't want to become a dictator, just someone who shows the way and is placed at the top of the order for his efforts. If people had to be persuaded to see the light, as it were, then so be it.

He has always had the more unusual hobbies compared to the rest of his peers. Astrology was one that has always taken his interest. He had developed the ability to draw up superb birth charts in very short spaces of time for anybody who wanted one, and this is what made him laugh; this is what started off his belief that people's insecurities were ripe for picking, even if they didn't realise it themselves.

For example, even those that criticised astrology, and said that they couldn't believe in it, would be likely to ask him for a birth chart. Because, they said "it's only for a laugh isn't it?" Well no, now that you ask, when you bear in mind this hypocrisy, the majority of people have deep seated fears; some are well hidden, but they *are* there. And if and when somebody comes along and plays on these fears, and shows a morally and spiritually better way of being, then it would only take the extremely strong willed, or people from another planet, that could resist it.

He narrowed his forehead and it's wrinkles almost increased the power that was emanating from him. He now felt at one with the earth, relaxed, calm and sure that what he was doing was right. Right for him, and right for those who needed some sort of salvation in their little lives.

His life had been little. Oh God yes, a little life that would've gone absolutely nowhere if others had had their way. But one day when standing naked in front of his bedroom mirror, he had felt, no he had seen the room around him change colour and he had known that his mind had been the cause of it. No explanation, it was just a freak of nature . . . . maybe. No pains from his eyes or in his head, just a warm glow that came from somewhere within, and the search for a better way had begun in earnest.

It had taken a lot of studying, and a lot of time blocking out nearly everybody else in his life, but it had been so worth it. He had met a lot of fascinating people on his lonely journey, and a lot of disturbing people too, but now he had the way forward. Now the world could be a more fulfilling place and with a little help from those who had learnt a little of the way from him, he could almost taste the satisfaction the success was going to give him.

From what seemed a million miles away, he thought he could hear a voice, and as the voice became nearer and clearer he realised that it was one of his assistants; one of the people that was, for now, going to help him on his epic journey forward. From the gaiety in the person's voice, it was probably Burn, and just as well—he had something that he needed to say to that character.

As if with a blink of his eyes, the light around him stopped completely and the room reclaimed its black surround. He felt refreshed and back on focus, and as he stood up, his erection almost screamed to him how much he always enjoyed these sessions.

Adjusting the front of his trousers, he stood, stretched and made for the bolted door, but his state of excitement never wilted—sometimes, even the most regrettable parts of his leadership could be thrilling. Whether Burns would agree to that notion he doubted very much. But that was besides the point—he was the one, the power and types like Burn were not going to forget it. He slowly opened the door and as the man's voice got louder, the adrenaline started to pump through him so strongly, that he could almost hear the sound of its rush tingle through his eardrums.

Burn swept around the corner and faced the man who filled him with a maelstrom of emotions. He looked at his face, and felt his smile crash to the floor.

CHAPTER TWELVE

He wasn't having the greatest of days, in fact he wasn't having the greatest of lives, but hey, who was there to complain to? To be quite honest, the feeling of having wasted a precious hour or so of his life had occurred to him, but if we can get anything positive from the experience it was in a good cause. Well, it *was* in a good cause wasn't it? Chasing around after a woman who doesn't know that you exist? Might as well be racing around Southend looking for Kylie Minogue, ask her out for dinner maybe, a little nightcap back at his five star hotel and bingo! The envy of every man with a pulse! No, maybe not, but the way he felt at the moment the chances of seeing his lost love again were just as likely.

After looking around backstreets in pursuit of the bob-haired woman, Mick had finally come to rest on the Promenade. He was leaning on the railings looking out past the amusement rides to the sea. He was trying to imagine what this place would look like without all the tourist attractions, without all the people in their football shirts, without the screaming Essex / London accents, and just quiet, tranquility, the sea and the town in perfect harmony, wouldn't that be nice?

He supposed that there were places like that in these green and pleasant lands, if you bothered to look for them. Just jump in your car and explore, if you like, and you would eventually find the tranquil utopia that took you away from this madness. And to think, he came here for a break! Honestly Mick, you just make more trouble for yourself, don't you? Well, he didn't know why he specifically wanted to come here. He could've gone anywhere for some sea and sand; the idea of coming to this particular town just strongly appealed to him, and he truly couldn't for the life of him think why.

He turned and started to walk along the seafront, not going anywhere in particular, just ambling along and maybe some attractive eighteen year old beauty might take pity on him and tell him how sad he looks, and could she do anything to cheer him up, anything at all, just tell her what you want and she will do it for you. She loves you, you see, always has done, ever since she saw you a few minutes ago at the railings. Please say that you'll marry her and take her away to your own little world, please do!

As he focused his vision ahead of him, not really looking, just enough to see what direction he was going whilst dreaming his own little dreams, he didn't become aware of the man also standing at the railings, not in a too different stance to how he looked a little time earlier. Only this guy didn't look so lost. He looked angry. He looked like he wanted to shout and scream at someone, but he couldn't quite find the person to do that to. Well, now was his chance, as Mick's right shoulder barged him with not inconsiderable force.

"For fuck's sake, watch where you're going mate!" Paul felt quite a bit of anger being discharged in those few words, but a few more wouldn't hurt either. "Bloody hell, all I'm doing is standing here, minding me own business, and a prick like you fucking nearly knocks me over!"

"Hey, I'm sorry mate, it's my fault, not looking where I'm going. Sorry."

"Shit, if it ain't the women trying to knock me down, it's a bloody stranger doing it too."

Mick, being the world's greatest expert on women, immediately picked up on Paul's words, and in an attempt to make light of the situation jokingly gave his point of view.

"Ha women! Yeah, I know what you mean mate. They get you down sometimes don't they?"

"What are you talking about mate? I don't think there's anything funny going on here. You taking the piss?"

Oh fuck, even when he is trying to be charming to a *bloke* he gets the wrong reaction. Was there *any* point at all in him being so *nice* to people? Maybe he should just tell the bloke to fuck himself and be done with. Mind you, he could get a smack in the mouth as a reward, the guy did look fed-up.

"No mate, I was just saying . . . . oh never mind."

Mick turned to walk away when the guy spoke again. His words made Mick look down behind him.

"Oi, you've dropped your pen mate! Look, I should apologise, I shouldn't have a go like that, no harm done eh?"

Mick bent and picked up the black biro he always kept on him. No reason why he should always carry a pen, apart from when he doodled on napkins in some sad, lonely cafe somewhere, or when he bravely completed The Sun's coffee time crossword. Maybe artists always carry some writing or drawing implement on them? Well he did anyway . . .

"Thanks. Shouldn't keep it in my back pocket anyway. I always lose them when I put them there. Er no, no harm done anyway. I shouldn't poke my nose into other people's business. I mean, I was only joking about the women getting you down and such, but anyway, you know what I mean!"

Paul couldn't help but smile as Mick expertly stumbled over his words.

"No I know mate. You were right though, women can be a pain. Doesn't stop us from loving them though does it. I mean, just take a look at that will ya?"

Two girls, maybe in their early twenties, walked by in bikinis of the same design, although one was red and the other yellow. Both though, came very close to their bikini lines, and the tops weren't doing too good a job at holding in their bouncing breasts. They smiled at Paul as he waggled his fingers at them in a friendly hello. Paul's smile to Mick became broader.

"I mean for God's sake, that shouldn't be allowed should it? And yet, I get told off by the missus if one of them even crosses my eye line! I can't help it if they walk in front of me can I? I think they want to be looked at, so I look at them. I'm not chatting them up or ravishing them in broad daylight, just looking. I mean, I don't complain when she looks at a bloke's arse—human nature innit?"

Mick watched as the girls walked majestically along the promenade before coming out with one of his truths to this stranger who seemed a bit happier for seeing a bit of young, female flesh.

"I know what you mean. Mind you, I'm single and yet I probably wouldn't stand a chance with that sort of totty." Did people still say *totty*? Oh well, this guy hadn't noticed so maybe it was okay.

"Why not? You can't be that old. Well you don't look it. My excuse is that I'm married, but if you're single why don't you just say hello to them and see what happens. I just waved at them and they smiled, so I don't think they would bite your head off."

What the guy was saying was all true of course. He had always known of his stupid weakness in that department. The truth is Michael, women just don't approach *you*. Especially attractive, young ladies like the bikini twins.

"I suppose so. I've always been a bit slow in that department. You know, I'm the type of guy who has had many an unrequited love, only to see the fancied girl run off with some other bastard. My fault I guess, but I never did quite get the hang of the chatting up lark."

Paul was a little surprised at Mick's frankness with him, but it took his mind off of his problems with Maria and Emily, and anyway this guy looked alright. He understood how difficult it was to chat up women, although he couldn't remember suffering from endless bouts of unrequited love.

"So what do you think you do wrong then?"

"Well, as I just said. I watch from afar as the girl I like is swept off her feet by someone else, and then I go and get myself pissed in frustration or have a good sulk listening to some really sad songs. 'Everybody Hurts' is one of my faves. Must be wearing that CD out by now."

Paul felt a mixture of pity and humour at Mick's attitude to women that he fancied. To be honest, it didn't quite match up to his own endeavours in that field, but he guessed that there were guys with such low confidence. He was curious though.

"What, you mean you never told them that you liked them?"

"Er . . . I don't suppose I did. Look, I know it sounds really stupid, pathetic even to someone who is married, but when you've been hurt like me, then it takes ages for you to jump back into the chatting up mode again. Probably too long for me."

"How long is long?"

"Well I suppose I've been in this state of mind for about eight years now. I mean, I had a fling or two, but they came about through work or through a friend."

"So, what makes you think that you won't meet another girl through work or a friend?"

"I may do, but that isn't the point. I suppose I just wanted to be able to go out there and pick and choose like most blokes do. For example, would you chat up a girl you found really unattractive?"

"No, but then you didn't have to have a fling with those girls that you met through work or a friend, did you? Same thing isn't it?"

Mick shook his head with a face that told the story of a man who had lost all hope in working out this particular problem.

"No it isn't really. I shouldn't have to wait months or years at a time for someone to enter my life by chance. I should be out there choosing a girl to meet. I don't think you understand do you?"

Paul sighed but couldn't help smiling at this guy's words.

"I *do* understand and I don't! I understand that you want to be just like any other guy and chat up some women. I don't understand because there is nothing to stop you from doing this. Look at her over there, her by the ice-cream kiosk. I dare you to just go over there and ask for a bit of her ice-cream."

Mick looked at the girl Paul was pointing to. Another young lady barely wearing her bikini, but this time showing a bit more bum than the other two girls. Very pretty though, and one that Mick wouldn't turn down should she ever demand a long-term relationship from him. He looked at Paul.

"You want me to ask her for a bit of her ice-cream?"

"I don't *want* you to do anything. I just thought it would be a good opportunity for you to get to know her. You don't know her at all at the moment. If you speak just a few words to her now, then at least you can say that you knew her for a few seconds of her life! Go on, give it a go!"

"What if she has a boyfriend?"

"What if she has a *girl*friend? What if she is has a boyfriend *and* a girlfriend? What if she is into shagging inanimate objects like that bloke in the paper the other day? Who cares? You're not asking for her hand in marriage, sorry what's your name?"

"Mick."

"Mick. I'm Paul by the way." The two shook hands. "You're not asking her for her hand in marriage Mick. Just go up to her, smile, look at her ice-cream and say "So, are you gonna give me a lick of that?" If you're lucky, she might think your talking about her tit! But you better hurry up, or it'll start dripping."

"What, her tit?" Mick laughed.

"No prat, the bloody ice-cream! Go on quick, she's getting away!"

So Mick the brave, the mighty knight in shining armour, approached the girl with the ice cream. As he walked up to her, he had visions of the girl screaming at him, the way a woman would scream at any bloke that was stalking her. What if she screamed so loud that people would jump on him and beat him to a pulp for harassing a girl? But his thoughts had to stop as the girl caught his eye. He was just inches from her and remembering what Paul said, he looked at the girl's cornet with flake. Well, he nearly looked at the ice-cream. Unfortunately for Mick, the girl moved in time for him to look directly at her cleavage, so when the words "So, are you gonna give me a lick of that?" came out, he really did look like he was asking for a more personal favour.

The girl looked at him in horror, and with the words "Fuck off you dirty bastard, I'll get my Sean onto you," raced off towards a group of people standing not a million miles away from where Paul was now laughing, doubled-up, as if this was the funniest thing he had seen in years.

Mick felt the blood race to his face. A wave of sickness had suddenly hit him, but he quickly ran back to where Paul was holding onto the railings again, but this time for support for his laughing frame.

"Fuck, fuck, fuck! I'm getting out of here. She *has* got a boyfriend, and what's more, she thinks I'm a fucking pervert! Shit, why did I listen to you?"

Paul, with tears in his eyes, quickly followed the graphic designer as he strode past the glaring girl and her friends, and towards somewhere away from a possible beating up.

"Hey Mick, hold up! No seriously, you did well mate! Hey hold on, I wanna tell you something. Listen!"

Mick stopped and turned. His face was still red, and he looked as if he was about to cry. Paul saw the guy's distress immediately and realised that this really wasn't a joke to Mick. He tried to stop the laughs that seemed to come from his stomach, and spoke in a trying-very-hard-to-be-serious sort of voice.

"Hey mate I'm sorry! I was just trying to help. Look, you have to admit that it was bloody brave of you to do that. You just did what other guys do all the time . . . . it just went a little bit wrong, that's all!"

"A *little* bit wrong? I now have to leave Southend in case I'm branded a perve, and you think it went a *little* bit wrong? I think *you're* taking the piss now! What do you want to tell me?"

"What? Tell you?"

"Yes, you said to wait. That you wanted to tell me something. What is it?"

"Oh that! Well, did you notice the reaction of the girl's friends? They were laughing."

"Yeah, at me, thanks very much!"

"No, you don't get it! They thought that what you did was funny!"

"Yes, and what other pearl of wisdom can you offer me? They thought I was funny for asking if I could lick their friend's tits! Funny, ha-ha, I'm laughing!"

"Yes! No! Shit! What I'm saying is that they weren't laughing at you for being a pervert. I mean, admittedly one of the guy's looked a bit pissed off at first, he must be the boyfriend, but even he started grinning. He saw the funny side."

"At his girlfriend being propositioned by a pervert?"

"He knows what guys are like. So do her friends. They admired your guts Mick!"

"Oh come on, how can you tell just by looking at them?"

"Bloody hell! The bloke wasn't exactly chasing you was he? You could *tell* that they thought it a funny, blokeish thing to do. Come on, you have to admit, her face was a picture." At the thought of the girl's shocked face, Paul started laughing again, and this time Mick laughed too.

"Yeah, I suppose you're right. It *was* a brave thing to do, wasn't it?"

"You *know* it was! You're alright Mick. I tell you what, fancy a pint? I think you deserve one, that's if you haven't got anything else to do?"

Mick agreed that a pint would be just the thing at the moment, and at the recommendation of Paul they headed off to one of the pub's where he used to go with Maria, many years ago. Mick allowed himself a smile as they walked. Was that all there was to it? It was embarrassing, but he *was* still alive. He wondered what other pearls of wisdom Paul could tell him over their pints.

Maria walked up the street with Emily skipping beside her. Thoughts of talking to her aunt about her new problems just didn't seem right to her. She and Paul were old enough to sort these things out without any help or hindrance from others. Her aunt Lyn was a lovely woman, but a bit too keen to push her own point of view upon you, and she really didn't need that at the moment.

Instead, she had popped back and taken Emily off her hands with promises of a milk shake. On the way to the cafe, she decided to ask Emily questions in order to try and understand whether her little sister really had meant what she had said. The worrying thing was, that Em had repeated her accusations in a rather careless manner a few times since that episode in the hospital. Was she telling the truth, or was she, as deep down she suspected, just seeking a bit of attention?

"So, shall we go and see Pauly later on then?" Emily had shrugged her shoulders.

"When are we going home again?"

"Later Em. You haven't answered my question. Shall we go and see Pauly later on? I know that he misses you when you aren't around."

Emily had shot Maria a look with furrowed brows that suggested that she didn't totally agree with this statement.

"What's *that* supposed to mean Em? Don't you love your uncle Pauly?"

"I used to. But he is horrible to me now. Why do you love him?"

"Why do I ? . . . . Emily that is a terrible thing to ask me. Why are you saying that uncle Paul has been hitting you? I've never seen him do that to you. Why are you saying that?"

"He does it when you're not looking. He pretends he loves me but really he doesn't. Why do you love him?"

"Stop asking me that. When was the last time he hit you then?"

"Can't remember . . . . but he did. Do you love Paul, or do you love someone else?"

"What? Emily Willows, you stop that talk right now or you won't get a milk shake. You'll get a shake, and a smack, but no bloody milk shake!"

"Don't care! You don't care so I don't care!" Emily had stopped in the street and now was looking up at her sister. Maria looked at the girl's blue eyes and felt that something was wrong with the child. This wasn't her Emily. The girl that was staring at her with a blank, emotionless stare was not her lovely, bubbly sister. For the first time in her life, Maria looked at Emily with a feeling of fear. Not necessarily fear of her own flesh and blood, but fear that the little girl was being something that she wasn't. It was hard to explain. Surely that look isn't spite is it? Why would Emily spite her? Whatever it was meant to convey, the stare that Emily was now giving her sister made her feel uncomfortable. And yes, even a little scared. This was ridiculous. She didn't need this hassle either.

"Oh for heaven's sake. Do you want a milk-shake or not?"

"I suppose so," and with a sudden beaming smile, "a banana one!"

"We'll have this conversation later little miss, but we will get to the bottom of it, I promise you."

Emily again had shrugged her shoulders. The smile had vanished as quickly as it had appeared.

They has carried on their walk to the cafe, but the feeling of uneasiness in Maria was still there. She couldn't help it. The way Emily looked at her, the way she now she spoke of Paul, right down to the way she walked—as if she were walking with a purpose to some place she needed to go to in a hurry—just wasn't synonymous with her sister.

In the cafe Maria ordered Emily's banana milkshake and a cappuccino. Emily sat opposite her and started drinking the milk shake whilst playing with a napkin. Folding it one way and then another. Any attempts to converse with the little girl proved fruitless as Maria tried to understand just why Emily was so distant at the moment.

"Nice shake?" Emily nodded. "You used to like vanilla didn't you? Why do you like banana now?" Emily shrugged her shoulders.

"You looking forward to going back to school?" Emily shrugged again.

Maria looked up in annoyance and felt angry at her sister's stubborn attitude. But she just knew that to do her nut with Emily now would make the girl all the more difficult to communicate with. Sometimes, sometimes, she felt that her wish for children of her own was just a ridiculous whimsy that should never be encouraged.

Emily had drunk half her milk shake when she jumped out of her seat with a shot. She stood upright in front of her older sister and stared straight into her eyes. For only a second she said nothing, although to the startled nurse, it felt like minutes. Then with an abrupt tone she spat out the words . . .

"I need the toilet!" before marching off to the ladies.

Maria stared down into her cappuccino. She turned her spoon around and around the drink, watching white circles of foam turn and dip and tried to think of what to do next. She felt that she knew Paul better than anybody in the world. He didn't have many relatives still alive so it wasn't like she had much competition in that department.

She tried to imagine Paul getting angry with Emily. Tried to imagine him leaping up off the sofa or something and giving the little girl a smack across the bottom or the back of the legs. To be honest, Emily was a bit too old for that sort of treatment, so it seemed unlikely Paul would do that. So what was she referring to? She certainly couldn't imagine him punching her or threatening her in any way. Paul was no coward when it came to violence, but there wasn't any way that he would raise his fist in anger to a child, especially little Em. Okay, he wasn't what you would call *close* to the kid, and sometimes he looked as if he could well do without her around, especially when she was making a noise. But even he would admit that in a funny sort of way, he did actually love his mini sister-in-law.

Oh Emily, she thought to herself, if this is a forerunner of the kind of behaviour you will show in your teenage years, then maybe they should find a way of stopping you from turning thirteen? If only it was that easy!

Maria gazed at the half-finished milk shake and looked at her watch. She was taking her time. Surely she had been in there for over five minutes? If she didn't come out soon she would go and see if she was alright. She didn't want to barge straight in if Emily was on the toilet. If there was one thing that she felt shouldn't be done at the moment, it was to patronise her. Emily may only be nine years old, but you couldn't tell her what to do as easily as the nine year olds of the past!

The waitress came to the table and picked up the milk shake glass. "Is this dead?"

"No, not yet" replied Maria, "although my sister will be if she doesn't come out of the toilet soon."

Both her and the waitress smiled as they looked towards the still closed toilet door. What on earth was she doing in there?

Mick was handing over money to the guy behind the bar. Paul had bought the first two pints and a second round was considered to be an excellent idea considering how well the two strangers were getting along.

There hadn't been much talk of the ice-cream incident. Instead, information about careers, ambitions and then the state of the England football team had been exchanged. In fact, the football talk had taken up much of the time. It had struck Mick as funny how the international language of football could be so handy when anywhere in the world. Wherever he had travelled in the world, his knowledge of football had always been a useful ice-breaker when talking to blokes he had just met, especially when talking of his beloved Arsenal. It did help when your team had such well known players such as Fabregas or Theo Walcott.

"Ah yes!" would be a usual reply. "Walcott, England eh? Good player! He plays for Arsenal? Your team is good, yes?" or something like that anyway.

Well, Paul may not be foreign, but his support for Colchester United was impressive considering how everybody else who didn't support the Gunners seemed to support Manchester United or Chelsea, regardless of where they came from. And it is always good to speak to someone when you knew how superior your team is to theirs. Quite patronising when you think of it, but satisfying in a bizarre sort of way!

"So Mick," said the Colchester supporter, "do you think you will ever have kids one day?" Mick raised his eyebrows and grinned.

"I think I would need a woman first! I dunno, sometimes I think it would be great. I'm told that there is nothing like being present at the birth of your kids. A guy at work has a picture in his wallet of him and his wife moments after the birth of their son. He said that the feelings in the room were so emotional that he had to take a picture for posterity. Whenever he now feels that life is being a bitch, he just takes out the photo and all those proud feelings come rushing back. Very therapeutic he says, and it always makes him realise how precious life is. So I guess that there must be something in having kids. What do you think?"

"Well we don't have kids of our own yet, although she always drops hints about it. We do have a kid in the house though, Emily, the wife's sister-in-law. We took her in after the sudden death of the wife's mum. She's nine years old and full of energy. She keeps us busy, well, busy enough until we have our own, if you see what I mean?"

"Who's the wife then?"

"Who's the wife? Oh you mean her name! Maria, yes her name's Maria. Not in her good books at the moment. We had a bit of a barney, that's why I looked so pissed off earlier on. I was trying to work out what I had done wrong *this* time!"

Mick had momentarily paled as he heard the name. He always did whenever he heard it. He wished he could treat it the same way as any name, but it always made his heart race just that little bit quicker. He had just got himself together again when the feeling returned at Paul's next sentence, but this time it was a thousand times worse. Even Paul noticed that Mick was holding his pint glass halfway to his mouth, in mid air.

"She works as a nurse. We usually get on really well, but I don't know, her sister said that I've been hitting her and Maria believes it. Well, I think she believes it the way she's acting. Are you okay? I think your glass needs to get a bit closer to your mouth if you're going to drink your beer!"

"Yes, I was just thinking of your wife's name. I used to know a Maria that's all and the name triggered off some memories. You know what it's like with ex's."

"Liked her, this Maria you went out with? What happened to her?"

"Oh you know, the usual thing. "I think you're really nice but . . . ." that sort of excuse. To be honest I'm not sure that I do understand what drove her away. I think I really loved her, but obviously that wasn't good enough."

"You *think* you loved her! How can you *think* you love someone?"

"Okay, I had really strong feelings for her. Maybe if it had worked out then I could've said that I really loved her. I'm trying to be realistic here, but it's hard when you really, really fancy someone. Am I making sense?"

"A bit! No seriously, I think what you're saying is that you wanted to be with her long term, but she had other ideas, and now you aren't sure if you loved her or if you just had a really strong crush on her, yeah?"

"I don't think *crush* is the right word. I had a crush on my social science teacher at school, but I didn't want to marry her!"

"Just shag her yeah?"

"Yeah!" he laughed at the memory of the young teacher who would bend over when checking their work and who clearly had no bra on. All the boys had fancied her. Well, fancied her cleavage anyway!

"Okay," Paul continued, "crush is a bad word. You *really* fancied her but maybe the real love thing would've happened if you two had stayed together."

"Something like that. God, I really wanted her though, thought about her all the time. It nearly drove me mad!"

"All part and parcel of maturing as an adult my man. It'll happen again for you, and next time it will put all your thoughts about Maria into perspective. You'll laugh about it one day."

"I hope so. God, what do I sound like! I don't normally talk about my miserable love life to people I've just met you know. Sorry mate, I think it's the beer talking."

Paul laughed and finished off his pint quickly.

"Don't worry about it! We've all been there! All I know is that I'm enjoying this Mick me new old mate, and I'm gonna enjoy it just a bit more! I'm on holiday, and that means getting pissed, especially when the wife has given me a good reason to! You could use another one too I think!"

Mick looked down at his half full pint and was about to ask for just another half, but Paul was already about to talk to the barman.

It was only after Paul had asked for two more pints that Mick became aware of the door of the pub banging open. A woman with short brown hair was rushing towards them, and judging by the look on her face something was seriously upsetting her. She got closer to them and grabbed Paul's shoulder, making him turn around to face her. Mick looked at Paul's smiling face in bemusement, and then looked at the woman's face in alarm as she spat out her words. He felt his body weaken, his adrenaline pump and his face pale, and this time he knew that it definitely wasn't the beer that was affecting him.

"Paul, where the fuck have you been? I've been looking for you everywhere! Why was your fucking phone turned off!"

Paul's smile disappeared and he glared at his shouting spouse.

"What's going on now? Don't start on me Maria, I really don't need this crap . . . ."

"Emily is missing Paul! We were in the cafe, she went to the toilet and then disappeared! We've lost Emily!"

CHAPTER THIRTEEN

From the pub, Paul, Maria and Mick had intended to go straight to the police station. They had certainly rushed out of the pub with purpose with Maria screaming at Paul about his lack of responsibility and how useless he was at being around when she needed him.

Mick had tagged along, trying to keep pace and staring with a mixture of disbelief, pleasure and panic. Never in his life had so many feelings raced through him at one time. From the moment he had seen Maria's panic-stricken face in the bar, it was as if the moment he had always dreamt of had finally happened—he was in the presence of Maria again. It could've been in better circumstances though—this was not good, not good at all.

Maybe he was bloody selfish because he had felt rather pissed off that she hadn't said a word to him. Sure, she had noticed him alright—her eyes had lingered on his face a bit longer than normal right? Even in these circumstances they had lingered, he was sure of it—but apart from that her attention was totally on her anguish and her anger with Paul.

Paul had tried hard to ascertain what had happened, where they had gone, when she had noticed that Em had disappeared, how long had it been since then and had she told the police yet? It seems that Maria hadn't told the police. She had felt that Emily couldn't possibly have gone far and had looked all around the streets near the cafe. People hadn't been very helpful, looked at her like she was mad she had said, bet they would've been more fucking helpful if it had been their kid. Anyway, she couldn't find her. She thought that she might bump into Paul as well—should've known that he would find his way to the pub.

Paul hadn't been impressed with this attack on him. He had told her that it wasn't *his* fault that Emily had gone missing. Yes, of course he was bloody worried, worried sick actually, but her ranting at him wasn't going to solve anything. As for him going to the pub, when did he actually have the time to go the pub at home? He thought he was having a break. First the accusations had continued and now this.

Maria had ignored Paul's attempts at justifying his trip to the pub and had screamed out her sister's name. Apart from the bemused looks on passers-by there had been no response until they were standing across the road from the McDonalds. It was there that Mick had noticed the approaching policeman. As he walked he had spoken into his walkie-talkie and Mick had felt that he had seen Maria's anguish and was telling the station that there could be a problem. As he got close, Maria had noticed his approach and had raced up to him. Her speech babbled as she had tried to tell him about her missing sibling. The policeman had tried to calm her down.

"Now Madam, if you would be so kind as to just step over here out of the way of the public trying to get by you, then I'm sure that we can sort this out calmly."

It had been at that moment that the situation had become surreal. According to the policeman, they had noticed Maria and the two guys racing along in obvious distress five minutes before. As it happens, they had in their care a little blonde girl matching the description of Emily. That she was unharmed and quite happy. She had been seen wandering near the cafe and had been taken to them by an old lady. Would they like to be taken to her?

Maria had sat down on the pavement in her relief, the whole incident obviously taking most of the energy out of her.

Now they were sitting in the back of an unmarked police car outside the police station. They had been in there for over ten minutes with Maria growing more and more impatient. She looked at Paul in annoyance.

"Paul, will you go and find out what's going on? There must be a problem if they haven't come out yet." Paul sighed and tried to think of a reason not to go into the station.

"It's only been a short while Maria. I'm worried that they'll smell the beer on my breath and arrest me for something. You know what they're like. They'll be out in a moment, I'm sure of it."

"What? Unless you really have done something wrong then you have nothing to worry about. For God's sake, even policemen drink beer you know, just go in there and ask if there's a problem. They know how worried I am."

"Yeah, but I'm sure that they'll . . . ."

"Forget it, I'll go myself!" She had opened the door, but before she could jump out, Paul had quickly opened his door and jumped out before her.

"Okay, okay I'll go. If I'm not back in five minutes, call the police!" Maria hadn't been impressed with his humour.

"Prat!" She closed the door again and sat back in her seat, sighing loudly.

There followed the most painful few seconds of Mick's life. He was so close to the woman he had adored so long ago and yet the situation was so awkward. Why hadn't she said anything to him? Surely she recognised him, he hadn't changed that much. As Maria was in the front seat, all he could see was the back of her brown hair. He wondered if it still had the smell of henna in it and was very tempted to smell it out of curiosity. Just below the hair was the start of her neck. Oh how he had kissed and caressed that neck in the past. It hadn't changed—she hadn't changed. To Mick's eyes, she was just as beautiful as ever. He had to say something, he couldn't just let this moment pass with nothing said, as awkward as it was. He thought hard about what to say, his heart pumping so hard he was sure that she could hear it in the closed space of the car.

"Not the best time to see you again Maria." Maria hadn't turned her head.

"I don't really have anything to say to you Mick. I have enough on my mind as it is."

"I'm . . . . I'm sorry. I'm sure that Emily is safe. Try not to worry." Maria then did turn her head.

"Try not to worry? You haven't changed have you? Always did have a naive attitude to the word Mick Rogers. Shit, just don't speak to me, okay?"

Mick had always thought that he would see Maria again somehow. But this wasn't how he thought it would go. In his dreams, Maria had said that she was now aware of her mistake and could he ever forgive her? It hadn't mattered to him if Maria had put on ten stone in weight and had seven kids—he still would've taken her back. The fact that she had hardly changed didn't help the pain he was starting to feel. She was even wearing the same perfume.

"I never meant to hurt you Maria. I'm sorry that I loved you like I did. You are right, I was naive. You have another life and Paul's a nice guy. I'm sorry. I'll shut up now." Maria's face softened. She didn't hate Mick. She had no dislike of him at all. He hadn't done anything wrong, not really. But she hadn't been able to reciprocate the feelings that he had had for her. It had been difficult because he had been so devoted to her, and she knew that the way she had left him was wrong. But it had all been in the past. She never thought that their paths would cross again. She turned to him.

"Don't keep apologising. Things are different now Mick, you know that. Please, I don't want to speak about anything at the moment."

As she turned away, Mick felt that never in his life had he ever felt so hurt. The truth was that Maria was right, life *was* different now, he *did* know that. But what could you do when your heart kept rebelling against you? He thought about getting out of the car, but the thought of staying in her presence for just a while longer kept him there. This was ridiculous, he kept telling himself that, but for the life of him he just couldn't leave her at that moment.

"I've only just met Paul. We met at the promenade. I nearly knocked him over. Nice guy. Good sense of humour."

Maria didn't reply to this but just stared through the windscreen, lost in a million different thoughts.

The door opened and Paul jumped back into the car, closely followed by the policeman they had spoken to earlier who jumped into the driver's seat. Mick had been trying to figure out something in the back of his mind since they had got into the car and it finally came to him.

"Tell me officer, why are we in an unmarked car?"

The officer had turned to look at him.

"No particular reason sir. All the squad cars are out at the moment and one of the CID lot kindly let us take this for our little journey. Just sit back and enjoy the ride and you should be reunited with little Emily in an hour or so."

Maria looked at the officer in surprise.

"An hour or so? Surely she couldn't have got *that* far officer?"

The officer started the car, and as he released the handbrake, he replied to Maria's startled query.

"She didn't go that far by herself, it's true madam. No, the old lady in question took her to a colleague of mine and they took her to London. It wasn't that long ago actually."

"London? Why the hell London?"

"Why the hell? Indeed madam, London could be likened to hell by some people, but that is why we are going there. Trust me madam, sirs. It will all become clear to you at our destination. Emily is safe, that is all you need to know."

Paul grimaced at Mick.

"Back to jolly old London we go then! Mind you, what about my car?"

"Oh I think I can get you to your sister-in-law much quicker sir. You'd be surprised, at least, you will be when we get there!"

Maria turned to Paul and then Mick. Their faces gave the same questioning, puzzled expression. Okay, Emily was safe, at least that is what the officer said. So why was the guy's expression so odd? Where on earth was he taking them?

Emily, on the other hand, couldn't have been happier at this turn of events. She had come out of the toilet to be met by a lady in a pretty, patterned scarf, who had held out her hand in a request to lead her away. Emily had taken the hand with a broadening smile on her face, and after a quick look towards her sister, who was staring, hypnotized by her cup of coffee, had slipped out of the cafe.

She had got into a car with the lady, and after a quick drive to the local airport had been taken to a helicopter. What a thrill that had been, flying over fields and looking down at the tiny people below. After the helicopter had come another short ride and now she stood in a big, dark building.

The old lady with the scarf had been with her every step of the journey, but she had then left her with yet another lady, a taller lady who was dressed in a frilly, white blouse. She handed Emily a can of coke.

"Just in case you need a drink after your journey. Did you enjoy the helicopter?"

"Yes, I've never been in one before. Where are we?"

"This looks like quite a scary place doesn't it, but don't you worry, you are with a lot of people that will take care of you Emily."

"How do you know my name?"

"Well, the lady that brought you here told me it."

"Oh. What's your name?"

"Dorothy. You remind me so much of my own little girl, but she's grown up now."

"Do you work here?" Dorothy laughed at the little girl's query.

"No darling, I don't work here, but a lot of work is planned here. Actually, I've brought somebody to see you, someone you may remember."

From out of the darkness stepped Thomas Burn. As he stepped into the light from the candles, Emily recognised him as the man she had first met a couple of months ago. He had been in the park with a very tall man, and she had been playing Frisbee with her best friend Amy. When the Frisbee had gone near the two men, Burn had passed it back to her, but he had also asked her about her sister. Emily, thinking that he knew Maria, had therefore spoken to him. After the meeting, she had felt strange. Not ill or anything, but somewhat spaced out. The man had looked into her eyes and said something, but she couldn't remember what it was. She had felt compelled to go and see the man in the park again a week later. He had been with a woman then, and they had bought her an ice-cream and said a lot of things to her, most of which she couldn't remember now.

Now the same man stood before her, but he looked a little different. There was a red mark on his face, right next to his nose. It looked painful, and had what looked like some ointment on it. His voice however, sounded the same as before.

"Hello again sweetie. You do remember me don't you?"

"Yes. I can't remember your name though."

"I don't think that I told you my name, but you can call me Tom."

"Okay Tom."

"Dorothy has introduced herself I think? Dorothy is a lovely lady and I'm sure that you two are going to be the bestest of friends, don't you Dorothy?" Dorothy stood behind Emily and placed her hands on her shoulders.

"Oh yes Thomas, I know we will. Are you hungry darling, I can get you something from the McDonalds across the road if you like?" Emily wrinkled her nose and shook her head.

"No thank you, I ate something before that lady brought me here. I'd like a burger later on, if I can have one?" Thomas Burn smiled.

"Of course you can sweetie, I'm sure that Dorothy will get you whatever you want. In fact, Dorothy is going to look after you during your stay with us, Anything you want, just ask her and she will get it for you."

Emily smiled and nodded.

Thomas turned to Dorothy, the smile on his face dropping. Even in the dark, Dorothy could see that Burn had a look on his face that was unnerving and his words didn't help her feel that something had upset the man a great deal.

"I won't be going to the meeting. Something has come up that I need to deal with urgently."

"But won't the leader be expecting you? He won't be pleased that you haven't turned up will he?"

"I suppose not, but I can't seem to do anything right as far as he is concerned, despite everything that I have done for him and this cause. Why he calls it the 'cause' and not a proper name is beyond me."

"You're not changing you mind are you Thomas? You can't, he won't allow it."

"No, no, I just need to make something clear to the man. He may think that he has all the ideas, but if it wasn't for me then a lot of what has happened wouldn't have happened. No, I just want to be respected a bit more that's all. He's always maintained that respect for all is important, well, I just want some of that for me that's all."

"But he values you, I know he does."

"With some of that respect Dorothy, I know him a lot better than you do, and I know how he values my contributions."

Dorothy sidled up to Burn, and ran her finger down his face, whispering so that Emily couldn't hear what she said.

"That really is a nasty injury Thomas. Would you like me to kiss it better? Or would you like me to kiss some other part of you better? I'd *love* to you know." Thomas moved away towards the door.

"Very nice of you to offer Dorothy, but I really have to get away. Make my apologies to the leader please. I shan't be far."

Feeling hurt at this rejection, and frustrated at not being able to perform an act that Stephen had never wanted, Dorothy looked at Emily and smiled.

"Well young lady, I suppose we better get you to the hall eh? You have an important man to meet."

CHAPTER FOURTEEN

"How is security? Have we made sure that the little problem we had earlier on isn't going to happen again?"

"No sir, I guarantee that this time we have seen to everything. I don't understand what happened before. Mr Burn said that nobody would notice our occupation, bearing in mind that it's only temporary like."

"You've seen Mr Burn have you? Maybe you should speak to him about sloppy behaviour. To be honest, I am wondering if I am not better off finding others to help me with my task. The incompetence and liberties that you people find so interesting are beginning to tire me. This is an important evening Roscoe. We have come a long way and brought in a lot of people. We cannot fail now. Everything must be perfect, understand? Perfect."

"Yes sir, I totally agree. Don't you worry sir, I know that tonight will be a big success. I know that the rector has been busy and that all our subjects know the address."

"And the time? We must start promptly."

"Yes sir, that was made quite clear." With this remark, Roscoe put two hands to his hat and straightened it to his specifications.

"You won't be wearing that in the service will you?"

"Well I thought that . . . ."

"No, you really won't be wearing that ridiculous thing. Where is the girl?"

"Mrs Tarmint is bringing her?"

"Who the hell is Mrs Tarmint? What sort of name is that?"

"I don't know completely sir, but apparently she is a very annoyed housewife. Was quite easy to get to apparently. I saw her work and was quite impressed."

"Well as long as the girl is here. There is someone that I need to meet again and the girl being here is imperative."

"Why do you need to meet this person again? What is so special about him?"

"I don't expect you to understand anything I choose to do Roscoe, but suffice it to say that we have quite a bit in common. He could be very useful to have on my side, providing we dangle the right carrot in front of him. Quite an attractive carrot too I think."

"What carrot would that be sir?"

"Enough of this. I think I would like to make my way to the service. Blow out the candles as you come out, there's a good chap."

"Yes sir, my pleasure sir. Absolutely. Blow out the candles."

The two men walked down the damp, dark corridor. There were doors to either side, all of which looked like they hadn't been opened in years. As Roscoe walked he looked around and saw paper peeling off walls and patches where paint had been steadily peeling away over the decades. The only light came from more candles that had been placed carefully along the corridor. With no electricity in the building candles seemed to be the only option, especially as their leader had ignored any other options like battery powered lamps or torches. Their leader liked candles, and that was all there was to it.

It wasn't long before they came to the staircase. A more grandiose staircase Roscoe had never seen before with its cantilevered iron stair. Stone angels and demons set in terracotta watched their every move as they went down, the gothic splendour totally lost on the man who followed his leader towards the great hall.

Everywhere they walked there were brothers and sisters of the cause creeping around the darkness, their torches gleaming like on-coming tube trains. Now and then there were men in grey, double-breasted suits. These men were important to the leader, for they had not only managed to secure the building, getting rid of a few too curious security men in the process, but word had it they had perfected some interesting ways of stopping people from speaking, should they feel like splitting from the cause and telling the world as to what they had gone through. Fortunately, there hadn't been many of these cases.

As they walked, Roscoe was aware of just how many more people there were in this decaying building. It didn't seem like so long ago that the only people that were here were the leader, himself, Burn and the Rector. Now the Rector stood waiting in the hall, a hall that was evidently not empty anymore. The sound of crowds of people talking became clearer, the buzz reaching Roscoe's ears as they approached their destination. Eventually they stood besides a huge, open door and peered into the hall.

It was as if they had gate-crashed a party for somebody very popular. There were people laughing, drinking, smoking and generally enjoying the candlelit atmosphere of the hall. It had taken Roscoe and four other helpers ages to set out and light all the candles, but he had to admit that it looked rather spectacular. It had him thinking of the Christmas services that he was dragged to as a kid. The only thing missing was a tree. He mentioned this to his leader, who gazed impassively at the crowd.

"But I'm sure that your presence will light up the proceedings sir."

"Shut up Roscoe! If your tongue goes any higher up my arse I will clench my cheeks and rip it off."

A skinhead in front of the newly arrived twosome looked around at the threat and immediately smiled and nudged the person to his left. This in effect led to other nudges, smiles and whispered comments before the entire congregation had stopped what it was doing and looked in unison at Roscoe and his leader.

At the front, standing on a stage of wooden blocks that looked not unlike the sort that you would find in a school's assembly hall, stood the Rector. He was holding his hat, a huge, round hat, and one that made Roscoe think that they wouldn't necessarily need a tree if he was to put the hat on. The rector was tall, very tall, and the hat would give an impression of a tree's canopy in the darkness. Upon seeing the leader, the rector threw the hat into the corner and clapped his hands together.

"Ladies and Gentleman, I have the honour of presenting you to the great man responsible for our wonderful coming together. The man that has made this great occasion happen and to whom the entire world will one day cherish and be thankful to. You are truly blessed on this day, for ladies and gentleman, I give you your leader, Mr Theobald Leonard. Mr Leonard, sir, if you would come this way."

The quietness had changed into a hum as the people digested the name of the man who had only been known before as the great leader, before a round of applause broke out, interspersed with cheers and whistles.

Roscoe looked just as surprised as everybody else at this revealing of the great man's name and for a moment felt as if some of his mystery had been taken away. But Leonard's face was one of cool acknowledgement as he carefully skirted his way through the throngs of people. Shaking hands with some and uttering words of thanks to others.

Leonard was directed to a chair to the left of the stage, and there he sat, legs crossed, hands clasped, and eyes flickering between the crowd of people and the beaming Rector on the stage. He nodded his head briefly; the Rector hushed the people with his hands and started the speech that he had rehearsed in his head for many days now. At last, the time had come.

"Ladies and Gentlemen. I warmly welcome you one and all to this special occasion. May I say that I am honoured to not only be in the presence of our great leader, but to be present in front of you all. Like most of you, I have waited a long time for today and if it were ever needed to be shown that patience is a virtue, then today, this great day, has proved that very thing."

A round of applause again rang out at these words, and the Rector smiled at Leonard, his captive audience and raised his hand to silence those that now hung onto every word that he said.

"Yes it's been quite a journey but here we all are. Now, I know that each and every one of you has become close to at least one new member of our brethren. It may well be the person who introduced you to our movement, the person who has tried to help encourage the latent powers that each and every one of us possesses. Failing that, they will have at least helped you realise that your life is not as helpless as you may think and that things can change. You are now among people that will help this change to come about. You are all truly blessed."

More applause. Leonard sat as impassive as before, until his eyes rested on the little blonde girl near the front. Emily smiled at him, and responding to his gesture, climbed the stage and sat on his lap. This action resulted in even more applause, with the Rector himself taking part this time. He coughed for silence and continued.

"Ah it is so gratifying to see the young respond so positively to our cause. There are quite a lot of us in this hall that are in despair at the way the youth act today. With their baseball caps, hoods and violent, brainless attitude, these fools are raised by parents who cannot control them or who are blind to their children's faults. Make no mistake ladies and gentlemen, the rot set in a long time ago. But we have youth here today that are proof that the task we have is not a futile one. We shall succeed in eradicating these problems and many others of the same ilk. Our techniques may be a little brusque at times, but we *shall* succeed."

This time the ovation was louder, with whoops and cheers not unlike those overreactions on an American sit-com. A man near the front screamed out "We are right with you on that one Rec," before high-fiveing with the young guy next to him. The Rector looked at the man in bemusement.

"Rector will do if you don't mind. The term 'rec' reminds me of the word recreation, and I assure you I have nothing to do with playing games." He looked at Leonard when speaking these words and was rewarded with a stony gaze that bore straight through him. A little unnerved by his leader's response he carried on as before.

"Indeed, I know as well as you all that there are many things in this cruel world that have been ignored for far too long now. Tell me people, why do politicians get paid astronomical wages while nurses and teachers toil for hardly anything? Yes people, a question you have heard so many times before, but what has actually been done about it? Does it *really* matter who you vote for? Is this really democracy? Well, I think that we know the truth don't we? People like these useless politicians must be removed and replaced and with enough people on our side then we can do it. No class systems, no police, no courts, just one law for all from one great man. It is time for action. What we have to do is not ideal, but nevertheless it *has* to be done."

Yet more applause started to sound in the hall, but was abruptly halted by the sight of Leonard approaching the front of the stage. Emily sat in his vacated chair, her legs swinging back and forth looking as if this was just an enjoyable day out for her. The Rector stepped back with a look of surprise—this wasn't in the script; the leader was not due to speak to the people just yet. However, he wasn't going to argue the point just now—Leonard did not have the look of a man open to discussion.

"I think, Rector, with thanks for your kind words and respect for your loyalty to the cause, that you are dawdling somewhat, especially when it comes to what needs to be done. Yes, it needs not be said that each of you has been chosen because there is something about this world that distresses you, but let's be honest, if we don't make others out there see that they *must* be encouraged to join with our cause and defeat the sources of our discontent, then what the hell are we doing here? I think it is time to be blunt don't you? If anybody here has got any doubts as to going ahead with our plans, then you may as well turn around and walk through those doors now. There is no going back after today."

Waiting at the doors were two men dressed in the same grey double-breasted suits as before. They opened the doors and gestured towards them, but nobody moved. Instead they look back to where Leonard stood.

"Good. Then we can continue. Boys, make sure those doors are shut tight. We seem to have a loyal following here. Very pleasing. Ladies and gentlemen. Some of us standing here have already taken the step that I am going to speak of, but I suggest that you listen carefully, for you may well have to take the very same step yourself. It is a sure fact that not everybody will be convinced of our motives or of our actions, but *we* know that they need to be fulfilled. Later, we have people standing by on either side of the hall that will take you to separate rooms where you will be conditioned further to the cause. Trust me, it is painless, but it is just a little *booster* if you will to enhance your capabilities. It will certainly boost a more positive reaction to what I am going to show you now. Emily, if you'd be so kind as to come to the front."

Emily jumped off the chair and walked to where Leonard stood. She showed no fear of the crowd but seemed to enjoy being in the spotlight. Leonard knelt slightly as he spoke.

"Tell me Emily, are you happy to be here?"

"Yes Mr Leonard."

"Good. Where are your parents?"

"Dead."

"I see. We are sorry to hear that. Who do you live with then?"

"My sister."

"Is she good to you?"

"Yes. I don't like my uncle though."

"Ah interesting, why is that?"

"I used to, but I think he is horrible to my sister. I want her to be happy but he doesn't always make her happy. He doesn't want a baby, my sister does. I think another man would have a baby with my sister."

"How do you know that somebody else could love her more than your uncle?"

"I didn't at first, but I knew that my uncle was making my sister sad. I didn't like that."

"So do you think that there are other people like your uncle in the world?"

"Yes, I watch the news and there are always people hurting others, just like my uncle hurts my sister. Well, not exactly the same, but sometimes my sister looks so sad. I get upset when she is sad."

"What should we do with these people Emily?"

"Make them go away. The world would be better without people like my uncle."

"Do you remember how we can make people like your uncle go away? Do you remember what I taught you, Emily?"

"Yes. I remember."

Leonard stood up and looked towards the audience. He swept his eyes across them, from left to right, from the back to the front, before settling his vision on a young man laughing with a friend. The man was wearing an Iron Maiden t-shirt, with a particularly gruesome picture of Maiden icon Eddie on the front, and Leonard pointed towards him and asked him to join them on the stage. The man pointed towards himself.

"Me sir?"

"Yes you sir. Let's have a look at your t-shirt shall we?"

The man made his way to the stage and climbed up till he was standing next to the great leader. Leonard prodded the man in the chest.

"Interesting design. A favourite of yours, this band?"

"Yes sir. I am a big heavy metal fan."

"I see. What is your name, heavy metal fan?"

"Ricky. Ricky Talbot."

"Well Mr Talbot, would you mind taking that unusual t-shirt off for a moment?"

"Eh? But I'm not wearing anything underneath it?"

"Oh come now Mr Talbot. Ricky. Nobody is going to judge you on your chest are they now? This is an unusual request granted, but you are helping me make a point that is essential to be put across in as graphic a way a possible, if only to make my meaning a little clearer, a little more meaningful if you will, to all of our friends here."

Ricky looked around him feeling increasingly nervous. He didn't have a problem with strange people seeing him topless, but it was just the request to take his shirt off now that worried him. Yes, it *was* unusual, but it was also the look in Leonard's eyes that bothered him. Still, what could he do in front of all these people that was so bad? There was bound to be a good reason for it. Wasn't there?

As Ricky pulled the t-shirt over his head, Leonard knelt quickly to hand Emily something. The crowd were so busy watching and whistling at Ricky's topless body that nobody was aware of what exactly it was, although that would become clear in just a few seconds.

"Very good Mr Talbot. Perhaps you'd be so good as to just give the t-shirt to the Rector. I'm sure he'll look after it for the moment."

Ricky threw his t-shirt underarm at the approaching Rector, who looked uneasily at the leader. He knew what was coming next, but this really was too unexpected. There were times when he felt that Leonard acted on a whim. Well, if this didn't make the crowd sit up and take notice, then nothing would.

"Okay Mr Talbot. For the sake of role-play, you are going to be Emily's uncle okay? Emily tells me that his name is Paul, so for the moment you are Paul, understand?"

"Er yes, I understand."

Leonard looked to the side of the stage and nodded at two of his grey-suited assistants. Both men came onto the stage, and before Ricky could protest had grabbed both of his arms.

"Now Ricky don't be alarmed. All shall be explained. You have just told Emily off. You are really angry with her, so much so that you have come very close to hitting her."

"But I wouldn't dare do such a thing."

"I know Mr Talbot, but right now you are Paul, remember? And from what Emily tells me, Paul definitely would, do you see?"

"Right, I er . . . I see."

Ricky winced as the two men gripped his arms harder.

"Now, you are so angry that a couple of neighbours have heard the noise and rushed in to calm you down, hence the boys here. Now Emily needs to tell you how much she is hurting. Okay Emily, tell your uncle why his behaviour is hurting you. Why it is hurting your sister who you love so much. Tell Uncle Paul why you hate him so."

"You don't love my sister, you pretend you do but you won't have a baby with her. I've seen her crying and so I know that you don't love her. You are a liar Uncle Paul and I hate, I really, really *hate* you!"

Now it became apparent to Ricky why he had had a feeling of fear. Now it became apparent why the crowd were now staring wide-eyed at what Leonard had handed the little girl. She moved forward quickly and produced from behind her back a knife with deep serrated edges.

In one swift motion, Emily Willows plunged the knife deep into the stomach of Ricky Talbot. Ricky looked down in horror and screamed.

"Nooooooo! For fuck's sake nooooo!"

Leonard gripped the chin of the Maiden fan and turned it towards the silent people in the crowd.

"Yes you bastard. I'm sorry Ricky, but life is one huge role-play, didn't you know that? Unfortunately, this was also your audition and you failed. Did you think that I didn't see you taking the piss out of me in the crowd? You shouldn't have come you shit." He let go of the man's chin and turned towards the crowd. "Still, I suppose he has served one purpose for the cause eh? *This* my people, is the only way to deal with those that get in the way of our cause. I offered you the chance to turn back, now it's too late. You must continue with everything that has taken place so far. You must do it with compassion, but with ruthlessness should people totally fail to agree with what must be done. There will come a day in the not too distant future when our numbers will be so great that the toppling of those that run this sordid world will be dispersed with too, just like this fool here. Now, you know what I am asking of you. You know that my visions are of a world far greater than this, without people who know nothing patronising us every single day. But in order for us to be totally absorbed in the process, we must increase the power we have already been shown by other members of the . . . . brethren, as the good Rector puts it. It is now your duty to go to the other rooms we have prepared where you will be greeted by my staff. They will help you and when that is done, they will give you a list of instructions that are to be carried out. Lists of people that you may wish to bring into our cause. Some of the more senior members of our cause shall be targeting council members, politicians, senior policemen etc, but your task is easier. Start with family, friends, neighbours, those that ridicule or hinder must be dispersed with like Talbot here. Go, for you all have plenty to do. We shall meet at a later time in a larger arena, where we shall see for ourselves the progress we have made. Thank you ladies and gentlemen."

A final thunderous applause broke out as Leonard, the Rector and Emily joined hands and raised them together in a sign of solidarity. When this ovation had subsided, grey-suits mixed among the crowds and counted heads as groups were made and led off to other candle-lit rooms.

Roscoe, who had remained at the back of the room, rushed forward, tripping over others as he came, and breathlessly spoke to his leader of his admiration.

"Fantastic sir, truly inspiring. What would you like me to do next? I can help move the groups around if you'd like sir. The people here do know that I am a senior member of the cause don't they?"

"Roscoe, I can't tell you what these people will think of you, but they are fully aware of the task ahead of them so just let them get on with it, okay? In the meantime, get rid of this fool here, he's bleeding all over the place. You may need to finish Emily's job first though, I can trust you to do that can't I? Where the hell is Burn? He should've been on the stage too."

Leonard kicked the gasping body of Talbot before taking Emily's hand and leading her off the stage.

"As for you my dear, we have an appointment with some people you know well. I do hope that they will be able to keep it."

CHAPTER FIFTEEN

After their journey, Maria, Mick and Paul found themselves being led into the Victorian building that had once housed the cream of society, but it was also a place where the spirits of people that had died in strange circumstances still stalked the rooms and corridors.

It was this fact that Leonard had enjoyed so much. There was a mystery to the place and a feeling that despite its past as an hotel, there was still an air of eeriness that the gothic decoration only enhanced.

The police officer had uttered some words to the men standing at the main doors and the threesome walked into what Mick thought looked like the inside of a church. The truth was that all three of them knew the building they were in, but they had gone past it so many times without giving it any thought. They certainly didn't think that they would be taken there by a police officer on the trail of a missing sister. The mood of the police officer was mirrored by that of the people in the building. They all looked busy; as if they had a purpose, but when you looked into their eyes there was no individuality—they could've been robots if you hadn't know that they were flesh and blood.

Maria was the first to speak the words that were also in Mick and Paul's heads.

"What the fuck is this? Where is Emily? Why have you brought us to this godforsaken place?"

The officer quickly came over as Maria's questions echoed around the entrance and brought austere glances from those walking by them.

"Can you not swear please, there are young people in this building and we don't need them growing up using swear words thank you very much. Keep that sort of language for outside, for when you talk to those that enjoy living in a spoiled environment."

"Oh sor-ree!" Maria's sarcastic response brought another stern look from the officer. But to Mick, this appeal was quite a fair one. How many times had he been annoyed at the way that young people spoke these days? No, it was a fair request—it just didn't sit right with the whole atmosphere of the place, that's all. It was his turn to ask questions.

"What sort of place is this mate, and to repeat what my friend has asked you, where exactly is Emily? What has she got to do with a place like this?" Calling Maria a 'friend' had felt odd to him, and he had hoped that her face would show a little smile at it—but of course it didn't. How stupid of him. The officer replied as he showed them up a long, wide flight of stairs.

"If you had been here a little earlier then you would've seen for yourself, in fact I would've like to have been here myself had I not been tied up with you three. Still, all in a good cause I suppose, and we can't all be in the same place at the same time. These people that you see around you have just been rejuvenated by a speech from our leader, and in fact I was just informed by a brother that your sister took quite an active part in the proceedings. I'm sure she will want to tell you all about it. Come this way, she isn't far from you now." Paul looked confused.

"Brother? You have relatives working in this hole? What sort of malarky is this?"

The officer looked behind at Paul and shook his head in derision, which just confused Paul all the more. Mick looked at his new friend and smiled grimly.

"I don't think he appreciated your joke there mate?"

"Joke? I wasn't joking. He said brother. Unless he meant . . . . oh fuck, don't tell me he means like a brother in a joint cause, you know, a cult type of thing?"

Maria couldn't help display her feelings at this suggestion, her voice getting higher as she spoke.

"Cult? Don't say that Paul! We don't have cults in this country."

"So what's going on then?"

"I don't know! All I want is to get Emily home—I just hope that this bloke isn't taking us for a couple of prats."

Mick again felt a pang of hurt as Maria used the word 'couple' instead of saying something like 'us three'. Was she that determined to hurt him?

As they walked along a corridor, Mick felt that he would show that he really cared and that he would show this woman that he wasn't the loser that she obviously still felt he was. He'd show her that he really could be a knight in shining armour, monster or no monster.

"If we have to grab her then you Paul and Maria try to grab her. I'll try to stall them, get in their way or something."

Maria looked unimpressed.

"Yeah, okay Mick, since when have you become superman uh? Let's just find her first okay?"

Paul looked at Maria's face as she said this. It was the strangest thing. To Paul, Maria spoke to this guy like she'd known him for ages, but that couldn't be possible. And what did she mean, 'since when have you become?' Did she know this guy? Then the realisation hit him. The name of the guy that she had mentioned in the arcade. The ex that she had grown to hate because of his bitter ways. It all made sense. From his chat with Mick in the pub it was obvious that the guy was very bitter at the way his life had panned out. *And* he had said his ex was called Maria! This was just too much of a coincidence.

"Hey hold on a minute!" He pulled Mick back, causing Maria and the officer to stop and look back at them.

"She knows you doesn't she? You know this guy don't you?" Maria sighed in annoyance.

"It was a long time ago Paul. I don't think now is the time to discuss this do you?"

"But you spoke to me all that time, knowing that years ago you'd shagged my wife!" Mick tried to reason with him.

"How the hell could I know that you are married to the Maria that I knew?"

"Well, what were you doing in Southend? A bit of a coincidence isn't it?"

"What are you talking about? You guys live in London don't you? I live in London too! When I loved Maria, we lived in London then! And I don't think that we're the only people who live in London that go to bloody Southend for a holiday!"

"But you knew that Maria comes from Southend. You knew that she has family there."

"And? What is your point? That I'm *stalking* her? Christ, I know that I loved her once, but as she will tell you herself, she doesn't bloody love me, in fact, I don't think she ever bloody did!" Maria's head shot up at this remark.

"Oh don't be so bloody pathetic Rogers. Whatever I felt for you, love, hate, indifference, it's all in the sodding past. Can we go now?" Mick pointed to Maria as if his argument was now rock solid.

"There, told you! She loves *you*. You are one lucky bastard, but I don't dislike you for it. You're a good bloke Paul, and you look a great couple. Believe me!"

Maria was just about to repeat her last phrase but was stopped by the intervention of the officer who stood by watching this conversation with a bemused look on his face.

"When you two children have finished, can you please take yourself into this room here. The leader, Emily and her carer will be with you shortly. Make yourselves comfortable." However, Maria had picked up on the word 'carer', and was not impressed with it.

"Carer? *I'm* her fucking carer. What d'ya mean *carer*?"

"Madam, I have already told you to stop the foul language."

"*Don't* patronise me you fucking weirdo. I don't know what sort of fucked up operation that you're running here, but if I don't get my sister back right now, then I'm gonna do more than swear, you see if I don't!" The officer grabbed Paul's arm and spat words into his face.

"If you don't shut your wife up *sir*, then you won't see Emily again. I promise you that. Now get her into that room and keep her quiet." Maria was not to be deterred.

"Oh, you think that he's *my carer* do you? I will go into this bloody room, but you better bring me my sister. I'm warning you!"

Paul smiled sheepishly at the officer as he pushed his wife into the room, where they found themselves in a bare room with one large window opposite the door. The sunlight streamed onto six chairs that had obviously been set out for an impromptu meeting. They sat down with Mick putting a couple of chairs between himself and the couple.

"Well, isn't this cosy? They obviously haven't had the decorators in." Maria growled at her partner's remark.

"Paul, how can you be so unmoved by all of this. Do you know, I haven't seen any indication from you that you are angry about what's happening. I don't think it has even occurred to you just how fucking bizarre this is, has it?" Mick tried to side with his ex.

"I'm just biding my time. I'm just giving them a chance to return your sister. Otherwise . . ."

"Otherwise what Supermick? I always said that you were a dreamer and that hasn't changed, and as for you Paul, words fail me. I can't believe that you're just going to let me do all the work by myself. I won't forget this!" Paul stood up.

"Right, that's enough! Do you know what your problem is Miss fucking always-right? You just jump straight in and bollocks to the consequences! You *assume* all the time. You *assume* that I'm not angry because I'm not charging around like a fucking madman at all the fuckwits in this building. You *assume* that I don't care because I can't scream and cry and wear my heart on my sleeve. You *assume* that if Emily is complaining that I've been assaulting her then it *must* be right because Emily doesn't lie, does she? I don't know what you and Micky boy here did in the past, to be honest I couldn't give a toss either way, but I wouldn't be surprised if you have *assumed* that he wouldn't care too much if you just left him, despite him being totally fucking besotted with you! And why do you *assume* all these things Maria? Because when it comes down to it, you are only concerned with yourself and Emily. I don't know if your dad pissing off has anything to do with it, whether *that* has made you such a hard-hearted cow, but *now* I see it, *now* I see beyond that girly facade that you have been hiding behind all these years. You accuse me of not caring, but really, apart from what happens to you and Emily, it's *you* that doesn't care. I tell ya, for a nurse you really are quite something. I know that nurses have to be cool and professional, especially as they could get too close to patients if they are not careful, but you really take the biscuit. *You* carry on with this approach at home as well! Do you know what you are Maria? *You* are a fucking hypocrite!"

With that, Paul got up and stormed out of the room. Mick sat slack-jawed at Paul's show of resentment. As Maria's tears flooded down her face, he shook off his dazed expression and moved quickly to where Paul had been sitting. He moved the chair a little closer and uncertainly put his arm around her shoulder.

"He didn't mean that. He really is upset, he just can't show it that's all. Come on, you know what us men are like."

"Yes, that's the problem, I *do* know what you bloody men are like. Just who the hell do I trust, tell me. I thought we could trust a policeman to take me to my missing sister, but all he did was lead us to this bloody place. I don't get it. I thought that Paul would at least get angry with these goons, but . . . oh I just don't get it."

"He *is* angry with them Mezza. But you have to admit, this is weird, really weird. Hopefully, once we get Emily back we can get out of here. Then when we are clear of this lot, I'll say goodbye to you both, and walk out of your life forever. Let's just see what happens eh?" The choking noises Maria was making as she cried stopped at Mick's use of the name 'Mezza'. Nobody had called her that in years, and a rush of past images swept through her mind. She recalled the look on Mick's face when she had told him that she couldn't see him anymore. If ever there had been an image that summed up the term a 'broken heart', then Mick's face at that moment had been it.

"You apologised for hurting me Mick, but as usual you were just being your normal Mickish self!" Mick laughed at Maria's remark.

"Mickish? What's Mickish mean?" Maria smirked too.

"I don't know! I can't think of an appropriate adjective that could describe the way that you are. One minute you're bitter at the world, the next loving and unselfish. You are an enigma Mick Rogers. You are Mickish in temperament! But I couldn't deal with an enigma, and I know it hurts you to hear this, but I felt that you were just too immature for me. You could be different now, I don't know, but as I keep saying, it's all water under the bridge. We can't change how we felt back then and I wouldn't want to because I would be lying. It's how I truly felt. That doesn't make you a bad man though. Maybe I wasn't good enough for *you*, have you ever thought about it that way?"

"So there is no chance of me impressing you with my Rambo act then?"

"Do you want to? Aren't you impressed with *my* Rambo act?"

"Rambolina you mean!"

"Or Rambette!" They laughed at the silliness of their word play.

The two ex lovebirds were so engrossed at this momentary forgetfulness of the situation, that they didn't see the three figures as they made their way into the sunlit room.

"Oh very nice," said the grinning Theobald Leonard, "very nice indeed, now, I believe we have some business to discuss don't you? Mr Rogers, I am delighted to finally meet you."

CHAPTER SIXTEEN

Paul walked along the corridors of the building, his footsteps echoing beneath him and his face set in a tight grimace. He couldn't remember ever feeling this angry with Maria before, and with his genuine worry about Emily his felt that his mind was a heaving, mixed-up bag of emotional stress. How could Maria accuse him of not caring? Maybe it *was* his fault? Maybe he didn't show the emotions that he felt, although, he did kind of hope that he didn't need to with his wife; he had hoped that she knew him well enough to know that he did have problems wearing his heart on his sleeve.

A moment of extra worry flittered into his head as he remembered that he had left Maria alone with Mick. He had liked this guy, despite him being screwed up about his past association with his wife, but would this Mick try it on with Maria now? Would he try and step in and give her support, and would Maria, being as pissed off with Paul as she was, respond to the help and start to like him all over again? No, that couldn't be. If he knew one thing about Maria, it was that she never went back. If she had decided that a relationship, any relationship, wasn't worth pursuing then she wouldn't. She was loyal to her friends, and would often defend them through thick and thin, but she genuinely didn't suffer fools gladly and if she had had enough, then she really *had* had enough!

He remembered the way Mick had squirmed as he had spoken of Maria in the bar, and that settled his mind. Mick was a nice guy, and he may well have loved Maria deeply, but he was too weak to do anything about it now especially with Emily in such danger.

By now, he had come to the top of the long staircase that they had climbed earlier and looked down it carefully. There were a lot of people rushing about below, and he didn't particularly want to bump into that policeman again, or anybody else that might want him to stay where he was.

The staircase was quite wide and Paul stood to its far left and started to inch his way down. As soon as he started though, two guys began to make their way quickly up the other side. They were laughing and appeared quite normal to Paul, well, as normal as could be in this freaky place. Everyone else seemed as if they were on an important mission, but these two looked quite friendly, and he decided to use them for his enquiries.

"Hey, excuse me lads, you couldn't give me a hand could you?"

One of the men started clapping his hands, and grinned at his friend.

"Aren't you gonna give this chap a hand too Mr Morris?" The other guy laughed and clapped his hands too. He spoke in a fake posh accent.

"So sorry Mr Jackson, my manners are simply awful. Yes, jolly good show old pip. Excellent, simply superb! So, what are we giving this gentleman a hand for?" Jackson put his hand on Paul's shoulder and moved closer to him. This time he also spoke in a fake posh accent.

"Sorry old bean, got carried away with the giving you a hand bit, so much so, that I forgot to ask you something. What exactly do you want a hand for? A magic trick? A little dance maybe? How about that lovely shirt you are wearing?" Paul looked down at his shirt as the two guys laughed at his expense. He started to become more pissed off.

"Oh sorry, I didn't realise that I was in the company of the greatest comedy double act since Morecambe and Wise. Your material is obviously from their era too. Never mind children, I'll ask somebody else in this fucking stinking place."

The two guys stopped laughing and with the smiles still on their faces, but with a strange seriousness now in their eyes, the guy called Jackson moved away from Paul and looked him up and down.

"Fucking stinking place? What, don't you like gothic architecture? This is one of the greatest buildings in London, if not the whole United Kingdom. Quite a coup it was for our leader to get access to it. A grand building for a grand scheme, a grand plan of action. Well we like it anyway, don't we Andy?"

Andy's eyes had been fixed on Paul's throughout Jackson's words and he still held them firm as he replied.

"Yes Jacko, although maybe this gentleman doesn't like it because he doesn't have plans to stay? Were you about to leave us then?"

Paul realised that the two men were starting to get suspicious of him. Funny how three words like stinking, place and fucking can have an affect on people really, especially if the people were obviously not what they seemed. At least, not in this place anyway. He knew that he had to quickly gain their trust somehow if he was going to get anywhere. He laughed nervously.

"No, no, of course I'm not going anywhere. Why would I want to go anywhere when it's all happening here eh? No, sorry, we have obviously had a little bit of a misunderstanding. I said fucking, stinking place because I have always had a touch of claustrophobia, and when I feel hemmed in, I get tetchy and little bit too jumpy at times, hence my words. No, you're right, it is a fabulous building. I'd love to know how our . . . leader managed to get in, don't you?"

The two guys looked at each other quickly. Paul quickly corrected his last words.

"What I mean is, it looks quite secure from the outside, doesn't it?" He didn't know this for sure, but if it helped to back up his argument then anything was good just then.

Jacko looked carefully at Paul's nervousness and finally smiled. At his smile, Andy smiled too, although he still didn't look as convinced as his friend. Jacko slapped Paul on the shoulder.

"I think I know what you mean, although if you suffer from claustrophobia then why haven't you asked one of the elders to help you correct it? After all, they can help us enhance our mental powers in other ways, so why not use their methods for curing your problem? I'm sure that they could help you, I mean, even if we do all move to a bigger place, there is no guarantee that it will be any lighter than this place. The leader seems to like this style of building, and apparently he isn't a great fan of too much light anyway. Tell you what, we'll ask Mr Burn. He's quite a superior actually, but I get on with him quite well, and he is much more approachable than the others. Has a good sense of humour. Likes the ladies! If he can't help you then nobody can. Let's see if we can find him."

The two guys started to go back down the stairs, and Paul knew that he had to follow them if they were to stay unsuspicious, but even the name itself had him worried. Mr Burn? Did he *want* to meet this Mr Burn, and even if he was as *helpful* as this Jacko has said, then what *kind* of help was he prepared to give? Enhancing mental powers? Elders? This sounded weirder by the second, and what with the leader and his love of dark places he wasn't sure that he really wanted to know. But what about Emily? How could he face Maria and honestly say that he hadn't tried to find her? He felt apprehensive, but he knew that he had to go with the two men. Who knows, he may bump into his little sister-in-law on the way there? He quickened his pace and moving down the stairs he caught up to the two men.

"So, have you guys had the lucky chance to meet the leader yet?" He felt the inclusion of the word 'lucky' might make him sound more convincing. It seemed to work as Andy replied.

"Meet him? What as in speak to him personally?"

"Well obviously he means speak personally to him, because in a way we all 'met' the leader this morning. Even learnt his name! Didn't know he had one! Stupid really, we all have a blooming name, but I still didn't think he would worry about such a thing!" Jacko responded.

Paul thought hard about his next question. So this leader had a name. Of course he had a name, what was this Jacko blabbing on about? But he didn't know what it was because he hadn't been to this great 'meeting' of the leader. He tried to delve a little deeper.

"Blimey, how many people do you think were there then?" If one of them now said four or ten even, he would feel really stupid and they would realise his mistake. He held his breath as Andy replied.

"All of us I would like to think, I don't know as I wasn't counting, were you Jacko?" Jacko shook his head with a smirk. "Hundreds probably, but bearing in mind how many there will be of us, whatever the headcount was today is gonna be really small in comparison." Jacko stopped still and held up his finger.

"Minus one of course." The two men laughed. Paul laughed too. At what he didn't know, but it felt polite to do so just in case. He delved even deeper.

"Ha, yeah minus one. There's always one isn't there? What do you do with that one eh?"

"Well," said Jacko, "I don't know what I'd do, but even so, it was pretty amazing how that girl just thrust the knife in wasn't it? Could you have done that Andy?" Andy shook his head.

"Don't know Jack, although Talbot had been asking for it I think. I always thought he was a little bit strange, not into the cause as the rest of us, a bit too lairy if you know what I mean. Didn't know he was called Talbot until today, but had seen him around a few times and well, he just didn't fit in. What else could the leader do? But you're right; I wasn't expecting the little girl to do it. He obviously likes her a lot, almost fatherly in a way. Wonder why he favours her so much?"

The mention of a little girl and how she had thrust a knife in somebody caused Paul's face to pale. His heart beat fast, and the uncertainty he had always felt in this place was now beginning to grow into genuine fear. This wasn't right. Surely somebody wasn't murdered in here? And a little girl? Not Em, please God let it not be Emily. He needed more answers. He thought hard and fast as they walked down another endless, darkened corridor, passing faces that looked busy and yet half alive.

"Er, yeah it is strange isn't it? I mean, there are other little ones around aren't there?" He looked around as he said this, although there weren't that many people in this part of the building to justify his remark. To be honest, he hadn't seen many children, if any, and he started to think that he had just asked an ill-informed question. At this rate, they would find him out. He felt sweat start to pour from his forehead.

Cold sweat. Sweat associated with fear, and not heat, because it sure wasn't hot in this ancient building. It was Jacko that looked at him quizzically.

"Well if you have matey, then it must be your 'claustrophobia' making you see things, because I sure as hell haven't seen many. I'm sure that there will be some joining us soon, but it is early days, don't you think? I think this particular little girl must have something special about her, because she even sat with the leader, and very few people have done that. Most of us haven't even looked at him close up."

The way that Jacko had said the word claustrophobic now had Paul worried. It was the first real hint that these two men didn't totally believe his story. If this was so, then where were they taking him? Paul tried to carry on with his questions. Even if they became more suspicious, he needed to know the girl's name.

"I was at the back and didn't quite hear what the leader called her. Did you from where you were?"

Andy now looked at him strangely.

"I think your 'claustrophobia' has affected your hearing too mate, cause the leader had a little microphone attached to him, didn't you see it?"

"Yeah, I mean I know, but people were muttering, what with the appearance of the girl and everything. I think I did hear it but I can't remember it. What was it?"

"You can't remember it or you didn't hear it?"

"Yeah, I mean I can't remember it. I mean come on guys, it was the first time that we had met the leader, the excitement of it and all."

Andy didn't look convinced at Paul's stuttered explanation, but looked at Jacko for back up.

"Emma, wasn't it Jacko?" Paul felt his heart sink at this, but then felt it collapse completely as Jacko corrected his friend.

"Ha, and you accuse him of not listening! Emily, you twat, her name is Emily! Lovely little thing. I wonder why she hates her uncle so much?"

This was too much information for Paul. Now *he* was being dragged into this sordid scenario. Emily hates him? So much that she stabbed somebody? His legs felt weak and his adrenaline pumped harder and harder. By the time the three of them has stopped by a large, wooden door, he felt that maybe he wasn't going to do this all by himself after all. Jacko pointed to another door a few feet away and as he made his way towards it, he looked behind him.

"You just stay here with Andy, and I'll see if Mr Burn is in this room here. Look after our friend Andy, I won't be a minute."

Paul looked at the searching face of Andy. He noticed that the guy had no gap between his eyebrows, so that it looked like one, long eyebrow. According to his mother, that was the sign of a serial killer! Sometimes, little nuggets of information like this weren't welcome in his head at such worrying moments. He physically shook his head to rid the thought.

"No? Why are you saying no?"

"Oh I wasn't, just a little effect of the 'claustrophobia' I guess. Shaking the mist away from my brain!" He had said the word claustrophobia in the same mocking way that the two men had, in some bizarre sign of solidarity. If he had felt that this would lighten Andy's obvious mistrust of him though he was seriously wrong.

"I don't think you are into the cause like us. Well, you might be, but not in the same, one-minded way as the rest of us. I think Jacko senses this too, although he is a friendly guy, so you wouldn't know if he thought it or not. I, on the other hand, think that you have a problem with this. If you don't want to be here, then why don't you, how did you put it? Leave this fucking, stinking place?"

"I don't know what you mean mate. I guess I do seem a little strange, but I was always the sort of person that laughed at the idea of leaders and cults and such. This is all a new experience and I'm just adjusting to it. It doesn't mean that I'm not into it as much as you guys."

"Cult? Who said anything about a cult? You don't seriously believe this to be some sort of weirdo cult thing do you?"

Paul cursed his loose tongue again. He really wasn't making a good job of this. Maria had always said that he was a bad liar and now he was beginning to think that she was right. What would he now say to the increasingly annoyed Andy?

"No, that's what I mean. This isn't a cult, so that's why I am taking it seriously. I just need time to adjust that's all. Look, I don't like buildings like this. Does that mean that I don't believe in the . . . cause?"

Andy wasn't convinced, but took his eyes away from Paul's face and tried to sound appeased.

"Maybe you would be better off doing the work outside. I suppose it is an imposing building. Not everyone can like this sort of place I guess."

"Do you really like it then? It seems full of ghosts to me."

"So what if it is? There are ghosts everywhere mate. Not just in gothic style buildings. Believe that and you may as well believe in Caspar the ghost."

Paul didn't even smile at this. Andy was not joking and he could tell.

Paul turned to look carefully at the door. It had a huge, brass knob and underneath this was a keyhole. He tried to turn the knob, but it didn't open the obviously locked door. He was about to ask Andy if he knew what was in this room, before the question was unexpectedly answered. He felt his arms pulled behind him tightly, and as he looked around in shock he saw two grey-suited men. One was pulling his arms; the other was bounding them together with wire. Jacko appeared suddenly and with a large key opened the door. It creaked open, and Paul just noticed that it was barely lit with a small, high up window and that it stank of dampness, before he was pushed inside.

He landed on the dusty floor. He had just enough time to notice a cockroach scurrying away before the door closed to leave just Jacko's nose poking through it. He laughed as he spoke.

"Well matey, if that doesn't cure your 'claustrophobia' then nothing will. Cruel to be kind and all that! Try not to scream, there's a good lad!"

The door closed completely and Paul heard it lock and footsteps walk away. They hadn't gagged him, who if you were a fan of horror films was a surprise to him, but looking at how thick the door was, it probably wasn't a good idea to shout anyway. Even if he did, would anybody come? He seriously doubted it.

He tried to stand up, and after a few attempts he finally managed it. So, they had seen through his lies. Not as stupid as they looked obviously. So now what? The lovesick Mick was with his hysterical wife, Emily was apparently knifing complete strangers and he was stuck in a stinking, dusty room, with just enough light to see his wrists all bound up behind him.

He hadn't given it much thought when he had stormed out of the room upstairs. Maybe he felt that he really would see Emily somewhere. And if he had, what would he have done then? Christ, who was the dreamer here, him or Mick? He would calm down a little and think about things. Take a few deep breaths and put his situation into some sort of context. This wasn't good, but they couldn't leave him here forever, could they?

He sat underneath the window, his back to the wall and breathed deeply. The sound of his breathing calmed him and he started to feel more rational. Until he heard the sounds of breathing from elsewhere in the room. There, in the corner to his right. There in the darkness, was somebody else, or something else breathing.

Paul was not alone.

CHAPTER SEVENTEEN

Thomas Burn walked slowly around the dank, musty room. At least it used to be a room. An ordinary room in what used to be an hotel. Now, despite the people filing in and out of it, it would not have been out of place to call this scenario a chamber. A mouldy, damp, rusting chamber, years of non-use bringing one of the ex hotel's finest rooms into this almost sinister state.

Yet, it was probably the case that this chamber had never been so busy either. Burn considered it rather ironic that this building had served the public so well all those years ago, and now it was the first of many bases that would change the public to species that would eradicate all the hypocrisy, selfishness and downright lies of the world today. How Leonard would eventually fulfil all of his ambitions was yet to be seen, but he didn't doubt that he would and he thought it very fortunate of Leonard that he should've met somebody like him to help the cause. He knew that Leonard disliked his ways; he was very aware that the way he used his powers to satisfy his more natural urges was seen as being against all that Leonard stood for, but considering that it was he that had taught Leonard a lot of what he knew he didn't consider the leader's view to be anything more than a slight inconvenience.

But would he step in once Leonard's aims had been realised, or would he just watch, knowingly, from the background, and pick off what pleased him, as if he was picking the ripest apples from a tree?

Knowing the little girl had stabbed that moron in the crowd was something unexpected. Sure, he had done some horrendous things in his time, often using the innocent minds and bodies of other beings to do it for him too, but the little blonde girl looked, even to his mind, sweet and innocent, and something didn't seem quite right with what

Leonard had made the little thing do. Was he beginning to soften? No, impossible. Such a thing just couldn't happen to him. Maybe to the thousands of people that surrounded him in the place where he now walked, but certainly not to him. He was emotionally incapable of it.

He was just about to look for the useful character that was Leonard when a skinny, red-haired man of no more than thirty ran sweating towards him. He was flustered and panicking and looking as if he didn't know whether to speak to Burn or not. His eyes darted back and forth as he finally spat out what he dared to say.

"Mr Burn . . . . Mr . . . Burn, I'm . . . really, really sorry . . . I swear I dunno what happened . . . it just . . . well it . . . sort of worked but she's not . . . . christ . . . ."

Burn stared deep into the eyes of the animated man before him, making the red-head even more nervous than before. A slight grin broke upon his thin lips before he spoke.

"Christ? No, I'm not even close to that particular person, but thank you all the same. Now young man, perhaps you'd like to calm down before you explain to me why it is you're so stricken with worry."

"Well . . . as I said . . . it was going well until she just jumped up and started . . . . well screaming I suppose . . . I really didn't think that . . . ."

The man's speech was halted by the appearance and the noise of a woman who was racing towards Burn and the gibbering red-head, her arms waving and her teeth chattering wildly as words spewed out of her open mouth.

"Noooo, keep away, get me out of here! Don't fucking touch me you dirty, dirty fucking perverts. No, help me somebody. HELP ME!"

Burn glared at the shaking red-head. "So this is your work is it? Well done, we really need this, don't we? How did you manage it? She was perfectly fine when she was handed over to you, wasn't she?"

"Yes, yes Mr Burn . . . . sir."

"So how the fuck, sorry, how on earth did you manage to mess this up? Surely you have done it many times now?"

As Burn questioned the terrified red-head, the screaming woman had been tackled by two men in grey suits. They pinned her to the floor and in an attempt to stop her screaming one of them tried to push her chin towards her nose, in a clumsy attempt to close the orifice that the noise was emanating from. The wildly thrashing lady was having none of it, and with a swift turn of her head, she bit down on the finger of the man trying to silence her.

"Shit! You bitch, you fucking, spiteful bitch!" And in a show of pseudo male superiority, the now bleeding guard used his powerful, ring adorned fist to close the screaming mouth once and for all. The lady's head jolted back against the floor and she went silent. Burn was not impressed by this show of machismo.

"Oh very good, that was right out of the Homo Sapien book of how to treat a lady, wasn't it? Are you usually so tactful with the opposite sex, is that how you normally manage to entice ladies into accommodating your shrivelled penis between their parted thighs, or was this just a one off show to impress the audience before you?"

The bleeding guard stood up slowly, his now worried eyes focusing on Burn. It wasn't Burn's words that had bothered him so much, although there was no doubting the malice in them, rather than the now bizarre look on Burn's face as he gradually stepped towards the suited guard. The guard stood still, as if he didn't quite know what to do next, and when Burn was barely a foot away from the guard, he spoke the last words the suited gentleman ever heard.

"You see sir, while I appreciated your motives, I mean, the poor lady was obviously distraught, no thanks to this gentleman here, (a quick glance towards the red-head told Burn that that particular man was still terrified, and in a perverse way, that made Burn feel even better about what was to happen next) but anyway, there's no going back now, is there? No, absolutely not, now let me just say, that this could be a lot worse, but as you've been so useful to our cause, I'll be quite the lenient one . . . this time."

The last two words were not just directed to the guard but to the red-headed man too, and the malevolence in them became more apparent as Burn's hand reached around the throat of the motionless guard.

It seemed to the racing mind of the red-head that Burn hadn't really gripped the guard's throat with any real strength, as least it didn't seem from the guard's face that he had. What was horrific though, was the way the guard's face suddenly grew redder and redder. Still there was no noise from the guard's mouth, just an increasing redness that seemed to be spreading from the guard's head to every inch of his body. The second guard had already made his exit at this sight of his friend's plight, but the petrified red-head still couldn't avert his eyes, and before long, it wasn't just his sight that was being insulted but his sense of smell too. The smell of burning flesh was not something the red-head could honestly say he was accustomed to, but the stench that now reached his nostrils couldn't possibly be anything else. The guard was literally burning up in front of him and the power was coming from the grip of Thomas Burn.

Sixty seconds passed before the bright red body of the guard slumped to the floor. There was steam coming from the mouth and yet, the guard had not made a single sound.

Burn looked down at the corpse and casually kicked it as if it were nothing but a heap of rags. He walked towards the red-head, whose bladder had taken the opportunity of emptying itself, and placed his hand, palm down, on his cheek. The red-head felt that death was imminent, and just hoped that it wouldn't hurt as badly as it looked. He had only just registered the fact that the hand on his cheek was the same that had gripped the guard's throat, and that contrary to logic, it was ice cool, when Burn smiled his enigmatic smile and spoke calmly.

"Now my friend. You have just witnessed something quite unique I am sure you will agree. You would be amazed at the powers us mere mortals have, and yet I would like to assume that you are looking forward to the day, when we all have more access to such powers than anybody could've thought possible, is that right?"

The red-head nodded dumbly. All he wanted was to live. Yet, as he stood there, the intense fear he was feeling had triggered something in his mind. He wondered how he had got himself into this position. He couldn't remember ever meeting Burn and his colleagues before, yet surely he must've done? But where though? And when did he sign up to help this cause? His wandering thoughts were halted by the searching eyes of Burn. He felt their blackness burning into his brain. He felt, physically, that Burn was reading his mind. It was as if there was the tangible feeling of a spider's legs traversing across the front of his brain. He shook his head.

"I wouldn't worry too much about what has happened in the past if I were you young man, just keep remembering how you are now part of a great scheme that has been long overdue. Keep thinking this and all will be well. As to this lady before us, when she wakes, you will, with the help of some less violent colleagues, restrain her and try to finish off the job that you so badly screwed up. Maybe she was just less susceptible to our methods. Whatever, you have a second chance, so don't mess it up, not everybody gets one you know. Oh, and I would get a change of trousers if I were you."

As Burn made his exit from the room the red-head looked around. Other people were now staring in from the rooms attached to the one that he was in. Their faces were emotionless. He looked again at the lady on the floor, and feeling the strength in his legs desert him, he slouched down beside her, his mind not sure what was happening next or whether he was capable of anything like normal thought again.

Two more grey suited men walked towards him and nodded towards the unconscious lady, and without any word, they dragged her off to the room she had fled from in such a panic.

Burn had gone off in search of Leonard, but at that moment Leonard was having an interesting time of his own. He was sitting in the bare room with Emily, Dorothy Trollope, Maria and Mick. Emily stood by his side as he stared at the perplexed Mick. Maria was desperately trying to encourage Emily over to her, but her sister just stared at her blankly and hugged the arm of Leonard. Leonard grinned.

"I really wouldn't take it personally Maria. Emily has done a lot of growing up in a very short space of time and sometimes that can unbalance a lot of the information that we store in our heads. She'll come around and go to you . . . eventually." Maria ignored the fact that Leonard knew her name and stood up fiercely, only to be pulled back down onto her seat by Mick.

"What the fuck are you talking about? I'm not totally stupid you know. I do have medical training, and I can honestly say that you are talking absolute bollocks. Information in our heads? I know what you have in your head mate, crap, that's what, and it's spilling out of your mouth as well!" Leonard grinned at Mick.

"Feisty isn't she? Foul mouth but feisty . . ."

"*Feisty* am I? Foul fucking mouthed am I? You don't wanna . . . ."

"QUIET young lady! Stay quiet now and maybe, maybe, you'll get some answers. But until you close that foul mouth of yours and *listen*,

then you, your boyfriend here or your sister won't be going anywhere."
Mick looked up at this last remark.

"I'm not actually her partner, he's . . . he's gone off somewhere.
Looking for a toilet I think . . ." Leonard laughed and stared steadily
at Mick.

"Hmmm, okay, if you say so. I am usually a good judge of character.
Although, knowing you Michael, I would say that you would *like* to be
Maria's boyfriend, wouldn't you? Wouldn't he Emily?"

Little Emily started laughing at this. Mick looked towards the little
girl and was surprised to feel a little fear creeping into his mind. He
couldn't put his finger on why, but there was something about the
child's eyes that made him feel uncomfortable. Maria, on the other
hand, was obviously unaware of any changes in her sister and would've
been still trying to call Emily to her, if she hadn't become acutely aware
of something that Leonard had said.

"Knowing you Michael? What does he mean Mick? How does this
weirdo *know* you? Well? Enlighten me with something else that I don't
know about you. What have you been up to? Why the fuck have we
been dragged into this?" Leonard intervened.

"I think you misunderstand Miss. Nobody has said that Mick here
knows me or indeed anybody else in this building. But we are very
aware of him. It's his type that we find particularly interesting. Why
don't you *enlighten* us of your feelings about life in general Michael?"

Maria turned to face Mick, her face one of confusion and
expectation, as if anything that he was about to say would make the
current situation understandable. However, Mick just shrugged his
shoulders and stumbled over his words.

"I . . . I really don't know what you are talking about. I'm no
different to anybody else. I really don't think that what I have to say or
think is anything to shout . . . ."

"Oh come Michael," Leonard interrupted, "what goes on in that
mind of yours when you walk down the road every day? Don't be shy,
let us have some insight into why the world is such an unfair place.
You know exactly what I'm referring to. Admit it, this world gets you
down, and yet you keep all these grievances to yourself. Well, now is
the chance to get them off your chest. Now is the time to do something
about it Michael. Come now, tell us about something that gets you so
irate. What about women? How is it that you have never been lucky

with women? What do you *really* think about women Mick?" Maria was still staring, her eyes ever widening at her ex-boyfriend.

"Yes Michael, answer the nice man. What do you *really* think about us nasty women?" Mick blushed and still struggled for words.

"Look mate, I don't know who you think I am, but you've got this seriously wrong. I mean, okay, I admit, I have been pissed off that all the nice girls like a bastard."

"Ha! That old chestnut!" intervened Maria. Mick continued, still blushing madly.

"Why the hell would you understand when you're a woman?"

"Oh, so you had noticed all those years ago? What, was it the tits that swung the decision for you, or the fact that I don't have a small prick like you?"

This latest insult, coupled with the ridiculous situation he was in, finally did for Mick and he turned towards the nurse who was clearly enjoying the sarcastic remarks she was firing at him. "Oh right, making me feel like shit all over again isn't enough, is it Maria? Never mind *my* old chestnut, you have to be a fucking woman and use the old small dick line don't you? Did I ever mention your saggy tits? Did I ever mention you can't give a decent blowjob? Did I mention the two front teeth that could open beer bottles? No, and why? Because even though you hurt me, even though you were responsible for some of my darkest nights, because even though you behaved like a complete and utter BITCH, I still felt, somewhere deep in my heart, something like love for you. I was never going to get you back, I knew that, I accepted that. But unlike you, I can't just turn off my feelings when I get bored with them or when something better turns up. And you may think all this stupid, but maybe that's me. Maybe I will always be this way. That's what's gonna be on my tombstone. Here likes Mick Rogers RIP TS Rest in Peace, terminally stupid. And you know what, I don't give a toss anymore, I really couldn't give a toss."

Throughout Mick's tirade, Maria's anger had subsided into shock. She had never seen Mick Rogers in such an angry state before. Even in his most annoyed moments, he wouldn't even raise a voice, instead just settling for a creased brow or some under the breath mutterings. Maybe if he'd shown a bit more life like that then she'd have thought differently about him? But, wasn't that what he was ranting about? Wasn't she suggesting that if he'd been more of a bastard, then she'd have liked him more? She looked at the graphic artist as he stalked around the room, his anger still bubbling within him. She then noticed Leonard, who was staring at Mick with approval. His smile suggesting that this was exactly why Mick would be good for whatever twisted *cause* they had. She made a point of now redirecting her anger at the odious Leonard.

"And this pleases you, obviously. Is this what you deal in you freak? Other people's anger? Is this what you need to fuel your little perversions? Probably, judging from your moronic grin. Just tell me weirdo, why me? Why Emily?" Leonard's smile never left his face as he replied.

"Ah, why, why, why. So many questions, but are there any answers? For your information Maria, I don't actually like the foulness that comes from your and Mr Rogers' mouth, and I know that it insults Mrs Trollope here and certainly shouldn't be for the ears of little Emily."

"Yes, I know but . . . ."

"But you are angry, with Mick, with Paul, with Emily even for frightening you with her disappearance. But really, you're a caring person aren't you, or you wouldn't be a nurse. But, like all caring people there are moments when you've had enough too. You and Mick are very similar in that he's had enough of quite a few things in his life and not only connected to his feelings for you."

"His feelings for me? Oh for crying out loud, I'm sorry, okay? Is that what you want to hear, I'm really, really sorry. Now, can you tell me why you sickos have kidnapped my little sister?"

For the first time since she entered the room, Dorothy Trollope, nee Chatsworth, decided that a bit of politeness was in order, if only to stop the cursing that was flying around this empty, cold room.

"Well, if I may just say at this juncture that I am not involved in the *kidnapping* of anybody, especially not this delightful little girl. Have you seen any distress on her angelic little face?" Mick turned to the ex-housewife.

"No, we haven't actually, and I have to ask why that is. Why would Emily suddenly become such good friends with such a bunch of cultish losers? What have you done to her?" Leonard stood up, and trying desperately to control his anger, responded to Mick's question.

"*Cultish?* You think we are some sort of cult? Is that how far your ignorance goes Mr Rogers? Is that really the best your intelligence can come up with, oh, you disappoint me, I really thought that you would appreciate our cause."

"There it is again," Maria was now stalking towards Dorothy Trollope. "Your cause! What cause? And you are part of this farce are you missus? Shouldn't you be at home baking a Victoria sponge or polishing your husband's shoes?" Dorothy cringed at this remark.

"Don't you dare mention my husband. You know nothing about me young lady. If it wasn't for people like Mr Leonard and Mr Burn, then I dread to think what kind of life I would now be living."

"Mr Burn? Oh this is priceless! Where's Mr Evil or Mr Torture, I suppose they are skulking around this cesspit of a place somewhere too eh?"

"*You* don't know what you're talking about. I think little Emily is right to choose us as you clearly aren't capable of caring for her. I'll take her away now Mr Leonard if that's alright with you, she shouldn't be with these people."

As Mrs Trollope took Emily by the hand, Maria saw the blank look on her sister's face and felt that she was losing her. However she had gotten into this situation was irrelevant, all she knew was that Emily was being taken away from her and that unless she did something now, then maybe she wouldn't see her again. Anger replaced despair and sense of purpose replaced helplessness as Maria sprang forward aggressively to take Emily away from this town mouse woman who had no right to even touch her little sister.

Dorothy screamed as Maria first landed a fist on her cheek and then bent back her fingers to release her grip on Emily's hand. Pulling the little girl's arm away from the reach of the wailing woman, she grabbed Emily with her other hand and went to rush through the door that Mrs Trollope had intended to pass through only moments earlier.

Such was the speed of all this that Mick and Theodore Leonard watched in a sense of slow motion before it occurred to them what was happening before their eyes.

Mick's thoughts flashed through his mind in a matter of seconds. Thoughts of him fighting the scaly dragon and rescuing the damsel (or damsels) in distress. Well, there was no time for high factor sun cream this time, in fact there was no time at all, just grit your teeth and do what should be done . . . whatever that is, right Mick?

The graphic artist looked at the bent over figure of Dorothy Trollope, her face red with pain as she ignored her freshly bruised face and clutched her assaulted hand. Then he noticed Leonard, about to sprint after the departing Maria and Emily, his voice desperately trying to sound calm, but still not able to disguise the slight panic in it.

"No, you are wasting your time young lady. Do you seriously think that you can get out of this place just like that? I will ensure that you apologise to Mrs Trollope before you get anywhere near the outside, I promise you that. Security, security, stop that woman and child, stop . . . ."

Leonard didn't get any further with his plea for assistance as he suddenly felt his head being dragged backwards by his hair. Mick had grabbed the first thing he could of the shouting man, and now was trying to pull him back into the centre of the room. He didn't quite know what he would do next, and the thought of Dorothy Trollope jumping on his back did occur to him, but Mick's problem was conveniently solved as Leonard tripped backwards and smashed his head on the corner of one of the chairs. He laid motionless, blood trickling from a head wound, and with Dorothy Trollope now moaning by his side.

"You brute! Are you happy now? What have you done, what have you done? All he wants to do is help us and you do this to him? Oh I wouldn't be in your shoes now young man, you really have done it now!"

Mick, now shaken and white with shock, took one glance at the stricken woman before making the effort of finding Maria. He saw her disappear around a corner and was just about to start the chase when he was stopped in his tracks by a scream. It was Maria, and whatever had happened to Maria, or whatever Maria had seen, he knew that he wasn't going to like it.

CHAPTER EIGHTEEN

Paul struggled with the wire that was crudely, yet effectively keeping his wrists together. He had intended to sit and think this situation through, to be calm about it and see if these freaks would see sense and open the door; maybe it was just a joke on their part? They certainly acted as if they found it all rather amusing, or maybe that was just their way? Maybe they took enjoyment from causing people grief, in which case, he now had a problem.

Unfortunately, the shuffling noise he heard had made him realise that he had even more of a problem that he had originally thought. In the darkness of the cell (room, cell, it was all the same to Paul at that moment) there was also a faint sighing noise that was getting louder. Not only was it getting louder, but it was getting closer, and not only was getting closer but Paul realised with mounting dismay that the sound was almost human, and a human that didn't sound too healthy either.

As the snuffling, wheezing sound got closer and closer, Paul tried in desperation to crawl away, gradually forcing himself to the door. He tried to stand and shout for help, asking, even pleading for somebody to come and free him from this mess. But even though he knew that people were passing the door, nobody took the time to even stop, never mind ask what his problem was.

The wet, panting sound was getting closer and Paul felt that now he could smell the breath of the thing creeping relentlessly towards him. Every time Paul moved, this creature moved with him too, and that smell was definitely getting stronger. The odour was of tobacco, and Paul recalled this smell from an uncle who had smoked roll-ups when he was a kid.

Finally, Paul could take no more of the fear that was now gripping him by the throat, and he screamed at the thing in front of him, hoping to sound scary himself but knowing that he really sounded as wet as last week's lettuce.

"Get away, I'm fucking warning you, I'm not joking, get away or I'll hurt you, go on, fuck off!"

Whether the voice that came from the creature was a relief to Paul, whether he was pleased that at least it was human he wasn't quite sure, especially when the words of the creature started to register in Paul's brain.

"Get away?! Why? Why should I? Tell me why? Scared of me are you? You should be? I have power too you know, they told me I had, they told me I would have too, but I know what they meant. All my work for them, all my work, all my devotion, and this is how I get treated, all I wanted to do for them. Well, I DO have power, I'll show you shall I? Let me show you now!"

The words, coupled with the wheezing voice sent Paul into panic of the sort he had never experienced in his life before. He kicked out at the creature (the man?) before him, making contact with something soft. The man recoiled, if only for a moment.

"Urgh! So like that is it? Want to be like the others eh? Like you're really in a position to be like them aren't you? Well, we'll see who the boss is here, shan't we?"

Paul found himself being forced down as the foul smelling man crawled over him.

The pain he felt as his bound hands were squashed against the floor because of his own weight and that of the man's was becoming unbearable, and yet no amount of screaming was ever going to get this lunatic from off of him.

Then, for the first time, Paul saw the face of the man, dimly in front of him, the tobacco breath assaulting his face and the madman's nose almost touching his. The smell of the rank breath became even worse with every word the man said.

"Now, look into MY eyes, yes, look into MINE. Oh yes, I can do this too, I can and I will, I'll show them, oh they will regret losing my devotion. Look into my eyes, look, LOOK!"

But I can't see your fucking eyes properly, so you're wasting your time now fucking get off me! You're hurting my fucking arms!"

"No, no pain, no pain allowed, just look at me. What do you see? Do you feel it? Do you feel the power? Do you see the light? Do you? DO YOU?"

"No, I feel only the pain in my fucking arms, get . . . the . . . . fuck . . . . off . . . . ME!"

With as much effort as he could muster, Paul tried to force himself up, making the man lose a little balance, but enough for Paul to wriggle free of the man's weight. The raving man's voice became louder as he realised that his efforts had had no effect on his intended victim.

"Nooo, you can't go yet, I won't allow it, no, you must feel the power, it's all for the cause, it's all for the good of the world. Come, join me, join us, join everyfuckingbody!"

As Paul was about to yell for help yet again, the sound of unlocking came from the door and one of the guys that Paul had spoken to earlier poked his head around the creaking door as it let in some light.

"Well hello there, having fun are we?" Paul almost spat his reply at the grinning Jacko.

"Get me the fuck out of here! What did I do uh? What did I do to deserve being tied up and thrown into a stinking cell with a fucking madman!" Jackson found Paul's hysteria amusing.

"Ah yes, sorry about that, a slight oversight. We clean forgot all about Mr Roscoe. Nice man when you get on his good side, although not many people have found his good side yet."

As if on cue, the mentioned Roscoe appeared and dragged Paul down to the floor by his shoulders. Paul screamed as Roscoe again attempted to sit on top of him, yelling maniacally into his face as before.

"I'll show you, I'll show you. You, you boy, you watch and tell Leonard, tell Burn, tell them that I can do it, that I CAN do it!"

Jackson walked quickly into the cell, and it was only in the spilt second that it took to connect with Roscoe's jaw, that Paul noticed that Jackson was holding a large, adjustable spanner in his hand. Roscoe yelped and slid off Paul's chest for the second time and laid on the floor moaning. Jackson passed the spanner to a grey suit waiting outside the cell door and turned to Paul.

"Girls, girls, do we really need such bad feeling amongst us? Tut-tut Mr Weston, is it all really necessary? Anyway, despite Mr Roscoe's strange attraction to you, I've been told to take you upstairs to see some of our staff for conditioning. Although, I've a feeling that certain questions need to be answered before that. You're not all that you pretend to be are you?" Paul gazed at Jackson, a thousand questions of his own racing through his head, although he did have an immediate one . . .

"How do you know my name?"

"It wasn't that difficult for me to find out, just ask the right people the right questions."

"And who are these *right* people? I don't get it. Where is Emily?"

"Ah, the young lady whose name you couldn't remember. Funny how a bang on the head can help you regain your memory, albeit someone else's bang on the head, eh Roscoe?"

"Just tell me Mr Joker, where is my wife's sister?"

"Your wife? I hear that we have a couple of more people currently being questioned, by none other than our esteemed leader no less, seems he's quite interested in one of them, but the lady he's with, well, I *think* she's okay, not heard any screams in any case!" Paul's face creased with confusion.

"Mick? What's so bloody fascinating about that bloke?"

"Mick? Is that his name then? I'd like to meet this Mick myself. I agree with you Mr Weston, what could be so fascinating about him? Anyway, we have somewhere to go. James, give Mr Weston a hand will you?"

Paul cringed as the grey-suited James grabbed hold of the wire that was bounding his hands and pushed him out of the door.

As Paul was frogmarched along the dusty, dank corridors, he felt that everybody in this bizarre building was concentrating on some sort of errand, as if they were totally ignorant of anything else apart from their duty. There was the occasional bit of laughter, and the occasional smile, but as with Jackson and his friend earlier it didn't sit right with normal behaviour. Almost as if the smiles were masks. They seemed to be saying as a collective, 'look at us, we're absolutely fine, no problems here, it's quite fun at times, but we need to do our job too.' Paul shook his head as this vision flooded his head and he started to wonder what this atmosphere was doing to him.

At one point, Paul, Jackson and James walked past what Paul thought would've been an entrance or exit to the building. There were chinks of light coming through it and it was heavily guarded by more men in grey-suits, only these suits were holding pistols. Jackson noticed Paul's straining neck as he was walked past this 'exit'.

"I wouldn't worry about that at the moment matey, you've got some training to undergo before you can go that way again."

"What sort of training?"

"Good training. I've been through it and I've never felt better. At least, I *think* I've been through it. You too eh James?"

"Uh?" muttered the guard.

"Exactly. See, no problems there at all. Don't you go a-worrying matey. Just enjoy yourself!"

"Yeah, enjoy myself. My hands are killing me and I've been set on by a raving lunatic. I'm having the time of my life. Where are you taking me?"

"I told you, conditioning. But some questions first. Don't listen much do you?"

"And conditioning is? . . . ."

"Conditioning is . . . . conditioning I guess. Hey, you'll see when you get there. Mind your step, these stairs can be awkward sometimes."

The threesome made their way up flights of stairs before they turned right onto a corridor. Paul noticed that there was a bend in the corridor ahead of them and he realised that this was the way he had come before when he'd stormed away from Maria and Mick.

They walked towards the bend, Paul only just aware of raised voices ahead of them. Jacko smirked.

"Well, someone isn't a happy bunny-wunny are they?"

"I know who they are." replied Paul, gradually despising the cockiness of Jackson's constant remarks.

"Friends of yours eh, well in that case I . . . ."

Jacko didn't get a chance to finish his latest smart remark, as the sound of a man screaming, a man growling, came racing up the ancient stairway. It grew closer and closer until eventually it culminated in a loud, ear-piercing roar that swept past Paul's right shoulder.

"You bastarrrrd! You bastaaard! I'll teach you, I'll fucking teach you!"

There was a sickening, bone crunching sound from Jackson's direction, followed by a low moaning as Paul felt someone reel against him, knocking him into one of the corridor's damp walls before falling heavily to the floor.

Paul looked down, and there before him was the crumpled body of Jackson, and standing over him was the menacing figure of the guy that had been in the cell with him. He had the adjustable spanner in his hand and was about to bring it down again onto the head of his victim.

Paul Weston looked on, as if life was being played in slow motion, as the grey-suited James grabbed hold of the ranting Roscoe, only for the ballistic lunatic to elbow him squarely in the jaw knocking him forcefully backwards. Roscoe stood over Jackson a second time and this time he finished the job that he had intended to do moments earlier.

As the spanner smashed into the side of Jackson's head, once, twice, three times, blood spurted all over Paul's shoes.

Then a scream, a loud, piercing scream jolted Paul from his stupor and he looked up to see his Maria, the woman he loved, staring at the scene of bloody murder before him. It was all he needed to wake up from the unnatural daze that the events had led him to, but he quickly realised that it wasn't the assault on Jackson that was making Maria scream, but the sight of Roscoe, spanner covered in blood, advancing on her husband with an obvious intent to kill.

"Now you, now you you bastard, now I'll show you, now I'll show them, now I'll show them that I can do just as well as that bloody little girl, just a good a job as that fucking Burn, you need to fucking die! . . . ."

As Maria's screams became hysterical, Paul bent his head down, a desperate attempt to somehow defend himself, to somehow deflect the blows that he knew were coming. Maybe he could dodge the spanner somehow? Maybe it won't hurt as much as he hoped? Or maybe, maybe the first one would just knock him out cold and all of this madness would go away and he'd wake up in bed, back home, awake from this nightmare he was enduring.

Paul closed his eyes in sheer, desperate anticipation, wishing that whatever was going to happen would happen quickly. That tobacco smell was again close to him as Roscoe got closer, he could almost feel Roscoe's arm going back to swing a blow down onto him, he could hear Maria's tear-choked screams in the background . . . . but the blow didn't come. He waited some more seconds, but still it didn't happen. Instead he heard scuffling coming from the left, and as he looked up, James, blood still trickling from his mouth, had grabbed Roscoe's spanner holding arm and was smashing it against the wall. Roscoe screamed as the spanner flew from his hand and crashed to the floor.

Paul tried to think quickly, could he get the spanner? Should he get Maria and run? But before he could decide on anything, someone had run towards James and the shouting, fighting Roscoe. This person punched Roscoe forcefully in the stomach as James held him and as Roscoe doubled over in pain, he grabbed his head by his thinning hair and brought it down with a sickening crack onto his raised knee. Roscoe slumped to the floor, and this new assailant limped away, holding his knee.

"Fuck, fuck, that fucking hurt, what the fuck did I do that for?" Paul stared astonished as he realised that it was Mick that had silenced the crazy madman that had nearly killed him.

Mick looked over at Paul, his face still creased with the discomfort of his aching knee. "Well, thanks Pauly. You could've helped us."

"How? Just tell me how? My hands are fucking tied, or can't you see that?"

As the two rivals in love looked at each other, they forgot the advancing figure of James, as he wiped fresh blood from his jaw and towered above them.

"Where's the leader? How come you got away from him?" Mick coughed and looked at the floor as he replied.

"Yeah, good question. I thought he was right behind us . . . . maybe he got distracted . . . or something?"

James's face suggested distrust and this soon changed to surprise as the voice of Dorothy Trollope came screeching from the room that contained the unconscious Theobald Leonard.

"They've killed him! They've killed the leader, our master, my beloved leader! Get them, for God's sake get them!"

Paul winced as James grabbed his bound hands with one hand and spoke on a walkie-talkie with the other. "Guys, we have a 1-8 on our hands. Get to floor three now, I repeat a 1-8, floor three!"

Mick looked around him. James trying to hold Paul and yet block his passage at the same time, Maria now holding Paul's face in her hands (a sight which hurt him, even now in these bizarre moments, it really hurt him) and the bodies on the floor of Roscoe and . . . a man that he knew, a guy he knew too well. He raced to the lifeless, blood covered body of Jackson and turned it over to see its face more clearly.

The sight made him feel sick. Not sick because of the blood, because of the injuries caused by the spanner, but because it was his friend, the annoying but good friend that was Jackson.

"Noooo, not you too Jacko, why you? Why did you have to get dragged into this fucking nightmare? Why Jacko?" Paul stared in disbelief at Mick.

"You *know* that bastard?"

"He isn't a bastard!"

"No? He wanted to take me for, what did he call it? Conditioning, yeah, that was it. I take it you know what conditioning is then Micky boy? Maybe you're not telling us the truth eh? Hear that Maria? Your lover boy here is working for these goons."

"Working for them? How d'ya work that one out? Do you really think that I want to be here too?"

"Well, let's face it Micky boy, this leader, whatever his name is, seems to be very interested in you. What if we give them you in return for Emily then maybe they'll let us go. We'll be home and you can play with your little friends, how about that Micky boy?"

"For a start, stop calling me Micky boy, and secondly, that just about sums you up doesn't it you prick! What a fucking hero you . . . ." Maria screamed as James looked on in astonishment as the two men argued.

"Stop it! Just stop it! You're both as bad as one another! Christ, I was so worried Paul, I really thought that lunatic was going to bash your brains out and yet you're still as fucking childish as ever."

Mick registered this remark. To hear Maria call Paul childish when she had often aimed such a remark at him made him feel, quite bizarrely, quite a bit better. Paul winced at his wife's insult.

"Well, just as well that Micky here was able to save my brains from the bashing they quite clearly deserved." Before Maria could respond in exasperation to this retort, James had decided that enough was enough.

"Right, get back in that room all three of you, I hope for your sake that the leader isn't dead or you too will wind up fucked. Now move!" Maria doubled checked James' remarks. You three? But with Emily there would be . . . ? She looked down. In all the panic Emily had disappeared again. Maria screamed her sister's name in horror.

Mick looked around. He heard running footsteps and realised that James' friends were responding to the 1-8, whatever the hell that was. Well, he wasn't going to go like a little lamb to the slaughter. Knocking out that guy, who oddly enough seemed very familiar to him, had stirred something inside him. He didn't fancy another meeting with Leonard, and even worse, he didn't fancy a bullet in the head if Leonard had died. Trying to work out from which direction the footsteps were coming, Mick ran down past the room in which lay Leonard, in a guess that they weren't coming from that direction. Maria screamed at him, tears running down her face.

"Where are you going? You'll get yourself killed for God's sake!" Mick took one look back at her.

"And your point is? What the hell does it matter to you anyway? Someone has to do something Mezza, and it quite clearly ain't gonna be your husband, is it?" As Mick ran, he came to another landing with more stairs and not knowing which direction was best he ran downstairs, hoping that at least that way it may be nearer a way out.

CHAPTER NINETEEN

He carried on running, down stairs, along corridors, trying desperately hard not to be noticed as somebody trying to find a way out. He thought about the woman he had just left behind and felt an old sickness, a feeling of never seeing her again, one that he had felt before and one he wished that he had never felt in the first place.

Well, they say that everybody has a soul mate, right? And where's yours Micky? Married to somebody else, that's where. Good isn't it? Doesn't it just crease you up Micky my lad, just make you feel that your whole life has some sort of meaning to it? No, why not? Surely you see the irony in this situation don't you?

Even in bizarre situations like these, it seemed to be part of Mick's personality to have these arguments running through his mind. For most of his life he had tried desperately to make sense of what was happening to him and the world around him but somehow he seemed to place all the negativity on himself. Why this was he didn't know. His father had been a man that had never shown any kind of overt emotion, although Mick felt that it was there under the surface, and sometimes Mick felt that he was always trying to please his dad, even all these years down the line and yet never quite making it. Was that why he always felt guilty? Was this why no matter what he was thinking of, the blame always, somehow, even inexplicably laid down at his doorstep?

He became more and more aware of people staring at him as he rushed along, not sure where the hell he was going, just knowing that sooner or later he would be stopped, asked some awkward questions, grabbed and bound and placed in a room, anything but be allowed to get away with running around this bizarre, gothic building.

As Mick ran he looked left, right, back and forwards in an effort to see something, anything that would give him a reason to carry on in this stupid position he was in. It was as he did this, as he looked through an open doorway to his left as he ran that he collided into another person, a smaller person and failing to keep his balance he fell sprawling to the floor.

He laid back on the floor. The bottom of his spine was aching where he had fallen and he was rubbing it in an effort to make it feel better. As he did this he looked up and there overlooking him, looking down with a totally neutral look on her face, was a small, blonde girl. She said nothing, just stared at him, as if she was trying to read his mind. This lasted for at least half a minute as Mick tried to find some words to say to the girl, something along the lines of 'are you alright sweetheart?' but all he could do was gaze into the cool, blue eyes of the youngster staring right at him.

Then a name came from nowhere into his head. Suddenly, the lights in his mind went on and he realised who he was looking at.

"Emily? Where did you get to?" There was no answer from the little girl. Instead she turned around as if to walk away. But Mick couldn't let her go. If there was anything that had ever happened to him in his life that made sense, it was the knowledge that he could not let this little girl just walk away from him. In a flash of seconds, Mick thought of all the good that could come of 'rescuing' the child that intended to walk away from him. Maybe for once, just once in his life, he really would be the hero, he really would be fighting the metaphorical dragon and loving the attention as the man who saved the day. Maybe his father would be proud of him after all? Maybe Maria would see another side to him, the side that she clearly didn't know existed. Maybe he could even avenge the death of Jackson? Now that was something, being the avenger! Maybe the comic books he used to read as a kid would have some sort of link to reality after all?

He pulled at the arm of the girl who immediately span around and spat at him. He looked down at the spit as it ran down his shirt but he didn't relinquish his grip on her arm. Seeing that spitting hadn't done anything, the girl tried to pull her arm away and in a sudden burst of energy she lashed out with her legs, trying to kick Mick in the shins as hard as she could.

A voice came from the open doorway he had past not so long ago. "Emily? Emily my love don't run away again. We need to make a move. We need to leave quickly."

Mick could make out that the voice was coming from a mature lady, but he didn't stop to see what she looked like. Instead he used all the strength he had left to grab the kicking and resisting Emily. He put his hand across her mouth in case she tried to scream but she didn't scream, she just bit down hard on Mick's forefinger. Now it was Mick who was trying not to scream, but with visions of knights on white chargers rushing through his head, Mick wrestled the unhappy Emily up the corridor until he saw another door that was slightly ajar. Not stopping to think that someone else could be in this room he dragged Emily through the doorway and closed the heavy door behind them. He leaned against the door, Emily still kicking and about to bite again. This time though Mick made his feelings felt.

"Don't little girl, just don't you dare bite me again! Once was painful enough but do it twice and I'll hit you, I swear I'll fucking hit you back. Don't fucking dare!"

Whether it was the shock of an adult swearing, the threat of being hit back or just the manic look that was now appearing in Mick's eyes, Emily stopped her kicking and stood still. She resumed the strange, statuesque, staring position that she had shown in the corridor only moments before. Mick rubbed his sore shins and feeling sorry for himself looked at his bleeding finger—he felt that this ridiculous nightmare had better be worth all the physical and mental pain that he was now suffering.

Mick looked around the room. It was full of wooden tables and chairs. The chairs had been pushed aside from the tables that gave the impression that people had been sitting there but had now evacuated the room. Whatever has happened here before at least it was empty now.

Outside the lady's voice was calling for Emily. She started to sound like an annoyed parent after their child has run off for the tenth time without permission, her voice gradually sounding more stressed. But she moved past the room Mick and Emily were in and he heard her footsteps fade up the corridor. He had thought about putting his hand across Emily's mouth again in case she had tried to call out, but the thought of another bite and the stoney look on the child's face had stopped him in his tracks. Instead Emily just kept up that gaze, her eyes burning into Mick's face.

He looked down at her blonde hair and her angelic features. He couldn't believe that this little girl could be involved in such a ridiculous farce as what was going on in this building. He suddenly felt paternal towards the girl and gently this time he led her towards one of the chairs. Without any kicking or trying to get away, Emily let him sit her down on one of the chairs, all the time keeping her blank gaze on Mick's face.

He knelt in front of her still feeling uncomfortable at the way the child was looking at him.

"Ok Emily, we need to sort out what is going on. Now how did you get here? Who brought you here? What on earth have you been doing here?"

The girl didn't answer. Some answers may have given him some idea of the situation they were in, but getting them was not going to be easy. He stood up, grabbed a second chair and placing it close to Emily sat on it the wrong way round, his arms and chin resting on the back. If this was going to take time then at least he should make himself comfortable.

Maria winced as she felt the tight rope cut into her bound wrists. James' friends, all equally suited and booted had arrived not long after Mick's disappearing act and they hadn't taken long to re-capture the nurse and her protesting husband. Paul looked around at his distraught spouse and tried to reassure her.

"We'll get her back Maria, we will I promise you!"

"*You* promise do you? And what do *you* intend to do next superman? At least Mick had the guts to get away and do something."

"Do what? What do you think he's gonna do? I'll tell you what, he's going to fuck off out of this place that's what. Some fucking boyfriend he must've been."

Paul's sneer at this remark caused Maria to feel something hurt inside her. Whatever Mick was, whatever he had been, he clearly had felt something strong for her and just because she hadn't welcomed the strength of his feelings, he had only meant well for her. He didn't deserve the caustic remarks that were now coming from her husband.

"I have never questioned the types of women you went out with Paul so don't question what I had with Mick. *You* are the man I married and that should be enough for you. If it isn't then maybe I made a big mistake,"

James, still rubbing the jaw that had been assaulted by Briscoe, smiled sarcastically at the couple as they marched along. He turned to look at Maria.

"No darling, *you're* mistake was trying to act all tough and not let things happen naturally. We are all going to benefit from the leader's visions. However, after what you did to him I would be very surprised if you will see anything in the future. If you had killed him then you would be dead now yourselves. As you only wounded him then you are going to see some of what we are doing instead and be lucky enough to take part in some trials. Well, I say lucky, maybe privileged would be a better word."

The other guards laughed at James' remarks. Maria looked at Paul suddenly realising that something bad was lined up for her and her husband. Through an increasingly shaking voice she begged her sister's case.

"I don't care what you do to me, just let my Emily go. She is too young to go through all this, she doesn't understand, just let my little sister go, please."

James's grin didn't drop as he replied. "No darling, again *you're* mistaken. Emily *does* know what is going on. You are showing your sister a great disservice by ignoring the intelligence that she has. If anything she knows more about our cause than me and my friends here. Our leader thinks a great deal of her you know, almost fatherly he is to her, she has a great future, unlike yourself."

The word 'fatherly' filled Maria with a feeling of sickness more so than the threat that had come at the end of James' words. She felt the anger come back once again.

"Fatherly? Emily only had one father, the same one as me. Don't you dare suggest anything else you freak." James stopped the party before a large door and turned towards Maria fully now, his nose only inches away from hers.

"Now I'm a freak? You'd be surprised at what *freaks* can do missy. You are going to be educated beyond your wildest dreams, in fact, the whole experience is going to blow your mind! Totally blow . . . your . . . mind."

Paul and Maria held their breath as the door opened. Then their breath drained away as they saw the horrendous vision before them.

CHAPTER TWENTY

"I don't understand what is happening here. I don't understand why I am here, why your sister and brother-in-law are here and why, in the name of God, why you are here and why you are caught up in all of this mess. I also don't understand why I am explaining this inability to understand to someone as young as you, but there you go. Now, could you, please Emily, tell me what the hell is going on and why you felt the need to bite me."

Emily's face was still retaining the stony look as before as Mick tried to make sense of things and he felt that deep down he wasn't going to get anywhere with this little girl, at least not in her current state of mind.

He couldn't help but see some sort of irony even in this situation. He had never had much success with women; they always saw him as a 'friend' rather than a lover. It was always the line of 'I'm really sorry Mick, you're really nice but I'm sort of seeing someone/I have just finished with someone/I like you as a friend' etc etc that met his desperate attempts to ask 'someone out'. Now here he was trying to communicate with a little version of the species that seemed to ridicule him and he still couldn't get a point across!

He placed his forehead on the back of the chair and closed his eyes. Mixed up thoughts raced through his mind. If he didn't get any answers soon then he just knew that someone would find him and drag him off somewhere but this little girl looked stubbornly against any form of communication.

After a couple of minutes of silence, Mick sighed and got up out of the chair. He walked a couple of paces towards the door before a small voice piped up behind him. He turned towards the blonde hair girl that it had come from.

"I don't like being told what to do, that's why I bit you." Mick looked down again at the bite marks on his hand.

"I wasn't trying to tell you what to do Emily, I only want some answers. I only want to get you out of this place."

"Why? Why get me out of here?"

"Why? You mean you don't know?" Emily looked quizzically at the tired graphic artist.

"My friends are here. They don't tell me what to do. How do you know my name? I don't like Emily anyway. Uncle Theo says that I should call myself Clara. He says that Clara is a nice name and I like it too." Mick sat back down on the chair close to Emily, straddling it back to front as before.

"Look, I don't care if you call yourself Emily, Clara, Sarah or even Dewdrop, all I know is that your sister calls you Emily and so I call you Emily. As for Uncle Theo, well he isn't your uncle. If anything Paul is more of an uncle, although strictly speaking he is actually your . . . ." Emily interrupted him.

"Paul isn't my uncle. I hate Paul. He isn't my uncle because he tells me what to do. They don't tell me what to do here. Uncle Theo is my friend."

"Ah you remember Paul eh? Look Emily, between you and me, I don't like Paul either . . . well, I think I don't. But whether you like him or not he *is* your relative. I think you'll find as well that older relatives have a habit of telling younger relatives what to do, that is what being part of a family is all about." Emily looked down at the floor.

"My family is here. Auntie Dorothy is nice to me. She tells me stories and we tell each other jokes. Paul doesn't do that."

"Whoever Dorothy is isn't important. Your *real* family are here Emily and they are in trouble. They need your help. Don't you care for Maria? She loves you Emily, she really loves you. Don't you want to help her?" Then Emily spoke words that wounded Mick to the quick; that made him rock back in the chair and reinforced what he had always known.

"*You* love her. *You* love her a lot. Why don't *you* help her then?"

"What do you mean *I* love her?"

"I know that you love my sister. She doesn't love you though. Why would you want to help her when she doesn't love you?" Mick felt himself physically wincing as he found himself trying to justify his feelings to this indifferent child.

"Because I . . . . because it is . . . . well, because regardless of what I feel for your sister, she and her husband, the man I know she loves, have been dragged into something that has them in trouble. And what I find horrific is that you don't care, you don't care one little bit. What's wrong with you for heaven's sake?"

"Why do you love her so much? Why are you here with her now? Why do you think that you can still make her love you?"

"What? I don't! I've never said that I could make her love me! I don't think that she would . . . ." Mick's response was checked by the way that Emily was staring straight into his eyes. He felt his mind tingling as her crystal blue eyes seemed to search his mind for answers. He tried to continue his protestation against what Emily had said to him.

"Okay, maybe I felt that it was some sort of destiny that we would, eventually, get back together."

"But my sister doesn't love you. She won't love you. I think you are wasting your time." Mick winced again as Emily's words became arrows that pierced his heart and soul.

"How would you know little miss know it all? You can't even see how much your sister loves you otherwise you would stop playing these stupid games, realise how much trouble you're in and help your sister get out of here."

"She told me about you. Well she told Paul. I heard her talk about you once in the kitchen. She was laughing about you. She called you 'pathetic'. She said that you sent her stupid letters and that she must've been mad to ever like you because you act like a child."

"Yeah, you heard her talk about me! And how do you know it was me she was talking about? What were you doing listening anyway?"

"She said your name. Your name is Mick isn't it? Mezza and Pauly had had an argument that day and I heard them making up in the bedroom. Yuck! But then they were laughing in the kitchen about how they loved each other and the stupid people they had been out with before. Mezza talked about you. She thinks you're stupid. Do you still love her now? Do you still want me to help her now?"

Mick shook his head as he tried to get the image of Maria and Paul making love out of his head. Why such an image should hurt him he didn't know; there was no logic to these feelings anymore and yet they were still there, after all these years. Emily seemed to sense what Mick was thinking as she continued her diatribe of ridicule.

"I think you're changing your mind now. I bet it hurts so much when you think of Maria never loving you that you now think that maybe it would be better to just not help her, after all, she doesn't care about you, does she Michael?"

Michael? It was bad enough that Emily was speaking like a girl much older than her years, saying things that no child of her age would ever say and yet now she was calling him Michael! But how did she know that he was called Michael anyway? He stood and walked closer to the girl and looked down at her.

"Wait a minute, you ask *me* how I know *your* name and yet you call me Michael? Not even my mother calls me Michael anymore! How do you know *I* am Michael and who said that you can call me *Michael* anyway?" The first semblance of a smile crossed Emily's lips as she replied.

"I didn't know your name until Uncle Theo said it. They had a picture of you. He was talking to Uncle Thomas about you. They were saying nice things about you. They said that you would understand what they want to do. They said that you would join us. I think you *should* join us, after all, Maria doesn't love you. What is the point of helping her?"

"But I don't know who Uncle Theo and bloody Uncle Thomas are! How can I understand them when I don't know them! Look Emily, I don't mean to be funny but surely even you can see that this is wrong." Emily ignored this and carried on attacking Mick's Achilles heel. She seemed to almost enjoy the pangs of hurt that Mick felt when talking about her sister.

"Maria doesn't love you. Maria doesn't love you. Maria doesn't love you. Get it?"

"I think if anything little girl that I would rather hear that from Maria anyway, not that I need to hear it."

"Maria doesn't love you. Maria doesn't love you. Give up Michael."

"Give up? What have I got to give up anyway? I think that all the feelings that I've kept for your sister were kept for a reason. I think that I have *hurt* for so long for a reason. I think that if I spoke to her, tried to make her realise that for a person to love for so long under such pointless circumstances, then maybe, maybe she would see that I am sincere. I have nothing against Paul, but he will never feel for her what I feel, never. I hope that you never feel the pain that I've felt Emily. I hope that one day you find true love and you hold it to you for ever and ever. Don't ever let it go, no matter what anybody says. The moment you feel it slipping even slightly, grasp it even tighter, because otherwise you will lose it forever and hurt forever. Contrary to belief, destiny can be changed and when it does it hurts, I mean really hurts. My destiny has always been with your sister. Oh, why am I telling you, a child anyway! This is pointless." Emily momentarily looked confused but carried on.

"Your love is pointless too. She will never love you."

"I think that's a lie. I don't believe your lies Emily."

Emily smiled and grabbed the sleeve of his jacket. He looked down and he suddenly saw not some malevolent being trying to destroy him but a mischievous little girl. Why this was such a surprise was bizarre, but it had really seemed like this blonde child had been trying to get inside of him, to pierce his very being with her sarcastic comments and her penetrating blue eyes. Now Emily was just a little girl. Misguided true, and obviously heavily influenced by the freaks that were roaming this building, but still, essentially, a little girl. Emily sighed as she looked up at Mick and spoke in an almost resigned manner.

"So you *still* want to help her?"

"What do *you* think Emily? Yes, I want to help the woman that loves *you*, never mind me, that loves *you* more than anything in the world. Whatever you think of Paul, whatever *I* think of Paul, don't you think that her love means something? It is something that I would pay for in blood and yet it is the blood that you and Maria share that makes her love you and care for you so much. What did she ever do to hurt you Emily, what did your Mezza ever do to hurt you?"

Mick felt that the last line, if he said it with enough emotion, might get some sort of reaction from her, although the child had been so stony faced that it was a slim chance. But suddenly Emily's face softened and her eyes started to well up. She didn't cry but she did now look as if the message was getting through. She stood up and took Mick's hand.

"I *do* love Maria, honestly Mick, I do. I don't know why I felt like it didn't matter but I think I know that what you have said is . . . true now."

"You agree with me now? Why?"

"I don't know! I feel tired Mick. I feel like I do when I wake up. My head hurts. I feel . . . strange." Then her voice turned to an increasing, sudden panic. "Where is Maria, Mick? Where is my sister?"

"I don't know Emily, but we are going to find out. Are you gonna behave yourself? You're not going to run away from me are you otherwise you could mess up everything?"

Emily shook her head. She was trying to smile but Mick could now see that this little girl was changing. There was something in her face, as if a veil was starting to lift. Now she *looked* at Mick whereas before she looked *through* him.

"I won't run this time Mick I promise."

"What if you see Uncle Theo? Auntie Dorothy?"

"I'll . . . I'll just tell them that I want to see Maria." Mick inwardly smiled at the naïve remark of Emily. Now it seemed that her vocabulary was more becoming of her age. She was almost becoming a child again before his eyes. Why he hadn't seen this before he wasn't sure. Maybe he was too worried about the whole situation to register how Emily had really looked when they came into this room? However she had looked, now she was a little girl who wanted to know where her sister was and this knight was going to help her get her back."

"I don't get this Emily, I don't get this at all. I don't know if I even trust you to be honest but what can I do, quickly, follow me."

Emily went to follow Mick out of the door but suddenly she stopped and pulled him back. She looked up at his baffled face as she spat out her words.

"Mick! Stop!"

"What *now* Emily?"

"You need to know something."

"Do I?"

Feeling more and more tired of this game, Mick knelt down so that his eyes were opposite the little girl's.

"You need to know what they do Mick. I know what Uncle Thomas does. You need to know what I've seen."

Mick felt his stomach turn over and the adrenaline pump through his veins as Emily's description of the events in this building became more horrifyingly clear to the man who now wished he had never left Walters Associates. The little girl spoke calmly and without hesitation. Mick on the other hand was now frantic. If what this little girl said was true then they were in an even more dangerous situation than he could've ever believed. And there were sights waiting for him that he just didn't want to see.

CHAPTER TWENTY-ONE

There was a strange smell in the room. It was difficult to distinguish whether the smell was iron-like, blood-like, the smell of burning, a strange smell that seemed disconcerting and yet you would not be able to say why.

The room was also full of people. It had been lit with an extraordinary amount of candles and because of this some parts of it still remained quite dark, yet it was obvious that this was the busiest part of the building and nearly everybody in it was busy, eyes focused ahead of them as they went about their tasks. *Nearly* everybody. There were some people who weren't busy at all . . . not in the way that the others were. Some were wired up to machines that loosely resembled metallic bathroom cabinets on stands. The 'cabinets' were shaking slightly, the wires were shaking quite a bit and the people wired up were shaking considerably. To the observer they were receiving some sort of power source which was obviously flowing freely through their bodies.

Next to each of these cabinets stood a person in a white coat, some men and some women. They carried a clip board which they referred to every now and then. To the onlooker's eyes these people resembled a doctor doing their rounds, although it would also be clear to that onlooker that this white coated person wasn't exactly offering a medical opinion.

The most startling figure of all was a tall man. This man looked nearly seven foot tall, was dressed in black and wore a very wide rimmed hat. He was moving around the room, swimming in and out of the throngs of people, almost graceful in his movement as if he was on wheels. He was speaking to nearly every person that he met, speaking in a low manner and with a slight smile on his face. The people that he addressed would also respond with a slight smile but without speaking in return. If he wasn't speaking to people, the tall, dark man was looking with interest at the people wired up to the cabinet style machines, where after an almost sympathetic shake of his head he would utter words to the person in the white coat and float on to his next destination.

Even in this seemingly chaotic room there was a semblance of order going on. If you were to look down at the scene before you, you would see that the cabinet style machines had been laid out in a certain way. They were almost in rows. The rows at the back of this room were only manned by people in white coats, while the rows at the front of the room, the rows you would see as you came into the room, were manned by more than just a white coated pseudo doctor. The machines at the front had people that were strapped into their chairs and were bucking and fighting the power a lot more than the people in the other rows. These people were distressed and it was these rows that offered the most chilling sights. It was these front rows that greeted Maria and Paul as they were ushered into the gloom of the hall.

For all the anger that Maria felt, for all of her protestations and brave outbursts against her captors, what she witnessed in front of her became a permanent, dark memory for the rest of her life.

For the first spectacle that greeted Mr and Mrs Weston was so obscene in its unique perverseness that the fact that the people around it were carrying on as if nothing was wrong just made it all the more sickening.

It triggered off memories in Paul's mind of a method of execution in the USA, only there didn't seem to be a direct intention to kill. At first sight, these people were monitoring with great interest what was happening to those sat down, it looked like they were enjoying the results as some of the strapped down people calmed down, were released from their restraints and were hugged by people around them.

Unfortunately this wasn't the case for some others, especially those at the front near the door and it was these others that dragged your attention kicking and screaming to what was happening. Even if you didn't want to look, this obscene rubberneck reaction had you looking at what you didn't want to see—one of the darker sides to pure human nature.

But even if the Westons didn't want to look, in this case they didn't have much choice. Their heads were being held by James' colleagues to look in the direction of those screaming at the front. Even closing their eyes wasn't an option as James pointed out.

"I'd look if I were you. Close your eyes and we'll dispense of you here and now. There is no point in you living any longer if you don't take in all that is going on. I'm sure you wanted to understand why you were brought here, well, now you are going to get some answers. Open your eyes and see what is going on, you never know, you may even like what you see!"

Maria shuddered as James gave a short laugh at the end of this statement and reluctantly looked at what was going on with the poor souls in front of her.

In front of one screaming man there stood another man who had quickly looked around at the newcomers before going back to what he was doing. Paul had registered the dark, jaggedness of his eyebrows and the almost serene look on his face despite the noise before him. This man was talking as the victim shrieked in pain and as his eyes bulged larger and larger.

"Don't fight it, don't fight it. I implore you to relax and let it all change you, change you for the better. You know it is right, don't fight the change young Jeffrey, calm down and accept."

A white coated figure spoke to the man with jagged eyebrows. In response he received words of comfort.

"Don't worry my friend. If I had done this myself then I think the result would've been much the same. I can't be everywhere as you know. It is just another person who is obviously more resistant than even he realised. Ah, sometimes you can't change the subconscious mind, no matter how much you may want to try. You creatures are so complex! Jeffrey please accept, please relax for you are leaving it far too late. My friend I fear for you."

The screams became louder, the restraints on Jeffery's arms threatened to cut into him as he fought what was going on and then the screams became more gurgled in nature, as if Jeffrey was drowning. The serene man shook his head and still tried to reason with the helpless soul before him.

"No my friend, no please, it is becoming far too late. Just relax, it is your last chance, relax now or it is too late."

Whether Jeffrey could hear the serene man was debateable but Jeffrey's gurgled screams stopped and his body became rigid. His eyes became hideous protuberances as they tried to escape his skull and blood trickled out of his ears, nose and mouth. His skin changed colour, first red then a purplish colour then a dark, charcoal grey. The serene man walked away from what was happening, shaking his head.

As Maria and Paul stared in repulsion at the fate of young Jeffrey, they felt as if heat was coming from the desperate being in front of them. The hall was cool but Jeffrey clearly was not. James squeezed Maria's arm and with a curious look on his face mumbled "now watch *this* missy."

Jeffrey's skin stayed grey but it started to move about, it started to slide up and down as if Jeffrey was just covered in a loose grey garment. Then to the Westons' disgust Jeffrey's skin started to break up, gaps appeared in his head and arms where all that could be seen was first bubbling blood and then the whiteness of human bone. Maria screamed and battled against those holding her as the spectacle before her became more and more dreadful.

What used to be Jeffrey's eyes had ceased to stand out and instead had become a light greyish liquid that was seeping from the eye sockets and mingling with the ever separating, ever liquefying flesh. There was a strange smell of burning material and something else which the Westons couldn't explain as Jeffrey's clothes and hair smouldered and yet they didn't catch fire.

More and more flesh slipped away from Jeffrey, some of it seeming to go down the front of the smart open necked shirt that he had on, some of it sliding onto the chair and onto the floor where it lay like the most obscene jelly. More blood bubbled into nothing and more bone became apparent. Slowly but surely, what used to be a honourable man named Jeffrey became a sitting skeleton. The clothes and hair giving the sight a sickening bizarreness to it.

Paul let his eyes drop down, away from the disgusting vision that was before him. He heard his wife retching. For all the sights she had seen as a nurse, he could guarantee that nobody deserved to see what had just happened to a fellow human being.

A suited man dragged Maria to one side as she tried to throw up all the sickness that she felt, but a lack of food and drink meant that the process was painful and she was eventually taken back to where Paul stood, her face red from the effort. Then there was a voice next to Paul. He hadn't seen anybody approach him and the effect of the voice startled him. He figured as the man spoke that he must have been too concerned for his wife to notice the man sidle up to him, although something told him that surely he would've noticed. As he looked at the man he noticed that it was the serene natured man who had seemed so keen for the late Jeffrey to relax. As before his voice was calm and strangely soothing.

"I am sorry that you had to be forced to see such a sight, but to be honest with you my friend the people here have become strangely numb to it." He motioned to four men and a woman that were removing the remains of Jeffrey and attempting to mop up what was left of his skin. There was almost an helpless sound to the man's voice as he tried to discuss to his audience what had just happened.

"I try my best I really do. I don't wish for such a thing like this to happen but . . . ."

The man's voiced stopped as more screaming came from along the front row.

Maria and Paul had become so horrified by what had happened to Jeffrey that they had failed to notice that something similar was happening again only this time to a woman in her mid forties. Her screams were even louder than Jeffrey's and she was being calmly spoken to by one of the people in white coats, in a manner which the serene man had shown only moments before. The man turned to James.

"Bring them this way, into my pathetic excuse for an office. They don't want to see that again. I'm sure they wouldn't want to be subjected to it either, would you? A purely rhetorical question of course. I can't imagine you *wanting* to go through that." James looked confused.

"But Mr Burn sir, I was given orders to bring them here. For conditioning."

"And where do we initially take our new faces James?"

"Well . . . upstairs sir . . . but I assumed . . ."

"Assumed what James? Why should our friends be treated differently? Anyway, our new amigos need to have a chat with me in any case. Before we introduce them to anything, they need to help us a little bit more than normally. I take it they have seen the leader?"

"Well yes sir . . . but unfortunately there was some trouble and . . . ."

"Trouble? Well, why doesn't that surprise me. What is it that you people say? If you want a job doing, do it yourself? Ah what can we do. Honestly, doing good can be so relentlessly unrewarding sometimes."

Paul tried to get closer to Thomas Burn at this remark and spat out his feelings close to Burn's face.

"Doing good? How the fuck is *that* doing good? What sort of fucking freak are you? What fucking freakshow is going on here?" Burn merely smiled, wiping away flecks of spittle that had projected from the angry mouth of Paul.

"Did I say that you would appreciate what we are doing here, did I? Did I at any point say that you would like what you would see at the front of the room? I don't think so. Yes, good afternoon Derek . . ."

Burn had turned to people passing them as he spoke, directing his words to another suited man who was smiling and escorting an equally pleased looking man who was dressed in casual jeans and a button down shirt. Paul figured that whatever was being done to those people in the hall was about to be done to the man escorted by this Derek, although he didn't seem unduly bothered. In fact, he seemed quite pleased to be going in there. When Paul thought about it there wasn't any sign of struggle in the hall at all. The people doing their jobs were obviously transfixed by their duties and keen to do them and those that were being wired up did do voluntarily. It was only those poor souls at the front, the ones who wouldn't *relax* as this Mr Burn put it that showed any sign of fighting what was happening to them. It was all too confusing. It was obvious that some sort of mind conditioning was going on, some kind of brainwashing, but what was with those machines, and how could they lead to such a peculiar yet horrifying death as Jeffrey's?

Paul had looked at his wife. Maria was ashen faced and looking more tired than he had ever seen her. But it was Derek's response of "Good afternoon Mr Burn," that had injected some new life into her. It had long been a kind of proud fascination of Paul's that his wife could be so mentally resourceful. He had never known such a person that would always seize the initiative whenever possible and he had always joked that if there was ever a job to be head nurse of all the world then his Maria would probably go for it. She was tired, emotionally and physically but her resources still held an emergency tank of anger and action.

"Mr Burn? Hold on, you were called that in that room as well."

"Well, it being my name I am not totally surprised."

"Ok don't be smart. *You* were mentioned earlier on as well when we were upstairs. *You* are one of the main men here aren't you? *You* know exactly what is going on. Well Burn, whatever dodgy operation you have got going on here is of no importance to me. All I want to know is where my little sister is, so tell me where she is you bastard!"

Thomas Burn walked silently up to Maria Weston and put his hand on her shoulder. She felt warmth from his hand and felt a dizziness sweep over her. She stayed conscious and upright but this warmth and the strangest smell emanating from Burn had her in a daze. Paul noticed the change of look in his wife's face and tried to get to her but was held back by his suited guards. Burn's voice was as calm as ever.

"Bastard? In a way I am. I believe that your language has a definition that wouldn't be a million miles away from what I actually am. But really Maria, do you think that I and my colleagues would hurt such a little sweetheart as your Emily? Trust me Maria, you and yours have nothing to worry about. Why, pretty soon everyone in this country is going to be so much calmer and you will realise that this charade that you and your husband are playing was such a mistake. But we shall explain that in more detail in my . . . . office. I shall explain in much more detail for I fear that without explanations and without your total support then I worry that you too will have more in common in Jeffrey than just an over casual taste in attire. Are you feeling ok now?"

Maria nodded her head. She felt drowsy but at the same time didn't wish to sleep. She just felt that to comply would be less hassle and maybe bring about some positive results. Maybe this Burn was alright after all?

Paul looked at his Maria in bewilderment as they were led into the room that Burn obviously had a problem with. He didn't know what Burn had just done to his wife but this was not good, this was not good at all. If he didn't know better he would say that Maria had just been drugged, but how? Soon they were sitting in front of a leather topped desk, their suited guards by their sides. Burn sat behind the desk, reclining on a chair with casters and his feet up on it. Behind them, atop a tall stool sat a carousel filled with slides and on the wall was fixed a white, pull down screen. Burn pointed towards the carousel.

"Before we start my friends, I need to show you some pictures. A little bit of light entertainment if you like before we discuss the real meat of the matter. In fact, I understand you may know one of the stars of the show, how exciting is that? Sit back, relax and be entertained then, for all will be much clearer to you after this little treat."

Paul looked as the carousel was switched on by James. Then as the machine warmed up and Burn used a remote control to switch to the first slide Paul's features creased in anger as a now familiar face appeared on the screen.

CHAPTER TWENTY-TWO

After a cup of tea, the man with the very wide-rimmed hat known as the Rector sat down at a long wooden table, clasped his hands together and closed his eyes. It was a bit of a struggle to get his long legs under the table but with a little bit of a struggle he finally managed it. His knees were still rubbing against the top of the table but he was comfortable enough to just sit and relax.

In his mind he was replaying what he had just seen in the great hall, the sight of people been conditioned to fully accept all of the ideas that Mr Leonard, the great leader, had been spouting for as long as he had known him. It wasn't that he didn't believe in what Leonard said, he just wondered if it was worth all the pain that accompanied some of the efforts. In a way he had become used to the deaths that had taken place in order for the cause to be realised, but that didn't stop him from thinking that maybe there was another way to accomplish the objective.

In his hands he held a Bible. When he had started to become involved in this process he hadn't been what would be termed overly 'religious'; to be honest, the whole idea of a God was something that he felt, that he *knew* just couldn't be. But there was something in the book's message that had him thinking, after all, wasn't it all down to your beliefs? If you believed strong enough then that was all you needed to help you survive all that life could throw at you. People didn't need proof as such, it was pure faith and surely if you have faith in anything then surely you can only succeed?

And wasn't that what they were trying to achieve here? For people to just *believe* and have faith in what they were doing. There really shouldn't be any strain on the subconscious to see that essentially the message they were spreading was good and not a million miles away from the good book in his hands.

He thought of Mr Leonard. Whilst there was no doubting the differences when comparing Leonard to himself and Mr Burn he felt that if anybody could bridge the gap between the people here and the likes of himself and Burn then there couldn't have been a better choice. Leonard's beliefs and his way of doing things were sometimes naïve. He had seen for himself Leonard's attempts at harnessing the power in his head, when all that Leonard needed was a candle, a mirror and a dark room. Sure, he had had a lot more success that other mere mortals here but that was only because he had been helped a great deal by Mr Burn. The question was, how long would Burn accept the treatment that Leonard gave out to him? He knew Burn better than anyone and there were times that after a meeting with Leonard, Burn's eyes were just a dark shadow, nothing underneath that shadow mind, just darkness that people looked into at their peril.

They had made mistakes too. Trying to get a lunatic like Roscoe involved was not something that he had agreed with. Fair enough, the young man had been keen, but he had started to believe in his power just a little bit too much. How they hadn't initially seen this madness was difficult to explain at the time but now he felt that there was something about the people here that had to be learned; that the differences in personality and differences in how the individual brains dealt with events was far more powerful than they could've realised and this brought him back to the events in the great hall—if ever he or they needed proof of this then that was it.

He stood up and walked to the large window that was bringing in the ever darkening light of an early evening. The view from this window was excellent, one of the reasons why he liked to come in here. He could see for himself the way that people rushed here and there and he felt good that there were now so many people down there that were happy to help their cause. He pulled up the window which creaked in protest at his efforts and leaned out of the window as far as he could. Making sure that his hat wouldn't be blown off he looked down and saw what used to be the main entrance to the building. There he saw suited guards issuing people in and out of the building and this too made him smile. With every person that they conditioned the task at hand was becoming ever closer to fruition.

Looking across the main road he became aware of something that grabbed his attention. A man in a pin-stripe suit and holding a suitcase had been thrown against the wall of the bank. His assailants, a man in his thirties and two women in their twenties were shouting at him. They were pointing in the direction of the Rector and after a few choice punches to the man's stomach and head lifted him up and pushed him towards the main road. The suited man was having none of it though. He tried to retaliate and defend himself with blows to the man and women until the attackers were joined by two youths. These boys also started to punch and kick the man until the pin-striped businessman was cowering on the floor.

The rector said words under his breath and grasped the Bible in his hands. He had a feeling that this hideous sideshow was not over yet and as he looked on his feelings proved to be correct.

One of the women who had started punching the man was now holding a weapon, what looked from the window to be a knife with a very long blade. As the youths now held the attacked man his attackers spoke some words to him. They were not pleased with the response as the beaten man retorted with shakes of his head. To show their anger at this the girl with the blade approached the held down man and without any compassion slid it slowly and calmly into the throat of the now panicking, kicking and screaming businessman. Blood started to gush from the throat but the majority of the people around this scene didn't even bother to look. There were a few horrified citizens, people who obviously couldn't decided to look at the man or not, but even they seemed fairly determined to hide their fear and walk away from the sight of the murder.

It was these people that got the Rector thinking. It was obvious that these people hadn't been taken in yet and were trying to keep a low profile while the other members of the society, the ever increasing number that had been through the first phase of conditioning, calmly went about their business, now conscious of the good that was going to be done via the great leader. And if they had to wipe out certain individuals that were determined to cause problems? Well, he couldn't say that he agreed with this action, he would've much preferred a less violent way of dealing with things and he had told Burn this on numerous occasions, but Burn had always smiled that enigmatic smile of his and reassured him that deaths like these were always going to be few and far between. If what was going on in the hall was anything to go by then he wasn't sure that this was entirely true and sights like the one in front of the bank just added to his doubt as to Burn's and Leonard's methods, but there was little that he could do about it. He may well be a part of the machine, but he certainly wasn't anywhere near the engine room.

He closed the window and tried to blot out the image of the man whose life blood was seeping away from him. When he had been out and about trying to convert people using the methods that he and Burn preferred, he had genuinely felt that he was doing these wretched creatures a favour. But how would the continued role of death affect the already fragile state of minds that had been conditioned? This was all new to Burn and him and he knew that Leonard had never had dealings with such an operation as well, despite his own inflated views as to his own abilities.

Pretty soon they were going to have to leave this gothic creation and move some place else. Next on the menu was a trip to the west of this island and see whom they could find there for their cause. It was a shame really as he rather liked where they were, although he felt that Leonard's insistence on candles was a bit too over the top.

He turned around and made his way to the door just in time to hear the sound of a man shouting, a man almost screaming with sheer panic in his voice. The voice came nearer and nearer until the Rector could see that it was one of the suited guards who was referred to as Shorty on account of him being over six foot seven. Despite the size of the man, he had a face so stricken with revulsion that the Rector knew that something had gone horrible wrong. With all the sights that could be seen in this building, for somebody as big as this chap to be worried spelt trouble . . . unless Burn had been up to his tricks again.

Shorty spotted the Rector and as he reached him he stepped back and leant against a peeling wall. Sweat was cascading down his face and his hands were shaking. He tried to speak but he had obviously been running and he was finding it difficult to form words.

The Rector grasped Shorty's shoulder and tried to get him to calm down and speak, to get across to him just what had upset this huge bulk of a man.

"Speak slowly now my son, take a deep breath for you are upset. Something has upset you. What is it?"

"I . . . . I . . . . oh Rector, I don't know what happened but there has been a mistake, something has gone wrong and . . . . oh my God!"

"What has gone so wrong that you need to ask for the help of our Lord?"

"One of the . . . no two of the people that have been conditioned, that have been through the second phase, that came off the machines and seemed perfectly fine."

"What about them?"

"They . . . they were fine, honestly Rector. They were working and helping others and they were talking of going outside to bring in some of their friends, to bring in some fresh people, to make the leader proud of them. They were so looking forward to . . . ." The Rector looked on impassively as Shorty broke down into tears. When the suited hulk eventually looked up there was a different look on his face. Now Shorty was looking at the Rector with a puzzled look on his face. He was still shaken by whatever it was that he had seen but now it was as if he was trying to recollect something. The Rector saw this change in Shorty and feared that something wasn't quite right in the way Shorty had been conditioned either and put his hand on the guard's shoulder.

A few seconds passed and Shorty started to stand upright. He was looking straight into the Rector's eyes only now the Rector didn't have the eyes that were familiar to the other members of the cause. Now there wasn't even what could normally be called human eyes. Now the Rector's face had a dark mist below his forehead and it was into this mist that Shorty was looking intently.

From out of the Rector's mouth came noises that were unearthly. It was a mixture of hisses and crackling but Shorty was nodding his head as if he understood. Eventually the Rector took his hand off the guard's shoulder and his dark eyes returned. Shorty was now standing upright and the Rector spoke to him in his calm, gentle voice.

"Now young man, what was it that had upset you so much? Think carefully now and explain what has gone wrong."

"It was two of the brothers," Shorty calmly responded. "They were talking about helping the cause. But then as one of them was downstairs near the entrance there was a terrible smell of burning and then one of their heads caught fire. There was no reason for it, it just caught fire. The brother didn't have the chance to scream either."

"What do you mean . . . . 'caught fire'?"

"Well, just like I said Sir. Started at the top of the brother's head, near the temples I think. Bluey-yellow flames that flickered around the top of the head. But the brother didn't scream or anything. He just stood there motionless as the flames engulfed his head more and more. His friend looked on as if he was watching a car crash—he didn't or couldn't do anything, until the fire totally covered the brother's head. The smell was awful Sir, so, so awful. Then the brother fell forward and the fire around his head died out, just died out. All that was left was a black, charred mess where the head should've been. The brother's friend staggered back against the wall and clutched his head, he was complaining of pains. But the guards, they took him away and started to remove the dead brother's body. What happened Rector? What happened to that poor guy?"

The Rector had walked over to the window again and watched impassively as scenes of the Police surrounding the dead pin-striped man washed over him. He was thinking hard. Something was wrong about this. He had gone along with the methods used so far but he wondered if Burn hadn't allowed things to go too far; if he hadn't allowed his bizarre partnership with Leonard to ignore the fact that things could go wrong. Alas, such was their conviction that they were right, oversights such as exploding heads had obviously not been contemplated. And in what could be called his heart, the Rector felt that if someone was going to make this whole operation go more smoothly, then surely he was the one to do it. Surely?

The Rector turned to face Shorty, who to his eyes was starting to doubt what was going on. Even the use of hypnosis, despite the initial calming influence, was seeming to buckle under the obvious distress of the guard.

"It is, I will admit my friend, a very unfortunate occurrence. I can assure you that this wasn't planned. It seems to me, that in order to make big leaps forward, we may have to suffer what is commonly called, by your people, collateral damage?"

"Collateral damage? I see Sir. But what do you mean by *your* people? Forgive me sir for being naive but I don't understand what you mean by that. Aren't we all in this together?"

The Rector cursed himself for the slip of his tongue. In his desire to be comforting to this soul he had almost let himself become careless when it came to some truths, truths that Shorty and his kind were just not ready for. The fact that he had almost been careless annoyed him; made him feel that maybe he wasn't ready for these transformations that had taken place in this small part of a naive, underdeveloped planet. The look on Shorty's face was one of questions and a desire to be told that everything was ok. But it was the questions part that bothered him.

As he approached Shorty, he outstretched his arms, the Bible in his right hand, in a pose to suggest warmth and understanding. Shorty would soon feel warmth, this was true, he would feel a great deal of warmth. But if it meant that the Rector could somehow make up for his lack of tact and do something more positive for the cause, to help keep things on track as it were, to nip any questions in the bud, then that was what he had to do. He didn't totally agree with this, but the bigger picture had to be considered. After this, he would speak to Burn and try to get him to see some sense.

Shorty's face looked at the Rector in a mixture of confusion and fear as the tall gentleman before him got closer and closer and wrapped his arms around the helpless guard.

CHAPTER TWENTY-THREE

He had no idea where he was heading to. All he knew was that he had to find Maria and Paul, and somehow, with little Emily in tow, find their way out of this bizarre place.

If he was to think about it logically, this whole situation was unreal. Talk about the blind leading the blind; it would be so much easier if someone could just hand him some instructions as to what to do next, but then, life wasn't like that was it? *Welcome to the world little baby, we would give you instructions as to how to deal with all the crap you are going to face in this life, but we thought it would be so much more fun if we didn't! No real reason, we just can't be bothered! Isn't this fun?*

Down yet another musty corridor, past rooms that had their doors shut and maybe just as well considering what he had seen of the place so far. Emily held onto his hand, not struggling anymore, just content to see what Mick was going to do to help them out of this bizarre situation. Mick was just happy to see that she had lost the 'zombie' look that had been across her face earlier on, although he did feel that if she could lose it so quickly, then maybe she could regain it just as quickly too. Whatever the state of the little girl's mind, they could deal with that later, just as soon as they were in the 'real' world . . . . whatever that meant.

The one thing that was a little bit disconcerting, although in a way that he didn't quite understand, was that there didn't seem to be many people going past him, that he and Emily hadn't yet met anybody that was questioning where they were going. After all the hubbub he had noticed in this building, surely there should be more people around? He could hear that things were going on around him, but he didn't see anyone yet.

Just as he was contemplating this conundrum, footsteps came from around the corner of the corridor that they were heading down, footsteps that were moving fast, running, in a hurry. Mick looked down at Emily who looked up at him calmly, a nondescript look on her pale features. Then, turning around 360 degrees, Mick looked for somewhere to hide before the ever louder footsteps turned into actual people running towards them. All he could see in that split second was the same dismal looking doors to God knows where that seemed to line these corridors.

Trying to act quickly, Mick reached out to one of the doors and turned its handle but it wouldn't open. He tried to push the door but it wouldn't move. He lashed out in frustration and kicked the door hard with the sole of his foot but still the door wasn't going to open for him.

Moving further along the corridor, he was about to give another door the same treatment when he realised that it was too late, whoever was coming down the bending corridor was here and there was nowhere for him and Emily to go.

He stood with his back to the wall and held out his hands as if they were bound together with invisible handcuffs as suited guards approached them.

"Okay, I give up! Take me to your leader!"

One of the guards shot Mick a look of annoyance, but to the bemusement of the artist and his little companion the four suited and booted men that were the owners of the footsteps didn't stop, although one of the others did offer a "very funny, now get back to your duties."

As he watched the retreating backs of the guards, Mick felt an overwhelming feeling of confusion. Confused that he didn't know where he was taking Emily; confused that he didn't know what he was going to do once he had found Maria and Paul, and now confused that people he considered to be the 'enemy' weren't remotely interested in him.

It was Emily's observations that stirred Mick into some sort of action, although an action he didn't think that he would take. As she watched the disappearing guards she looked up at her new friend and in a matter of fact way uttered:

"They seem to be worried Mick. They look like they are going somewhere fast. I wonder what has happened?"

Mick thought about the faces of the guards and had to admit that Emily had made a valid point; normally the people around here looked calm, cocky even, to the point where you wanted to give their self satisfied faces a slap. And yet, the guards that had just run past them looked, well, panic stricken. Where were they running to?

Now there was a different conundrum in Mick's mind. Should he make the most of this opportunity and carry on looking for Maria and Paul then get out? Or does his curiosity get the better of him and he tries to find out why those guards looked so worried? Did he actually *want* to get Maria *and* Paul out? Surely he only wanted to get Maria out and to hell with Paul? Then again, before he knew who Paul was, he actually thought that he was a nice guy, so what to do?

It was the scream that did it. From down below there was a noise that was definitely a scream but it also had an unearthly moan to it as well; almost as if the woman responsible was afraid and yet astonished at the same time. Even Emily, who until now had looked so calm and serene, showed a look of uncertainty at the bizarre noise from down the stairs.

Well, if ever Mick Rogers was going to be brave, then let it be now! A decision is going to be made so sound the trumpets and wave the flags!

Taking Emily by the hand again, Mick looked around and then made the decision to follow the guards, to see what had caused them to look so panic stricken.

It took a few minutes of walking, of constantly looking around to see if they were being followed or watched, before one of the ex-hotel's grandiose staircases came into view. As they reached the stairs, it became even more obvious from the sounds that were floating up through the stairwell that all was not good, that not everyone or everything was as calm and as businesslike as it first seemed. Feeling even more curious now to see what was so different than before, Mick led Emily, carefully and stealthily down the stairs. Each step more cautious than the one before and taking Mick and Emily to a scene that was as bizarre as it was disgusting.

This wasn't going according to plan. At least he didn't think that Mr Leonard would've ever have envisaged such a problem as this one. Personally he had seen worse, much worse, in fact he had been rather instrumental in a lot of the worse things he had seen, but whether he was to blame for this little problem . . . well . . . maybe a little bit, but then, he would've gone about things a lot more directly. Some people might say with less tact, but he would say that if you were going to do a job, then always do it right.

A woman in her late thirties, wearing what could only have been described as some throwback dungarees from the 70s was wailing. She had started off screaming, but had gradually descended into a wail and much to the annoyance of Burn she had seemed to trigger off something in the others who, even though they weren't screaming, were staring in horror at the bloody pulp that was spread out on the floor before them.

To Burn, the whole point of the game that Leonard called 'conditioning' was to persuade these pathetic little individuals to see some sort of sense and live in a better world, a world where there was no anger, no fighting, no hatred. All very nice he was sure, and the fact that the 'leader' of this whole new movement would have been Leonard himself was purely coincidental. At least that is what Leonard would have you believe. You didn't have to be a genius or a person from another planet to see that Leonard's vanity and ego played a huge part in this and that while he had genuine reasons for feeling the way he did (otherwise, how else would they have tapped into his psyche?) that maybe Mr Theobald Leonard was over his head in this operation. Yes, Leonard had accessed a way of living that many humans could access, if only they believed and took the time, and a way of living that would actually gain them much more credibility across the whole universe. But now, looking before him, seeing the despicable mess on the floor that used to be a human, had made him think that maybe things were getting away from Leonard and that something had to change.

The machines that did the 'conditioning' had been suggested by himself and the Rector; if himself and his esteemed colleague had to do all the converting themselves, then it would've caused suspicion amongst the followers and taken up a ridiculous amount of time. This way, with their machines in this building and in other parts of the country, the converting would be quicker and achieve their objectives more satisfactorily as well. Well, the objectives of the Rector and him.

Whether Leonard would appreciate the end product was another thing entirely.

The woman in the dungarees was now kneeling. Her hands were flung to the heavens and she was pleading to her God.

"Why did this happen? This wasn't supposed to happen. He was only doing your work. They told us we are doing your work, so why? Tell me whyyyyy."

Burn felt that something had to be said. He moved forward towards the hysterical woman, skirting around the red pool that had fragments of skull and brain mixed within its smoking concoction. He was aware that the people here were afraid of him and he liked that.

The woman stopped moaning as she looked up and started straight into the dark eyes of Thomas Burn. Burn was smiling and reaching out to her. As he got closer and closer to her, the woman felt warmer and warmer, as if somebody had just directed a sun lamp towards her. The people around her had also started to back away, gazing with a mix of awe and fear at the man they knew as Burn. Burn reached the woman in dungarees and lifted her up from her kneeling position, almost effortlessly. Her eyes met his as he spoke.

"Now, whatever you have just seen my dear is nothing for you to worry about. I know, it is not very pleasant, and it must be distressing to see such . . an unfortunate occurrence happen to a colleague . . .."

"Colleague? That was my boyfriend!"

"Boyfriend you say? Is there any room in your heart for anything other than the cause then? I must say that I am disappointed by this revelation."

The faces on the people that gathered around the woman and the mess that used to be her boyfriend showed that they had seen the change in Burn's expression. He had seemed so concerned initially, but after hearing the woman mention her boyfriend, his eyes became hard and his body seemed to tense up. The woman was now silent and Burn reached out and put his hands on her shoulders.

Looking around momentarily, Burn focused on one of the suited guards that had appeared and was standing a few feet away from him. The guard understood what it was that Burn was saying to him and started to usher people away from the scene, from the blood and gore and from Burn's interactions with the woman. As he started to do this, a few more grey suits arrived and pretty soon the area was empty apart from Burn, the guard that Burn had communicated with and the woman in the dungarees.

With another motion, Burn sent the guard away and turned once more to the woman who was now pale faced and trembling.

"I wasn't trying to create trouble Mr Burn, I wasn't trying to create trouble. I felt strange that's all. I saw my boyfriend dissolve and I felt strange. Angry, distraught, I'm sorry for screaming, please don't hurt me, please Mr Burn sir."

Burn carried on standing in front of the woman, his hands still on her shoulders, but now his forehead went closer and closer to her face as if he was about to kiss the now petrified female before him passionately. But as his nose was barely touching hers he spoke in a low, rasping, crackling voice that made the woman lose control of her bladder.

"I had to rush down here to sort out the mess that you and your boyfriend caused. I was about to show some friends of mine something very important, important to me, the leader and the whole fucking cause, the reason why we have ignorant fuckers like you in buildings like this all over this fucking island and soon the world. I was about to enjoy the reactions of my friends and hopefully encourage them to join us in our, what shall we call it, our crusade. Yes, that's a good a word as any. Your people liked crusades didn't you, many years ago. Maybe even now?"

"I don't . . . know . . . . what you mean sir . . ."

"No, no, I don't suppose you do my dear. Wasn't anything to do with you was it? Only it was my dear, it was very much to do with you and all your kind. But you never listen, never learn from your mistakes. So you have lost your . . . . boyfriend, so he reacted badly to the help we have tried to give him, but let's face it, does he really matter? In the whole scheme of things, does HE really matter? No, your kind have lost so many for so little, so when something goes wrong that surely, means a few, how would your kind put it, casualties of war, then surely, surely it doesn't mean a damn thing when the outcome is for the positive. Isn't that what your race has taught the universe?"

Urine was now in a puddle around the feet of Burn and the woman, but he didn't seem to notice, and as her legs started to buckle in fear, he held her up without any effort and continued to press his forehead against hers.

With abject horror, the woman noticed that smoke was starting to emanate from Mr Burn, but she couldn't tell from where on his body it came. The smell was appalling, an acrid, metallic stench that was stinging her nostrils, but she couldn't move her head, her whole body from the grip of Mr Thomas Burn and she felt her head swimming, her body temperature rising and darkness appearing over the horizon.

As she felt consciousness start to desert her, as she felt so hot that she could almost smell her dungarees start to scorch, from a distance she heard a voice, a man's voice and then bizarrely, what sounded like the shout from a little girl. As soon as the voices stopped, she felt a sudden coolness in her body and consciousness starting to wash back over her like a stream coursing over a river bed. She was no longer shaking but standing still, so still, like a statue. Afraid to move, to blink, to breathe. She was only now just aware that Burn had moved away and was ten feet from her and facing where the voices had come from. Moving her eyes slowly, she saw standing on the bottom step of a huge staircase a man who was holding a little girl's hand. She knew the little girl, had seen her around the building quite a few times, but the man? Whoever he was, he was now being approached by Burn who was holding out his hand in a strange gesture of welcome.

Whether it was Burn's actions or just pure relief and fear, blackness enveloped the lady in the dungarees and she became faintly aware of her legs buckling beneath her and the floor coming up towards her. In just a second's thought she knew that she was going to faint and she felt grateful for this release.

CHAPTER TWENTY-FOUR

"Well, well, what a turn up for the books eh? Lots of lovely piccies of Micky boy! Well, I am sure that you really enjoyed that uh? Although, and I don't mean to be funny here, but why the fuck have these bastards been taking pictures of your ex? Don't you find that interesting?"

Maria's face was downcast during Burn's picture show and during Paul's words, but it was the sheer sarcasm of his tone that made her stand up quickly and launch into her response.

"And you think I know do you? For fuck's sake Paul, you just can't get it into your tiny mind can you? Look, I'm not going to go through the same old crap with you over and over again. All I'm going to say is that I haven't got a fucking clue why they have pictures of Mick and what's more I don't give a toss either. My only concern is Emily and getting out of here. I don't know where that weirdo just went to, but as far as I'm concerned I want my sister and I want out of here. If you wanna argue or be oh so smart then good luck, personally I think we have more important things to worry about."

"And how do you suggest that we get out Maria? It may have escaped your notice but there's a hulking big bonehead standing outside this room. I don't think he is going to let us go anywhere do you? Whatever these people are doing, whatever fucked up shit they intend to unleash on the world, Emily has been dragged into it and Micky boy is in the middle of it too! Although what they would want with someone so fucking miserable is beyond me, did you see those bloody pictures?"

Paul was describing how Burn's slides had shown Mick in a variety of places. From leaving Walters Associates to putting a key into his front door to him leaning over a bridge and gazing into a stream in what looked like a large park somewhere.

It was the bridge picture that had got to Maria. She thought that she knew her ex boyfriend well, but there was a look on his face in that slide that made her feel that he was hurting; that he was the most lonely person she had ever seen and that maybe her actions towards him in the past had contributed towards this.

Looking at her husband now, it would be easy to feel, if only for a short second, that she may have made a mistake somewhere and that she could've been a bit more patient towards the guy who she knew had loved her unconditionally. But then, what would be the point of that? She did love Paul. She just wished that Mick hadn't loved her as much as he did. She knew that deep down he was a nice guy, so why didn't he let other women know that?

The 'bonehead' that Paul had referred to had entered the room and was now standing in front of the closed door and facing them. His arms were folded and he wore a smirk that suggested that he was the one in control here and there was nothing that they could do to change that. And looking at the way his bulk seemed to fill up the frame, Paul was very much inclined to agree with him. Maria though had other ideas and walked up to the man whose head was almost touching the top of the door frame.

"So, what is your role in all of this? Here to keep the peace? Do your leader's bidding? Who is the leader by the way? I've met a few nutcases in here and I'm confused as to who is running this fucking show? The lovely named Mr Burn maybe?"

"You will find out everything soon," responded the guard.

"Oh that old chestnut? A need to know basis uh? Look mate, think about it for a second uh? Whatever is happening here is not good, understand? *Not good!* You know as well as I do that eventually your little gang are gonna get arrested and you will be slung in prison for so long that by the time you get out you will be a wizened old man who needs a Zimmer frame to get around on and incontinence pants to stop you from pissing yourself."

If this was meant to provoke an angry reaction from the guard then it didn't work as he stared straight at the nurse with that smug smile still on his face.

"Yes Maria, upset our host why don't you? That is really going to make things better isn't it?" protested Paul, as he cringed at his wife's attempts to communicate with their captors.

"It isn't really me that you should worry about upsetting," said the guard, "because as you have mentioned lady, I am here to serve my master's bidding. I just do my job. If you keep quiet and do as you're told then everything will be ok."

"Or your version of ok," suggested Maria. "You still haven't said who is running this show. And why my sister eh? What has she got to do with all of this?"

"And Micky boy," continued Paul.

Moving his stance from one foot to another the guard, still smiling, let out a sigh before responding to Maria's question.

"As I have said, you will find out soon. As for your sister, I have no idea why she is here. I would've thought that if she wasn't here then she would be in one of the other places. Everyone will go through the same process eventually."

"What other places?" exclaimed Maria, "what do you mean everyone will go through this process as you put it? You don't mean to tell me that there are more of these fucking weirdos about do you?"

"Maria for fuck's sake! You just aren't helping! Why do you have to shout your mouth off all the bleedin' time?" Paul was looking more and more uneasy at his wife's outbursts. He understood why she was so angry, of course she was angry, who wouldn't be in a situation like this? He also understood that Maria had a foul temper when she felt like losing it. But he was becoming increasingly irritated by her lack of tact. Or was it that he was just scared? If it was that, he would never admit such a thing to his wife.

As if she was reading his thoughts, Maria, looking coolly into the eyes of her husband, walked up to him until he could smell the faint odour of chewing gum being breathed into his face and whispered to him words that were clearly not meant for the guard at the door.

"Look Pauly, you know as well as I do that this is getting silly. Sometimes we have to do things out of character to get us out of situations so please don't take this the wrong way, just go along with it okay?"

Before he had the chance to ask her what the hell she was talking about, Maria pecked him on the cheek, turned around and went back to the guard at the door. This time though, Maria's attitude was different, this time she wasn't angry, at least not on the outside. If anything, Maria Weston was strangely calm and looking like she had a sense of purpose.

To anybody else, this sudden change of temperament would've been bizarre and unexpected, to Mr Paul Weston, it was all part of the course in his marriage to the woman that was now standing very close to the guard, looking up at him as he gazed down at her, still, even now, with that grin on his face.

"So, what was your name again?" Maria asked, not really knowing what the guard would reply, although she was guessing that it would have something to do about waiting and seeing, and doing his duty for the leader or whatever. As it was there was no reply and the guard carried on looking down at the brunette who was smiling sweetly up at him.

"I didn't mention my name." the grinning guard eventually rasped.

"No, so you didn't, but wouldn't you like to tell me it? I mean, I could tell you a lot of things, that's if you wanted me to . . ." As Maria breathed these words to the suited gentleman in front of her, she let fingers wander down the chest of the guard and down towards where his belt was. The guard just smiled with that seemingly immovable smile, not seeming to care what Maria was doing or trying to do. Maria though didn't let the guard's reluctance to go along with the situation distract her from her intentions. She carried on tracing her finger down the body of the guard until she was kneeling down in front of the guard's flies. It was then obvious to Paul and to any man or woman of the world what his wife's intentions were and he didn't like them.

"No, I don't think so Maria, just don't even think about it! I don't know what you think that will achieve but just forget it!"

As he approached his wife, with feelings of disgust in his stomach, Maria looked up at him with anger again spread across her features. The guard on the other hand was now looking at Maria and Paul in amusement and spoke with a laughing tone to his voice.

"Ah now, I am sure that whatever your wife was about to do wouldn't have made any difference to the eventual outcome of things, although clearly I would have liked it. Ha-ha. Then again, maybe when you two eventually give up and accept the inevitable then me and your missus can get together later on. I mean, I'm sure that the leader won't mind love being spread around in that manner."

"Oh fucking really?" screamed the now furious Paul, his face a mixture of anger and frustration at this ridiculous situation. "If you seriously think that I'm gonna stand here and let you give that monkey a blowjob then you are so fucking wrong missus."

"Well," responded his smirking wife, "if you feel that you could do a better job . . ."

"Now hold on a minute!" The guard's smile dropped at Maria's remark as he moved away from the kneeling nurse. "I don't let guys anywhere near there. You sick or what?"

"Sick?" exclaimed Maria, "You have the fucking nerve to call *me* sick? Who works for the sick goons that are trying to change the world uh? Who is the monkey, as my husband politely puts it, who clearly thinks that his employers are the best thing since sliced fucking bread? You're the sick one boy, you and your little friends are the sick fuckers around here!"

"Don't call me a monkey you bitch, and don't call me and the leaders sick."

"Or what monkey man? Spread the love you said. Surely hitting a woman isn't spreading anything but hate isn't it? I wonder what the lovely Mr Burn will think of your nasty attitude?"

"Who said I was gonna hit you?" spat the grey suited guard who was now approaching a slowly retreating Maria, "you just need to learn some manners."

"And how do you intend to do that monkey man?" joined in Paul Weston. He had noticed that with every step towards his wife the guard was leaving the door unguarded. He wasn't entirely sure what this meant and how this was going to improve things but something told him that annoying the bulky guard might, somehow, help matters. That to get him angry was a lot better than the annoying, self satisfied bulk that seemed an immovable object by the door. And anyway, the sight of seeing his wife kneeling in front of the brute's crotch had stirred feelings of hatred towards this guy even though the idea was clearly Maria's. When he called the guard 'monkey man' he meant it, and he would've called him worse if the thought of self preservation and the guy flying at him had not occurred to him also.

"Well now, perhaps I should show you a little eh?" replied the guard. "I won't have as many scruples in hitting you than I would in hitting your pretty little wife here. I can always say that you were causing trouble and that I had no alternative. I'm sure that the leaders will understand that. I've been a good servant to the cause so far."

"Oh lovely," said the sarcastic nurse, "that is so good to hear. I mean, we could've been looked after by an absolute beginner, but to know that our host is a good servant, a good worker, a good little boy, well, that makes all the difference. Do you get a nice certificate for your good behaviour. Will you be given a lovely clock when you leave? Don't you feel better knowing all of this Paul?"

Paul looked at his wife and from the look on her face he realised that she had come to the same conclusion as himself; that if they were going to get out of this room, then they had to annoy this guard to the point where he lost control of the situation. After all, there was two of them. He couldn't deal with both of them, could he?

The guard looked at Maria and then at Paul. He then stared at Paul as he waited for the response to his wife's taunts. But when he realised that Paul wasn't going to say anything he felt his anger subside a little and he started to backtrack towards the door again but this time he had reached inside his pocket for his walkie-talkie.

"I don't know why I'm letting you two get to me. What the hell can you do? However, maybe if I get someone else here to help me *look after* you two then maybe you will realise what a hopeless situation you are in. Unless you change your ways of course."

Maria looked at Paul again. They both seemed to realise that this wasn't part of the plan, a plan that was unspoken but one that they had both seemed to think of all the same. The nurse tried to stop him from speaking into the walkie-talkie; to call someone else to the room would mean that they would never get out of this depressing room, not until they were lead to whatever lovely place the so called leader had in mind for them anyway.

"So you can't handle us then? It's going to make you look pretty stupid isn't it? A big boy like you not being able to control a little woman like me and a slightly built guy like my husband?"

"Slightly built?" Paul began to interject.

"Of course darling. Not that is a bad thing. You are just not as . . . well . . . ready for a punch-up physically as this chap here, do you know what I mean?"

Paul felt himself shrink at this comparison between himself and the guard but bit his lip regardless. He seemed to realise that his spouse was now trying a different tactic. From the insulting to the praising of the guard's attributes. Or was she just being sarcastic again? If there was one thing that Paul Weston knew of his wife it was that she could charm the pants off a prude, even when she was taking the piss. Whatever she was doing, the guard had briefly stopped from operating the walkie-talkie.

"It isn't about being able to handle you, lady. I just don't want to get into trouble just because you two trouble makers can't be bothered to see sense and just do what you know is right." The guard spat out his retort while looking at the married couple with a mix of anger, annoyance and bemusement.

Maria walked slowly up to the guard and much to Paul's horror started to tickle the tall suited one under the chin. "Oh no, you poor liddle boy. Will the nasty men give you smacks on the bottom. Will they send you to beddy byes with no dinner winner. Ah, come to Auntie Maria and give us hugs."

"Tell your wife to not push her luck mate." Paul looked at Maria as the guard spoke to him with an increasing sense of anger. It seemed that whatever plan she had in her head it was now the opposite of trying to praise him. Maybe she was just playing with his mind, confusing the guy to not know how to take this woman in front of him. Maybe even convince him that she was a little bit out of control too? Maria had always read books that Paul had referred to as 'psycho-babble,' books that dealt with the ways that people thought and acted in times of trouble or stress. Maybe she was using some of her new found knowledge to good use in this bizarre situation? If he didn't know his wife better, he would swear that Maria was actually enjoying the way that she was messing with the guard.

Looking around the room, Paul felt that whether the guard got help or not, he and Maria were going to be taken somewhere else probably not very nice in a short time. Not only that but he was bored with the guard, his pathetic attitude and Maria's own brand of psychiatry. If only Maria could get out of the door then that would be something, regardless of whether he went with her, and feeling that he was about to make a huge mistake, Paul Weston inched his way towards the grey suited keeper of the door.

"Come on then monkey man, enough games, let's see if you can handle this *slightly built* guy shall we? Let's see if you are all muscle and no brain which quite frankly I think you are!"

The guard also inched towards Paul with a grin on his face. "Oh, feeling brave are you Weston? Do you really want your wife to see you splattered across the room then? Maybe save the leaders a job because personally, I think you will be splattered all over the place anyway."

Maria, looking anxiously for fear of her husband's safety, decided that as worried as she was, she must go along with what was happening. Now was a time as good as any to get out of this room. She just hoped that Paul wouldn't get too hurt in the process.

"Yeah Paul, use your, you know, your karate stuff on him. He won't like that. Honestly monkey man, you have met your match in my husband. He may be slim but he'll make you pay for being such a knob."

After hearing his wife's words, Paul didn't know whether to stand his ground and let the guard get nearer to him or to make up some ridiculous pose that suggested that he really was a black belt in karate or origami or whatever it was that Maria was suggesting that he was skilled at. Whatever his predicament, the guard didn't look impressed.

"I think a little slap will suffice, just to shut you up and make your slut wife behave yourselves. I'll teach you to be so fucking awkward. Come here you little shit."

With every approaching step towards Paul, Maria looked at the door and at her worried husband. He could see what she was thinking and nodded slightly, his eyes moving to the door and to her, telling her to try it and get out.

The guard raised his fist and Paul had enough time to see a huge gold ring upon his forefinger before the ring and the fist made a crashing connection with his unprotected face. Maria screamed her husband's name but with the taste of blood seeping into his mouth he shouted to her "now!" just as the guard grabbed his collar and delivered another smash to his jaw.

Paul fell backwards, staggering slightly before his legs gave way and he just evaded an orange plastic backed chair before his backside hit the floor and he felt the pain of the blows rack his face.

Maria had opened the door and was clearly unsure whether to go through it or not, but a slight breeze through the doorway alerted the guard and told him that the door was open and he left his victim on the floor and turned towards the nurse. His roars made up her mind as she shot through the doorway and after a second of indecision turned right down the musty, candlelit passage.

"Come back you bitch, come back here or I'll really hurt your fucking husband!"

She knew that the guard *would* really hurt Paul too if he really wanted to. Paul, for all of his bravado, was never going to be a fighter. She wanted to turn back and stop him from getting hurt, but she also wanted her sister back and to get out of this dreadful building. As she headed towards a staircase she thought she could hear her husband's voice telling her to run. It sounded like he was repeating it a few times before it was suddenly stopped.

There were people passing by her, staring at her in confusion, but the feelings of fear and desperation in her body pushed her on. She wasn't sure where she was heading or what she was going to do, but she was determined to find her sister and find some answers. Someone, somewhere must have some answers. Someone, somewhere must help her end this bizarre nightmare.

CHAPTER TWENTY-FIVE

Walking around the ex-hotel; looking around what he guessed could be called his own dominion and maybe even called the starting place of all that he desired and felt was needed by the world, Leonard still felt a sense of unease. People were going past him in increasing numbers now and all of them treated him with reverence and with the same style of respect that he felt the Royal Family demanded.

But despite the feeling that more and more people were appearing in the building and despite assurances from Burn and the Rector that other bases in the country were also proving profitable for the cause, Leonard still felt that something was missing.

He thought of Dorothy who had been so concerned when he had been hurt earlier on and he thought that maybe if he'd had a female partner, someone to look after him while he did his work, then maybe that could fill this strange hole in his life? But when he thought about it, he had never been successful with women. He seemed to be the sort of guy that women generally found easy to forget. The fact that his interests seemed to be at odds with everybody else's could be a reason for this, but ultimately he felt that he was only worried about the world in general; that the obvious social decay around the world was not being dealt with by the powers that be; that it would take something or someone different to grab society by the collar and change things for the better. He knew how people would perceive him, but he lived by the saying that what is now proved was once impossible. It is possible to make this world a better place with no violence, no teenage killings, no religious hatred, no blinkered politicians, it would just mean making people in general believe in these things differently than ever before. And if that meant a bit of, what did the armies call it? Collateral damage? Then so be it. It isn't perfect, but it would be fantastic when it works and he would be seen as a hero to the people.

However, he mustn't get carried away. As nice and as well deserved as it would be to be called an hero, one mustn't become so power crazed and develop a despot personality.

He started to think of Mick Rogers. He still remembered the day when Burn had spoken to him of this young man, of how here was a guy who thought in exactly the same way as they did but who didn't know how to channel his grievances in the correct way. Burn had been watching him for some time. How he had initially found him he hadn't been prepared to say, but then Leonard knew that Burn was not the sort of guy to ask too many awkward questions to. He had used some of the power he had been given by Burn sparingly although he had been tempted to use it against him such was his dislike of Burn's careless nature, but he had to admit that Burn and the Rector made him feel uneasy.

By all accounts Rogers was an angry young man, a guy who also saw how the human race was heading down a slippery slope towards anarchy and how he was also scared of how the current crop of hoodie wearing teenagers were going to be tomorrows adults and wage earners, that's if they got off their 'give me respect' high horse and actually looked for work.

Maybe, just maybe, with the right sort of help, Rogers could be as powerful as him, Burn and the Rector. He certainly couldn't be any worse than the late Roscoe; if ever Leonard had totally misplaced his trust in someone then it had been with that screwball. Why he had felt that he had seen some kind of intelligence in amongst the clutter of Roscoe's mind he was unsure of, however that chap was no longer a problem, not to anybody or to himself.

Feeling in need of some fresh air, Leonard had found his way to a fire exit which had been opened for him by one of the grey suited guards. Upon his exit the guard had told him to "take care sir," a phrase which amused him, because he wondered if anybody actually meant it when they said it?

He eventually found himself in a busy road; cars, taxis, lorries, coaches all rushing up and down past office blocks, shops and fast food outlets.

People were rushing around in a manner which wasn't so different from any other day. It made him wonder if what the Rector and Burn had been saying was wrong, but then, why would they lie to him? Surely they were using him as much as he was using them?

As he turned a corner he brushed the arm of a middle aged guy wearing an England football shirt. The guy's head snapped around at Leonard as if he was about to challenge him for daring to knock his arm, accident or not, when the guy's face changed quickly from swift anger to one of calm acceptance. He stared at Leonard for a few seconds almost motionless before speaking.

"Oh sir, I am sorry. Didn't see you coming around the corner. Please accept my apologies. Hey Jimmy, look who is here amongst us!"

Jimmy turned out to be another obvious football fan but one who was wearing an Arsenal polo shirt. He sidled over to the England fan and he also stared at Leonard.

"Sir, we are honoured that you are here. Is there anything you wish for us to do for you?"

Leonard stood looking at the two men who were standing subserviently in front of him. A certain excitement ran through him, a strange rush of endorphins as he realised that he was genuinely being treated as a leader of men; the man that he knew he would one day become.

He was about to answer that things were fine and that they should just carry on their business when he noticed that a small crowd of people, clearly those that was working for him and the good of humanity, starting to build up just behind the football fans. They were looking intently at Leonard and waiting for him to say something in return to the two guys whose attention he had initially taken. However, there were also more people looking at him as they walked past; what was disturbing to Leonard was the mixture of responses that he was getting. Some acknowledged him as someone who was clearly important, but others were just staring at him as if he was the local oddball who was trying to gain attention. It was when Leonard overheard an elderly lady say to no-one in particular, "some people, tut!" that he felt that things weren't going as smoothly as he had wished. Clearly it was going to take more time to get the vast majority of people thinking the same way as him, Burn and the Rector.

Burn had likened it to a rolling snowball. Starting off very small and then getting bigger and bigger as more and more people become stuck to the object that was heading towards and over them. Picking up people, picking up tools for the cause. Apparently, according to Burn, it had worked before. But he didn't say where exactly. And surely it couldn't have been such a success if he hadn't heard of such an exploit before?

Leonard walked slowly down the main road, trying to ignore the faces of people that recognised him or wanted to point him out to their friends. Maybe it would've been better if he had come out with a guard or two, just in case people tried to touch him? He shook his head as he thought of all the world's rock stars who sauntered through life behind dark glasses, regardless of the time of day or the weather, who clearly saw themselves as far more important than the minions that had bought their records and had put them in their position of fame in the first place. They had their guards too in case, God forbid, one of the unwashed should attempt to communicate with them in some dangerous way. Did he really want to put himself across as shallow as them? Wasn't that the sort of behaviour that was causing him to feel so angry and disillusioned with the world? Wasn't that what this whole new movement was about? No, he was right to walk without a guard and what would be, would be.

After five minutes of walking, of looking steadily around the streets and the faces of the passers by, Leonard found himself outside a pub. He looked at his watch and noticed that it was 6.05 pm. He wasn't fully aware of how popular pubs were at this time of the day but this one seemed quite busy. As the pub's main entrance open and closed a couple of times he could hear the music of a 70s hit song get louder and then fade as patrons of the establishment came back and forth.

Leonard felt that part of the conditioning process was to somehow deter people from places like public houses. Clearly, this pub was full of people who wouldn't have a clue as to who he was, although he was sure that their time would come. As far as he could remember these sort of places caused him annoyance. Partly because he felt that to him they looked like places for the out of control of society, and partly, and maybe this was the main reason although he wouldn't openly admit it, because they were full of people who were with their friends and who were enjoying themselves. Leonard had never had real friends, instead keeping himself to himself, immersed in his rooms and enveloped in his own views of what was making this world an increasingly dark place to live in.

The door of the pub swung open for the fifth time and out stepped a young lady. She looked in her early twenties and was wearing a short pink skirt that allowed you to see her long legs that were covered in white stockings. She had long, flowing blonde hair and was wearing enough make-up to keep Max Factor in a nice little profit for the remainder of the year.

As the girl tottered out, on heels that made her look at least a foot taller, Leonard couldn't help but stare at her legs. He let his eyes travel up them until they caressed the roundness of her skirt covered backside. He then noticed that she was wearing a thin sweater, also pink, that was gently adhered to the shape of her breasts. Then he noticed the cross that was resting on the top of the sweater just above her cleavage.

He wondered whether the girl actually believed in God or whether she wore it as a fashion accessory? Maybe it had been a present from a relative? A boyfriend? Whatever the reason the girl had gone from shouting behind her, clearly a goodbye to someone in the bar, to now looking at Leonard with disgust on her face. She took hold of her cross and tucked it into her jumper as she spoke.

"Oi, having a good look at my body are ya? Dirty fucking sod!"

Leonard shuddered at the words. She was accusing *him* of being some sort of a pervert. Since when was looking at a chain such a bad thing, especially the symbol that many regarded as their proof of salvation in such a wicked and stressful world. It was his sense of outrage that caused him to state his case against this unfair accusation.

"I'm sorry young lady. I was only looking at your cross. I wasn't attempting to look at your body in any other way I assure you."

"Yeahhh, like women haven't heard that excuse before. I wouldn't mind if you were at least honest about it but like a typical man you perve at the girls and then deny ever doing anything wrong. Pathetic little prick!"

With this final insult the girl glared at Leonard and went her way along the street leaving the leader of the new world staring at the dirty pavement, somewhat abashed and yet somewhat increasingly angry that after all that he was doing, such a cheap little tart should accuse him of being what he so abhorred.

As he looked up he saw the girl stop and start talking to a shaven headed guy. He was stroking her face and looking at her with obvious tenderness. Leonard wondered if it was him that had given her the cross? He thought about the girl's accusations and went cold as he felt that maybe he had been guilty of some misdemeanour. After all, didn't he let his eyes look at her legs? Didn't he feel the need to trace the outline of her backside? Was it sheer curiosity as to the girl's outfit or was it something else; something that he had let stay hidden for so long? Maybe he was right and that finding someone to share his vision of the world wouldn't be so bad? He thought of Burn and knew that he was always using what power he had for his own pleasures. Leonard had despised this and even though he knew he would never take it that far, maybe he could use, just once, the powers that he had been blessed with to find an outlet for these thoughts that were creeping into his mind more and more every day.

Leonard looked up from these thoughts in time to see the shaven headed guy coming towards him. This time there was no look of tenderness on his face as Leonard realised that the girl must've said something to him about the innocent incident that had just taken place.

"Hey mate, my girl says you were perving at her. Why don't you stop hanging around there and fuck off before you get hurt?"

This wasn't what Leonard thought was going to happen when he decided to get a breath of fresh air. What was it the guard had said? Take care? Did that large man know something then that he did not? Well, it clearly wasn't a good idea to stay where he was otherwise he would be at risk not just to himself but maybe to the whole process.

He turned around and gazed briefly at the approaching guy with an intent to move away and depart this unfortunate scene, but the guy took his look to mean something else and got even closer to Leonard.

"Don't look at me like that pervert, I'm not the one with the dirty, fucking problem. Go on, fuck off, get out of here you dirty bastard!"

Leonard had stopped his retreat as he turned back and looked at the verbal assailant. His body facing the direction he intended to walk and his face facing the ever more aggressive boyfriend of the pink skirted woman. Years of feeling like the odd one out and the 'weird' one raced through his mind and to think that even when his plans were seeming to take shape there was still room for idiots like this guy to spout their ill informed garbage to the public.

"Look, I don't know who you think you're talking to but I can assure you that this is just a misunderstanding. Now, if you don't mind I have business to attend to."

Despite Leonard's offer to depart it seemed that the shaven headed gentleman was still having a problem with him.

"What do you mean who you think I'm talking to? Whatever dirty business you have perve then fuck off and do it now, but you're starting to piss me off tosser!"

After watching the result of her handiwork, the pink skirted girl decided that enough was enough and that her boyfriend should now leave the guy she had insulted alone. She raced up to him and grabbed his arm.

"Leave it alone Lee, he ain't worth it! Come on, I wanna go and get some chips, I'm starving."

"What? You tell me that some geezer's been gawping at ya and when I tell him to fuck off you want me to stop? Make your mind up girl. I mean look at him, he's clearly up to no good. Hey, ain't you gone yet?"

Feeling that despite his warnings and his girlfriend's beg for clemency, Leonard needed help to move on, so Lee decided to show his intentions by showing his yellowing teeth in a snarl and by pushing Leonard in the back, an action that caused Leonard to stumble forward but he was able to just catch his balance and stand up. He turned to Lee and stood very still.

"Not a wise move sir, now leave me alone before you cause me to react in a negative way. Please leave me alone to my business."

"Ha, what's the matter perve, can't take a hint? For fuck's sake, you talk like a fucking weirdo as well."

The pink skirted girl looked at Leonard's face and felt something inside her start to shrink. She hadn't noticed it before but there was something in this man's face that seemed, she couldn't quite get it, somehow scary in an unusual way. It was almost like he wasn't scared of Lee, who to be honest did have a reputation as a bit of a hothead, and that he was about to do something bad to her boyfriend and it wasn't going to be pleasant.

Leonard on the other hand was feeling a strange maelstrom of emotions. Should he confront this caveman and be forced into actions that went against his better judgement? Should he walk away or run away and risk the guy and his girlfriend laughing at him, which he just knew would cause him to revisit the scene over and over in his head later on and make him wish that he had done something braver? As he ran over these thoughts in the seconds that he stood facing Lee it seemed that the said gentleman was going to show his lucky girlfriend what a great, tough guy he is and how she is lucky enough to go out with and sleep with him.

He grabbed Leonard by the jacket collar and growled into his face, telling him in no uncertain terms how scum like Leonard shouldn't be on the streets and that if he wouldn't get off them when told to then maybe he needed a little prompting.

Leonard initially didn't move a muscle but stared into the man's eyes, and without considering his options anymore felt his hand come up and grasp Lee tightly but without great force on the right side of the angry man's neck, his forefinger just overlapping Lee's earlobe.

Lee was perplexed by this odd move of Leonard's but he didn't show it by making a joke of what had happened.

"What's this you fucking loser? Think that by rubbing my neck and giving me a little kiss then things will be better? You pathetic prick, you really are a fucking weirdo aren't you? Well, I know what to do with muppets that stare at innocent girls."

Leonard had smelled alcohol on Lee's breath as his face had closed in on him and he felt that judging by the way that Lee didn't have a problem invading his personal space that it was *him* that wanted the *little kiss*. But he let this odd thought fade away as he then closed his eyes and concentrated on the hand that was gripping Lee's neck. He was used to imagining golden light surrounding him when he was relaxing, recharging and trying to encourage his brain to use the power that he knew that he and other humans didn't usually touch. But thanks to Burn and the Rector he had learned, after many years of trying on his own, how to harness this and though using it for this particular purpose was against his principles he felt that there was no way out. Lee was clearly beyond help, beyond understanding, beyond being anything other than the type of person that was dragging 21st century England down into the depths of disorder.

Thinking these thoughts suddenly made Leonard feel better about doing what he was about to do. For a moment, everything that made him angry about life was being channelled into the hand that gripped Lee around the neck and he felt a warm glow disperse from the centre of his head and down through his arms, flooding his right arm and hand with a hot but strangely pleasant sensation.

Lee looked at Leonard as if he didn't know what to do next. He expected this guy in front of him to show the fear that others felt when being confronted by him and to maybe beg to be let go. He thought this weirdo would do this at first but now he wasn't so sure. This pervert was staring at him in the eyes and he wasn't sure if he was imagining it but his neck was feeling warmer and warmer. And not only that, but it was getting warmer where this freak had put his hand.

The pink skirted girl ran towards her boyfriend. She was initially pleased that Lee had showed this guy that he couldn't stare at girls the way he did and she always got a thrill from knowing that not many people could deal with her Lee, but this time something was wrong. She had never seen another guy, not even Lee's mates, put their hand around his neck like that and it seemed to her that Lee didn't know how to react to it, for he was now staring, his eyes increasingly wide, at the guy she had felt had been staring at her body.

"Lee leave him! Just leave it! He isn't worth it, just come away!"

The girl expected her boyfriend to react somehow to this plea. Usually another sarcastic remark would come from his lips, but this time the reaction was different. It looked like he was trying to turn his head towards her but failing to do so. He was shaking slightly and staring more and more wildly at the suited man that was holding his neck. Her panic increased as Leonard was now looking at her lover with such intensity and this coupled with what looked like steam coming from the hand of Leonard and the neck of Lee and the strange burning smell that now started to insult her senses, it was all too much and she ran to the two men and gripped the arm that was connected to her Lee's neck.

"Let him go you fucking freak! Let him go or you'll be fucking sorry!"

Neither Leonard or Lee looked at the girl. They just stared at each other but their eyes were telling different stories. Leonard was now in a trance like state with his eyes almost stuck in one position, totally focused on Lee's face; while Lee's eyes now showed alarm and it was this and the spittle that now escaped from Lee's mouth that made his girl lose control.

"Noooo! Let him go you bastard! Let him go! Lee! For fuck's sake hit him, will you fucking hit him!"

The shrieking of the girl was so loud that passers by now stopped to look at what was happening. People rushed from inside of the pub and as they rushed out the way they stopped still before the sight of Lee and Leonard was almost cartoonish as if they had all put on their emergency brakes.

The girl felt that Leonard's arm was made of steel. It was attached to her boyfriend's neck in such a manner that it seemed that it would never come away and the look on her man's face was now causing gorge to rise from the stomach of the woman that loved him. Lee's face was red and becoming redder. Blood was seeping from his nose and from the corners of his eyes. His skin had gone from his normal flushed pink (caused by many years of lager sessions with the lads) to a greyish pallor and for a few horrifying seconds the loyal girlfriend felt that she saw her man's skin start to loosen around his cheekbones.

The crowd around them had started to increase and yet they all stood still, unable to move, to divert their eyes from this increasingly bizarre and disturbing scene and totally unable to intervene, if not from the shock of the scene then from the fear that they too would be set upon by this suited man that was now staring at Lee, with eyes that were becoming bloodshot and protruding as far on their stalks as a pair of eyes could possibly go.

Lee's girlfriend had stopped screaming and with her hand loosely on Leonard's arm was whimpering, tears smudging the mascara that she had carefully applied that morning. She couldn't scream no more, she couldn't even speak, she was struck dumb by the fate that seemed to be heading full force towards her petrified boyfriend.

Leonard was feeling good. He never thought that his body had ever enjoyed such a rush of endorphins as what he was feeling now. He was exultant and even though he knew that his victim was falling to pieces in front of him there was a certain justice to this that just excited him all the more. He had been vaguely aware of the girl screaming at him, what it was she was screaming he wasn't sure, but he was sure that he had felt her trying to tug at his right arm, however, this whole process had left him momentarily within his own world. It wouldn't have surprised him so much as during his moments of contemplation in front of a mirror in many darkened rooms, hours had passed by without his being aware of it. This seemed part of the deal when you were tapping into parts of the human psyche that had never been touched before. To the eyes of Theobald Leonard, there was a golden glow that was emitting from the centre of his forehead and flowing down his neck, through his right arm and to his right hand where it glowed around Lee's neck. This was good, this was normal, this was what he had been preparing himself for over the past few years.

But from a million miles away there was another voice. It become louder and louder as his senses started to lock onto it. There was no ignoring this one as it seemed that it's whole tone was insisting that he should listen and take heed. Slowly, Leonard noticed the sounds of people groaning in disgust and of the moaning of the young, pink skirted girl who by now was crouched at the feet of both men. His eyes started to focus and he saw blood trickling from the orifice's of Lee's face and run down his chin until it dripped onto his pale blue shirt. And now the voice that had grabbed his attention became louder and with a ring to it that he started to recognise.

"Desist Leonard, desist from this action this instant. What are you doing man? Have you not learned anything from what we have taught you? Are you willing to destroy everything? Let this boy go. Desist and return to our base. We shall discuss this back there."

The Rector was speaking in a voice that was not quite the calm voice of reason that Leonard was used to. This time there was an edge to it that he had not been aware of before, a resonance that suggested that Leonard had to obey this order despite any feelings that he may have of being the leader of this operation. He looked up at the face of the speaker and straight into the Rector's burning eyes. Where there should have been sclera there was blackness. Where there should have been sockets and eyelashes and eyebrows there was shadow. Leonard let the feeling of unease pass him by and slowly let go of the suffering Lee to walk in the direction of the Rector's pointing finger, the direction of the building he had left half an hour before.

After being released Lee slumped to the floor and was immediately set upon by his distraught girlfriend. She lifted his head and looked up at the Rector.

"Can you help us? Please, my boyfriend is dying, please do something, call an ambulance, anything, pleeeease!"

The Rector bent down as much as his long body would allow him and placed his hand on Lee's forehead. The girl looked on in perplexity as first of all the Rector's face darkened and then he tipped his head downwards so that she could no longer see what expression he had on his face. Then her boyfriend's body stiffened slightly, as if something was moving within him. Looking around, she noticed that people had crowded in and were now looking on not far from where her, Lee and this strange man were. Then from the back of the crowd someone who had not long joined the throng shouted.

"It's the Rector! People, it's the Rector, so everything is going to be ok. He will save this guy! Let us leave him to save this soul and get back to our work."

"Who's the bloody Rector? And what is *he* doing to that bloke? I think we should stop him. Hey, help me grab that bloke!"

The response from a man in baggy jeans did not go unnoticed by the Rector who continued to work on the unconscious Lee, but he did not allow his head to change from the position that it was in.

The man in jeans and two 'helpers' rushed forward in their concerned effort to save Lee from the Rector but as they got within a few yards of the tall man of God he raised his hand to them, no words from his mouth, no raising of the head, just a motion to tell them to stop.

The crowd looked on and were under the impression that this Rector man must have one hell of an aura about him as the three men stopped still. But what they didn't appreciate was that from the raised hand of the Rector there exuded an electromagnetic force that was causing the men to become unable to progress another inch. Whatever the frequency was of this phenomenon, it gave the impression that the three heroes were shimmering slightly and it was the fact that they weren't as still as statues that caused the watchers to think that they had obviously stopped at the Rector's bidding.

Some of the crowd weren't happy with this development and made their views clear to all and sundry.

"What's stopping you guys? Bloody grab him then!"

"Don't let him stop you. God knows what he's doing to that guy!"

"What do they think they are doing? So much for the bloody superhero act eh?"

As soon as these viewpoints were issued other people now among the crowd issued their opposition to these words. Among them were the men in the football shirts that Leonard had encountered earlier on. These two gentlemen had been on their way to a house close to the pub that the girl had come out of and had become caught up in the throng that had been watching Leonard, Lee et al.

"Leave the Rector alone. He knows what he is doing. If those three want to get hurt then that is up to them."

A man in his late fifties and who was wearing a leather jacket he had bought in the 70s turned to the man in the Arsenal polo shirt who had uttered those words.

"What you mean get hurt? The only person who is hurt is that poor fucker on the floor. Jesus, what did that lunatic do to him?"

"I don't think those three look very healthy at the moment, do you?"

"Eh? They are just standing still, aren't they?"

"I don't know, are they? What do you think my friend?"

The Rector listened to these conversations impassively but allowed himself an inner smile. All these references to God and Jesus intermingled with words like 'bloody' and 'fuck' amused him; if only these creatures were aware of the hypocrisy of their lives that was so borne out by their everyday speech. It was an idiosyncrasy that he didn't understand but one that he recognised as a serious weakness in mankind.

He looked down from behind a dark mist to the face of Lee as his eyes flickered open and he started to cough, blood shooting from his mouth and just missing the long black jacket of the Rector.

"Whoa there young man. You are okay now. We will take you somewhere safe. Somewhere where you can't suffer such an indignity again. Young lady, help your friend up. Come with me and I will ensure that he is totally cured."

The girl's face had gone from the deepest despair to unbelieving joy as the eyelids of her beloved Lee had opened and after the initial bursts of blood from his mouth she had bent down and cradled him in her arms. She looked around to thank this clearly respectful man when she properly noticed the three men that were standing mid-run just before them. Such had been her grief that she had assumed that they had just stopped still but now she saw, as close as she was, that they weren't moving at all apart from the glow around them, a glow that reminded her of a heat haze on a rare English summer's day.

"What has happened to them? Are they alright?"

"I do assure you that these three gentlemen are fine. They just need to have a little chat with me and some of my associates. The important thing is to get your friend here to a place of safety. Come with me."

As he went to move off with the girl and the now staggering Lee, the Rector turned to the three men and made a downward motion with his hand. Upon this sign, the three men that had meant to grab hold of the Rector slumped to the floor, moaning to themselves and holding their heads.

More people in the crowd, upon witnessing this new bizarre sight, decided to make it known what their feelings were, and these fresh outbursts were met, as before, by opinions to the contrary. Soon, as the Rector and his new 'friends' made their way past them, the swarm of people was a fusion of judgments.

"What did he do just then?"

"Yes, we told you that all would be well! Thank God for the Rector!"

"We better make sure those three men are ok. That man is a fucking maniac."

"Hey, you don't call the Rector a maniac. You hold your tongue and show some respect!"

"Respect? For a fucking nutcase like him?"

"You don't call the Rector a fucking nutcase my friend."

"I'm not your friend mate. You mean to tell me that what has gone on was normal?"

"For fuck's sake, if nobody else is going to do something then I will!"

This last statement came from a man in a beanie hat who rushed forward to where the Rector, Lee and his girlfriend were making their way towards the causes HQ. The Rector was even taller than he initially thought he was and it took a bit of an effort to reach up to the man's left shoulder in order to spin him around to face him. But this he did, and the Rector looked at him momentarily surprised as the man verbally spat in the direction of his face.

"Ok mate, what did you just do and where are you taking these people? If you don't give us some answers then I'm going to call the police. This is too weird."

"Weird you say," responded the Rector after a few seconds of collecting himself, "you wish to call the police? And tell me young man, what makes you think that your *police* will help you hmm? We already have quite a lot of those people helping us at the moment and to be honest you would be better off joining them. Instead of being so aggressive why don't you just come with us and see what good work we are doing. I assure you that my friends here are just going to be looked after. Wouldn't you like to be looked after too?"

With an attempted poke in the ribs of the Rector, the beanie hatted man tried to underline his point of view. "I'm not going anywhere mate and neither are you. I don't trust you, know what I mean?"

"And how do you intend to prevent me dear boy?"

"Well . . . . I'll make a citizen's arrest. And anyway, I don't think anybody here is going to let you just go off." With this he pointed his thumb backwards at the increasingly noisy crowd standing near the pub, a crowd that was now causing more and more passers by to stop and stare and wonder what on earth was going on.

The Rector looked at the girl that was encouraging a slowly recovering Lee to walk by himself now and then at the crowd that the beanie hat man had referred to. He hadn't taken too much notice of the sounds that were coming from this bunch of people before but now he realised that they were arguing amongst themselves; that there were clearly people in this mass that had been conditioned and that whilst they were clearly using words to argue their points of view, the others were now becoming more aggressive and had grabbed some of the conditioned people by their jackets or shirts and were talking in ever louder voices into their faces.

He looked around at other people who had stopped in the street and noticed that some of them were talking into their mobile phones, no doubt that at least a couple of them were phoning the police and telling them of this incident near Kings Cross Station.

This wasn't how it was supposed to go. Indeed, he felt that so far, even though there had been some incidents which had angered him things were going quite smoothly. When Burn had spoken to him and their people about using the resources on this rock for their own needs he had been a little bit dubious. Their previous infiltrations on other planets had been successful but then they had been less ambitious. This was never going to be easy but after a great deal of research it had been decided by those on high that if they took their time and used the naivety of this race to their advantage then in time they would gain all that they wanted. Theobald Leonard had been an absolute find, a man that showed complete and utter anger towards his people and who was certain that he was the one that could change things. With some conditioning, or training as he called it, Leonard had proved to be the natural 'leader' to the whole operation. There was something dark about him and what he practiced that made him stand out from others but now after this incident he felt that maybe Leonard was starting to believe his own hype.

When Burn had told him of another such man, this man they called Mick, he seemed a natural choice to be roped into the cause, if not as a deputy to Leonard then maybe, in time, as a successor. This Mick was bitter, confused and ripe for the job in hand, although from what he had been told, nobody had told Mick of this little proposition as he was currently making it clear what he thought of the people currently involved in the cause.

Involving the little girl, her sister and the sister's husband had been unfortunate, but according to Burn it was as good a chance as any to get Mick to the HQ without any hassle. Apparently, Mick's passion for the sister burned brightly and they were sure that someone with such strength of feeling for one person, coupled with his clear distrust of all around him, would be able to direct it to other more worthwhile means.

But for now the increasing noises around him shook him out of this brief reverie and he noticed that the crowd by the pub were now using physical violence and that the beanie hatted man in front of him was still shouting at him in an increasingly hostile manner.

Leonard. Leonard had caused this ridiculous scenario. Where the hell was he now? People were becoming more angry, more on edge and now he heard the sounds of sirens from in the distance. He felt, for the first time since arriving on this planet the emotion that they called anger. It rose up from the pit of his stomach and towards his throat until the heat of it caused his long body to shudder.

So they wanted weird did they? Needed something to take their mind off their petty arguments? These people didn't deserve what they had been trying to do for them and as he grabbed the shoulder of the beanie hatted man he felt all the irritation and resentment that had been building up in him for quite some time. He gazed down at the man who had now stopped shouting. Instead he was gazing up, slack jawed into the space where this man's eyes should have been. Instead there was a mist and as he realised this there was also another challenge to his senses as he became aware of an acrid stench that was creeping up his nostrils and that was definitely coming from this increasingly tall man.

Lee's girlfriend stopped, now a few paces ahead of the Rector, as she too became aware of the tangy odour that was emanating from Lee's lifesaver. She turned back and saw that the Rector was holding a man with a beanie hat by the shoulders and that the man was starting to shake.

She didn't want to know what was happening, she wasn't sure that after seeing what had happened to her tough boyfriend that her brain could handle it, but sheer curiosity made her want to approach the Rector and as she got nearer she felt heat, heat that was somehow unnatural, like the dry heat one would feel in a foreign climate. Hot but in a way that you couldn't put your finger on.

She walked up to the Rector and the man, leaving Lee standing shakily, still a bit fuzzy in the head but now becoming more aware of his surroundings once again. Her mind became full of confusions as she heard the increasing arguments from the crowd, the sounds of aggression versus the less violent responses from people that were trying to back up the actions of the Rector and the sounds of bodies being punched, dragged and slapped.

Then the view before her. The man in the beanie hat. He was shaking more violently and as she looked up at the Rector she could no longer see his eyes. She saw the mist and yet there was now more. Like the clouds parting to show the rays of the sun, this greyish mist now divided slightly to reveal a bright light. From this she looked at the shuddering man and was just able to see that there was a circle of light between his eyes and from what she could ascertain in her muddled state it was coming from the direction of the Rector's mist.

The noise of the fighting crowd, the sounds of ever closer sirens, the shuddering man and the sight of the Rector's face, all culminating in a feeling of such fear now that she felt that her full bladder, the result of an afternoon of serious spritzer drinking, was about to relieve itself in an embarrassing fashion.

The beanie hatted man lost his hat as his body shook more and more violently and now the acrid smell became stronger and more potent and she felt the insides of her nose were on fire. She covered her nose with her hand but could not avert her eyes as the shaking man went dark pink, red then a dark mauve, his eyes starting to bulge until with a sickening squelch they were forced from their sockets. The man's mouth was open as if in a silent scream but the only sounds she could now hear was the fighting crowd and now screams from the other side of the road as this disgusting spectacle became more and more obvious to all.

The sirens got louder and this seemed to have an effect on the Rector whose face tensed up and power seemed to travel along his arm that was connected to the now eye-less man. With the smell from the Rector becoming stronger the shaking man's body gave a sound that in her frazzled mind reminded her of boots trying to free themselves from a pool of deep, wet mud. Then the shaking man shook no more and his body which had also become dark mauve started to dissolve before her very eyes.

Chunks of flesh slid to the floor and clothing of the now late man in the beanie hat collapsed to the same dirty pavement straight after its unfortunate occupant.

Like looking at a condemned tower block brought down by the local council, Lee's girlfriend felt sick rise into her mouth as her eyes refused to stop staring at the steaming pile of flesh and cloth that was now piling up in front of her. The Rector stood still, his arm still outstretched and with a slight shudder to his long body until he became aware of the sound of the girl retching and bringing up the soda and wine that she had so happily imbibed earlier on that day.

Voices from the the crowd that had been fighting amongst themselves, people screaming horror and frightened abuse from the bus stop across the road, and the flashing blue lights as two cars belonging to the local constabulary finally reached their destination. The Rector looked about him and realised that even though there were people there that clearly approved of what he had done, they were easily outweighed but those that his act had sickened. He stepped backwards involuntarily as the police cars stopped and the officers jumped out to ascertain what the hell had happened here.

One officer ran over to Lee who was crawling on the floor, his recent recovery obviously proving too much for him and leaving him to try and make his way somehow to his girlfriend that was now dry heaving close to the tower of gore that had been a human being.

Another officer, PC Aaron Coupling, was staring wild eyed at this gore tower, his face a mixture of questioning, sickness and fear. He was a young man of 27 and hadn't been in the force long. He thought that having already witnessed the effects of three stabbings, two gunshot wounds and the victims of an arson attack he had seen everything already. This, though, would haunt him for the rest of his life.

Other officers were making their way to the crowd by the pub, a crowd that had stopped their in fighting but were now renewing their arguments over what the Rector had just done to an innocent man.

"You are going to die for that you bastards."

"We are all going to die you stupid man."

"And we are going to make sure that you die now. You fucking freaks are sick!"

Sergeant Robert Dickins waded into this potential flashpoint and demanded that there should be quiet.

"Enough! You lot be quiet! We'll sort this out my way if you don't mind. Now, who's responsible for this . . . . mess?" After having seen the pile of steaming flesh too and PC Coupling's reaction to it, Dickins wasn't quite sure what to call this situation. *Mess* seemed like as good a noun as any in the circumstances.

Voices screamed at him in response to his question, so much so that to the ears of the long serving copper there only seemed to be a steady buzz. What he could work out was that there was people in this place that seemed quite pleased by what had happened; they were praising the efforts of the perpetrator, whilst the majority of the others were trying to get at them and enact their revenge. Dickins felt that if his men had arrived a minute later then there would be even more bloodshed and God knows what else.

As it was, Dickins felt that he wasn't being heard. One or two people at the front of this increasingly hostile mob looked at him wide-eyed as if in surprise but the rest of their associates carried on with their arguments and Dickins winced as a middle aged woman was head butted by a geeky twenty-something with wild hair.

"Hey, *that* is assault and you are *nicked* my son! Grab him lads!"

Dickins' authority and orders to his officers was totally lost on the crowd as the limited amount of police tried to wade in and arrest the geek who had taken offence at the lady who had called him "a moron that was just as bad as the other morons who didn't know good when they saw it."

This attempt at arrest only incensed the mass more. As far as a lot of them were concerned what had happened to Lee and the beanie hat guy was vile and if the coppers were going to arrest those that didn't agree with that then *they* were just as bad as those that did agree with it.

Endeavours at grabbing the geek proved fruitless as others got between him and the officers, telling them to arrest that bastard in the long, black coat and the freaks who thought he was so bloody good.

Traffic on the York Way Road that separated the people at the bus stop from those fighting slowed down to barely a crawl as more and more people arrived to see what was going on. Cars had gone from doing 40 mph and swerving past the curious that had inadvertently stepped onto the road because of the amount of people on the pavement to now travelling at walking pace. The backlog of traffic started to build up and the traffic lights that were only a few yards before the bus stop and which staggered the traffic at the junction of York Way and Pentonville Road were deemed useless as beeping horns illustrated the jams that were now starting to occur. Soon the scene would be a mass of annoyed and increasingly aggressive citizens and traffic not going anywhere.

Dickins looks around him feeling increasingly worried. This was supposed to be a shout to break up a drunken fight outside a pub. There were quite a few involved so a couple of squad cars had been enlisted to help but this wasn't what he or the other officers were expecting to be involved in. This was now out of control and as he looked around he noticed people rushing across the road and from both directions of York Way joining in with the fight. He listened in wonder as some of these people were screaming to "leave my brother alone," and "you shall pay for this with your sinful lives." Other similar shouts were met with those he was used to such as "yeah, come on then, you're gonna get your fucking head kicked in." All in all this wasn't right. Whatever the argument was about something had gone horribly wrong and to Dickins' trained intellect it was all about what had happened to that pile of gore that was still steaming just yards away from him.

As for this 'bastard in the long, black coat'? He didn't know who they were referring to but clearly he was the main suspect in this case. As he shouted helplessly at the multitudes of people to "calm down" and "you will all be under arrest," he strained his head to see if he could glimpse this man but there was no sight of a long black coat anywhere.

Dickins looked sharply to his right. There walking towards him, zig-zagging through the throng was a young constable, his helmet slightly askew through being dislodged by more and more animated people.

"You need help sarge?"

"Do I need help? Do bears shit in woods? Get on the radio and call for reinforcements. A *lot of* reinforcement. We've got World War Three here and I don't wanna be on my own when it goes off big time. I'm trying to get these fuckers to calm down."

The young PC strode up to the sergeant and looked him cooly in the eyes. With only an arms length between them he brought out from behind his back what Dickins had just enough time to notice was an M26 Taser gun before he felt his younger subordinate press it against his right temple and fire.

Dickins did not know that the officer had held it to his head and fired for quite a few seconds. As the jolt went through him he had no knowledge of time or that as he passed out he was about to be trampled on by more pairs of feet than would be good for him.

His final view was of the PC and the PC's moving mouth.

"No sarge, I asked if *you* needed help. But don't worry, I can help you. Then we call help all the others too."

Sergeant Robert Dickens, father of three and keen golf fanatic was engulfed as the brawl spread outwards, now growing more violent and more malelovant as others appeared and became involved.

While just around the corner, slumped behind two huge metal council bins, sat a man in a suit and tie, rubbing his head and hearing in horror as the sounds of screams and obvious violence reached his ears. The smell of exhausts grew stronger as he urged his aching and exhausted body to stand up.

Managing to get to his feet he noticed beyond the bins that hid him more and more people running past in the direction he had come from ten minutes before. Some looked excited, some looked agitated and some looked just plain curious. The important thing to him was that he wasn't seen again.

He was wondering what the hell he was going to do next when an arm snaked around the bins almost from nowhere and grabbed his hair. His face was heading towards the dirt and smell of the bin to his right and he knew that this was going to hurt.

CHAPTER TWENTY-SIX

He didn't know want to know what it was that Burn was doing to that young lady. Whatever it was it looked nasty. Although bearing in mind that it looked weird as well, Mick tried hard to think of a word that was synonymous with nasty *and* weird . . . . but he couldn't think of one.

What he did know was that the lady looked terrified and she was looking at Emily as if trying to place the name of a long-lost friend. Emily just looked at her with what appeared to be no expression in her face, but then she decided to raise her hand to the shell-shocked lady and give her a little wave. Mick shook his head slowly in utter bemusement, an action that Emily caught and she looked at him as if she was being wrongly admonished for being naughty; a little scowl that creased her forehead and wrinkled her nose.

"Ah she is such a sweetheart isn't she Mr Rogers?"

Mick didn't have time to register Burn's knowledge of his surname as he came towards the artist, hand outstretched in an offer of a friendly introduction. He ignored the gesturing man's hand and stood where he was, not sure whether he should be afraid of this character or not.

"Yes indeed, she has been a pleasure to have around this here building. And she has such spirit as well! What she did to that young man in the meeting was quite something. But then, I don't think you were here to witness that event were you? Such a shame. You would've appreciated the irony of it I'm sure."

"Whatever Emily may or may not have done is of no concern to me now. I fully intend to get this girl out of here and *you* aren't going to stop me, okay? Not you, not your goons in grey suits, not anyone."

Burn smiled enigmatically as he stared serenely at the graphic artist.

"I didn't say that I was going to stop you from doing anything my friend. Hey Emily, would you like a lollipop?"

From the inside of his jacket Thomas Burn produced a round, orange lollipop that resembled a mini belisha beacon. He crouched down slightly and held it towards the little girl who first stared at the sweet and then at Mick. She then gave a little smile and moved forward slightly as if to take the offering from him.

"Stay there Emily. Don't get too close to him."

"But it is Uncle Tom. He is okay. He has a lollipop for me."

"He is *not* your Uncle Tom, Emily."

"Who is he then?"

"God knows who he is, but I know he isn't related to you. Now, just be a good girl and stay there. I can get you as many lollipops as you like later on."

Emily smiled at the thought of more than one lollipop but the smile on her face broadened even more as Burn coughed aloud to gain her attention. She looked around to see him put his hand in his pocket and then take out three, four then five lollipops, all of different colours.

"Which is your favourite flavour, Emily?" asked the smiling Burn.

"I like orange."

"Ah, I thought so, how did I guess my child?" With this, he put the lollipops back into his pocket and then removed four more, all of them mini belisha beacons. Emily gave a tiny squeal of delight and would've moved to retrieve them if Mick hadn't been holding onto her shoulder. For some unknown reason, Mick couldn't even feel a little surprise at this magic ruse. Somehow, it didn't seem strange that someone like Burn could perform such trickery.

"Let go Mick! I want those sweets. Let me have them, pleeeease!"

"Yes," responded Burn "let the sweetheart have her sweets. What harm could a few little sweeties do? I fear Mr Rogers that you have misunderstood my intentions here entirely."

There were constant voices in the building as people rushed here and there but Mick could still hear footsteps coming towards him. Because of the building's acoustics it was unclear to him from which direction they were coming from, but he wasn't prepared to hang around and wait for the answer.

"Intentions? You know what mate, from what I have seen of this place and from some of the weirdos in it, present company included, this is no place for me, my friends and especially this girl. Now, as I said, we are going to leave so you carry on doing what you need to do and we'll let you get on with it."

"But why the hurry Mr Rogers? You seem to have made your mind up about us already and yet I just know that if you bothered to actually talk to us then you may see us in a way that would . . . interest you. In fact, I am absolutely sure of it. Look, I shall make a little deal with you. Come and talk to me. No pressure. Let us go somewhere where we can discuss what we are all about and why the likes of little Emily are so important to us. If you don't like it then . . . you are free to go about your life as best you please, as best as you can in this world. What do you say?"

From behind Mick there were screams and voices shouting. More footsteps now but these were more hurried and seemingly without any real order to them. As if in response to this, a grey suit rushed from where the din had come from and addressed Thomas Burn. He stood there, shaking slightly, his head covered in perspiration and looking to Mick that he wanted to use the toilet quite badly.

"Sir, I am so sorry, but it's happened again."

"What's happened again? For heaven's sake what is going on back there? Can't I leave you people alone for five minutes without you screwing it up?"

"It's the same as before. Fire started to come from one of the brother's head. He was taking a brother to the conditioning room, just calmly talking to him, when he fell to the floor and his head . . . . his head was just covered in flames. He didn't scream or anything. What the hell happened to him sir?"

"And I take it that the noise that I am now hearing is a result of this . . . . accident?"

"If you mean the screams, yes sir. It was pretty bad. What shall we do sir? This wasn't supposed to happen, was it?"

Burn looked up at the high ceiling of the building that he was starting to resent. It seemed to him that turning this whole endeavour into some kind of religious party was turning out to be a big mistake. It was Leonard that had known of this structure; it had fallen out of use as one of Victorian society's most elaborate of hotels decades before and it did have a certain murky charm to it, but now he was feeling trapped and frustrated and if there was one thing these people didn't want, it was him feeling trapped and frustrated.

He looked at the horrified guard and felt a momentary pang of compassion for this wretched man. For all of his bulky size, for all of his pseudo machismo, he was just as helpless as when he was a baby boy. He was helpless without someone to tug his forelock to and it amused Burn how the majority of beings in this world always had someone to answer to. He was Burn. He was Burn alone. He could fool people like Leonard into their thoughtless thoughts of leadership, but when all was said and done, when their aims had been realised then it would become clear to them all who was running this show.

But for now there *was* a problem. A sound akin to the rumbling of an approaching train was heading in their direction, shrieks imitating brakes rubbing the steel of a track, but this was no locomotive.

Then from the big double doors at the back of this chamber, doors that led to many of the building's rooms and halls, including the hall that was being used for the 'conditioning' of the tens if not hundreds of people that had come through the doors to a better way of life, came the first batch of panicking brothers and sisters.

There was no order to this rush. In amongst the multitudes of people there was evidence of grey suited guards and people in white coats, holding some back, lashing out at others but ultimately failing in their attempts to hold back a mass of people that were showing increasing signs of dread.

Then in a cloud of smoke staggered not just one, but three people who were silently clutching their heads. Blue flames licked around their facial features and the hands that uselessly held the melting body parts. They were surrounded by others but these others were trying desperately to keep away from their burning counterparts, afraid that they too should suffer a similar fate and gagging also at the fiery, unnatural odours that came from them.

Forward they came. Rushing through the corridors and chambers, some scraping against the walls that still had gold Fleur de Lys wallpapers glued to them. Then into the area where Mick, Emily, the guard and Thomas Burn were discussing Mick's desire to leave this place. A stampede that threatened to overcome anything or anyone that was in its path.

Thomas Burn straightened his body and to Mick Rogers it seemed that this guy had actually grown a few inches. It was also obvious that Burn's face was darker, more shadowy and with a definite hint of malice in it. Emily noticed this too and she spun around and clung to Mick's right leg. Every now and then she would peek around at her 'Uncle Tom' but it was clear that she was no longer interested in any orange flavoured lollipops.

Indeed the confectionary was nowhere to be seen now. Burn instead was now standing with his arms slightly outstretched and his palms upwards. His gaze steadily focusing on the hoards that were heading full pelt towards them. When he could see the whites of the eyes of the people in front, Burn's hands went from palm upwards to facing the rushing pack. Mick Rogers wasn't sure what this action from Burn meant but he dragged Emily to the side and behind one of the building's many gothic pillars. He pushed her down slightly towards the geometric ceramic tiles in a strange but caring attempt to keep her out of the way of the approaching mob and also so that she was unaware of anything that Burn was about to do.

Nice one Micky boy, why not just dig a little hole and push her through that as well uh? I mean, what the hell is this supposed to do? You really are an absolute twat when it comes to dealing with kids aren't you? Gawd help any living being that should spring from your loins.

Mick pushed these unhelpful opinions of his sub-conscious away as best as he could. Now was not the time for a self analysis session.

He looked up and saw that the crowd has stopped. They were becoming silent. They had noticed Thomas Burn standing there imperiously and were all staring at him as if they fully expected him to say something. They were not to be disappointed.

"Now, refrain from this madness. What is the cause of this rebellion? We must have calmness and order. You must return to your jobs and to aid our most worthy cause. We have so much to do and this will surely hold us back."

A woman in a red short sleeved t-shirt was the first to offer her explanation.

"Mr Burn. There have many more people in trouble. They have been catching fire for no reason. Our heads are starting to hurt and we are worried that we will suffer the same fate. We want to help the cause

Mr Burn, but we are scared. What is happening to us? Please tell us what we need to hear."

Burn was about to respond to this impassioned plea but Mick noticed that there was a man in black cords, standing only a few yards from him that was in trouble. He wasn't on fire but he had both hands on the sides of his head and was shaking it back and forth as if he was trying to clear water from his ears after a long session of swimming. He staggered forward, his eyes red and watering and glazing his vision so that he knocked into and stumbled over the people around him. He was moaning and shouting and these noises became louder as the crowd gave him room to manoeuvre his way to the front where Burn gazed at his haphazard way of approaching him.

"We shouldn't be here! There is no reason to this! For God's sake, what have you done to me? My head, Christ my head is killing me!"

"No my friend. Stop trying to fight it. We have told you over and over again, you must not fight what you have now become."

"I'm not fighting anything you fucking idiot! This is happening to me no matter what I try to do. I don't know who I am! Who the fuck *am* I? Someone help me! I have to get out of here. These bastards must be stopped!"

Others from the crowd then rushed forward to support the screaming man. They feared his head blazing like the others that they had seen but right now this guy needed support and a mix of the conditioning and their own human nature meant that some of them were willing to give this. Burn looked on at the guy and tried hard to keep some of the calmness that the majority of the people here associated him with. But as he glanced to a pillar to his right, he espied Mick Rogers sloping away from it, dragging Emily by the hand. The little girl's face was pale and it then occurred to Burn that whatever they had done to Emily hadn't held. This was a little girl that had killed in the name of the cause but now she was allowing herself to be taken away by a guy that had more reason than most to support the whole shebang.

How could this have happened? What was causing the heads of conditioned people to catch alight? Where was Leonard? When all of this was kicking off, where was the self proclaimed leader of this exciting new movement?

In the meantime, the man in black cords was getting closer to Burn and now others were starting to agree with what this pain addled brother was trying to say.

"Mr Burn, please don't just stand there. This brother needs help. What is the reason for us being here if you don't help those that are helping you? What *is* the reason for this? What *is* the . . . ."

The speaker couldn't finish his words as he suddenly gripped his head in the same manner as the man in black cords. He opened his mouth but nothing was coming out and the people around him backed off leaving a little space for him to writhe and moan. His eyes rolled around his head like marbles on a flimsy piece of plastic and his right arm reached out to Thomas Burn.

Burn looked around the crowd before him. He noticed the mayhem that was taking place before him as more and more people came through the double doors and these were joined by the curious from the floors above, cascading down the great, fancy stair cases, intermingled with men in grey suits that were pathetically trying to tell them what to do, some on their walkie-talkies, but mostly looking as baffled and as helpless as anyone else here.

Fury was not an emotion foreign to Thomas Burn but in the past he had never felt the need to show it for fear of losing his self control. But standing here in this now despised building, looking out at people that were asking too many questions, watching people drop to the floor with blackened heads that no longer showed any facial features, this was too much. To make matters worse he then noticed that he had been so distracted by the mob in front of him that he had lost track of where Mick and Emily were. They were gone from the pillar where they had been crouching and the pent up frustration and bitterness started to overflow. The one person that Burn really wanted to believe in him was getting away, was refusing to play ball. It was as if Mick had a stronger power inside him that shielded him from what they were trying to achieve here.

Looking at the staircase he saw her, leaning over the banister and looking around in open mouthed bemusement; Maria Weston. He thought of Mick and Maria and started to feel rage. This time he couldn't help himself. This time he was going to show these weak beings in front of him who they were dealing with.

Burn tensed his body and stared into the distance. The crowd before him went quiet as they watched this man that they had shown such a devotion to look beyond them into a place that clearly wasn't there. The only sounds in this cavern of a room came from the whimpering of the people holding their heads and even these unfortunates were aware of the change that had started to take place in Thomas Burn.

A mist appeared across the forehead of Burn. His eyes, or what had been his eyes, were enveloped in this smoky grey fog.

His arms were outstretched again and his palms outwards. From them came a power that was initially invisible to the naked eye but when you looked more closely it was like the air around Burn's hands was like the gentle ripples of water that flow outwards when a stone is dropped into it. These power waves increased in their frequency as Burn tensed even more and to the horror and amazement of those gathered there in the chamber Burn started to rise up from where he stood. His feet left the ground until he was at least five feet away from his starting point, his eyes still fixed ahead of him.

The waves from his hands now spread out and wrapped themselves around the first fifteen people in front of him, including the two that were holding their heads and still moaning at the sickening pain they were feeling. As the waves hit them their bodies froze until the people behind them, backing away all the time and causing those behind them to fall and become trampled on, saw them in a twitching haze, not totally still but clearly unable to control their bodies. Now the moaning men were quiet and from the trapped fifteen the only sound was a slight crackle that you may get from a plug that was about to blow.

Maria Weston looked on. Her face was like stone as she tried to understand what was happening. When Burn started to rise from the floor she gave a little gasp but she still couldn't change the way her face was set. Thoughts of finding Emily were momentarily displaced as she tried to understand what was going to happen next. She felt that Burn had noticed her and she had almost ran down the remainder of the stairs to hide behind the crowd that had assembled but now it seemed that he was busy elsewhere.

Next to her, also leaning over the banister was a guy dressed in a casual shirt and chinos. He was at least 6ft 4in in height and to Maria's eyes he must have been approximating 30 stone in weight. She moved slightly behind this man, peering around him, using him as a shield, a shield against what she didn't know, but her instincts told her that if there could be some sort of barrier between her and Thomas Burn then that had to be a good thing. She noticed that the big man's grey underpants were sticking out from the top of his trousers and that as he leaned over he was showing the start of a massive bum cleft; Maria allowed herself an inner giggle that was totally at odds to the situation she was in, but for that split second everything had seemed less strenuous.

Then all thoughts of the big man's attire left her as Burn opened his mouth and the voice that came from him wasn't the voice she had heard before.

Thomas Burn was a quietly spoken man. He had obvious charm, dark good looks and charisma and if Maria had met him in different circumstances then she would've understood it if his silky tones had been the undoing of many bras and suspender belts. In these circumstances though his tones had been more sinister; his serenity adding malice to what was a troubling and disturbing situation. But the being that was now speaking was not Thomas Burn, at least not the Burn that she had been conversing with. Now, from the mouth of the floating, dapper gentleman came the noise of a demon, the noise of spite, evil, pain and malevolance. Low grumbling laughs and wet, wheezy breath accompanied each word as it spat from the mouth that was the animal that was known as Thomas Burn.

"Silence you cretinous fools. You selfish, ignorant, whining, weak spirited beings of this spinning rock of stupidity. Now watch and wonder and learn."

All eyes now on the fifteen trapped in the waves of power emanating from the hands of Burn. Their bodies shook more violently as the waves became more prominent and now seemed to darken in colour. Then the smell of fire, of smouldering, an acidic stench that caused those in the chamber, Maria included to grip their noses and breathe with difficulty through narrow mouths.

The waves became more tangible and as the face of Burn misted over completely the fifteen people at the front of the mob that had run panic stricken to the revered Burn to beg for help disappeared completely in a spiral of greys and dark reds that rushed around them clockwise. Even those closest to the fifteen could not see through these spirals and despite their speed they gave off no wind, no rush of air that logic suggested you would get from such an occurrence.

Then a roar from Thomas Burn. An obscene growl that lasted long and low and then tapered off into a gurgling laugh. The mist separated from the face of Burn and there beneath was a being that wasn't the gentleman that had seduced Dorothy Trollope with such ease. There floating in the air, looking repulsive as it waggled atop the smart suit and tie that Burn would always wear, was a bright red face with a deep indentation across where the eyebrows would normally be. There was no hair but steam fizzing off it in a style that Medusa would have approved of and a lipless mouth that showed two of the sharpest fang like teeth jutting down from the mouth's opening.

Maria gripped the chinos of the big man in front of her, fear gripping her being and exposing more of the eternal bum cleft, but neither he, Maria nor anyone else would have noticed such a sight as this being that used to look like Thomas Burn throbbed in front of them. This was the adjective that Maria immediately thought of, this creature was throbbing, and the face didn't just look hot but she could swear that there were the waves of a heat haze pulsating from it.

As the gurgling laugh subsided, the spirals that had encompassed the fateful fifteen started to slow down and fade from greys and reds back to the twitching haze and then disappearing completely. To Maria's shaken senses she saw that it wasn't just the spirals that had now departed—the fifteen people that had been swept up in them were gone as well. All that was left was fifteen piles of ashes and Maria knew that even someone without all of her nurse's training would be able to ascertain what those ashes used to be. The Burn creature spoke in its wet, drooling tones.

"You *will* now get back to your duties. You will *not* show disobedience. You *will* suffer the same fate as these fools should you try and deviate from any path other than that which you have all been conditioned for. Fight the programming and suffer the consequences. Show resistance and your pain will be unbearable—*I* shall make sure of that. Be gone, be gone to your positions and work. We shall soon be moving on and we have lots to do. Be gone."

Why wasn't anyone screaming or panicking at this sight? Sure, people looked on in horror and fear but they were doing so calmly as if this was always going to happen and that maybe their own stupid reactions had caused it. How could *normal* people be so blasé about this monstrosity before them?

Maria's eyes had looked up the stairs as this creature spoke, her attention briefly drawn by the moans of "oh my God, what the fuck is that?" coming from a teenage girl, who was shaking her head from side to side and starting to slide down to the stairs as if she was suffering from heat-stroke. Maria's nursing instincts battled with her desire to find Emily and also her need to lift the girl up and try and ease the suffering she was feeling. But then she looked back at Burn as he finished his words and she saw that the creature that had throbbed with its red, malicious face was gone and that the Thomas Burn that she knew was back and now returning down to the ground.

"I'm sorry," said the nurse to the teenager. And feeling that it was against her calling to just leave someone in distress, Maria moved between the people standing on the staircase and down to the ground floor level.

Thomas Burn, now back to the image that these people usually had of him, stared out again at the people in front of him. Some were making their way back to the back of the chamber and those big double doors, helped and directed by the guards in grey suits who wore faces as stunned as those walking, others were standing there, seemingly unsure of what they were going to do next.

Burn wondered whether to dispose of these people there but then caught the attention of other guards. Beckoning them to him with his finger, they approached him cautiously and with distrust in their eyes.

"Take these people away. Put them somewhere safe and I will deal with them myself personally later on. What are you waiting for? Take them all away now!"

Using his walkie-talkie, one of the guards called more of his colleagues for help and the process of removing those that were stunned by what had happened. The guards careful not to walk in the ashes of those now permanently departed, either through disgust, respect or both.

As Burn spoke to the guards, Maria had swiftly and quietly made her way through the passing people and was soon on the other side of the chamber and heading in the direction, that unbeknown to her, Mick and Emily had departed not long before. As she ran she felt a cool breeze on her face and turned in the direction that it was coming from. There was no denying it. This was fresh air and the sweetness of it made her head giddy with excitement.

She had turned into a corridor that had paint peeling from the walls and even more so from the ceiling. There were closed doors to her left and she wondered if something would jump out at her from one of these portals at any given moment and drag her into her own personal hell. Maybe one of the steaming creatures that Thomas Burn was. It was as dark as the rest of the building but there, at the bottom of the corridor was a white rectangle to the right hand side with a shape that seemed slumped in front of it.

As she got closer to the light her heart stopped as she realised that the shape was a guard and he was sitting up against the wall to the right of what Maria now saw was an open doorway, a fire exit whose door had been opened wide and was resting against the left of the opening.

Slowing down her pace she approached the guard expecting him to look up from his position at any moment and tell her to stop. Her fears started to realise as the balding, stocky man did look up at her, but he did not speak. He moaned and Maria saw that he had blood trickling from his nose and ears and he was starting to rock back and forth like he was trying to lose feelings of pain and disorientation. He tried to open his mouth but all that came from it was spittle.

For the second occasion in such a short space of time, Maria felt the need to bend down and help this stricken man, but again she stopped short as she looked through the doorway, felt the cold air and heard the unmistakable noise of traffic and smelt the unmistakable bouquet of a busy, city main road.

Wherever Emily was there was no way that she was going to find her by herself in that place of the damned. For all of her bravery she had no desire to tackle Burn by herself again in case he decided to give her his own personal performance of turning into a fiend from Hell. She would go outside and look around, give herself time to clear her head and think. Then she could decide what to do next.

"I'm sorry to you as well," she said to the guard, who was now looking up at her with pleading eyes.

Walking through the doorway she found herself in a street that she knew was perpendicular to the Euston Road. She made to go around the front of the building and think about where Emily could be. The traffic was roaring past her, and the normality of the scene filled her with confusion. How could such things be happening in that building and yet nobody was doing anything about it? That's if they didn't know about it. Looking at some of the passing people, she wondered if they were actually in with the whole scheme and this thought chilled her even more so than the wind that was causing her bare arms to goosebump.

At the top of the street she turned left into the Euston Road and saw to the left the building of Kings Cross Station. It was then that she saw that maybe things weren't as normal as she thought after all. Judging by the way some people were running in the direction of the station and gazing at the major traffic jam that had occurred at the junction with York Way and Pentonville Road, this wasn't a *normal* scene at all. Not in any sense of the word.

CHAPTER TWENTY-SEVEN

They were standing outside the station, looking around them at the furore that seemed to be spreading in all directions. From their initial observation after they had turned into Euston Road it seemed that the focus of people's attention was around the corner in York Way, yet as they stood there and watched as the traffic slowed to a stop and the general public rushed hither and thither it struck Mick that this wasn't your average rush hour madness.

Sure, there were people who were clearly returning from work or going out with friends but what was disturbing was that there was a lot of talk as well and it seemed, from what he could hear, that you were either of one of two viewpoints: a) that you were going to kill or at the very least badly hurt those that were sick or b) that you were going to defend your beliefs and the way that it should now be. After seeing what he had seen in that Victorian building Mick flinched as he feared that he knew damn well what these conversations were about but still his logical mind refused to believe that all the nonsense could have spilt over onto the streets as well. Then he looked down at the little blonde girl that was holding his hand and looking about her in wonder, her head swivelling one way and then another like a curious little searchlight. Seeing her made him think of the trip to London with the policeman, the officer who told them that he knew where Emily was. Well, he hadn't been lying that's for sure, and if a copper in Southend had been part of that ridiculous charade then who's to say that others hadn't been affected too? He wanted to doubt this whole idea and put it down to an overactive imagination but screams and sirens from York Way made him pull Emily in its direction.

As they turned in and out of the people massed outside the station, they noticed being pinned against the window of the WH Smith a man who was shouting about 'vengeance being against those who refused to believe and help make the world a better place,' while two men in their thirties, sleeves rolled up and eager for action, pummelled him in the face and stomach, each blow rendering his words harder to understand and causing blood to spurt in their direction. The beaten man wasn't putting up much of a resistance and Mick dragged Emily away so as to spare her this brutal sight.

Others walked past this incident, not wanting to see it as, and this is what caused Mick so much sickness in his stomach, it *really isn't their problem, right?* Either that or they knew well enough what this was all about and were going to become involved in the argument themselves.

Judging by other tussles in the street that latter argument had some legs as he saw more and more people being punched and kicked the closer they got to York Way. Individuals were zig-zagging through stationary traffic to get to the obvious flashpoint of this scenario, others were coming from the directions of Pentonville Road and Kings Cross Road. Arguments were heard and flesh was assaulted and in amongst all of this genuinely baffled members of the public were either gawping, rubbernecking or remembering an important appointment on their way to the station.

A woman in a floral dress, in her late forties if not a day over fifty, came to an abrupt stop in front of Emily as she was purposefully making her way to where the fighting was kicking off. Her greying hair was in a bun but one or two strands were bobbing on her forehead looking as if they had come loose from her exertions to get to where she was going. Sweat beaded her forehead as she bent down and glared at Maria Weston's little sister.

"Well, looky here! It's you little girl isn't it? Little Emily! We saw you at the meeting when you helped get rid of that man in the nasty t-shirt. You are so well liked by the Leader aren't you, you lucky little thing. Not many of us will get as close to him as you darling. Hey, Margaret, look who's here—the Leader's little favourite!"

Mick looked in horror as he realised that this woman's loud voice and insistence that Emily be acknowledged was being clocked by a group of men that were standing by the bus stop that let people on and off outside WH Smith's. These guys, who were rather pleased at the aggravation that was taking place, started pointing at the woman and then at Mick and Emily and Mick heard one of them mention the words 'leader' and 'fucking weirdos'; this was not a place for them to be, and holding Emily by the hand even more tightly he turned one hundred and eighty degrees and headed towards the entrance to the main-line station.

"Where are we going Mick? Where is Maria? I thought you wanted to see my sister?"

Mick responded to Emily's question as he rushed them along as fast as he could.

"What *I* want isn't important anymore Em. Surely *you* want to see your sister uh? First things first though. Let's get away from this place and get away from those not very nice men that want to punch my lights out."

"Why do they want to *punch your lights out*? Have you done something wrong?"

"No Em, but it seems that because of your friend out there I have been tarred with the same brush as your other friends in that bloody building. Society is good at that didn't you know? Tarring others with the same brush, regardless of proof or reason. It makes the more insecure and less educated members of the public feel much more important."

"What do you mean *tarring with a brush*?"

"Oh I'll explain it to you later . . . maybe. We haven't got the time to worry about my cracked view of the world."

Looking around he saw the group of men weren't that far behind him and he worried that trying to drag Emily along wasn't going to speed up their escape either. He thought about picking her up and running with her but then realised that coming home with four bags of shopping usually exhausted him; carrying Emily and running would kill him, that's if those men behind them didn't do it first.

Queuing up for entry to one of the platforms was a line of people. A lot of them had seen through the archway that led from the platforms to York Way that trouble was taking place outside and they were keen to get on their train and away. However, as this queue snaked past a pillar that was next to a *photo-me* machine, Mick noticed that a small cluster of young men and women, all in their early twenties, were also staring and smiling at Emily. One of the young women raised a heavily bangled right arm and gave her a little wave, the sounds of the bangles jingling merrily as the gesture was done.

Mick's thoughts momentarily remembered Helen Walters, a large woman who loved wearing all sorts of bangled nonsense on her arms. During all of the recent events he hadn't thought of his work once which was one of the reasons why he wanted to get a breath of fresh air at the sea-side. Well, *that idea was an absolute humdinger, wasn't it eh? You certainly got a break from the bloody routine here didn't you? What next? Bungee jumping from the top of Big Ben with the rope attached to one of your pathetic little testicles? That should be fun and no doubt make you very alluring to women all over the world eh?* That aside, he wondered where Helen and Mr Walters were now? Maybe Helen and Burn would get along famously? He wouldn't have put it past that damn woman. Anybody that was remotely of good breeding and charm would love to be pals with her, she was sure of that.

With a jolt back to the real world Mick rushed over to the smiling youngsters. He didn't stop moving, but slowed down a little to get his message across.

"You know Emily uh?"

"Yes," responded the bangled girl, "we have seen her at the meetings and at the HQ."

"Well, guess what? See those men chasing after us? They want to take her away from the Leader. They don't like what he is doing and want to hurt her to hurt him. Can you believe it? I'm taking her to the Leader now—that's if I can get there!"

"But I thought that . . . ."

"Yes Em, you thought we were going to the sweet shop and we *are* matey. First we need to let the Leader know that you're safe uh?"

"They want to take Emily where?" A young man in an adidas sports top stepped forward to ask this question, but Mick, noticing the approaching guys who obviously had mischief in their hearts didn't feel inclined to stretch the point with them. He trotted backwards away from the twenty-somethings, dragging Emily as he went.

"Can't answer that now my friend. But if you want to gain some brownie points then maybe you should help us out here yeah? All sorts of crap is kicking off out there and *you* are needed. Quick, they're almost onto us."

Without feeling the need to add to this plea Mick and Emily rushed towards the start of Platform One. Mick knew that if they turned left onto this then there were pillars along the platform that may hide them from the guys chasing them. He also knew that towards the end of the platform there was an exit that led to York Way. This exit was used by Post Office vans when delivering post to the mail trains that left Kings Cross Station but local pedestrians also used it as a handy short cut.

As they started along the platform, Mick allowed himself time to look around and see if the youngsters had done anything to help Emily. Sure enough he noticed that the guys had been stopped by the people from the cause. They were pushing and shoving each other and it was obvious that the chasing guys were by far the more aggressive, but importantly to Mick and Emily they had been given more time to put distance between them and their would be assailants.

There was a loud shriek as one of the girls in the group leapt upon the back of one of the aggressive guys that was starting to get away from them to continue their chase of the artist and the Leader's 'favourite'. As Mick looked around at this he found it nigh impossible not to find the sight comical as the angry man tried to shake off the rather determined young lady on his back. She had wrapped her arms around his neck and linked her hands together and this 'chain' was causing her victim all sorts of problems. It made Mick think of articles he had read of how when humans really believe and are determined to do something then they can summon all sorts of strength and power that normally they wouldn't have. There had been examples of people lifting cars off of family members or friends or pets, of collapsed wardrobes being lifted by slight people to rescue others, of the breaking down of doors to get to those in trouble etc. Well, that young lady was clearly up for a fight because her fingers looked glued together as far as Mick could ascertain.

A few more paces up the platform and another quick turn around of the head and this time more people had gathered to see what was going on with Mick and Emily's chasers and the young people that were doing everything they could to stop them from carrying on with their task. This made it even more difficult for the aggressive men as now they also had dozens of people around them and in front of them some of whom wanted to help with the guys' arrest and some of whom, and much to Mick's sinking heart, wanted to help the aggressors shake their hindrances from them.

To their right approached the little opening that led to a small turning that inclined upwards towards York Way. Without any more observations of what was going on behind them but aware of the increasing yells and shouts of distress that were emanating from the site of the *photo-me* booth, Mick and Emily made their way to the main road.

"So what now Micky boy?"

For a brief moment Mick heard the sarcastic tones of Maria Willows and his heart stopped. Then a quick mental check and he realised that the words had come from Maria's little sister and not the woman that he knew he still loved. But looking at her, Mick felt that if Emily had been a short bobbed brunette and not a long, silky blonde then surely she would be Maria's mini-me? Then he registered the girl's question to him.

"Hey, enough of the Micky boy young lady. You may have heard your sister call me such a thing but that doesn't mean that you can too. As for your question, I think we better carry on towards Caledonian Road. I have a friend who lives near the swimming pool. He can hide us until we work out what to do next."

"But what about Maria? What about Pauly? They might be in trouble. I want my sister and I want to see her now!"

"Is that right madam? Well, it's a damn shame that you didn't think of your sister earlier on then isn't it? Oh no, you were too busy making bestest friends with Mr and Mrs Loony Tunes weren't you? Anyway, you don't like Paul, so why should you be so concerned about him?"

"What do you mean? I *do* like Paul. I have never not liked Paul."

"Really? Like him so much as to want to cause him physical and mental pain? You have a funny way of showing your affection Emily. I'm sure he will be made up to hear of how his little attacker wants to be friends with him again."

"Attacker? Why are you calling me that? I love Paul. He loves Maria and has made her happy. Why are you saying that to me?"

Ignoring the twinge that hit his heartstrings as Emily told him of Paul's love for Maria, Mick looked at the little girl's face after her last query and he realised that she wasn't just vocalising a question, she was also genuinely asking him this via the look on her young face. Her bottom lip was quivering and it was clear that she was about to start crying. Whatever it was that Emily may or may not have done to her in-law in the past, it was obvious that she didn't know what it was that Mick was referring to. *She doesn't know what she did to Paul. She really doesn't understand why Paul would be cross with her.*

"What happened in the hall, Emily? What did you do to that guy in the . . . . offensive t-shirt?"

The child looked down at the floor, staring at the yellow line that ran beside the main road, crossing a drain as it kept close to the dirty tarmac of the highway. Her hands went up to her head and she held her temples lightly. Looking up at Mick her eyes had gone a bright pink and tears were coursing down her cheeks. A little blob of snot was flickering in and out of her left nostril, keeping time with Emily's breathing rate.

"What hall? I don't know what hall you are talking about? Why do you keep asking me such stupid questions? Why aren't we finding Maria? I don't think you care about my sister. I don't think that . . . ."

Emily's words trailed off into a wail of tears and Mick, as if by instinct more than anything, brought the lamenting infant towards him, hugged her close and offered her what he hoped were words of comfort. All the time wondering just why on earth it was that Emily wasn't recalling anything that had happened to her recently.

"Hey champ! Come on, you have done well so far. I *do* care about Maria. I think that *you* know that more than anybody. Probably more than Maria herself. But I'm gonna be honest with you here matey, I am confused, I am worried and I am scared. I need help. *We* need help. We have to get away from those types that are in that bloody building we've come from and get some more people on our side. Can you understand that? Then we can start looking for your sister and Paul. Then we will have a better chance, I'm sure of it. Now, what do you say that we try and find that help uh? Come on, you know it makes sense."

With a huge, wet sniff that dislodged the snot from her nose and no doubt was making its way down her throat, Emily looked up at the contrite graphic artist and nodded her agreement; contrite because despite what he considered his next to useless plan of action, he was wondering if maybe he had just got Maria out of his system once and for all then none of this would've happened. Burn clearly wanted him to be part of something and if all of this was kicking off because of his own selfish views then how could he possibly forgive himself? Had he caused all this hassle? Had he caused the death of Jackson? Had he caused the woman he had always loved to be dragged into this horrendous state of affairs? And not just her but Paul (*God damn him*) and the lost little girl in front of him?

Turning left, Mick held Emily's hand and intended to walk to the junction with Copenhagen Street. A right turn there and they would be five minutes' walk from Caledonian Road and the safety *as long as it is safe; as long as his friend hadn't been got at as well* of the house opposite the community swimming pool.

But as they walked there was a rush of wind, a sudden blast of warm air as if a huge truck was bearing down behind them and was about to hit them hard and knock them into the middle of next week. There was no noise, no growl of engines, no smell of oil or dirt, but the force alone left no argument as to what was going to happen if they didn't jump out of the way right now. Emily squealed and Mick's heart hit his stomach, his face prickled with cold sweat as he switched his head around, expecting to see the oncoming beast with its huge windscreen, smoking hot grill and wheels the size of flying saucers bearing down upon them . . . . but there was nothing there.

This didn't make sense. He had felt it there behind them. Emily had too, otherwise why would she have screamed that way? It had come from nowhere but there was no doubting that something was about to push them out of the way. All he could see was the union of many types of traffic at the bottom of York Way at its juncture with Pentonville Road; cars, lorries, buses and taxis beeping at each other and now an endless supply of people rushing around like the proverbial headless fowl, either in despair, astonishment or aggression.

Momentarily hypnotized by this sight of increasing chaos, Mick felt something tugging his right sleeve. He ignored it at first, still trying to understand what was going on with the world, but it wouldn't leave off. It was getting stronger and stronger until he could feel his sleeve sliding over the top half of his hand and then from the back of beyond he tuned into the words of Emily Willows.

"Mick, Mick! Somebody wants to talk to you Mick. Mick? Somebody wants to *talk . . . . to . . . . you!*"

In what felt like slow motion Mick allowed himself to turn in the direction that Emily was clearly referring to and then for the second occasion in that short space of time Mick Rogers, graphic artist and grumpy old man from London experienced his solar plexus performing a triple somersault; then a feeling of sickness and cold panic filled his forehead and tricked down his face chilling his blood and making him feel dizzy at the whole sensation. There standing in front of him was the Rector and at his side Theobald Leonard. Leonard was bleeding quite badly from a gash on his forehead and every now and then he would wipe away trickling blood with a handkerchief that had used to be white and crisp and new and was now an increasingly soggy piece of dark pink and red material that couldn't possibly take much more blood flow.

"No. That isn't possible. You weren't here a moment ago. How the hell did you get here? What are you, some kind of weird magician?"

Leonard tried to smile at Mick but only managed a lop sided grimace. Whether it was because he was in pain from his wound or because he was clearly the one not in control here it was hard to establish. The Rector gazed at Mick and Emily as calmly as ever.

"Magician, my friend? No, I wouldn't say that I am a *magician*. To me, the definition of magician is somebody that is able to produce illusions by deception or even by sleight of hand. What I do is not based on illusion or deception. It is perfectly real I assure you. No conjuring, no sorcery, no enchanting or skills of a necromancer from my good self. Why, I look at your world's constant deceptions and lives full of illusion and see what grief and pain and destruction they cause. Why would I want to add fuel to the fire? Surely you know that for yourself Mr Rogers? I *know* that you feel the same way as me. As *us*."

"I *know* that whatever you have done to all those people that entered that bloody building, whatever you did to Emily, is causing more grief and pain than anything that this world could ever dish out. I don't care whether you consider yourself David Copperfield, Uri Gellar or Sooty, you have no right to screw up people's lives just because you feel like it. You are sick, *he* is sick and that Burn bloke seems to be the sickest of them all. *That* guy isn't right in the head, I just know that."

"He isn't a bloke, Mick."

The artist didn't understand what Emily had said. She was holding her temples again and looking at the Rector, then Leonard then back to Mick. "He *isn't* a bloke, Mick. I don't know what he is, but he isn't a man."

"What are you talking about Emily?"

"I don't know how I know. He isn't a bloke. And neither is he." Now the blonde girl was pointing at the Rector who was smiling as if this revelation wasn't news to anybody. Leonard, on the other hand, was now looking at the Rector with a countenance of bewilderment on his face. Mick noticed that Leonard was not only bleeding from his head but also from a straight cut on the right hand side of his mouth, and he spat out blood as he looked up and spoke to the Rector.

"What *does* she mean, Rector? What is Emily saying?"

"As if you didn't know my loyal friend, as if you really didn't know."

To punctuate this remark, a low, grumbling sound came from the mouth of the Rector and it took Mick a while to realise that this bloke, or whatever it was that Emily was referring to, was actually laughing. Although it was unlike any laugh that he had heard in his life.

Leonard looked at Mick who acknowledged the leader's gaze of dismay. Something had not gone according to plan for this man and it was only now that he realised that some sort of power shift was taking place; that Leonard's injuries had to come from somewhere and that the Rector's coldness towards the man that the people in the HQ had treated with such reverence was not in keeping with their earlier relationship.

Mick suddenly realised the awful truth. It was all across Theobald Leonard's face now and from the smiling eyes of the Rector it was almost that he sensed Mick's realisation, as if it was tangible and he was able to reach out and grasp it—Leonard was now a prisoner. He wasn't the 'numero uno' anymore; he was as helpless as him and Emily and Mick didn't know whether to feel smug satisfaction or pity for this man that looked increasingly broken in front of him.

"I think that you are a lot cleverer that you realise Mr Rogers. I think Mr Burn had you summed up correctly. You really see things in a way that isn't as black and white as normal people do. You really must talk to us but this isn't the place for such chit-chat. Come, I will take us somewhere where we will not be disrupted. It's a chilling little place but rather apt for what we need to discuss. It's not far either. Just 'up the road' as the local natives would say. Come."

Before Mick could say anything in reply, the Rector held up his hands, palms outwards. A feeling of coolness ran through his body and the surroundings seemed to shimmer slightly. Then they were moving. His legs were still but they were moving, all four of them, up York Way and then past the junction with Copenhagen Street.

He didn't know where this creature was taking them, his body wouldn't allow him to have a say in the matter, but when they arrived Mick was just as bemused as ever. What had he just done to them? How was it possible to move and yet *not* move? And why, in the name of all that is normal, would this lunatic have brought them here?

CHAPTER TWENTY-EIGHT

Clasping her head, feeling her body shake and a multiplicity of feelings and thoughts flooding through her mind, Becky Shaw looked around at the people around her. Most of them were heading back towards the double doors at the back of the chamber but there was no doubting that there was now a change in the atmosphere of this place. From feeling that she was involved in something good, she now felt that something had shifted in her mind; that somebody had flicked a switch inside her and she had gone from automatic and back to manual.

Shooting pains shot from her optic nerves to her fornix and down to her cerebellum. Sharp and piercing at what seemed to be two minute intervals. Through all of her doctor's training so far Becky had never come across any description of such pains. Even now, in the third year of her run-through training at the University College Hospital such an occurrence seemed at odds with everything that she had learned so far.

She thought of the people that she had seen whose heads had just combusted into flames. Why was it that when she had initially seen that unfortunate spectacle that she had blamed the unfortunates involved; as if they had been totally responsible for their ugly demise? No, no matter how she tried to square it with herself, she really had felt pity for them but also, and as dreadful as it now seemed to her, a kind of accusatory stance towards them, as if they were causing trouble.

There had been others who had screamed blame at the likes of Burn and Leonard, at the guards and those in the conditioning rooms, but they had been moved off somewhere, probably to re-condition them or calm them down. It had all made sense to her.

She thought back to her first meeting with one of the sisters of this cause. An elderly lady who was complaining of chest pains and also, *and I am very embarrassed about this lovey, trouble down below, you know? Trouble with the waterworks, can't seem to go properly. Can that have something to do with the chest pains lovey?*

She had an unusual surname, something to do with mint. She couldn't for the life of her remember it now, but she did recall that she was such a grandmotherly old dear. Kept touching her on the arm or the hand as she spoke. Every now and then she would look away as if she was thinking about something quite serious, and then she would be back again, smiling her slightly gummy smile and asking the trainee doctor all about her life. How was she coping with her work? Did she have a boyfriend? Was she happy with her life? Didn't she think that the world was such an evil place these days? She was so concerned about her that Becky was rather touched by it all. Shame that other patients didn't show such anxiety for her; no, she was more likely to be sworn at, told that she 'didn't know what she was talking about and that the patient was better off talking to a 'real' doctor.'

As she had left work following another fifteen hour shift, her eyes bleary from looking at too many patients' notes, her brain aching from trying to retrieve knowledge that she had mentally filed away from countless medical reference books, this 'mint' woman had been standing outside the hospital's exit doors, smiling and nodding at passerby and seeming as if she had all the time in the world. She had asked the pensioner why she was standing there when she should've been back in the hospital surely? What had been the result of her meeting with the cardiologist that she had been referred to? The 'mint' lady had merely laughed and told her that she didn't want to be such a *fusspot* anymore; that she was sure that there were younger people than her who needed far more important treatment. Anyway, she wanted to introduce Dr Shaw to a friend of hers. Apparently she had been talking to him about this lovely young doctor and he seemed quite keen to help her relieve the stress from her life. At the time Becky had felt the alarm bells ringing and good sense had told her that despite the old lady's kindliness that she would be better off with Phil, her boyfriend of three years who would be waiting for her at home with a bottle of Pinot Grigio, a homemade chicken lasagne and a night of unabashed, selfless nookie.

But the tall stranger that was friends with the pensioner had such a calming influence on her; had spoken so softly and intelligently and with such warmth that she had been completely taken in. And his *eyes*, his eyes had been, well, spellbinding was a good a word as any. Then life had switched onto automatic and she had felt that these good people were onto something that nobody had thought of before. She had met many more brothers and sisters that were also in on this wonderful opportunity to cure the world. And when she thought of it, wasn't that what she was training to do? *Cure* if not the whole world then at least the world that she inhabited?

But what about Phil? Jesus, she hadn't thought of her boyfriend since that time. Wouldn't he be worried about her? How long had it been since she had last seen him? The thought of this caused more sharpness to arrow through her brain and she felt more disorientated than before.

If she didn't know better she would've considered herself drunk. As drunk as she got on one of her night's out with the girls down the Punch & Judy in Covent Garden. It was always packed in that bar, could sometimes hardly hear yourself speak, but they loved the atmosphere of it and there were always some nice looking guys to be chatted up by—I mean, what Phil didn't know wouldn't hurt him, right? It isn't like she would've taken anyone up on their offers anyway, even if the other girls were free to do as they liked.

But she hadn't touched alcohol in what must be ages. They didn't like the 'devil's juice' in this place and that had made sense to her as well. You were talking to a doctor that had seen the effects of alcohol on many, many ignorant people in the A and E department so she wasn't going to readily argue with that point of view.

She had been standing on the first floor talking to a middle aged man that had come from conditioning twenty minutes or so before. He wasn't feeling good and it seemed that when the Rector had informed the others of her training then it made sense to ask her to comfort those that were feeling shaky after their stint in one of the conditioning chairs.

Then it had all kicked off. There had been shouts and screams from downstairs and as she had gone to investigate what was happening, along it seemed, with most of the others that were in the building at that time, she had had to leave the middle aged man where they had been talking. She had been unaware that as she had gone downstairs he had first sat on the floor and then curled up into a ball, moaning quietly to himself as he held his greying head.

There had been people rushing into the main hall from the double doors and there were also those crowding on the gothic staircase. As she had made her way down the stairs she had noticed that Mr Burn had been in a small clearing, facing a huge crowd of people that looked distressed and confused. Then Burn had changed and she saw something that she wasn't sure that her conscious or subconscious would ever forget; after staring at this creature before them all she had run from the staircase and into an empty, dusty room where she had been sick, her body heaving and trembling with the effort of her body's self evacuation and the remembrance of seeing that red, devil like creature rising from the floor of the main hall.

After composing herself but now feeling lightheaded and panic stricken, Becky had returned to the main hall to see the majority of the crowd returning through the double doors as if nothing had happened. *My God! Did they not see what Burn had become? Is nobody the slightest bit scared here because I know that I am! Oh God yes, I am fucking terrified and I want out!*

Becky looked around the scene before her, looking at all the people going back to their business but also aware of some of those that were standing there as if in a trance and some that were holding and shaking their heads clearly in pain. Then she noticed a brunette woman with a bob, a woman who was clearly not influenced by what had being going on in this building as she shot out of a doorway, clearly looking for some way out. *Maybe there are others here who know what's going on? Whatever crazy spell was put on me isn't affecting me anymore. I don't know what the hell I've been doing, but I know that it's wrong and I'm a good person aren't I? At least, that's what people tell me when they learn of my job. There has to be others here that feel the same way as me.*

She now immersed herself in the crowd, trying hard to be inconspicuous but grabbing people by their arms, their shoulders, their hands, anything to make them aware of her and what she was saying.

"Hey, you have to wake up! For God's sake, don't you see what Burn is? This isn't the way you have to be. They have been lying to us don't you see that? Please don't go back though those doors, please help me get us out of here!"

However, nearly everyone that she pleaded with just looked at her as if *she* was the one that was insane. She felt helpless and more scared than ever before. Well, if she couldn't help others then she was going to at least help herself. She thought of where that woman with the bob had gone and decided to see if she too could find an exit in that direction. If anything, she may find herself communicating with someone on her planet.

But as she made her way in the direction of the woman, Becky felt her arm being tugged violently and soon she was being pulled to a side of the main hall. She looked around and in dismay saw that one of the grey suited guards was now taking her somewhere and her heart sank; clearly her efforts *had* been noticed and now she was in trouble. Christ, what if he takes her to see Burn? Her mind couldn't deal with that, she would go insane first and her alarm overflowed from inside of her until she started screaming at the guard whose vice-like grip was causing her arm to hurt and yet he stared ahead his mouth tight-lipped and with purpose.

"Fuck off! Get off me you fucking brute! You're hurting me! Let my fucking arm go! I'm sorry okay? I didn't know what I was doing! I need more conditioning, I am happy for that to happen! Just stop fucking hurting me!"

To the right of the double doors was what looked like a room not too dissimilar to the one that Becky had thrown up in. The door was shut, but the guard grabbed the brass handle with his free hand and turned it rapidly to the right. He pushed and the door swung open with a rusty creak and Becky was pulled then pushed into the room, the guard following her and rapidly shutting the door behind him. He then pinned the trainee doctor against the wall, one of his hands firmly across her terrified lips.

"Shut the fuck up will you! Stop your fucking screaming and listen to me. *Are* you going to be quiet? Can I take my hand away?"

Becky stared at the guard wide-eyed and fought to gulp down air into her heaving chest, but she nodded acquiescence to the stocky man in front of her.

"Good, now I'm not going to hurt you, but if you had carried on the way you were then I was scared that you *would* get hurt. Listen, you can't help these people this way. I take it that the conditioning process hasn't worked on you?" Becky breathed deeply for a minute, trying hard to calm down her racing heart before replying to the man whose face was only inches away from hers.

"It did . . . . at least I think it did . . . . no, it must've done, otherwise why would I have been here all this time?"

"Is your head hurting?"

"God yes! What does that mean? I'm supposed to be a doctor but this is baffling me. I'm not going to burst into flames am I? Please don't tell me that I'm gonna suffer like those other poor fuckers."

"I can't answer that as I have been worrying about it myself. I've been getting pains in my head too. When did you realise you were, how can I put it? Back in the real world?" Becky didn't find this turn of phrase funny in the circumstances but maybe, maybe if she found her way out of this place she would have a little giggle at it later on, when she had her feet up in front of the TV, a devoted and clearly relieved Phil on hand to bring her whatever she needed as she settled down to catch up with the storyline of Eastenders.

"I don't know. All I really remember was talking to a guy on the first floor, hearing the commotion, then rushing down to see Burn become, Christ, what *did* he become? Why didn't anybody else react the same way as me? Did *you* know about this? You're one of their little helpers, surely *you* know what's going on? You *must* know what that freak is!"

Becky's voice became louder and more agitated as she recalled yet again what she had seen and she felt her outrage building at the liberty that these people had taken with her. The guard went to put his hairy hand across her mouth again but she pulled it away.

"You don't need to put your fucking hand across my mouth again. I'll keep quiet, I promise."

"Just as long as you know that I don't mean you any harm. I don't want any of the other guards coming in here and finding us. I mean, I might be able to bullshit my way out of it but I get the feeling that some of them are onto me and that won't be good for either of us."

"What could they do though? Re-condition us?"

"You think it's all about conditioning do you? Getting people to think for the good of the world? Yes, I have to admit that I was into that idea too. It all sounded so good and I couldn't understand why people like me were needed when surely nobody in their right minds could argue with such a concept. Then I was called to help Burn with a guy that was having trouble holding onto the conditioning process. He kept fighting it. *That* was bad enough as we have seen people just melt, literally melt before our eyes when they fight what they have been through. This guy though had somehow gone beyond that stage and he spat in Burn's face. Burn told me to hold him down onto the floor and then sat across his chest. His face went red, a bit like what has just happened out there but without the sharp teeth and smoke, pushed his face close to the guy that had been protesting but was now screaming in fear and breathed something into his mouth. It was like a shimmering mist. The guy's head went red too and then . . . disappeared; it broke down from melting flesh to crumbling bone to ashes. Then Burn became Burn again and dismissed me. But after that I wasn't the same. I started getting pains in my head and I keep bleeding from my nose and mouth. But most importantly, I realised that what was going on was wrong. I became scared and thought that if they found out about me 'waking up' then they would kill me too. I didn't want to die the way I had seen others die. This wasn't what the whole process was about was it?"

Becky focused on the guard's face and sure enough there were dried streaks of blood under his nose and around his lips. She was surprised that she hadn't seen them before but blamed the sheer panic and terror that she had been feeling.

"Anyway," the guard continued, "I don't know why I came out of the trance I was in but I can't help but think that it was after I saw Burn turn red and kill that poor sod that had spat in his face. If what you say is true then maybe after *you* saw Burn change you too became released from whatever it is they do to the people here."

"But *that* doesn't account for the rest of them that are mooching around like nothing has happened."

"I wouldn't be so sure. From what I can see there are quite a few out there that are bleeding, holding their heads and looking like they have woken up from a long sleep. Maybe they are like me and didn't know what to do and went along with the charade for the time being? When I saw you trying to grab those people I realised what had happened to you and knew that I had to get you safe before Burn or the guards or any other of their kind saw what you were doing."

"My hero!" responded Becky, slightly sarcastically but realising that he probably *had* stopped her from getting caught. Unless though she had made it out of the doorway that the brunette with the bob had gone through. "Did you see that woman with the dark bobbed hair? She looked pretty normal to me. She went through a doorway and I think she was trying to find an exit."

"If you're talking about Maria Weston then yes I saw her go. Thank God nobody else did though. She seemed to get out just after Burn had bedazzled people with his change of persona and people were too busy thinking about that. I hope she got out. And Emily as well."

"You know who she is?"

"Of course. The people here have been going on about her ex boyfriend for some time now, Mick his name is. They seem to hold him in really high regard. Emily was taken as bait for Maria in hope that this Mick guy would get involved too."

"But why couldn't they just approach Mick in the way they got others to join too?"

"Good question. It seems that they have been watching him for ages but why they didn't just put him in that trance like state I have no idea."

"Talking of them, where *is* the Leader and the Rector?"

"I believe they are out of the building at the moment. They clearly trust Burn to deal with any problems and from what we've seen you can understand why. Anyway, you can call me Dan. Guard to the loonies and ex-funeral director."

"What? Funeral director? You *are* joking aren't you?"

"I know! I hardly look the type do I? But I assure you that *is* my chosen career. Well, I say chosen. I work for my father's company, or should that be *worked*. I think I was always going to be involved in it no matter how I grew physically."

"You must care though, I mean, to have the empathy to do such a job?"

"Yes, I guess I *do* care. Let's face it, you would need a heart of stone not to, wouldn't you?"

Becky carefully studied Dan's face and believed that she saw, beyond his chiselled, macho features, the countenance of a person that really did want to think the best of people and help those that needed support. His eyes were dark brown but with a soft glow to them and Becky had always believed in that old adage of the 'eyes being the windows of the soul.' If ever there was no reason to judge a book by its cover then it was right in front of her.

"I'm Becky. Becky Shaw. Dr Becky Shaw, although I've not totally finished my training yet. Maybe the hospital gave up on me when I didn't go back and I won't ever qualify properly now?"

Dan smiled and for the first time backed away from Becky and made his way over to the door he had shut quickly behind them.

"Let's not be too negative eh? I know of someone else who is on our side too. If you come with me then I'll introduce you to him. He's a nice guy although he looks a bit bruised. Try not to let your doctor's training examine his wounds too much—I think his pride has taken a battering too and when you speak to him you may understand why."

Dan beckoned Becky over with his finger and when she got close to him he grabbed her arm again, although not as tight as before.

"Must keep up appearances eh?"

Soon they were back in the hall, now emptier than previously and with no sign of Thomas Burn. The ashes had been swept away and there were brothers and sisters walking around as before. A guard that was leaning against a pillar, talking into his walkie-talkie, acknowledged Dan with a nod of the head to which Dan responded likewise. He then led the young doctor back up the gothic staircase she had come down before Burn's change of face and up two floors to a small room in the very far left of the corridor. If Dan hadn't taken her to this room then she realised that she wouldn't have noticed it before, such was the doorway hidden in the darkness of the corner.

They stood in front of the door and Dan knocked on it five times.

Ten minutes had passed from the knocking on the door. At the time Paul Weston had been sitting at a wooden table, his thumb in his mouth as he nibbled at the nail. Biting his nails was a habit that he had tried to break ever since he was a kid but every time he felt a thick nail on the top of his finger then the desire to chew away at it until it peeled off was just too strong to ignore; especially when he was feeling as tense as he was now.

Every now and then he looked around at the mildew on the walls and at the darkened patches where dampness had collected behind what used to be raspberry coloured wallpaper embossed with the figures of lions, monkeys and giraffes. He was sure that in its day this decor looked rather fetching, somewhat cool for its age and in keeping with the high quality clientele that this building may have entertained. Now the room was tatty and empty apart from the solitary table and three cherry wood chairs with high backs and padded seats that were torn and dusty. Paul was perched on one of these, occasionally rocking it back and forth after he realised that one of the front legs was shorter than the others.

The only item in the room that could be termed modern was the pack of cards that were in a pile in front of him. He had played four games of solitaire but lost every time. Whether this was because he kept wondering what was going on with the noise from downstairs or because his face was throbbing from the beating he had received he wasn't entirely sure.

But now Paul was standing by a dirty window that if you could get past the thick, translucent grime looked down onto Euston Road. His eyes were on a lady in her mid twenties who was sitting in the chair that he had vacated and he was listening to the voice of Dan. Dan was the first person in this damned building that he had taken a liking to. It had been him that had burst into the room where Paul was being punched and kicked after Maria had run out on her quest for Emily. He had been on the floor, feeling the big man's neatly attired right foot making repeated hard contact with his liver and ribs. Even taking the foetal position hadn't stopped the brute from badly hurting him and he hadn't wanted to take his hands away from his face as that part of his body had already been used as a punch bag and he knew that the moment he did that then he would taste shoe leather and blood and feel loose dentine and enamel rolling around inside his hurting mouth.

Dan had grabbed Paul's attacker by the back of his jacket collar and pulled him back. It was testament to Dan's strength that he had managed to dislodge such a large man from the task that he was clearly enjoying. When the guard had spun around to face who had grabbed him, Dan immediately went on the verbal attack.

"*What* do you think you're *doing*? For God's sake, have you been given permission to kick the crap out of this man? Do you know what trouble you could get yourself into? Have you not seen what happens to those that go against the rules of this place?" The guard had looked at Dan oddly as if he wasn't quite expecting him to say such a thing, but Dan's face was resolutely frozen in a look of anger and the guard told

himself that it was only concern at a colleague's fate that was making
him so infuriated. The guard straightened his grey jacket and trousers
and stood almost to attention in front of Dan.

"I'm sorry, you are right. But you don't know what shit I have taken
from this git and his sodding missus. They kept winding me up and
winding me up and when she fucked off through that door I just lost
it. Sorry, don't say anything to the leaders will you?"

"What do you mean she 'fucked off'? Did you let her go then?"

"No! I mean, I didn't mean to. What I mean is, they kept taking the
piss and . . . well, I should've kept my cool and I lost my concentration
and she . . . ."

"Fucked off through the doorway. Yes, we've established that. Look,
I don't know what has happened here but I do know that battering this
bloke isn't going to help. It certainly isn't going to help you. You better
get a drink and calm yourself down. I'll take care of this joker."

"Yeah you're right. Try not to hit him though. He thinks he's clever
this one and he will try and wind you up."

"Ok, I have taken your advice. Do as I say and not as I do uh? Go
on, get lost!"

Paul had remained where he lay when that conversation took
place and despite the new guard's annoyance at Maria's husband being
beaten up, Paul wasn't convinced that this new hulk would treat him
any less lightly. He had been baffled when Dan had picked him up off
the floor by the arm and looked at his injuries with clear concern. His
bafflement had turned into complete confusion when Dan had told
him of how he was on *his* side before telling the story that he would tell
Becky Shaw later on. To the eyes and ears of Paul Weston, Dan seemed
genuine. Okay, he was wearing that boring grey single breasted suit
that all the other guards were wearing but you could tell that there was
a genuine sense of purpose in this big guy's manner and it clearly had
nothing to do with helping the cause any more.

And now in the room, after introductions and explanations were
Dan *and* Becky. Becky was absent mindedly turning over the cards that
Dan had left Paul to keep him amused while Dan answered the call
from his walkie talkie and went downstairs to the uproar in the main
hall. He had moved him to this new room because it was definitely
one, according to Dan, that nobody had ever used before and weren't
really likely too either. Although, from what he had seen, most of these

rooms looked as bare and musty as all the others so how would you be able to tell the difference?

As he listened to Dan's low but strangely comforting voice *do people who work in the funeral business develop naturally caring voices? Weren't they supposed to sound creepy, a bit like Uriah Heep? Or was that some misconception from a comedy sketch show he had seen?* he wondered why it was that if he and Becky had been zapped in the conditioning room, as he assumed they had been, then why were they now looking for a way out of this place? And they were both suffering from pains in the head. As if to emphasize this Becky dropped one of the cards and planted her hand on her right temple. She breathed in sharply through thin lips and her face grimaced. He had noticed that both her and Dan were prone to do this but this was clearly a bad shot of pain.

"Are you okay?" The funeral director looked at the student doctor with concern.

"Yes, I'm . . . . okay. Just caught me unawares that one did."

"You keep getting them though. Do you feel sick too?" asked Paul.

"No, well maybe a little bit, especially when they are as bad as that last one, but not all the time."

"Does it feel like a migrane?" continued Paul.

"Erm, sometimes. Ha, I thought I was the one that was trained to make medical diagnosis? Anyway, I can't describe it really. To be honest with you I feel that my brain is trying hard to break through my skull. There is a real pressure there. Back in the good old days of medicine doctors used to drill holes in heads to cure headaches. I think that if you were to hand me a drill now then I may be tempted to do that. Just a quick piercing of my frontal bone and watch the air escape and my face smile as the pressure subsides!"

"I can totally understand that. My head feels the same," agreed Dan.

"Okaaay. So that's two drills for my new friends then. Would you like chips with that?" joked Paul.

"Oh I will have chips," responded Dan, "I intend to have the biggest packet of hot, salty and vinegary chips that I can get my hands on. Trouble is, the chip shop is out there and we are in here."

"So why don't you just go out and get some then Mr Guard? Unless you are being held against your will?" Becky had asked a question that Paul was thinking of.

"Not exactly against my will. But Becky, you must understand as well as me that when you are under the influence of the conditioning then going for a nice bit of cod and chips isn't number one on your agenda. They feed us here and we do our duties. It makes sense when you are . . . ."

"One of the zombies!" completed Paul. Dan gave him a serious look and Paul felt that he had been out of order with that last exclamation, but before he had the chance to apologise in an abashed manner Dan's mouth went up at the edges and a deep laugh came up from the guard's chest.

"Yeah okay! I suppose to you we are zombie like in appearance. But that's another thing. I don't feel inclined to just run out of here and as far away as possible. I feel that I have been, if not an instigator, then at least an accessory to the crime. Surely I can do *something* to help the poor sods here?"

"And you are going to challenge the flying, murdering, alien vampire that is Burn are you?" queried Becky with a look of distaste on her face.

Paul looked up at this comment. "Sorry? Did you just say *flying, murdering, alien vampire?* Could you just run that one past me again?"

Becky looked as if she wished she had kept her mouth shut but with a nod of agreement from Dan she told Paul what had happened downstairs. Of the creature that Thomas Burn had become and of the victims whose only crime was to be standing at the front of the crowd.

Paul Weston walked back and forth across the room. His hands now gripping his hair and his voice starting to get higher with the force of his concern.

"And you never told me this before? What about Maria and Emily? They could be anywhere and now I know that it isn't just a mad man we are dealing with but a mad *thing!*"

Dan stopped Paul from his marching and held him gently by the shoulders.

"I told you that Maria went out the doorway. She wasn't affected by what Burn had become."

"But that doesn't tell me anything! That doesn't tell me that she is now safe and sound. God knows what other freaks there are in this hell-hole. If Burn is one then maybe the others are too. How do I know that she wasn't grabbed by someone and taken to Burn? How do I know that Emily isn't being subjected to all sorts of crap."

"Because you know that the leader thinks a lot of Emily. She won't be hurt."

"And Maria?"

"Your wife is strong willed Paul. We have all become aware of that, and while she is the sort of person that would wind even Burn up the wrong way I can't believe that the leaders would hurt her; why would they when she is Emily's sister?"

"Why *wouldn't* they?"

"My guess is that they don't want to affect the way that Emily has been conditioned. Maybe because she is young and her mind is so fragile. One thing I know is that any children in this place have not been harmed and if Maria was to get hurt then that may have a bad knock on effect in Emily's mind. As I say I'm guessing this, but from what I've been aware of I think it is an educated guess at the least."

Paul shook his head and moved away from Dan who was looking at Becky as if for some support.

"I'm sorry Dan. You seem a decent guy and you stopped me from being kicked half to death but I can't just let guesswork, educated or not, stop me now from finding my wife and sister in law. You gonna help me with this or not?"

Becky Shaw stood up and was soon standing by the panicking Paul Weston.

"Hey, we *will* find them. I think that if anyone can help you Paul then Dan is the man. He knows things about this place and that knowledge will be invaluable to us. As far as the others are concerned he is a guard doing his duty. Can you imagine how useful that is going to be?"

Dan looked at Becky as she spoke his name. He had been thinking about what Paul had said about guesswork and also what he had said about fragile minds; something about the connection of those words hit him hard. Not so much a light bulb moment but at the very least a mental whack around the brain cells with a neurological brick. Becky caught the new, wide eyed look on Dan's face.

"What Dan? What have you thought of?"

"I can't be sure that I am right. God knows I am no doctor like you Becky. But if I don't try this out then I may regret it for the rest of my life."

"Regret what?"

"We have to go downstairs. Not now but in a few hours time when most of the brothers and sisters are sleeping or out of the building. That room will be empty for at least a couple of hours, it always is. They like to stop the process to give the machinery a chance to cool down. I mean, they have used it enough times recently and Burn said himself that even something as 'genius' as that needs to be rested."

Paul's face was a combination of confusion and annoyance.

"Ok Dan, now talk to me in English. What room? What machinery? What bloody process?"

"Oh you know what I mean Paul," replied Dan. "You have seen it for yourself. We should hide out here for awhile. I'll get some food and drink and make sure that anybody coming our way is sent elsewhere. It's just as well you are a doctor Becky Shaw, as I think you may prove to be really useful when we start fiddling about with all the knobs and switches."

Becky looked at Paul and shrugged her shoulders but the face of Dan was resolute. Whatever plan was in his head, Paul reckoned that it had to be better than their current one of doing nothing.

Then he realised what Dan was talking about. There was only one room where Paul had seen lots of 'knobs and switches' and he suddenly felt very sick at the thought.

CHAPTER TWENTY-NINE

She had got as far as the junction between York Way and Pentonville Road, her eyes wide open in apprehension as she saw more and more people appear from every direction with so many of them either hitting others or being assaulted.

She wondered where the police were; surely there should be a whole band of them somewhere, holding their plastic shields, wearing their helmets and rushing forward en masse in a hopeful attempt at shepherding those that were disrupting the peace, like gangs of uniformed collie dogs intimidating their sheep and quarry.

There didn't seem to be any uniformed officers anywhere—but then she looked across to her left towards the magnolia painted walls of the snooker hall, a place where Paul had been a member in the past, a place for a good game of snooker, a pint or three and some burger and chips. But outside the club's small door (so small that if you didn't know it was there you would probably walk straight past it!) there were policemen fighting with the public (not *controlling* she had to remind herself, but actually *fighting*) and then, and more disturbing, another officer smashing a colleague around the unprotected head with what looked like a rusty metal bar. Blood spurted from the attacked officer as he went down in a slump, his face looking stunned and his ex-work mate rushing off to no doubt take a pop at somebody else.

To the right of the snooker hall, in the middle of the junction with Kings Cross Road and standing on a traffic island were two teenage girls, looking no older than eighteen. They had a guy in his twenties pinned against the metal barrier that stopped people from crossing the road at a dangerous place and were slapping, scratching and kicking him. The guy's face also looked dazed and it was bloodied with the effort of fingernails on skin; there was the impression that somebody else had already hit him and that the two girls were just 'finishing off' the job. What was bizarre and disquieting was that every now and then one of the girls would put her hand down the front of the guy's jeans, squeeze his package and then laugh maniacally at her friend before continuing with the beating.

Across from the island and outside what used to be the station for the Kings Cross Midland service, four young men and a woman that looked in her late fifties were being barracked by three gentlemen in sharp suits and carrying suitcases. They were clearly city types, their hair short and tidy, their shoes polished until they were mirrors and an overall impression of doing rather well for themselves. Their manners didn't seem to go with the picture though as all three prodded the men and woman, snarled and spat at them and made it quite clear that their sort weren't welcome around here. One of the city types was heard to shout in clipped tones that "you lot are nothing but pests, you think you can take over and spout your shit and turn others into morons too? Well, fuck you!"

There was no violent physical contact between that little crowd yet, but as one of the victims stumbled backwards against one of the ex station's glass doors, their legs slightly buckling underneath them, Maria Weston decided that she didn't want to see what was going to happen in that area and turned around to walk a bit further up the Pentonville Road.

Then from a turning on her left rushed a man in a baggy sweatshirt that had seen better days and khaki trousers that were clearly too long for him as the bottom of the legs covered the person's trainers. If it wasn't for the rounded, white, rubber toe cap giving the game away then it would've been difficult to know if footwear was being used at all.

This fellow had a mass of brown hair that was curly and clearly hadn't seen a brush or a comb in ages. He was moving at such a speed that he initially didn't see Maria and he rushed full force towards her. Maria closed her eyes tight and tensed up her body in preparation for what was going to be a painful collision. But just at the moment of impact, the guy stopped with such suddenness that Maria had felt that he must have some sort of breaking device in his feet that other less mortals are not blessed with. He wobbled a little bit forwards and then backwards as he held Maria's shoulders in an effort to steady himself.

The nurse backed away a little so that she wasn't being held by this rough looking character but she had the presence of mind to ask the burning question that had been buzzing through her mind ever since she had turned into the Euston Road.

"Hey, what's going on? Why is everyone fighting each other? For Christ's sake, it's fucking bedlam out here! And the fucking police too!"

Before he answered, the curly, dishevelled man turned to look at someone who was obviously his friend as they raced past him. This man looked just as scruffy as his mate but at least his blackened jeans fitted him and his grimy used-to-be-white trainers were available for all to admire.

"Come on Scaggsy! We have to get involved in this! It's fucking kicking off big time my son!"

"Yeah I'm coming, I'm coming, nearly knocked this bird over for fuck's sake!"

Maria ignored what she now considered the archaic use of 'bird' to describe the female form and felt a sudden rush of frustration as Scaggsy went to follow his partner in crime with relish.

"Hey, Scuggsy or whatever your sodding name is, I asked you a fucking question, you deaf or what?"

Scaggsy stopped in his tracks almost as quickly as he had halted before and turned his unkempt head around sharply.

"What you fucking say?"

"I said, what the hell is going on here? Where are you and your mate going to? What exactly is 'kicking off'? Why are people kicking the crap out of each other?"

Maria then thought that her impulsive comments were going to be her undoing as Scaggsy walked towards her and opening his mouth to speak he showed that he only had four teeth in his mouth: two yellowing, central incisors at the top underneath his scabby lips and two yellowing, chipped teeth at the bottom—a central incisor and a premolar.

To Maria's relief Scaggsy didn't go to hit her but it was obvious that he was pumped up (and on something?) and he responded to Maria's question with a jerky impatience.

"You're joking right? Where have you been girl? Haven't you heard of those dodgy geezers going around and trying to get people in that big church? They are well fucking dodgy and make out like they know better. And now someone has been splattered all over the floor by one of them. You *must've* heard about it. Everyone else has."

'That big church'? Was this guy talking about where she had just escaped from? How could the actions of so few have affected so many whilst her and Paul had been looking for Emily? But then, when she thought about it, had she really *escaped* from the building? Okay, so there had been guards there to insist that they went to certain parts of the building but when she thought about it there weren't exactly bars and cells to stop everybody else from doing what they wanted to. Actually, the people there seemed pleased to be doing their jobs, tasks, roles, whatever they were; there was definitely the feeling that people were pretty well coming and going as they pleased. And hadn't she got out without too much hassle? Apart from the sight of that agonised guard on the floor of course.

As these thoughts raced through her mind she had become unaware that Scaggsy had started to make his way back to his friend.

"Hey hold on! Hey, Scuggsy! Who's been splattered and how does *everyone* know about it?"

Scaggsy about turned once more and Maria could tell that he really wasn't in the mood to have a conversation with her.

"I don't know the name of the bloke do I? Bloody hell woman, we were told by our mates who were told by their mates who saw it happen. Fucking nasty apparently. Loads of people are bundling in now. They wanna watch it these twatting do gooders."

Do gooders. Well, she supposed that there was a self-satisfied smugness about the way the folk in that 'big church' had been. She knew now that those nasty looking contraptions in that large hall towards the back of the building had something to do with the way that they were behaving, but how do you explain *that* to so many people, especially when it seemed like World War Three was about to be a result of Leonard's wish for supreme leadership?

A cry or was it a howl from further up the Pentonville Road. Maria noticed that it was coming from a person who was staggering from the direction of the cemetery that had the burial place of Joseph Grimaldi. The pain ridden man was being helped along the pavement by a long haired woman who was staring at him with concern. It didn't surprise the nurse that he was holding his head, rocking backwards and forwards as he tottered along and that blood was coming from his nostrils in jets of claret. The long haired woman was pathetically attempting to control this blood flow with a scrunched up piece of tissue paper, bits of which were falling to the floor. The man's helper spotted Maria as they drew closer together and she sped up a little to get to her quicker.

"For God's sake sister help my friend. He is in so much pain. He can't stop bleeding and I think he's going to pass out. Help him please!"

Maria registered that she had been called 'sister'. Clearly the long haired woman had been got at by Leonard's gang and from the looks of him so had her friend. But seeing so much blood downpour from the man's nostrils made Maria think of that room with the special chairs again and she recalled the sight of the man called Jeffrey, whose skin had turned grey and had literally slipped off of him. She would never get that vision out of her head. If she didn't help this man would he suffer the same fate? She wasn't sure that her stomach or her sanity would be able to deal with such an experience.

"Look, I . . . er . . . I don't think that I am the person that can help your friend. He needs to get to a hospital and quick. Grab a taxi and get to the UCH, that's the nearest one."

But the long haired woman wasn't to be shrugged off as easily as that; she rushed forward and grabbing Maria's arm pushed her face forward until there was only a couple of inches between their noses.

"Noooo, you *can* help him! I have seen you around and I *know* that you can help him! Please help my friend. He needs your help sister!"

The woman's eyes were wild and to Maria, as far as her medical training would allow, it looked like her pupils were dilated just a bit too much. There were definitely red, jagged lines around the whites of the eyes, so vicious looking that they gave the eyes a pink glow about them. And the mouth of the long haired woman was set in a scowl and it seemed to Maria that if you had been watching her face with the sound off then you would've assumed that she was about to attack the nurse. Maria tried to release her arm from the increasingly passionate lady.

"You haven't seen me anywhere and I'm *not* your sister and I *can't* bloody help you!"

"You *are,* you *are,* you *lie* to us! Why do you lie to us?"

"Why the fuck do you think I'm lying to you? I don't bloody well know *you* so why the hell would I lie to you?"

"Ah, but you have been with the leaders and nobody gets to the leaders like that without being important. *That's* why I *know* that you can help us. So FUCKING HELP US!!"

With her long hair now tossing to and fro and sticking to parts of her face because of the sweat, the woman's face was starting to show signs of what Maria could only term as insanity; she was clearly concerned about her friend but surely to be challenging Maria in such a way was just losing the plot?

But what was all this about being seen? Christ, if this unhinged woman believed that Maria was in cahoots with the likes of Leonard and Burn then who else did as well?

"Hey, I'm sorry, I really am that your friend is in trouble, but I *really* ain't who you clearly think I am. I'm not exactly friends with Leonard or Burn or anybody else in that bloody building. I didn't ask to be there for God's sake! You clearly thought differently from me otherwise you wouldn't be calling me your bloody sister! Now get the . . . fuck . . . off . . . of . . . me!"

Wrenching her arm away, Maria turned back towards the direction of York Way and made to leave the ever manic woman behind. Then there was a scream and Maria just knew, even without turning around, that it had come from the long haired lady and it wasn't just a scream of frustration; this was also a scream of agony.

As she walked with ever increasing speed up the Pentonville Road, retracing her earlier steps, Maria slalomed past people that were either angry, scared or just non-plussed about the whole scene in front of her. If people weren't screaming with anger or fear then there was also the increasing sound of those bellowing in pain. Whatever had been done to these people in that room was having serious consequences for some of them.

The traffic was now at a complete standstill at the junction and the anger of drivers, getting out of their cars and road-raging their opinions about this situation just made the prospect look even grimmer. There were even drivers, who could clearly see from their positions that those cars in front of them couldn't go anywhere even if they wanted to, and yet they beeped their horns in fury and told the drivers in front of them that they doubted if they had had any parents and that they were clearly shit at driving.

Then there were those who were clearly revelling in the attacking of innocent people; those that, it seemed to Maria, who were going around with their own dubious opinions of right and wrong and were using whatever the hell had happened around here to let loose their own in-bred anger and spitefulness; idiosyncrasies that had always been there underneath the surfaces of these people but had been unable to come to the top because the right circumstances had not allowed them to; this was a circumstance, as weird and as scary as it was, that was manna from Heaven for these types of people.

Seeing these sights depressed Maria Weston even more, to the point where she wondered if the likes of Leonard may have hit upon something that made sense? *Just a shame that they had to go about it in such a despicable and stupid way though.*

The sounds of police and ambulance sirens rifled through the air but just where these vehicles thought they were going to stop was anyone's guess.

On the corner of York Way, outside the newly opened McDonalds and a building that used to be the very finest of grubby bookmakers (and one that outside its door you often noticed the local ladies of the night plying their services to those that needed secretive or desperate relief!) stood youngsters munching into their burgers, the flimsy paper that came wrapped around the food being allowed to fall to the floor without any notice from the devourer of the victuals. A normal sight under any condition; but usually you wouldn't see the said youngsters scoffing their patties in a bun whilst observing a pensioner standing between two squabbling men, one of whom was asking the other one what he had done to deserve a 'smack in the mouth' and that maybe if he had come with him to the meetings then he would understand why what he was thinking was so wrong. The other man was trying to get around the pensioner and 'smack the mouth' of the questioner once more but the senior citizen was doing a stout job in stopping the man from doing so.

"You were my friend! Why the fuck are you talking like that? I *knew* that something was wrong with you. You took me for a prick and I don't fucking like that!"

"I *didn't* take you for a prick Matt, I just wanted you to come with me to one of the meetings. I *know* that you would've enjoyed them."

"*Enjoy* them? For fuck's sake, they've really got to you man! Who are these bastards that have fucked you up?"

The pensioner was on tip toes in her fur trimmed slippers and was standing in front of the guy being threatened. She had to look up at

Matt as he towered over her five feet one height and as she spoke there was calmness in her voice and as Maria listened to what she was trying to say she felt that there was an undercurrent of malice in those tones. It was all too absurd; a sweet looking, innocent old lady and here she was comparing her voice to that of Christopher Lee when he was in his Dracula role heyday.

"This really isn't called for. Why do you want to hurt your friend when all he wants to do is help you? Now, please my dear, just listen to what he wants to say. Can't you see what is happening around here? It's all unnecessary. Please, let's be friends. Maybe we can stop all this fighting?"

"Yeah right! Maybe if one of your lot hadn't killed an innocent guy and tried to kill some others then this wouldn't have happened. You lot should've kept yourselves to yourselves what with your holier than thou attitudes. This has been coming for a while. Well, hope you're happy old girl because you lot are fucked!"

"Really, there is no need for such language! You should know better than to . . . ."

"Oh fuck off you old biddy!"

The pensioner had no chance to complete her sentence as Matt grabbed hold of her and with as much strength as he could muster he threw her to the floor. The elderly one screamed in shock as she hit the dirty pavement; her right hip first making contact before she scraped skin off of her right hand as she tried to stop herself from falling even heavier.

Maria rushed forward to the old lady as her professional instinct kicked in once more.

"My God, are you alright love? Let me look at your hand."

But the pensioner, as she sat up among the thrown away detritus of the capital city just stared at the nurse and as Maria bent down and lifted the hand that had little beads of blood and dirt speckled about the palm, she gave a little smile and reached out with her other hand and placed it over Maria's knuckles as if to stop her.

"That's very sweet of you dear but I'm fine, just a little scratch. *You* need to look after yourself, that's if you didn't know that already."

The intake of breath that the pensioner made didn't convince Maria that this lady *was* fine, but it had been her words that had stopped the staff nurse in her tracks; the old lady's eyes looked the way someone's might if they were enjoying the pain-killing after effects of a nice dose of pethidene or even morphine and that wasn't right. She looked subdued and despite the pain in her hip and hand it was apparent that Maria was now the sole focus of the lady's attention and feeling a shudder creep through her spine the nurse quietly stood up.

She ignored the sight of Matt punching his ex friend and the shouts of the youngsters who were encouraging Matt, through burger filled gobs to 'yes, fucking get the gay bastard' and walked back towards the station, now feeling more helpless and at a complete loss than ever before. What did the old woman mean by her looking after herself and that she should *know that already?* The only person Maria Weston should be looking after was her darling sister and look what a mess she had made of that!

Maria stood in the street, buried her face in her hands and allowed a few tears to trickle down from her grey eyes. Against the soundtrack of the melee that was going on around her she heard in her head Paul's accusation that she would always twist what he said and find 'ammunition' to use against him. She had also remembered the way that Mick had looked at her when they were in that building; after all these years, he *still* spoke and looked at her in the same way, as if all the intervening years had meant nothing and that to him time had just stopped still.

Paul had been hurt when she had questioned him about Emily's accusation and Mick was clearly still hurting about the way they had split up and his constant, unending it seemed love for her—not that she totally blamed herself for Mick's feelings. She couldn't be blamed, surely, just because somebody was suffering from a severe case of unrequited love, even if she had been the object of his desire? She supposed that she *could* have stayed with him longer, but in the end she would've started to resent and even hate him—surely he was intelligent enough to realise that she had made the decision for the good of them both?

Whatever the situation, it seemed to Maria that she was very adept at hurting people that loved her. Maybe *this* was a payback for what she had done? Maybe Emily's involvement in this escapade was somebody trying to prove that when it came down to it she wasn't the good person that she thought she was; that really, deep down, she was selfish, cold and not capable of appreciating the affection that others felt for her and certainly not capable of raising a sweet, darling girl that would always feel the loss of their mother just as much as her.

Mick. Mick bloody Rogers. Why and how did you get involved in this? Where were you now? What, if anything, are you trying to prove? She felt a few butterflies flutter in her stomach and fly up to her heart; she didn't want to go back to Mick, she loved Paul, but she *did* care for him, that there was no doubt. She realised that she *did* still love him, but just not in the way that he wanted her to. But Mick had been so, what was the word she had always used? 'Mickish', even after all these years he was still so sodding 'Mickish' and that still had an effect on her heart, whether she wanted it to or not.

She crossed the vehicle blocked road that was York Way and made towards the station again, looking around her for inspiration as to what to do next; a hope that maybe someone, *anyone*, could see the distress in her eyes and help her look for Emily. Christ, even Mick would've been a sight for sore eyes right now.

Then fear gripped her, fear, shock and pain as she felt herself falling backwards slightly and then being held; somebody was holding something sharp to her throat and was breathing hot air into her right ear. She could feel her hair on that side of her head being tickled by the person's breathing and despite her alarm she still felt the urge to scratch the itch that had been caused by it.

But the individual holding her had put their strong arm around her in such a way that she could not, or would not be able to raise her hand to do such a thing. The sharpness at her throat was hurting more now as she felt whatever was being used start to bury itself deeper into the softness of her skin that covered her trachea. Then Maria's assailant spoke.

"Ah, you wouldn't be one of them would you? You *look* like one of them. Would you like your Uncle 'Arry to show you what happens to your sort eh? Or would ya like to show your Uncle 'Arry how sorry you are first? Show me good and I *might* just let ya go."

With disgust Maria felt Uncle Harry's crotch bump against her backside and even through her denim jeans she could feel the unmistakable feeling of an erect member straining to be unleashed against her.

She looked around her, seeing people arguing and more and more people rushing to the scene to get involved in the ructions that had obviously started while she was in the church like building. And yet nobody was taking any notice of her problem. *Nobody* seemed the least bit moved by the fact that she had something sharp at her throat and something blunter but just as hard rubbing against her bum.

"I'm not one of them. I am just as angry as you are. Please let me go. I promise you I won't say anything, just let me go." Her words choked her and they came out in whispers but even these emotionally charged sentiments didn't affect the demeanour of Uncle Harry.

"Ah, you *say* that you are but how do I know that you're not? You need to show me darling. Prove to your Uncle 'Arry that you're a good girl. Now, walk towards the station entrance. I'm gonna take me knife away and you're gonna pretend that you're my girl okay. Try anything silly and I'm gonna cut ya, ok?"

"What? Where do you want me to go? I told you, I'm not one of these people that you think I am!"

"Never mind where we are going. I have a little place just a few minutes walk from here and that's where your gonna prove to me that you are a good girl and not just a fucking nutcase like one of them that's being going around here lately. Now move your arse. Mmm and a nice arse it is too my darling."

With her nerves and her body shaking, Maria started to walk slowly towards the station entrance, aware that the pointed object was no longer against her throat but that the disgusting man that wanted her was right behind. She cringed when he put his arm lightly around her waist and even though she could not see his face she just knew that he was smiling to anyone that watched this 'couple' walk by.

Maria tried to look at the eyes of strangers, at least those that were not involved in arguments, to try and tell them via her look that she needed help, but all she got in return were blank looks; the strangers weren't concerned with the fate of this woman, and why should they be? After all, wasn't she in the company of someone that was clearly proud of her? She is plainly absolutely fine despite the weird faces she's making, and if, *if* they had been witness to something wrong? Well, how were *they* to know? For God's sake, do you expect us to question every couple that walks past? No, she looked fine, no doubt about it!

They were now in the station. In here there weren't many fights going on although nearer platform one it was clear that something unhealthy was taking place, that's if the shouts and screams of the participants was anything to go by.

Towards the left of them were exits that led out to the Midland Road and it seemed to Maria that this was where her 'Uncle Harry' wanted to go.

As they walked, she felt his left hand slip down a little and then one of his fingers slipped into the gap between her jeans and her left hip; her head became dizzy with nausea as he fingered the waistband of her knickers, rubbing her skin there and then he went slightly lower and caressed their cotton material. Unless something happened soon, then Maria Weston was scared that he would try to caress more than just her underwear. She thought about screaming but then became worried that if she did that then this pervert might just whip out his knife and cut her throat just to shut her up; surely *anybody* that could approach a woman like this in broad daylight was capable of such an action?

The doors to the outside became closer and light spread in lines along the floor, lines that were occasionally darkened by the shadows of the pedestrians and passengers that came in and out of the station.

'Uncle Harry' had taken his finger from the inside of Maria's jeans and had hooked it around one of her belt loops, again on her left hand side. He let his hand dangle there in the way a boyfriend or husband or partner might. Maria felt the weight of this pull down that side of her jeans slightly and she felt the coolness of the day against the little bit of skin that became uncovered there. She thought of this guy trying to pull down her jeans totally in his sordid little room and the panic built in her until she felt it more and more difficult to breathe easily and then the prickle of more hot tears started to bleed from her eyes.

The automatic doors opened, the cool breeze rushed in towards them and they went to go through. But from behind them came a shout. Somebody was calling but at that moment it was difficult to ascertain whom it was that was being called.

Maria and her 'uncle' had just gone through the doors and they were just about to close behind them when the shouting grew louder. A name was being called.

A push in the back from 'Uncle Harry' told Maria to turn right and also to speed up. Then, almost as an afterthought, he gave her backside a quick squeeze and Maria felt that if she had eaten anything nutritious in the last few hours then it would've made an appearance on the pavement there and then. He put his mouth close to her ear and whispered.

"Lovely, very nice. Almost there now. Let's not be silly my girl."

There was a smell of alcohol coming from the man's breath but even that couldn't disguise the reek of decay that suggested dental hygiene was not high on this person's agenda.

As they carried on their journey, the nurse became aware of the whoosh of the automatic doors opening again and then that voice, still calling, now even louder and to the ears of anybody in the vicinity it was clear whose name was being called.

"Maria? That is you isn't it? Maria Weston? Yes, yes it *is* you! Hey slow down, I've been chasing you and I'm knackered!"

Maria went to turn around at the sound of her name, but 'Uncle Harry' pushed her forward with a thrust in the small of the back.

"Keep moving girl. Remember what I have and that I *will* use it."

The man that was shouting saw Maria and her 'friend' move away a bit faster but remained undeterred.

"Hey there! Maria! Where are you going! Slow down for God's sake!"

She was desperate to find out who was calling her; whilst that voice was shouting her name there was hope that she could get away from this weirdo that wanted to take her home. But 'Uncle Harry' was now marching her along, walking closer behind her with his hand resting just above her beltline.

Heavy breathing, but not from 'Uncle Harry'. This time it came from someone hurrying up beside them. This man stopped then stood in front of the anxious nurse.

"Cor, you're in a bit of hurry ain't ya? Didn't you hear me calling ya?"

Maria looked up after initially being at eye level with this individual's warm looking, cable knit jumper. She looked up into the handsome face of a man that was gazing down at her with blue eyes that she was rather embarrassed to admit that she found very attractive. This Adonis had five o'clock shadow and his brown hair was spiked up as if he had been at the hair gel that morning.

"Oh come on, you remember *me*! Don't try and tell me that you've forgotten me already Miss Willows, sorry, *Mrs Weston*! Blimey, hard to get used to that!"

The pervert's hand was now gripping the bottom of Maria's jacket, seizing it almost in his fist and the ex Miss Willows could practically feel the frustration discharging from the putrid persona of 'Uncle Harry'. Maria looked into her acquaintance's face and mentally rifled through her files of the hunks she had met with gorgeous blue eyes; but none came to mind. She would've remembered this handsome chap anywhere and yet he was convinced that he knew *her* . . . and he *did* know her name!

"We have somewhere to get to son, now if you don't mind me and . . . . Maria have to be somewhere. Give her a call, email her, twotter her or whatever it is you young people do these days uh?"

The speech of 'Uncle Harry' was rushed and had a degree of alarm in it too. It was also obvious that the way he had momentarily stopped at her name showed that he was just trying to sound like he was well known to the nurse, but hopefully this new arrival would see that he didn't know her, not really, that he was actually a complete, strange pervert who went about trying to molest women just to satisfy his own nauseating whims; she hoped that he would see that anyway.

'Uncle Harry' pushed her forward again and for a while Maria's dread seemed to return and triplicate as the distance between them and the handsome man started to widen. *Why won't he do something? For God's sake come and talk to me again you bastard!*

Nothing. No calling of her name, no chasing her down and smiling that lovely, white smile at her. 'Uncle Harry' had relaxed his grip on her jacket a little but he still held onto her like a father keeping a safe hold on their little child as they take their first steps.

He leaned into her again as they walked and grabbed her backside harder than before, squeezing it so that it started to hurt. She felt long nails digging through the toughness of her denims and she figured that they must be long due a cut if she could notice such a thing.

"That was lucky, wasn't it my girl? It's just as well for you that I was here as he looks a little bit dodgy to me. I've probably saved you from one of them eh? Now, what a nice thing to reward your Uncle 'Arry for eh?"

"But you think that I'm one of *them* too, *don't you?*"

"Now my girl, I never said that. I said that you *may* be and that I was giving you a chance to prove that you ain't. Remember? Now,

I'm not gonna hurt ya, not unless you make me. You may even enjoy yourself darling."

As if to emphasise the point, 'Uncle Harry' then slipped his hand into the left, back pocket of Maria's jeans and let it rest there, feeling her rear against his hand as she walked.

Maria didn't know what the most repugnant action of the two was: the suggestion that she may *enjoy* his ugly intentions or his hand in her back pocket. His hand was outsplayed there, open and receiving, feeling to the nurse as if she had some repulsive insect riding in the back of her jeans.

She wasn't sure how long had passed as they continued along the road towards some traffic lights. Maria was aware that a few more minutes and there at the top of this road there were some council flats; some 1950's fantastic view of futuristic, box shaped residences and which now looked old, run down and home to some of the less desirable members of Camden society. She started to wonder if this was where the pervert lived and where he intended to take her. Her hopes started to fade and she started to think of ways that she could fight off his hideous intentions when the time came.

But as they neared the traffic lights, ready to stop at the crossing and press the button that would trigger the 'come and help us' signal to the green man, the hand of 'Uncle Harry' that had been in her back pocket shot out abruptly. So quickly that it felt like it had been pulled out in a hurry. Then the pervading presence of that disgusting specimen, that smell of alcohol and dirt, that knowledge that something nasty was at your shoulder, that too was no longer there.

Above the roar of the traffic that was rushing in front of her, she could hear, a few paces behind her, muffled shouts. Dare she turn around? She hadn't had the courage to do so ever since she had been abducted. She wouldn't have known the dirty man's face from Adam in a line up of one, such had been her dread.

As she looked at the passing cars she realised that some of the passengers and drivers were looking behind her, their faces full of disbelief, mouths gaping and then their heads swivelling to look behind them as their carriages carried them away from the spectacle which had amazed them.

But still she didn't turn around. Her body refused to take any notice of what her brain was telling her to do and she wondered if she would spend the rest of her life frozen at the roadside of a dirty, north London neighbourhood.

Then the attendance of somebody else beside her. No smell of dirt, no sense of loathing, just the feeling that a 'normal' being was there looking down at her.

"Hey there again! Maria?"

This time she didn't just tell her head and body to turn, she forced it, she demanded it, because she didn't have to see the speaker's face; she could feel the gaze of those blue eyes on her face and after the filth of 'Uncle Harry' it felt as refreshing as a shower under a waterfall on a tropical island.

"Uh? Hey there! *Hey there? Did she ever say* hey there *to anyone? Had she ever done so in her life? Oh well, it must be catching. She had caught 'heythereitis' from her gallant rescuer!* Er, I'm not sure what to say, sorry. It's been a bit of a strange situation, you know?"

The liberator looked at Maria's pale face; she was shaken and dazed but he didn't let his jolly demeanour slip for a second.

"I'm sorry about your friend. He . . . er . . . had to go somewhere. Not sure if he wanted to at first but I understand that, nevertheless, he had a place to go anyway! So, Maria! How are you feeling? Would you like a drink, you seem a little bit knocked for six! Has my face proved so distressing for you? Ha!"

"Sorry, look, I really don't mean to be rude and especially after what you have just done for me and everything but, er, I don't . . . actually . . . remember your name!"

"You don't? Well, that isn't important right now. What *is* important is making sure that *you* my friend are feeling ok. You sure you wouldn't like a drink? Tea? Coffee? Something stronger, say a nice lemonade shandy?"

As Maria looked at the benevolent and yet rugged features of the gentleman, the tensions and the pent up dreadfulness of what had just happened to her finally tipped over the edge—she burst into tears and then buried her face into the guy's jumper, clinging onto its softness and becoming aware of the fragrance of a male perfume that she had once bought for Paul and which he hadn't approved of. *Men don't wear perfume, Maria! At least, not real men!*

"Hey there! Hey, what's all this about? Hmmm, I think you *do* need a little something to make you feel better, don't you?" Maria nodded her agreement, wiping her tears away with the back of her hands. "But first, I just need to take you somewhere. Don't worry, nothing too sinister! I have a feeling that when you get there you are going to be very, very happy and extremely pleased that we bumped into each other. Trust me, all is going to be great!"

A black Hyundai Genesis pulled up by the side of the road, just before it got to the traffic lights and its left back door opened, swinging until it reached the end of its hinges. The perfumed man held Maria away gently, walked towards the car and held out his hand.

"Come on! What you waiting for?" Then in a childish sing-song voice, "*I know someone that wants to see yooou!*"

Not sure what she was doing. Ignoring all that been told to her by her parents about accepting rides from strangers, Maria Weston slowly walked towards the waiting car. Just before she bent down to get into it, she looked up again at the man that had stopped 'Uncle Harry' from having his way with her. Then she looked around; her eyes sweeping the immediate area. *Where the hell had that dirty old man got to? He isn't anywhere in sight, and he should be! Shouldn't he?*

"Where did that horrible man . . . ."

"Shush my friend. Don't worry about people like that. You know that we don't approve of people like that, don't you?"

Looking at the man's blue eyes again Maria saw for the first time that they weren't a calming, soothing, gentle blue after all. There was an edge to the colour that was steely and sharp; then Maria noticed the blood vessels racing around the prominent blueness of the iris. They were redder and more vicious than normal and Maria Weston knew that she had seen something similar to this before.

The blood draining from her face, the nurse bent down and climbed into the car. Her rescuer gently guided her in with his hand on her back and smiled to himself as he settled into his seat next to her and closed the car door firmly shut.

CHAPTER THIRTY

With the taste of tuna and cucumber sandwich still in his mouth, Paul Weston stood outside the double doors of the room that he had had no intention of returning to ever again.

Quite where Dan had got their little snacks from was a mystery to him. He had never been aware that there could be a canteen in this place. The whole idea of there being a bright, clean, many seated environment, with fresh food, clean and disinfected tables, machines that sold crisps, cola or sweeties (should you wish not to queue up!) and smiley cashiers, their names on their badges, waiting to help you pay for your nosh didn't quite square with the dismal, candle lit, musty hole that he, Maria, Emily and that bloody Mick had found themselves having such fun in.

Dan had just smiled at Paul's query and said that 'they had to keep themselves refreshed somehow, didn't they? And while their version of a canteen wasn't exactly the Ritz, there were still kitchens where food was prepared and provided for the staff, brothers and sisters. They merely used the rooms that had been used as kitchens before, when this place was open to the public and was somewhere grand for people to stay. Wasn't that nice of Mr Leonard? To think of his admirers like that?' This last bit had been said with more than a hint of sarcasm, but when your brain had been scrambled for someone's amusement then he supposed you had a right to feel just a little bit pissed off.

Paul supposed that with the ridiculous amount of rooms in the place then the suggestion that there are places to eat shouldn't really be so strange, should it? It made him wonder what other places of intrigue and mystery could be found should he ever decide to take in the sights of this dreadful environment. Mind you, when he came to think about it, maybe *dreadful* was a bit too strong an adjective to use? Maybe if they got rid of those damned candles and got the electricity working in here? Maybe some bright paint for places where it was flaking? I mean, keep the 'posher' parts of the decor like the ceramic tiles, the Chaucerian mural, maybe even try and save the Victorian stencil pattered wallpapers, enriched with gilding . . . a bit of a job but you never know! Maybe then, maybe, this sinister abode for ghosts could be quite a pleasant place to come to?

One thing was for sure though. Whatever the large room before them had been used for a hundred plus years ago, it most certainly wasn't fulfilling that purpose now.

Two and a half hours had gone by since Paul had been introduced to Dr Becky Shaw. The light outside was darkening and Dan had confidently told Becky and Paul that conditioning always stopped at around the same time so that the machines could be rested, updated and fixed if needs be.

So here they were, the intrepid three, and as Dan reached out to turn the handle that would open the doors he made a quick look around just to check that there wasn't anybody to see what they were doing. Whilst there were people still wandering around, they were not anywhere near the area where Paul and his new friends were and the fact that this area was enveloped in shadows just made their cautious intentions easier to carry out . . . whatever their intentions were that is; Dan had seemed to have some sort of plan but he hadn't been totally forthcoming with it yet. Still, he wasn't going to argue with him—he had tried that with one of his equally stocky friends and looked what happened then!

The doors opened and from the widening aperture beyond came a concoction of smells that reminded Paul of the wards that Maria had worked on during her career—that indescribable, clinical mix of disinfectant and soap, but there underneath these aromas was the slight but troubling odour of something that had burnt; it wasn't overpowering but if you concentrated on your sense of smell it was definitely there.

Led by Dan, Paul and Becky slipped into the place that Paul had heard many times being referred to as the 'conditioning room.' Dan had stayed on the other side of the door as they came in and as soon as they were in he closed it—and darkness swept over them like a sea of black ink.

Nothing could be seen by either of the threesome. Paul waited for his eyes to adjust in the hope that he could become aware of something but it seemed that either his eyes weren't playing ball or that there genuinely was nothing to see but blackness in this place. Bearing in mind what he had seen before this just added to Paul's strong sense of anxiety; maybe the gruesomeness of that guy's death was just waiting to reach out and grab him and treat him to some of the same?

There was a shout from the left of the room. A yell of pain followed by a loud, crashing noise. Becky screeched in response and Paul responded with an odd noise that leapt from his mouth, a sort of panicked "woahwoah" noise that he had never uttered before. Paul felt Becky grab his arm and pull it close to her. She was trembling and he understood why as his legs had become seriously unstable.

Then silence. Paul looked around and he could just make out Becky's head doing the same. Suddenly Paul jumped as Becky spoke, not in her normal voice, but just above a whisper.

"Dan? What was that? Dan? What has happened? Are you there? For God's sake *answer me!*"

A brief silence, then the sound of movement. Footsteps were heard, a few paces ahead but still to the left of them; then another crash, the sound of metal against the floor that reverberated around the room, echoing off the walls and making Becky scream so close to Paul's right ear that his eardrum shook violently and sent waves along his ear canal. Paul stood rigid, tense and terrified at what he could not see.

The quick, closing shut of their eyes followed as bright, lurid light lit the room, dispersing the inkiness of before and causing Dr Shaw to shriek for a third time, again assaulting Paul's ear causing him to rub it as he squinted around at the newly lit area before him.

When he and Maria had been in here before, there had been people doing all sorts of bizarre 'jobs', including those that strapped 'brothers and sisters' into the chairs. What with the mass of people wandering around and the awful sights that their hosts had insisted that they should see, it had been difficult to appreciate every nuance of the room that he was now back in. All he knew was that it felt bad then and it felt bad now—regardless of whether there were people here or not.

"God, I'm so sorry guys. Shit, I should've been more careful. I was in such a hurry to get the lights on that I tripped over that bloody stool. Then I hit another one! Jeez, I think I've cut my bloody leg now!"

Dan was limping back towards them, every now and then stopping to lift up his right trouser leg and thereby showing Becky and Paul a rolled down black sock and a limb that did indeed have a gash across it. It wasn't bleeding as such but the gash did look like the leg was smiling a red lipped smile and it did indeed look sore.

"Here, let me have a look at it. I think you're gonna survive but I'll check it anyway."

Becky walked forward to meet Dan and went to bend down to check the wound but the guard just pulled his leg away and his face flushed as Becky, halfway to the floor, looked up at him with a bemused gaze.

"Nah, you don't need to do that doc. I mean . . . it's just a scratch. As you say, I'm gonna live."

"But I was only going to make sure you're ok. You sure?"

"Yeah! It's . . . nothing to worry about. I've had worse, Ha!"

"It's ok to feel pain you know Dan. You don't have to be the tough guard now you know!"

Dan tried to smile at Becky's comment and then carefully rolled his sock back up and straightened his trouser leg.

"Oh no, I know that Doc! I'm not saying that I'm trying to be tough or anything, but, well . . . . you know . . ."

Becky looked around at Paul and winked. Dan noticed this but said nothing. He was still flushing red and Paul found it amusing how someone so big and tough looking could be so embarrassed in front of an attractive young lady. He wondered if Dan had had a girlfriend before or maybe his idea of how a man should behave was stuck in the 1950s? He had said that he had followed his father into the family business; maybe this bulk of a man had also been told to work hard and not worry about girls for the moment? You did hear of such things, especially with family businesses run by control freak parents.

As Becky came back to where Paul was standing he heard her take in a huge breath and her cheeks puffed outwards as she released it. Despite the fun she was making of Dan it was obvious that the darkness and the crashing noises had freaked her out somewhat.

"Never mind the big guy Becky, are *you* okay? You nearly deafened me with all that screaming!"

"Well, it's a girl's prerogative isn't it? To scream when something makes you jump? Hope I didn't damage your ears too much!"

Becky's lips formed a little smile but she was clearly feeling just as edgy as he was. As for screaming being a *girl's prerogative*. Well, he knew of one girl that may disagree with such a sentiment; a thought which suddenly caused a feeling of lightness fill his heart as he wondered where he beloved wife was now?

He recalled the sickened, pained and horrified look on Maria's face when they had seen that guy die so gruesomely before them and looking at the room he saw the chair where Jeffrey had been so horribly dismantled. It was the same as the others in the room and without its bizarre purpose would not have looked out of place in a modern kitchen.

They were all made of a chrome like material but the bright lights gave them a strange, blue glow that Paul had never really noticed in chrome furniture before. They had a high back which resembled a noughts and crosses grid only at each intersection there was a star, what could have been termed by some a 'nautical' star, and going through it from upper left to bottom right there was an arrow.

Paul was obviously familiar with stars and arrows but to see an arrow pierce a star was a little bit different and he wondered if this symbol has anything to do with the people that ran this house of fun.

The legs of the chairs seemed quite short in comparison with the back, being at least two inches shorter giving the whole construction a dumpy appearance. It didn't look the most comfortable of fittings but Paul supposed that they weren't in them for long so what the hell!

Then he thought about the objects that he had thought resembled shaking cabinets. They didn't seem to be anywhere around. He looked around the room for these mysterious entities but instead his eyes lit upon the candles; these were scattered in no particular order in different parts of the room and then Paul recalled something that hadn't occurred to him before when Dan had flooded the room with light.

"But this place was lit by candles! You mean to tell me that they had electrical light in here all this time but instead they used all these bloody candles instead?" Dan just smiled at Paul's question and approaching him laid his hand on his right shoulder.

"Well my friend, they needed some of our earth's power sources to get these machines going, didn't they? I still don't know what the likes of Burn and the Rector are capable of doing but they are still practical people and if they could get the electricity running in here again then they would, and for people like *them* it wasn't that difficult to do."

"People like *them*?"

"Paul my friend, how can I put this without you taking offence? You *must* know by now, after *all* that you've seen, after all me and Becky have told you, that these people aren't like us."

"Yeah I got that but . . ."

"But accept it Paul. We are dealing with dangerous people here. Well, I say *people* as I don't know what else to call them! You think it's all confined to this building too? They have got places like this all over the country and I dare think of what havoc they have stirred up and what pain and bloodshed they have caused. All in the name of a *better society*. All in the name of Leonard's better world. And as for *that* geezer, it was all his idea, the candles and that. He has some bee in his bonnet about darkness and for God's sake I didn't think it was weird at all. I just thought it made sense at the time."

"Me too," responded Becky, "I know you find it hard to understand Paul, but when they initially get at you then all that we would normally think of as strange makes perfect sense, as Dan says. You are so lucky that they . . . ahhhhh!"

Paul rushed over to the trainee doctor as pain wracked her brain again. Her head was bowed and her hands were gripping each of her cheeks. As he placed his arm around her shoulders in concern he looked across at Dan whose eyes first looked at Becky and then at the floor in helplessness. His mouth had turned down and his lips were tight. Paul felt that Dan was trying to keep something in, a cry, a yell, something that would give voice to the fusion of feelings that must be speeding through him.

Then from the corner of his eye Paul saw something dripping. He turned to see blood trickling over Becky's hands and chin and falling to the floor, its impact making their own star like patterns on the tiles beneath them.

"No, no, nooooo, I don't wanna die yet! I don't wanna die like the rest of them! Oh God Paul, you *have* to help me!"

Paul Weston rifled through his pockets and found the handkerchief that he always carried with him, not necessarily because he had a continuous cold, but just in case his step-sister had managed to make another mess somewhere—many knocked over glasses of orange juice and many dirtied knees and elbows from falling over had made him realise that handkerchief carrying was always a winning idea, and to think that he hadn't long ago thought that only 'old men' carried such things . . . .

With his arm still around Becky he gently wiped the blood away from her hands and then moving them away and turning the handkerchief around in his hand he wiped the blood which he could now see was coming from her nose. Tears were now travelling down her face as well and trying to mix with the blood and Paul tried to wipe these away too.

"I wish I *could* help you Becky. I so wish that I knew a way of not just stopping *your* pain but also that of all the others too. A way of stopping all that has been going on in here and in all the other places. I wish that . . . ."

Paul ended abruptly as he realised that Becky's crying had stopped short and that she was now staring, her head upright and rigid and focused on what was going on behind them.

He followed her gaze and saw with horror that Dan had moved; that while Paul had been attending to Becky's bleeding he had gone to the back of the room again, moving in and out of the chairs and little trolleys on wheels that held a variety of items like clipboards, baby wipes and thermometers, all of which Paul could find no connection.

Dan had arrived at a door that Paul hadn't noticed before but which was in the back left hand corner. There was a sign on it that couldn't be read from where he was but whatever it said meant nothing to the guard as he took a few steps back then rushed at the door, shoulder charging it, using his considerable size and strength to weaken the dark, mahogany wood. Paul and Becky could only watch in sheer curiosity as their friend made four attempts at this and each time they could see that Dan was becoming more and more angry.

Then a fifth attempt. Dan stood still for a few seconds, stared at the door as if it was his worst enemy and with a roar that seemed to resound off the chrome chairs rushed forward again, a man who was channelling fury and frustration into his charge and this time the door splintered. It didn't break through as Paul had seen in many cop or hero films, but around its handle cracks appeared and flakes of wood spat from their aged home.

The ex funeral director lashed out with his right foot; kicking at the weakened wood and causing it to crack and disintegrate further. Then just as Paul felt that it was going to take quite a bit of violent kicking to get the door to open, it imploded upon one of Dan's furious assaults and amongst bits of dust and wood chips swung open. Dan didn't waste any time in pushing the broken door fully open and he hurried through into the room beyond it.

Paul looked at Becky and Becky looked at Paul. Without words they were clearly asking each other whether they should go after Dan? The man had shown such aggression towards the door that Paul didn't know whether he would be easy to talk to. And where had this aggression come from? He had seemed so calm, so docile even when he had initially seen Becky's bleeding.

"Let's see if he comes out, give him a minute or two." Paul suggested. Becky nodded in agreement.

Twenty seconds of silence and numerous looks between them and the battered doorway later, both of them ran to where Dan had been so determined to enter.

As they arrived at the destroyed doorway, Paul and Becky noticed the sign that they had not been able to read from a distance. It was a simple piece of A4, laminated and was now hanging off the open door by one corner; it read simply in large, red Times Roman script "KEEP OUT: NO STAFF OR FAMILY TO ENTER THIS ROOM. UNAUTHORISED ENTRY SHALL BE PUNISHED SEVERELY." Paul wondered how severe the punishment would be and why such a sign had been placed on this door? Well, they would soon find out and Paul and Becky drew in breath as they looked into the room. There at the bottom of this chamber was Dan, still in a state of agitation. But if the doctor and the nurse's husband were expecting more of the dark, mildewed and stale decor of the rest of the building then they were shocked to their core.

"You have been so good to me Thomas. You have made me reach heights of excitement and happiness that I never thought I ever would again. My, I feel like a young girl again! How do you do that? How do you make a woman as . . . ahem . . . as mature as me feel so young, so vibrant, so alive?"

Dorothy Trollope was buttoning up her blouse, her face flushed red and with fresh sweat streaked across her forehead. She was sitting on the edge of a four poster bed; 'colonial' in style and which had been made of solid mahogany. The wood was grimy, covered in dust and cobwebs, and the holed, torn and mould smelling mattress was sagging in places that would make it near impossible to get a good night's sleep on.

But sleep hadn't been on the agenda of Thomas Burn when he had appeared on the second floor of the building, marched into a room where Dorothy was chatting to Belinda and Mary, two 'sisters' that were excitedly discussing the uproar that they had heard downstairs, and with as little effort as possible dragged her down the corridor and into the room that they were now in. The two women had looked after them as they left and then looked at each other with a knowing look, a girlish giggle and a sense that Burn was just doing what Burn did and that this was acceptable and quite the honour too.

Dorothy had looked at Burn's nondescript face and had felt that she was in trouble. She tried to think back to what she had done since she had arrived and whether any of it could be construed by Burn as wrong. But feeling that her feet weren't even touching the ground, she was sped along and directed into the dark room with the four poster bed. The bed aside, the room was empty apart from the ever present lit candles that cast shadows where shadows would not normally occur and a walnut wardrobe that lurched slightly lop-sided against one of the walls; its oblong mirror placed between two doors that were fashioned in floral motives that had been embossed into the wood. At its bottom was a large drawer, slightly open and from which Dorothy could hear the tapping of tiny claws and she cringed at the thought of being in the same room as a rat.

However, the idea of rats and other such vermin had disappeared as Burn's face moved closer towards hers. She had just a moment to notice the smell that was coming off the skin of her friend; it reminded her of when she had visited one of Adrian's schools and he had proudly shown her one of his experiments in the school laboratory. There had been a strong odour that she had wrinkled her nose at and Adrian had laughed as he had told her to just *ignore that smell of sulphur, that you would get used to it after a while.* Well, she was certain that this was the same smell again only this time it was issuing from Thomas Burn's skin.

Then when Burn pressed his lips against hers she was near positive that now she could taste what before only her sense of smell had been aware of.

Burn had pushed his tongue into her mouth as he tried to undo the zip of Dorothy's skirt and this time the taste and the smell of this sulphur like substance was so strong that she gagged a little and tried to pull away, but Burn held her strong and as her skirt fell about her ankles and her 'lover' put his hand down the back of her knickers to caress her bottom, she felt that sensation of pure ecstasy that Burn had reintroduced to her life quite a few times now and when he laid her down on the bed Dorothy Trollope allowed herself to be the object of Burn's panting, forceful lust.

As soon as it had been over Burn had got off the bed quickly and it had been while he was straightening his tie in the walnut wardrobe's mirror that he answered Dorothy's question.

"Sometimes my dear Dorothy, a man has to release his stress in ways that only a good woman can aid him with. I am, or should I say *was* feeling very stressed, very angry even over certain events that have taken place. I needed relief and I knew that my Dorothy, a woman of substance, a woman of breeding and a woman that I feel knows me so well would have no problem helping me with. You *are* happy to relieve my stress, are you not my dear?"

"Oh well, when you are so charming, then how could, ha, a girl like me possibly refuse? But tell me Thomas, and please forgive me for asking such a question, and I don't mind what the answer is, I really don't but I am very curious about it, do you *relieve your stress* with other sisters in our current abode?"

Thomas Burn looked silently at his reflection in the mirror, the glow from the candlelight reflecting off the glass and his features giving him a sinister guise that he enjoyed and silently went to stand in front of the widow of Stephen Trollope. His fly was only inches from her face and she wondered for a moment if Burn wanted her to do something that she had tried only once in her life, and that was on her wedding night; that had been a disaster and neither she nor her groom had enjoyed it and the moment had never been discussed or repeated again. But, if Burn *really* insisted, then maybe she could . . . .

Her fingers slowly went to the top of Burn's trousers but they were halted by Burn's own hands and with relief she craned her head back to look up at her lover's face.

"I think Dorothy, that you know the answer to that question. Do you *really* need me to answer it and hurt your feelings? What is important is how much I am indebted to the way that you serve me, as serving me in such a way is more important to our cause than you will ever know."

"But Thomas, my dear Thomas, I am but an old woman, whose body lost its shape thirty years ago! My skin is saggy and I can't possibly compete with the firm, youthful bodies of those that are willing to serve you too? I am too old to be jealous Thomas and after the way you freed me from my life of torment with Stephen then I never will be, but as I say, I *am* very curious as to why you choose me?"

"Because," replied Burn, "when my body joins with yours I feel your years of experience flood into me. I feel all your knowledge and familiarities of years on this planet invigorating as my own body learns from you. I cannot get that from younger females. I can receive pleasure from them in a way that I have never experienced before in my years and never will again in the future, but with you and your maturity I learn as well, I learn and enjoy and respect your ways and your, dare I say it, body too. You see my dear Dorothy, where I come from, the feel of saggy skin or shapeless bodies means nothing for we don't associate such tangible or visual perceptions as stimulus for reproduction. When I came looking for relief, I knew it had to be from my dear Dorothy, only you, for I needed to be relieved and for my knowledge to be 'topped up' shall we say, and my belief in your kind reinforced. You have done that for me and I thank you."

As Burn spoke, Dorothy started to wonder by what he had meant by *belief in your kind* and *where I come from*. But then, Thomas Burn had always spoken with his own brand of eloquence that was certainly different from any man that she had met but which she had just put down to another of his own admirable personality traits. However, it did trigger off one query that now nibbled away at her conscience—where *did* this unfathomable man come from? And that smell of sulphur! It had to be sulphur, she couldn't think of what else it could be. Why did Burn smell of sulphur? Had he been messing about in a laboratory of his own? But then, it had come from his skin . . .

. . . and something else about his skin. During the throes of passion she hadn't been aware of it but now she realised that Burn's skin had been redder than before and somehow rougher to the touch; the sort of feeling a man's chin has after a day of stubble has built up but this texture had been all over his arms and his chest too. Burn had been warmer, rougher and had entered her with the thrusts and grunts of an animal; not the gentle and charming lover that she had been spellbound by before.

A dull ache appeared in the centre of her head but she ignored it as she tried to undo this mystery. Burn had been so different than before and despite his charm and his articulate words, the physical closeness she had just shared with the man was causing her to wonder.

As Dorothy looked up she saw that Burn was now eyeing her suspiciously. His gaze was centred on her forehead and she felt feelings like the ripples on water caress the front of her brain; a tickling sensation and yet it stayed there as Burn kept his steady focus on her face. Then his dark, bushy eyebrows knitted together. His eyes narrowed and yet emitted a glow from them that Dorothy saw as a reddish vapour. He moved towards her slowly and when he spoke Dorothy Trollope no longer heard the voice that she had allied with Thomas Burn, her leader, her saviour, her lover. This was a voice of a different mortal altogether and its wetness and sudden malevolance froze the professor's widow until she couldn't even feel herself breathe anymore.

"I read what you're thinking Dorothy Trollope. You know that I can do that, don't you? You know that I am a being of powers beyond anything that you or your pathetic fellow rock dwellers can ever understand. Now, why question me? Why put up barriers between us after the way that we have just enriched each others needs? Do you really wish to disappoint me? You *dare* to ask yourself such foolish questions? Oh my dear woman, I clearly need to put you right, bring you back to your senses. Come here my dear Dorothy, come and let me reinvigorate you further."

Dorothy Trollope couldn't move. The pain in her head was throbbing more forcefully now and as Burn lurched over her she saw that apart from the approaching creature everything else around her was a flickering, yellow blur. The red glow from Burn's eyes was pulsating, was reaching out to her, was transfixing her and she could make out that every now and then it was emitting a crackling noise that reminded her of bacon freshly laid in a smoking, hot pan.

His face was changing too. The area around his eyes seemed to be indenting somehow and yet she still couldn't shift any part of her body. His hands reached out towards her and she felt their warmth, their power as they clawed through the air and made for the sides of her head. And that smell again. She could sense more of that sulphur like smell only this time it was more acute, was causing the small hairs in her nostrils to tingle until she felt that this intrusive odour was actually hurting her; was flowing up her nasal passages and piercing the area between her eyes as if somebody was burrowing into her skin with a screwdriver.

Then as Burn's hands were centimetres from her face she knew that the crackling that she had recognised as coming from his eyes was now coming from his hands too and that noise accompanied sharp, pin pricks that were caressing her cheeks. Now even Burn was becoming a blur as the permeating stench and the increasingly painful sensations on her flesh caused her to fade in and out of consciousness, her body still straight and immovable but her mind in a state of flux that she could not control.

As if to show defiance against this onslaught of her senses, Dorothy's eyes pushed out tears and every now and then she felt their wetness—the only sign that her body was independent of Thomas Burn's motives.

Now his hands were on her and the pain that came from his fingertips completely covered up the increasing agony in the top of her head.

Then the flames of the candles went out. Then even when she thought that she could feel Burn in front of her there was still darkness and she knew that in a moment of irrational mood change, Burn had decided to do to her what the brothers and sisters had spoken of before; rumours that she had decided to ignore because Burn just wasn't that type of man—they didn't know him like *she* did and that knowledge had always made her feel safe and confident that her new life was going to bring her such happiness and rewards that Stephen Trollope could never have dreamed of.

But now there was darkness. Now there was pain coursing through her cheeks and flowing through the whole of her head. Then there was a breeze . . . .

As her consciousness went to leave her behind, Dorothy was incapable of seeing that the door to the room had swung open with force; it was the energy in which it had opened that had distinguished the candles and now the brighter candlelight from the corridor outside attempted to come in and reach her.

Thomas Burn turned around quickly to face the intrusion and there in the doorway was one of the guards. He saw the face of Burn and felt unable to communicate with his leader as he noticed the changes that had taken place on his face. Burn left Dorothy, her eyes opening slowly as his hands came away and her whole body hurting, and paced with spiteful intent towards the guard. The voice now even more malignant and biting.

"How dare you! How dare you interrupt me you ignorant boy. I'll make you pay for your ignorance, I'll make you hurt like you've never hurt before."

The guard could only stutter a reply and tried desperately to point in the direction of the staircase, but his arm felt like it was being dragged down by weights.

"B . . b . . b . . . but sir! T . . t . . t . . . t . . . trouble . . . n . . n . . n.n . . noise f . . ff.ff . . from the.r . . r . . roooom . . . ."

"What? You stupid, foolish creature! You *people* infuriate me!"

The last thing the guard understood was the feeling of Burn grabbing his chunky neck just under the windpipe. Then even though Burn didn't appear to be squeezing with his fingers the feeling of pressure dug into his soft flesh, restricting his breathing more and more until he could not breathe anymore. But there was no time to gasp for air as the guard's temperature shot up; his face turned pink, then red, then purple, his eyes bubbling then liquefying followed by a greyish-white fluid dripping onto his cheeks; his short, brown hair singeing and releasing a smoke that floated above his head.

The skin of the guard that had rushed around the building, looking for Burn, looking for Leonard, looking for any of the leaders finally went charcoal grey and then started to dry and flake away before the man that had only been following orders crumpled to the ground and where there had stood a large, grey suited man there was now only a mass of clothes and ashes.

Burn looked down at what had been one of his subordinates and kicked at the ashes, causing dust to fly up and swarm around the room.

"I don't know how much more of this nonsense I can take. Do you hear me Dorothy? *Can* you hear me Dorothy? I curse the day that the Rector, or whatever name he wishes to call himself, dragged us to this petty place and convinced me and our kind to undertake the transformation of you all and aid with our expansion. Your stupidity should make the job easier but all I now feel is frustration and resentment at your behaviour. And *you* my dear Dorothy, *you* have been my greatest disappointment. I wish that I didn't have to do this but you leave me no choice."

Dorothy had gained some consciousness as Burn had disposed of the guard and despite the awful pains that were shooting through every nerve and fibre of her body she was awake enough to see that Burn was coming for her again, his hands outstretched again and his face as ugly and as corrupt as before. The crackling noise started once more and Dorothy could only whimper, sobs escaping from her wrinkled mouth as the 'man' she had trusted approached to send her into permanent darkness.

Then Burn stopped. He stood upright and closed what were his eyes. Dorothy looked at him and wondered if maybe, maybe he was reconsidering his idea and in her mind she repeated the Lord's Prayer over and over again.

This creature stayed like this for a minute and she saw that he seemed to be listening to something and then she saw that his lips were moving a little as if he was inwardly talking. Noises came from his mouth but she couldn't understand them. If he was speaking then it wasn't in English; it wasn't in any language that she had heard before and she thought that after all the many foreign students that she and Stephen had kindly taken in and fed home-grown fruit and veg whilst they went to the local uni, she *should* recognise quite a few.

Burn opened his eyes, red mist now emanating not just from his eyes but seemingly from his entire head; the smell of sulphur became stronger and started to sting Dorothy's nostrils again.

He looked at Dorothy Trollope and when his hands outstretched again she felt that if he was going to kill her then please let him get it over with. *I can't bear this anymore. Please, just make it painless and quick.*

She wasn't sure if the screaming in her head was the sound of the pinnacle of fear; of the noise the brain transmits when you are about to suffer an end that isn't 'normal' and that will cause you more suffering than usual before you expire. All she knew was that this ear-piercing shrill was gradually getting louder and louder. Its intensity put her teeth on edge and made her fingernails dig into her fingertips leaving tiny little grooves where they had imbedded themselves.

Burn had stopped again and now was moving with speed to the outside corridor. As he stood there Dorothy became aware of brothers and sisters rushing past him, ignoring any appearance that he may now be presenting to them and holding their ears in pain. He was being jostled by those that had let panic overtake them but he did not react, instead he stood looking around him, steam still rising from his body.

As Mrs Trollope finally rammed her fingers into her ears to mask the awful noise that was shrieking around them all, she felt that she was finally going to lose her mind; that everything that had taken place from the killing of Stephen, to her seduction by Thomas Burn, her life full of good, meaningful promises despite being in this sunless edifice and finally to witnessing this alteration in the bearing of her 'lover'—it must all be getting too much for her senses for there in front of her Thomas Burn had started to float. She stared at this sight for a while longer, not wanting to believe this false information that her eyes were clearly communicating to her but there it was . . . it was indisputable . . . the man, the *fiend* that she had let have its way with her was no longer standing on the ground.

Moans escaped from her mouth once more but this time they were louder and full of a heartfelt agony that mirrored the horror and demoralization that she was acutely feeling throughout her conscious and subconscious self.

And then he was gone. One moment Thomas Burn had been rising from the floor, people still rushing past him in unadulterated dismay, and then with only the slightest of blurs he had disappeared. Shouts of protest and pain came from the corridor but the man that had promised so much only to want her dead was no longer outside the room where he had infiltrated her body for the last time.

With an increasing dull ache in her head and the sounds of the howling, jarring racket that was incessantly abusing the ears of everyone in the building, Dorothy made an attempt to stand up. Her legs ached as she stretched but her surroundings still kept fading in and out. As she reached out to steady herself, her fingers left her ears and the volume of the high pitched shriek perforated her mind. It was too much for this sensible woman's sensibilities and despite a sudden breathing in of musty air in order to clear her head, she felt her legs give way, the dizziness overcome her and her body fall forward. She didn't feel the impact of her head against the dirty floor as she blacked out and headed towards a place where monstrous spectacles and obscene noises would no longer insult her.

CHAPTER THIRTY-ONE

Clinical. That was the only word that could describe the room. Although, he only had a vague idea of the definition of that word! Something to do with *not showing much in the way of emotion*, he was pretty sure that was what it meant; in which case, it was perfect. It was the hard sound of the word that seemed to match as well; the two *kicking 'kers'* (as infants would call them!) making the word seem harsh as it clicked from the back of your throat.

This long room was definitely lacking emotion: *was* hard, *was* harsh and so different from the building that it was supposed to be a part of.

For a start it was all white and chrome. Not a single bit of dirt, mould and dampness to be seen; no candles . . . no lights at all. At least, not the sort of lights one may expect from this type of glare. Even in that 'conditioning' room it was obvious that electricity was being used to power the lights that had been installed on parts of the ceiling. But *this* was different. Paul couldn't see any light bulbs or strip lighting, no spotlights or fluorescent tube lighting. So where the hell was this brilliance coming from?

On the floor but resting along the walls to the left were long, white containers. They were about four feet tall and to Paul Weston's knowledge of life they slightly resembled the freezers that you would see, side by side, in a branch of *Iceland*. Only differences being that they were much closer together and had no glass to look through at the frozen chips, pizzas or ice cream and there were no handles to open them with. There was a line about an inch below the top of the repository that went along the front and the sides of it, thereby suggesting that it must be a lid of sorts.

The walls were also white, startlingly so, and to Paul's eyes this wasn't just a quick paint job to clean the place up; this wasn't your average DIY attempt to cover up the years of dirt and grime with a fresh lick of gloss. It appeared that these walls were *covered* with some sort of material. There wasn't any sign of screws to show where it had been put on but it was obvious that this shimmering substance had somehow been adhered to the walls. And that was the odd thing—this stuff was indeed *shimmering*.

It was as if he was looking at a piece of clean, white Formica that had been ducked underneath some water, with ripples flowing across it in the sunlight.

Becky seemed to notice this too and she went across to the right of the room where she rested her hand against the wall. She touched it for a second before pulling it off with a gasp. She looked at Paul quizzically and then went back to rest her hand on the wall for a second time. This time she left it there, her palm open and her fingers parted.

Paul looked around for Dan but he was nowhere to be seen. This didn't make sense as he felt that he could see all of this strange room from where he was standing. He let his eyes scour the room and shouted Dan's name, but there was no reply. He looked at the white containers and just about noticed that on the wall above the 'lid' there was a tube that went up from the back of the box and towards the ceiling. He hadn't spotted it at first as the tube was the same colour as the wall and very thin; the thing was practically camouflaged. Following the tube upwards he saw that it connected to another white box that was about an inch from the very tall ceiling, so far up that Paul felt his head go as far back as possible as he looked up. These boxes were perfect cubes and roughly ten inches in width. Paul allowed himself to wonder at this sight before his attention returned to Becky Shaw. By now she had closed her eyes.

"What is it Becky? What are you feeling?"

Becky didn't reply. She just stood in the same spot, and then Paul noticed that she had started to move from side to side, not in a wildly noticeable way, but in a gentle, undulating motion.

"Becky? What are you feeling? Why are you moving like that?"

Again Becky offered no response and feeling alarm at Becky's actions Paul sidled up to her and put his hand on her right wrist. But Dr Shaw carried on her sideways rocking and now it was becoming more obvious that her movements were more pronounced. Then from her lips came a humming sound, humming that went up and down in tone and Paul saw with dismay that its pitch seemed to follow the flowing movements on that white material on the wall.

This time Paul Weston shouted. "Becky! Becky for God's sake answer me! Open your bloody eyes, this isn't funny!"

Becky certainly wasn't laughing. She wasn't even smiling, so why Paul had felt the need to query her sense of humour was odd but in his panic words just tumbled from his mouth.

The humming from Becky's mouth grew louder, her movement more wilder, and then from behind him Paul heard something else. A noise that something heavy and wet was moving. But the noise was muffled. He listened again, trying to train his ear on where it had come from and as Becky hummed, that bizarre noise sounded again. Paul imagined a huge ball of blancmange or jelly that had developed its own life and was attempting to travel around leaving sticky substances behind it; the sound was sickly and was starting to make him feel nauseous.

Then Becky's mouth opened and from it came sounds that Paul had never heard of before.

"*Betor mundi, betor mundo, ai friz a mundo, ssssss.*"

Paul stood in front of the doctor and held her chin with his hand.

"Becky? What the hell are you talking about? Open your eyes, stop this bloody moving and talk sense."

"*Betor mundi, betor mundo, ai friz a mundo, sssss.*"

The slurping, slushing noise sounded again, still muffled but now in a state of great disturbance, it's unearthly movement becoming more obvious.

Paul grabbed the arm that Becky had rested against the wall. It seemed as rigid as the rest of her body was fluid. He instinctively knew that he had to get her away from this wall; to disconnect her from whatever power source had grabbed her when she had fixed her palm against its peculiar white surface.

"*Betor mundi, betor mundo, ai friz a mundo, sssss.*"

He faced the wall and being careful not to touch that surface himself he grabbed her wrist with his right hand and pulled. It didn't move. He used his left hand, putting it slightly above his other one and pulled again. Becky still remained glued to the rippling patterns on the white wall.

Her movements were growing wilder. The wet, slushy noise now moving with even more intensity and Paul Weston, trying hard to keep hold of Becky's arm as she rocked this way and that, grew more and more distraught in his attempts to drag her away from this unknown force.

"*Betor mundi, betor mundo, ai friz a mundo, ssss.*"

"FUCKING MOVE BECKY! GET THE FUCK AWAY FROM THERE! DON'T LET THEM GET YOU AGAIN, FUCKING MOOOVE!"

"*Betor mundi, betor mundo, ai friz a mundo, sssssss.*"

"I'M GONNA . . . MOVE . . . YOU IF . . . ITS . . . THE LAST . . . THING . . . I . . . FUCKING DO!"

Now he was pulling her forearm, her sleeves sliding up as he tried to get a good grip. As that nauseating slushy sound became more animated Paul switched his head around as he pulled at Becky's arm. Then it became clear. That disgusting noise was coming from the white container. Something was moving about in there. No, not just in *there*—in all of them! It was getting louder because the same movements were starting to happen in *every* white box. And their noise had only started when Becky had got herself stuck to that wall.

"Oh God, what have you done Becky? What . . . have . . . . you . . . . DONE?"

Pulling her arm with each and every frustrated word, Paul felt such panic that he could start to feel tears well in his eyes. A woman he hadn't known five minutes and he was crying over her! Or was it that he was going to cry over this whole sorry state. Over the fact that this young lady, who had already gone through so much, had now managed to get herself into more danger.

"*Betor mundi, betor mundo, ai friz a mundo, ssssss . . . . Betor mundi, betor mundo, ai friz a mundo, ssssssssssss . . . .*"

Pulling, heaving, trying everything possible to get the young doctor away from the wall, the disgusting, slushy sound now getting louder in his ears . . . . but Becky Shaw wouldn't budge from where she was . . .

"*Betor mundi, bettor mundo, ai friz a mundo, sssss. BETOR MUNDI, BETOR MUNDO, AI FRIZ A MUNDO SSSSSSS . . . .*"

. . . . then silence. Becky stopped speaking that peculiar lingo and the loathsome noises from the white containers also ended.

Becky's hand moved away slowly from the wall and she let it fall to her side. She turned to look at Paul and continuously blinked her blue eyes, her long lashes fluttering like a delicate butterfly. Paul noticed that blood was coming from her nose again but she stared at Paul and didn't make any attempt to wipe it away.

He had put the blood and tear soaked handkerchief back into his jeans pocket but now he took it out again and reached up to clean Becky's septum, wondering if he had actually pulled her away, if maybe he had been so worked up that he really had got the girl away from that magnetic material and hadn't noticed that his effort had finally succeeded.

But footsteps and heavy panting disturbed his deliberations as Dan raced up to his friends. During the whole of Becky's trauma Paul hadn't given Dan any more thought. But here he was, still looking frantic and clutching a thick wire. As he spoke hurriedly to them Paul saw that the wire was about an inch in diameter and was seemingly made of a shiny, black material that he had never seen used before. Dan was waving it about in front of them as if he was conducting an invisible orchestra. From both ends there was a smaller dark red wire sticking out and if you didn't look closely you could have been forgiven for thinking that Dan had an eel trying to wriggle and escape his chunky grip. Then Paul noticed that Dan's hand had a red, round uneven patch below his knuckles that went down to his wrist and which looked vicious. Whatever Dan had been up to he had clearly paid some sort of price for it.

"Did it work? Did it work? I didn't know what I was going to get at first and was just standing there like a tit in a trance. I thought I would know what to do but when it came to it I didn't have a clue. Then I heard the noises, the humming sounds, that . . . . chanting. Was that Becky?" Paul nodded and Becky looked at both of the men with her face bemused. "I just grabbed what I could. I grabbed quite a few of these wire things and one of the fuckers got me." He showed his friends the wound that Paul had already noticed. "Just made a cracking noise and spat blue fire at my hand. When I got over the initial pain I tried to grab some more things as I could still see what was going on. Then I grabbed this baby, it was hidden behind all the others. I thought the worst when I grabbed it as it seemed more alive than the rest and I thought I'd get an ever worse injury or even worse than that, but with a few bastard pulls I got the thing out and then I heard everything stop. Did it work then?"

"Well, Dan, my not so old friend. Let me put it this way. If you weren't such a brute with a bad hand I'd give you a hug. A *man hug* obviously! But more to the point. I was looking for you and I couldn't see you! Where the fuck were you?"

Dan looked at Paul with his brow narrowed and his eyes full of confusion. He was standing with his back towards where he had come from but he pointed backwards with his thumb as if he was trying to hitchhike.

"I was there you dope! I kept looking around at you. Christ, I even called your name for help when I saw you and Becky come through the door. Look, can't you see that bloody big silver box with all the wires coming out of it? Look!"

Paul looked in the direction that Dan was referring to but all he could see was a blank, white wall at the end of the room.

"Sorry mate, there ain't any box of wires there. Can you see anything Becky?"

Becky looked in the same direction as Paul and shook her head. Her voice was quiet, almost a whisper as she responded.

"No Dan, I can't see anything else either. Maybe you were in another room?"

"What *other* room? Can you see any *other* room? For fuck's sake guys, do I have to be daddy bear and point it out to you? Now, follow my liddle finger children and Daddy . . will . . . show . . . you . . the . . . nasty . . . b . . . oxxxx."

Dan's words faltered as he turned to where he had come from. There really was no box of wires to be seen. He turned back to Paul and Becky.

"But you *must* have seen me messing about with it! Come *on*! I was yards away! Don't tell me the damned thing just got up and walked away! Did it go past you? Did you see the sodding box make a run for it?" Paul looked at Dan's exasperated face and wondered if everything had finally got to the guy; that what with his brain being messed with and being part and parcel of this wonderful new way of living, he had finally lost the cheese from his cracker.

"Dan, I really didn't hear you and I really didn't *see* you either! What can I do to make you believe that . . . ."

Paul didn't finish what he was going to say. There was a loud hiss as if a steam engine was just about to make its way somewhere. Then a smell that was acrid and which stung their noses floated their way. To Paul Weston it was all too obvious where this sibilation originated from and he looked at the containers on the left of the room.

As Paul, Dan and Becky looked, all the lids on the containers started to slowly open. As the gaps they was making widened, red and grey steam seeped forth and started to swirl around the room. The stench was getting stronger and all three tried to pull their clothing over their noses in order to breathe more easily. But as the lids opened more and more fully, the odour started to become so unbearable that it made the threesome choke and splutter. Paul was doubled over but then the sound of squelching arose again and when he held his head up he saw that from the nearest container a red mass was starting to appear. It was luminous red and was of an extremely thick, sludge type appearance. Paul immediately thought of a plaything from his childhood—a green goo from a pot that slithered over your hands and made all kinds of shapes without actually sticking to you. But this stuff in front of him, its veiny, bubbled exterior twisting and slithering from left to right, was making his gorge rise.

Gradually, it starting to flow over the lip of the container and began to drip viscously to the floor. But just as it looked like this malevolent looking substance was going to try and slither its way towards them, its movement stopped. Paul looked along the other containers and saw that they also had this red slime half in and half out of them. Then the blaring started.

Paul, Becky and Dan were being gagged by the acidic stench from the containers and now their ear drums rattled and pulsated in their heads as this sharp screech pierced their consciousness. It was loud and almost tangible. They could feel its spiky fingers trying to jam into their ears and prod viciously at their minds.

His entire being swimming at this assault on his senses, Paul knew that they had to get out of this peculiar room. He looked towards the broken door and focused on making his legs head in that direction, but his head was feeling awkwardly heavy and looking at the way that Becky and Dan were crumpling to the floor it was obvious that they were in the same boat as him.

He grabbed Becky and clutching hold of her jacket he made a futile attempt to drag her up but the heaviness he was feeling in his own body and the weight of the doctor made it near impossible—his energy had ostensibly been zapped from him.

Saliva filled his mouth and his heart rate stepped up—there was no doubt that he was going to vomit and wooziness caressed his face and chilled his skin.

All three of them were sprawled on the floor, trying to block their ears and keep their noses under their jackets as that excruciating banshee wail went on and on and on.

Then almost abruptly the noise, that unspeakable, shattering piercing relented. The stench from the containers was starting to thin out a little too in the atmosphere and for a second the threesome could breathe in uncontaminated air. Their ears were screaming their outrage at the battering they had just undertaken and they heard a buzzing that was only in their heads but the relief at the ending of that teeth-itching noise was palpable.

Then Dan groaned. Paul initially thought it was just the effects of the aural and nasal assault they had just endured but he followed the guard's gaze and what he saw standing in the broken doorway struck his soul with terror—there was Burn, at least what *had* been Burn. If it wasn't for the man's suit and his shock of hair then Paul may have had more trouble recognising him. But this, this *creature* was Burn after a gruesome makeover. His face was bright red, his eyebrows had been replaced by a deep indentation that burrowed deep above his eyes . . . and the eyes, if they were there, were behind a red mist that swarmed out from his face and lingered about his head. The whole ensemble that was Thomas Burn was pulsating and giving off an energy that they all felt was perilous. And there was that smell again, the one that had come from the containers; Thomas Burn reeked of that pungent stench, it seemed to be coming from every part of him and Paul felt that sickness start to come back with a vengeance. This wasn't helped when Burn's deeper, wetter and inhuman tones spoke to them.

"Well, well. Haven't you done well my little heroes? Dan, I am so disappointed in you, I really thought that you had potential to be an important part of this operation. Doctor Becky, such a kind soul, such a sweet, attractive and attentive girl that would've gained so much from being part of the new order that Mr Leonard has so interestingly set in motion. And then Mr Weston. I thought Mr Rogers was an interesting specimen, but you really are not to be underestimated are you? But then, you are feeling rather scared aren't you? At least Mr Rogers is too narrow minded to feel fear when he's put in an awkward situation. I can see why you hate him so much. Tut, such jealousy can eat one up Mr Weston."

"Fuck you weirdo!" Paul didn't know that he was going to suddenly throw out this expletive but the thought of Mick being braver than him touch the rawest of nerves. But as soon as it was out he wished that he could gather it back in as Burn moved, *floated?* towards them.

Dan had stood up and had pulled Becky with him. He returned to the back of the room with the doctor, constantly looking back in trepidation at what Burn was going to do next. When Paul saw their retreat he knew that it was a pointless move but at least he would be with his friends. If they were going to die then he'd rather go with them than die all alone.

It was as they reached the part of the room that Dan had initially spoken of that Paul noticed something to his right. There was a large cabinet. It was perfectly square, about a metre in width and length, made of the same bluey chrome material that the chairs were made of and its door was wide open. On the front of the door, Paul could just make out in what he thought of as a hologram, the star and arrow symbol that was on the chairs. Wires of every conceivable colour spilled out and there were dark flash marks where fire had leapt out and stained the metal. Inside, Paul could see two ends of the thick, shiny, eel like tubing on each side of the cabinet. He looked at Dan who shrugged his shoulders.

"I told you it was here didn't I? You thought I was going mad didn't you? Where else would I have got that black tube from?" He pointed to the place where Becky had been stuck and the thick cable that was now on the floor.

"But, we couldn't see it. You noticed it yourself Dan! You asked me if it had run away! Come on, this is insane. It can't have been here and not here!"

"Oh but it can Mr Weston. You just don't understand that it isn't just you monkeys that have the intelligence to invent wonderful things, and I use the word *intelligence* very lightly. This was merely a simple security measure if you like, just in case somebody was stupid enough to get through the door. What you people would term an *optical illusion* I suppose but something that is a straight forward deviation of time and space for people of my kind. This box, as you think of it, wasn't to be seen by anyone in case it was tampered with and therefore damaged the little ones in those containers. Well, it seems that Dan here was party to this knowledge somehow, rather mistakenly I must say, and now you have permanently damaged my defenceless kin. You *will* have to pay for this, you do know that don't you?"

Burn was in front of them. Neither of them had seen or felt him approach but in a split second, Burn had made the trio a quartet.

"What is so disappointing is that we could have shared this knowledge with you all. If you had just relented then this planet would've become a safer and happier place with no more futile arguments and technology you could only dream about. It would have all been yours. But your typical human curiosity just had to screw things up, didn't it? We cared about you, didn't you see that?"

Becky looked into the mist of Burn, and Paul could sense outrage seeping from her pores. She spoke to this being in front of them but her voice, as brave as she wanted to sound, was shaky, her breathing shallow, her heartbeat racing.

"Care? Did you just say care? *I care* Mr fucking Burn, or whoever you fucking are! I have spent years training to show how much I *care!* Dan *cares*, at least he had a job where he cared deeply before you used him for your own sick motives. Now, you are a fucking ugly monster and I'm sure you have powers that we've never imagined before. I've seen what you can do and it terrifies me, in fact it was the shock of it that brought me to my senses! So do what you need to do. Kill us or fuck off, because to be honest you freak, you fucking stink!"

Burn reached out, his hand was now thinner and of a red, bubbled substance. There were no longer five fingers but a row of floundering tentacle type appendages that crackled and throbbed, steam pounding off them. He went to lay it on the shoulder of the brave, female doctor, his smouldering face giving a lipless smile that opened to show a dark cavern with what looked like steel needles where his teeth should have been.

Dan broke through his terror and grabbed this *hand* away from where it was about to rest. It felt strangely cool despite the steam; damp, sticky and unlike anything Dan had ever felt in his life.

"No you don't mate! You leave her alone! If you want a piece of someone then try me but leave her alone. It would be bloody typical of you to pick on a woman wouldn't it you fucking coward!"

Burn turned towards Dan, his snake like hand being held in the air by the guard, who despite his gallantry was definitely trying to keep it away from his own face. Burn sensed this unease immediately and pushed his captive hand towards the sweating, wide eyed face of Dan, the tentacles seeming to stretch and search as they neared the flesh of the ex funeral director.

Dan was putting as much of his considerable strength into holding the hand away from him but Burn was forcing it forward without any effort. Suddenly, thrusting the hand away, Dan let the hand go and leapt backwards in an attempt to get away from what Burn was attempting to do. As he did so he stumbled, his right leg buckling under him and he sprawled to the floor, looking up at the creature that used to be Burn as it paced forwards and towered over him.

"N . . n . . . n . . . no, Mr Burn, sir, please listen. I was only protecting Dr Shaw. Isn't that what you wanted us to do? To . . . to show kindness and respect towards others? Ok. I shouldn't have come here, I'm sorry, but . . . but . . . ."

"But what Dan? You don't know what to say, do you? You don't know what to say because you have made up your mind that we are the enemy, that what we are doing here is for our own benefit? Well, ok, I give up, I suppose that it wouldn't hurt for you to be trusted with another piece of information. You are right, absolutely right. We *are* here for our own gains and using the aggression and the narrow mindedness of the human race to gain it. And who can blame us when the whole universe is aware of the stinking hypocrisy that exists on your precious little world. *Kindness and respect* you say? Yes, all very nice. Of course, it is so much easier to deal with people when their aggression has been removed wouldn't you say? Now, I'd love to chat with you more, but I believe that you have destroyed something close to me and that won't do you moron, that won't do at all."

Becky and Paul had looked on in repulsion as Burn's wet, deep voice spoke and their hearts sank when they listened to what Burn had to say. As Burn finished speaking he moved forward towards Dan who had now backed into a corner but had nowhere else to go and as he reached down to him Paul rushed forward and leapt onto the back of this unearthly intruder, his arm hooked around his neck and feeling like he was desperate for an unreal version of a piggy back ride. Becky looked at this spectacle with shock at Paul's sudden bravery and in a split second she knew that Dan had only been trying to protect *her*; that seeing her bleeding so badly back in the conditioning room had finally caused him to lose his temper and she wondered if the guard had been fonder of her than he had let on? Now his life was in danger and she knew that she had to ignore the fear that was surging through her and help Paul get Burn away from the guy that really *had* tried to be her 'hero.'

But as she approached them, she could see that Paul was having no effect on the steaming, relentless progress of Burn; he was trying to pull the being back somehow, now using his own weight as a lever to maybe drag Burn down, but still he remained on the back of the thing that had now grabbed Dan under the chin and was lifting him up with ease.

It was obvious to Becky that the strength of this man was outrageous and that even if she was to fling herself upon him it would make no difference to the outcome. But these moments of uncertainty were moments that couldn't be wasted and now Dan had been lifted four feet off the ground and Paul was grabbing and pulling at the head of Burn; pulling with a face that showed total effort and what Becky saw as disgust because as his fingers dug into Burn there was a crackling noise which suggested that Paul was being shocked.

Instead, Paul was now looking at Becky as he started raining punches onto Thomas Burn and if he had had the time to speak to her he would have said that the only pain he felt was from the way his fists were punching something so hard that it might as well have been stainless steel.

Dan's face was growing redder by the second and vapour, steam, whatever it was that kept emanating from Burn, was now coming from him in clouds that enveloped Paul as he clung onto Dan's attacker. Paul was coughing, choking and that acrid smell was causing his sinuses to sting and tears to flow from his eyes and he felt his grip loosen around the neck of Burn as his head swam and all serious thought left his mind.

Now Becky saw that the guard's skin was starting to loosen around his face and his eyes were becoming so bloodshot that they seemed to be at one with the redness of his skin. His mouth was open as if he was screaming but nothing was coming out but gasps and spittle; flecks of it raining down onto his tie and bubbling at the corners of his mouth.

She looked around the white and chrome room, her head flicking this way and that, the only other colour being the red of the things that had slithered out of those freezer type vessels.

And still Burn stood there, motionless, lifting this big man almost above his head in ridiculous ease, his focus totally on the man who he had deemed to have killed the 'little ones' that were in those weird containers.

Paul couldn't hold on anymore. His fingers parted and he fell back to the floor, falling and landing onto his sacrum with such a force that the shot of pain that flared up his spine jerked some consciousness back into his mind. He sat on the floor, looked firstly at the plight of the guard that he could not help and feeling that he was useless in his efforts; then turning his head to the right, his ears started to perceive the slushy, aqueous sound that had been going on whilst Becky had been in her daze and he noticed that the doctor had gone over to one of the containers.

She was lifting the jelly mess that was one of the 'little ones'. It was slipping and sliding through her hands and over her arms leaving red stains on her clothes and despite it looking heavy and awkward to carry she hoisted and dragged this hideousness from its abode as red liquid followed this bulk and pooled around her feet. As she moved, Paul could see that this liquid was sticky as it clung to Becky's shoes, producing glistening threads between the soles and the floor.

"Hey Burn, is this one of your 'little ones' then? It don't look so little to me you freak! It looks fucking ugly to me. You sure it's not a mistake caused by one of your fucked up experiments?"

As Burn finally turned his head, the red mist pouring all around him, Becky felt her gag reflex wanting to work without any interference at the feel of the slithering, undulating, wetness that she was fighting to keep hold of. Then Dan fell from where he had been held, crashing to the floor in a heap, his legs and right arm underneath him and his face to the floor.

Burn swivelled around and Becky noticed that he was off the ground, that he was floating inches above the floor and its face was now so red that it was glowing like a poker that has been heating away in a roaring fire. The mouth was open and Becky noticed fang like teeth under what should have been its upper lip to complement the sharp, lethal looking needles that she had already noticed. And now Burn, this throbbing, steaming, vindictive animal was slowly making its way towards her as Paul raced to where Dan had fallen.

He lifted the guard's head, not sure what he would find and then dropped it just as quickly as he jolted backwards in terror; Dan's skin was sliding around his face and its gelatinous texture was causing some of it to stick to the floor, and as Paul pulled the head up some came away leaving patches of bone gleaming in the sharp whiteness of the room's light. As the guard's head hit the floor again, this time at an angle so it was resting on its right ear, the gooey white liquid that used to be eyes started to seep down the cheeks and mingle with the mess of blood, skin and bone.

Becky looked at Paul as he shook his head and with grief choking her she howled her anguish despite the oncoming presence of Thomas Burn.

"Nooooo! Why you bastard? Why did you have to kill him?"

"Put the little one back Dr Shaw."

"It's dead you freak! The thing tried to get out and died!"

"He killed them Dr Shaw. Put the little one back."

"Or what? Gonna kill me too? I've seen what you are trying to do Burn. When I put my hand on that moving wall of yours I *saw* what you want to do. I became one of you sad fuckers. I felt your motives and your desires."

"You knew no more than what you did before Dr Shaw. Put the little one back."

"Oh but I knew *nothing* before. When I came out of that trance like shit that you put us under I didn't remember a damn thing. But touch that bloody wall and suddenly I know what you bastards are up to."

"No human would survive the powers that we use in this sanctum. You lie Dr Shaw. Put the little one back."

"I *lie*? Use your powers Burn. Read my mind. Tell me again that I *lie!*"

"Betor mundi, betor mundo, ai friz a mundo, ssssss." Both Becky and Burn looked at Paul who had uttered that strange incantation and was walking towards them, even now being careful not to step into the liquid mess that was surrounding Becky's feet.

"What did you say Weston?"

Paul kept his eyes fully on Becky and took a deep breath as he answered Burn's question.

"Betor mundi, betor mundo, ai friz a mundo, sssssss."

"Where did you learn this speech?"

"From Becky. That's what she was repeating over and over again when the power from that wall was running through her."

Becky stared at Paul, her eyes narrow and questioning.

"I don't remember saying anything, I could only see what was going through the minds of these people."

"If you mean me and the Rector then you are mistaken Dr Shaw. You merely saw what was going through the *minds,* as you quaintly put it, of the little ones here."

"But I saw the spite, the hatred, the desire to wipe out anything that stands in your way. I *felt* it too. I have never felt such hatred in my life. You must be full of nothing but hate and evil. Jesus, you can't get away with this. Paul, they *can't* get away with this!"

"You are in no position to tell us what we can get away with Dr Shaw. Now I have asked you a few times to put the little one back but you have failed to respond to my order. I am sorry Dr Shaw."

Burn reached towards the red mass that Becky was trying to hold and Paul saw as well as heard the crackling of a bright blue force that came from Burn and hit the creature in Becky's arms. As soon as this force hit the bulbous, slimy mass it started to twitch and slowly undulate in the arms of the student doctor.

Noticing this disgusting movement, feeling the pulsating that now ran through it to prove that it was alive again, Becky turned and tried to push the red slime into the container that it had come from . . . . but she couldn't detach it from her hands.

The slime had been sticky, it had been difficult to handle, but she had been able to move her hands around it but now she was adhered to it, just as she had been to the glowing, pulsating wall. Her terror was indescribable and she cried, tears springing from her blue eyes as she screamed for help.

"Paul! I can't get it off me. Help me Paul, the fucking thing is stuck to me."

Paul rushed forward to help the doctor, the grief and panic in her face grabbing his heart and giving him no choice but to get that thing off of her. But he only took two paces when Burn held out his left arm and Paul stopped still. He stared at Becky in helplessness, trying to tell her that he was rooted to the spot, but he couldn't speak, he could only stare and breathe in the stinging, polluted air that came off Thomas Burn.

"Paul? Paul! It won't leave me! Fuck's sake Paul! Help me! HELP ME!"

Now Paul Weston felt sickness as well as helplessness as the red, palpitating creature seemed to drag the doctor into it; surrounding her arms, creeping up towards her shoulders, sliding down towards her knees.

"PAUL! HELP ME! GET IT OFF ME! PAUUUUL! PAUUULL!"

Paul tried to will himself to move but his body was denying his right to move his arms and legs. It was like someone was using a remote control on him and had pressed the stop button. His heart was aching with hurt as Becky Shaw screamed his name with such fear and anguish . . . and then her face went blank and when she opened her mouth again Paul knew that the lovely Dr Shaw was doomed and he desperately wanted to cover his ears as she moaned, hummed and then spoke.

"*Betor mundi, betor mundo, ai friz a mundo, sssss . . . . Betor mundi, betor mundo, ai friz a mundo, sssss . . . . Betor mundi, betor mundo, ai friz . . . .*"

She went no further as the gruesome 'little one' crept past her chin and smothered her mouth. Paul tried to scream Becky's name as it then rose up and covered the doctor's eyes, forehead and then her straw like blonde hair. Within a minute of being zapped by Thomas Burn, this red mass had covered young Dr Becky Shaw from head to foot, devoured her whole and was now slushing and creeping its way back into the container from which Becky had lifted it.

When the lid of the container was shut, Paul felt a jolt in his body and he was able to move. He turned to Burn, not noticing that he had resumed most of the human features that had been on show to all the 'brothers and sisters' and flew at him, fists raised and feeling nothing but an insatiable anger and a will to get at this monster that had killed Dan and then Becky.

But Burn just raised a hand and Paul stopped still where he was, before the hand was lowered and Paul felt that jolt again that knocked him slightly backwards and he was able to move.

"Pointless trying to attack me Weston. Do you *really* think that I would let you near me again? I could've dealt with you so easily when you decided to jump on my back and punch me. Which reminds me, how *is* your hand?"

Ignoring Burn's sarcasm Paul could not help himself from screaming what was in his heart.

"You didn't have to kill them you bastard. With all your wonderful powers you didn't have to kill them."

"I warned Dr Shaw that she should . . . ."

"Put the 'little one' back? Yeah I heard you. How was she to know that the fucking thing would come alive and kill her though?"

"That is irrelevant Mr Weston. She showed great disrespect and rudeness by refusing to listen to me. Most unlike what we wanted to provide in this establishment . . . . on this planet no less."

Paul's feeling of astonishment flooded through him.

"You don't mean to tell me that you are still bullshitting about your reasons for doing all of this are you? Whatever Becky saw or felt obviously was too near the knuckle for you otherwise you wouldn't have killed her."

"It wasn't me that killed her Weston, it was the 'little one'" This was said with a smile that just irritated Paul all the more. For everything that this Burn had shown and done he no longer feared him; he wanted revenge for the deaths of his new friends, for the brainwashing of the masses of people and also for dragging him and his family into this nightmare.

"Ha, you really are a fucking comedian aren't you Burn? That's if Burn is your name. Killer, bullshitter, face-changer and now a comedian. Anything else you can do before you kill me too? How about a nice song you tosser? How about 'My Way'? Shall I start it off for you? *And now, the end is near . . . ."*

"I have no intention of killing you Weston. Not unless you give me cause to that is. No, you are coming with me. I received a message from my fellow brothers and you my friend are taking a journey with me. Now come."

Paul didn't have a chance to reply as Burn moved forward and grabbed him by the arm. He effortlessly dragged Paul through the broken door, through the conditioning room and into the building, where 'brothers and sisters' of this unholy cause were now milling around in unordered chaos, recovering from the deafening alarm that had sounded and looking as if they didn't know where they were or what they were to do. Some of them bled profusely from their noses and their eyes, others were holding their heads and screaming in pain.

About a minute after leaving that clinical, secret room, Paul found himself being pushed down a passageway that grew steadily more and more darker, more and more colder and with a strong smell of dampness. Then they were by a locked door that was heavily padlocked, but Burn merely touched it and Paul was no longer surprised to see that lock melt away. They were through the door and down some stairs into what looked like a dark cellar, the musty odour now unbearably strong and as the door above them slowly shut close behind them Paul could only make out wires travelling along the dark, earthy walls and a darker, large rectangle to their right. It was this rectangle that Paul was pushed towards.

"I can't see anything. How am I supposed to know where I'm going?"

"Not important Mr Weston. *I* know where we are going and that's all you need to know. Now move, we have people to see, explanations to make."

Paul Weston was propelled forward into the darkness.

CHAPTER THIRTY-TWO

"You always took me to the nicest places, Mick. How nice of you to arrange my own car as well? *And* a reunion with Emily too! If I didn't know better, I would say you were trying to impress me!"

Mick looked ahead of him and decided not to respond to his ex girlfriend's dig. He was trying to understand what on earth had happened over the past half an hour.

Firstly, he and Emily had been whisked along at an unheard of pace to this building that Mick knew used to be the York Road tube station. Now it was abandoned and had been since the 1930s as far as Mick knew. He wasn't even aware that there was a way in until the Rector had taken him to the left of the building. Underneath the 'YORK' part of the original station lettering, still visible in dirty gold upon a maroon coloured background, and most bizarrely next door to a house that must have been built there twenty or so years before and as part of a new estate, was a large, fairly modern steel shutter. This was of a similar maroon colour to the station's original tiling and Mick had thought that somebody must've decided to paint it that colour in a strange attempt for it to fit in with the station's original, early 1900's, London Transport colour scheme.

It didn't really work but then who cared? London was full of disused stations like this one and when it became obvious that the Rector intended to enter this place then Mick had felt goose bumps on his arms and had tightened his grip on Emily. He had always had this irrational fear of closed down underground stations. Maybe it was because when he was a boy he had been on a tube train that had gone past the old Strand station, and young Michael had been peering out the darkened window to see what looked to him like a mini ghost town, with abandoned platform, posters, exits and bits of wiring hanging down from the ceilings. It had turned him cold and Mick, even in adulthood, was always aware of being in a tube station too late at night in case he got locked in. He understood how brilliant a concept underground travelling was, but then he also felt to be so far under the ground wasn't quite right either. *You spend most of your life worrying about your last breath and being put six feet under, and then here we all are, travelling around even further below that!* No, like with most things in this world, Mick Rogers didn't understand what that was all about.

The Rector had touched what Mick had felt must be a panel on or near the shutter because it started to roll upwards, slowly but surely, revealing dirty, dark brown brick work with a metal door in the middle of it. The brick work looked very dated and was crumbling in places, but the door was definitely not and its chrome sheen gave off a blueish glow in the glare of the streetlights, despite the late evening sky making everything look more sinister than usual.

After the door was opened, again with just a touch from the Rector's hand, Theobald Leonard, who was still looking subdued and touching the wounds on his head, was told to go inside. He had looked at the Rector as if he was insane, questioning him with his eyes, but the Rector looked down at him with such sudden malice across his darkening face that Leonard relented and stepping over a step went through the doorway.

When Mick and Emily joined him, they found themselves in a dusty room with old wooden benches all bare apart from the odd screw, nail and broken slithers of wood; also, bits of odd looking machinery scattered here and there and when the door shut behind them they were in complete darkness for a few seconds before the click of a torch went on and Mick saw that Leonard was carrying what could have been mistaken for a LED diving torch. The brightness was dazzling so much that to stare into it would've been tantamount to staring at the sun and to Mick it was the most impressive torch he had even seen, even if the light it gave out seemed to be radiating heat as well as light. The Rector had noticed him trying to gaze at this item.

"Just a little something from home. Well, no disrespect but we find your attempts at bringing light to a situation just a little bit . . . dim?"

"It doesn't bother me, but I am surprised, considering the way you people like candles so much? Your little HQ was the most miserable bloody place I've ever been in."

"Ah now, I cannot take the blame for such an arrangement. For that you would need to speak to my . . . . colleague here. Isn't that right Mr Leonard? *Our great Leader!*"

From behind the torch's glare Mick had seen the miserable face of Leonard and as the Rector spoke his words seemed to sting him as he flinched at every syllable, especially the last three in the sentence.

But now looking around, Mick could see that some of the machinery would have been used in the printing industry. Items like ink rollers and plate cylinders were to be seen, the torch's gleam lighting them up like they were being spotlighted in a museum exhibition. Then Mick remembered of how on the outside of the station, below the architectural arches that were a standard feature of stations from that era, was a yellow sign with black upper case writing that declared the VICTOR PRINTING CO LTD. Mick had always believed such companies to be on the upper floors of stations but then decades down the line he supposed that for there to be such a movement of old equipment shouldn't be too strange.

Leonard, uncomfortably, was pushed forward by the Rector and he and Emily had been urged to follow. As they made their way through the darkened station they arrived at the old ticket hall; Mick had noticed and shook at the sight of the old lifts, for through the triangular gaps in the shutters you could just about notice that there was no lift waiting to take you down but instead a drop into nothingness. He had never trusted the old style lifts of the tube stations, but the thought of a shaft without a lift alarmed him even more.

They had then been on a short journey down a winding, stinking emergency staircase, going deeper and deeper underground, before coming out of an aperture that led onto a small walkway that connected the northbound and southbound platforms . . . at least they would have done if the platforms had still been there.

Then a right turn onto the northbound 'platform' which was, as far as Mick could see in the torchlight, just a mass of dirt, rocks, old bits of paper and thrown away food containers including the odd coke can here and there before you came to the electrified track. Mick wondered how such things would've found their way down here after all these years and figured that maybe it wouldn't be so surprising if some of the local teens had found their way into the station and had come down here for a snog, snort or injection of something or even just to prove to themselves and their friends just how brave and cool they were. The fact that they were just yards away from an unguarded 400 volt rail that would zap them if they so much as touched it was irrelevant, because cool people like them were too clever to suffer such a fate, weren't they?

The Rector had told Leonard to swing the torchlight to the right of the platform and as they were marched along they went past huge cylinders and lumps of metal which no doubt had something to do with the running of trains but which Mick could never guess in a million years. Then as they had trudged towards the round, foreboding dark mouth that was a tunnel, a warm, dusty breeze brushing their faces and pushing back their hair, Mick could see that some of the old platform had been bricked off, providing a wall between where the platform had been and the track. This wall looked as if it had been built with white breeze blocks that went all the way up to the ceiling but which over the years had become blackened with dirt and smoke and also covered in splodges of green moss.

As they had walked behind this wall, Mick had felt slightly relieved to be away from the danger of the track and any oncoming trains, and the torchlight had shown a short, white staircase with a white handrail against the platform wall that led to a dirty white door; at the bottom of the platform there was the black rectangle of an old wooden door that had clearly been there since the station had been opened. Looking above them, there were white wooden beams that connected the breeze blocks to the platform's original wall and next to these were round, grey lampshades that for some reason reminded Mick of elephant's feet, albeit with thinner ankles. Mick figured there were at least ten of these lights and beams along this part of the platform

It was here, by the staircase, that Mick, Emily and Leonard had been told to stop. Emily had been clutching Mick's hand more and more tightly as they walked but to Mick's amazement and admiration had stayed quiet and seemingly calm in this decrepit structure.

Every now and then, the Rector had closed his eyes as if he was listening to something. At one point he smiled, at another his face had shown an anger that even Leonard had flinched at. Strange facial expressions aside, there had been no talking for a good five minutes.

A sudden rumbling that grew louder, more wind being blown through the abandoned platform, paper flying around their feet and dust rising up and causing them to sneeze, then the roar of a tube train passing by them on the other side of the breeze blocks, making them shake slightly as it made its way onto its next destination. Emily had blocked her ears in response while Mick and Leonard had stood still not daring to move and willing the train to go by quickly.

Then after what had seemed like an eternity, the Rector had shaken himself from his strange trance like state and grinned at his audience.

"Ah, it seems our group is now almost complete. Let the real tour begin, what do you say Mr Rogers?"

Amid the crunching of footsteps on dirt, Mick had turned to see Maria being pushed along by a handsome looking chap who must have been over six feet tall and had his hand on Maria's shoulder. As they got closer he could hear Maria's unmistakable tones of annoyance.

"For fuck's sake where are you taking me? What the hell are we doing down here? Will you take your fucking hand off of my shoulder you tosser!"

When she had seen Emily, she had screamed and rushed forward, picking her up, holding her tightly and smothering her face in kisses. When she had seen Mick her look had told him that she wasn't surprised that he was here too, and when she saw the miserable look on Leonard's face she then gave Mick a different look, a look that clearly asked *what had happened to him?*

Now Maria was standing next to Mick, leaning against the wall, holding Emily in front of her, her arms across her chest. Maria's escort had been dismissed and they had exchanged their tales of what had happened since their last meeting in the causes HQ, Maria getting more emotional when talking about 'Uncle Harry' and both of them had asked Leonard questions of what he intended to do with them—all of which were ignored by the self styled leader who had sat down on the dirty floor and drawn his knees up to his face. The Rector had made approving noises at these questions as if Leonard really did owe these people an explanation, his face a grinning mask that Mick didn't trust one iota.

"I feel, my friends, that Mr Leonard is feeling a little bit bashful at the moment. You see, everything had been going so well and then I feel that he got a little bit too confident, wouldn't you say so Mr Leonard?"

Leonard looked up at the Rector, his face a picture of misery. And then he spoke for the first time since Mick had seen him at their HQ, his voice was croaky and less confident than before, but there was still an undercurrent of pride there, as if he was still on a par with the lanky, dark clothed character before them.

"I have done what we agreed on. I have shown leadership and an ability to change the world for the better. Since the great day you approached me and saw me for the saviour that I am you have *known* that my ideals were akin to yours and we have achieved so much already. You have taught me and made me stronger, despite my own natural abilities, you know that . . ."

"Sorry, did you say *natural abilities* my friend?" interrupted the Rector. At this point he removed his ever present wide rimmed hat and threw it; it skimmed through the air before landing at an angle against the platform wall. "Okay, let me get this straight my friend. You had the ability to put yourself in a trance, or at least what you considered a trance. You used candles to give the feeling of a deepening of this state and I have no doubt that it relaxed you. Simple psychological process for humans I assure you. You have used candlelight to constantly keep this feeling of powerful relaxation within you and we have gone along with that idea quite happily as your state of mind was so easy to teach and instruct. You picked up your *powers* from us quite readily and without any barriers for you have, unlike many of your kind, made serious attempts to control the power that your little brains have and which many of your kind do not have the intelligence to use. We commend you for that Theobald. You *have* been an absolute boon to us my friend, but the fear was always that your ego would get out of control and you would believe your own hype. Your little escapade outside the station proved that. You used what powers we gave you regrettably and now we have been forced to rethink the plans we made."

Maria's eyes had widened at this dialogue and she looked at them all with exasperation, her voice high and not without a little bit of sarcasm.

"Did he just say *saviour*? He did didn't he? He just called himself a bloody *saviour*! I *knew* he was a fucking fruitcake! What did I say Mick? Now will you believe me? He thinks he's the second coming! For fuck's sake I've had enough of this!"

"Mmm, to be honest with you Mezza, even though I knew myself that Mr Leonard here was suffering delusions of grandeur, I'm more worried about his friends." Mick responded. "What is the point of this Rector? What do you hope to achieve with your brainwashing, your out of this world abilities? You have screwed up so many people, turned strangers against each other in shows of violence, and yet you made yourselves out to be so good, so peaceful, so God fearing and concerned for the well being of all. And why Emily? Why us? You and Burn and all your other cronies have a lot to answer for."

The Rector looked up the platform and smiled.

"Well, why don't you ask the question then Mr Rogers? In fact, why not ask Mr Burn yourself, for here is my friend and colleague now."

Thomas Burn and Paul had appeared from the wooden door at the end of the platform and were moving effortlessly, too smoothly across the dirty ground towards them. When they got within a few feet of them, Paul saw Mick and his face creased with all the frustration and anger that he had been feeling since the demise of his two recent friends.

"You! *You* have been the cause of this mess you bastard. Why the fuck couldn't you just stay away from my family? I'm gonna make sure you keep away from my girls, come here!"

Mick backed away as Paul rushed towards him, his fist raised and with every intention to connect with the face of the man he held responsible for his being brought into contact with the Rector and Burn. But what he didn't expect was Maria suddenly jumping between them and trying to grab his clenched hand.

"No you fucking idiot! Why are you blaming him? Leave him alone! You keep having a go at him and he isn't to blame! He is the one that got Emily out of that dodgy place so stop threatening him!"

Paul stopped, his body shaking with emotion and looked at Maria and Mick alternately. He saw Emily next to Maria. She had run between him and Mick as well and was clinging onto Maria's leg as she stood her ground.

"Yeah, so he got her out of that place and brought her here. Well done you fucking *hero*!" Paul's tone was calmer but still with that edge of hostility.

"Don't call me a hero Paul," Mick replied with more annoyance than he expected, "even when taking the piss, don't call me a hero. I only did what I thought was best for Emily. For all of you. It isn't my fault that this bastard and his leader friend stopped us and brought us here. I mean, if you're so bloody good, what the hell are you doing here too?"

Paul went to open his mouth in response but was stopped short by the deep, wet laugh of Thomas Burn. Burn's appearance was back to how he had originally appeared to them but his voice was how it had been when he had changed into that red faced, steaming creature from Hades.

"Ah children, children. How lovely to see the real faces of your kind! Mr Rogers, you are a star, do you know that? How I wish we had chosen you instead of Mr Leonard, but at the time Theobald was looking so good with his ability to channel his energies so delightfully. Why, me and the Rector are only surprised he didn't take astral flight as well, aren't we Rector?"

"You bastards!" Leonard's voice was audible above the laughs of the Rector and Burn and Mick knew that Leonard was now powerless. Whatever his role had been in this cause had come to an end for the two creatures before him now treated him with disdain. If anything, it was he that they seemed to be more interested in and despite the fear that was in the pit of his stomach there was also an undeniable feeling of curiosity.

"Now, you see the little staircase there? If you'd be so kind as to climb up it and go through the door. Maybe then we can finally put your minds at rest. Whether permanently or not could be up to you." The Rector gestured towards the dirty white door he had spoken of and like lambs to the slaughter, Mick, Maria, Emily, Paul and Theobald Leonard were encouraged to use it.

Paul groaned as they entered a chamber that was glowing white and chrome. It was circular and vast and he had spotted the pulsating white material that Becky had become stuck to covering all of the walls; there were also containers against parts of the wall that looked unmistakably like those he had seen in the room where Dan and Becky had met their ends. There was that acidic stench again permeating the atmosphere and which made the others hold their noses but which, oddly enough, he was becoming strangely used to. There were screens at the far end that looked like large, plasma TV screens, five of them in a row but blank and showing no images; they were slightly curved outwards as they clung onto the bend in the walls. Large cabinets, each about twelve foot high and six foot wide, all white apart from a chrome front which showed the star and piercing arrow symbol on the front, were also against parts of the wall and from these came humming sounds that every now and then would stop, start, stop then sound smoothly again.

There were two of the chairs from the 'conditioning room,' one of them on its back and another one that had been dismantled. Then close by the dismantled chair Paul saw one of the cabinets that had been attached to those being 'conditioned' and yet again he thought of the plight of the doomed Jeffrey.

"Ah, I wondered when I would have the joy of seeing one of those contraptions again. What you gonna do? Connect it to us and turn us into one of your pet zombies?"

The Rector approached Paul in response to his query and was soon looming over him.

"I wasn't aware that you took such an interest in them Mr Weston? Having said that, you seemed very interested in the workings of our little, what would you call it? Our little *nursery* back in the Hotel. Very interested indeed. Maybe we should *connect* you to it so that you can appreciate a lot more what we are about. That's if you wish that is?"

"What nursery?" Maria's ears had pricked up at this noun.

"Oh did you not know my dear Maria? It seems that your husband here made some little friends back at our hotel and they decided to go on a little wrecking spree, isn't that right Mr Weston? He and his new amigos found the *nursery* and damaged the control that was keeping our little ones alive and growing. Would you like to explain more to your dear wife Mr Weston?"

"You killed little ones Paul? Don't tell me you killed some infants? Please don't tell me that? And what bloody friends anyway?"

Paul found himself in the similar situation as to when Maria had insinuated that he had hit Emily back in Southend. He sighed deeply, ignoring the fascinated face of Mick Rogers and the shocked looks of Theobald Leonard.

"They weren't infants Maria! They weren't even human! They were some kind of red mess that slopped out of containers exactly like those. They stank so much and looked fucking evil. And anyway, I didn't touch them. It was Dan that screwed up their power supply and it was Becky that dragged one out of its box. Christ I wish she had left the damn thing alone. It killed her, just swallowed her up and killed her!"

Maria was looking at the containers that Paul was pointing towards but seemed more interested in the names he had mentioned.

"Dan? Becky? Who the fuck are they? Jesus, I should've known that you'd go off and make friends when me and Emily were in trouble! And what do you mean it *killed her*? What fucking *killed her*?"

Paul glared at his wife and for the first time in his relationship with her felt something akin to dislike. No, it was more than that, it was almost a burning desire to clap his hand around her mouth and tell her to shut up. 'For once you mouthy cow, just shut the *fuck up*!'

"They were two good people that had had their brains fucked by these bastards. Two, good, caring people from caring professions that managed to break free from their mental handcuffs, so don't start slagging them off Maria. Don't even *think* about slagging off people that you didn't and won't ever know. At least they tried to help those poor sods in that place, unlike some people I could mention."

Mick didn't even have to look at Paul to know who he was referring to and just exhaled the words "oh for fuck's sake!"

Maria was staring at her spouse. Never had he spoken to her with such an edge to his voice. Sure he had shouted and argued with her, she would always be the first to admit that she wasn't easy to live with, but this was different. The black look he was giving her and the anger in his voice quietened her and she stared at the floor not knowing what to say next.

While this exchange was going on, Thomas Burn had made his way to the five screens that were on the wall and was now sitting in a chrome office chair . . . at least it would've been an office chair had it had wheels. What Burn was sitting on was gently moving around without casters and was at least an inch off the ground.

He made a waving motion with his right hand and the screens flashed on causing his guests to all look around. He beckoned with his finger and the Rector held out his arm in an invitation to go and take a look at the movie show that Burn wished to treat them to. Burn's voice was still wet, deep and full of malice as he spoke to them.

"Please note on screen one the fighting outside Kings Cross Station. Note the aggression on the faces of your kinsman. Such a damaging and careless emotion and when seen from a distance rather, well, it looks rather pointless don't you think?"

"Now hold on a minute," responded Maria, "don't give us all that crap about people being aggressive. If you hadn't been screwing with people's minds with your stupid 'conditioning' or whatever you want to call it, *this* wouldn't have happened. So don't blame them, blame yourselves!"

"You are missing the point Mrs Weston, but bear with me and I'll explain more." continued Burn. "Now look at screen two. This was taken in our hotel before Mr Weston and his friends went on their little adventure. Note the calmness of the building. Note how the people there are so much happier with their lot."

"Note how they are walking around like zombies because of what you fuckers have done to them you mean." suggested Paul. "Funny how you haven't any footage of people holding their heads and screaming in pain, blood dripping from their noses. Or have you? Maybe you keep that footage for special occasions, like when you want to get off?"

Mick stifled a laugh at Paul's comment for given the circumstances it was rather funny. Paul just threw him a look as if he was going to shoot him at any given moment.

"Yes," answered the Rector, "I can understand your point of view. But Mr Weston, Paul, if we are guilty of one thing it is that we underestimated the ways that you people are so different from each other and therefore the *conditioning* process affected you all in different ways. It was a silly mistake on our part, granted, but it's one that we have definitely taken notice of. We will make sure that this won't happen again."

"Again? What do you mean again? You still think that you freaks are going to carry on with this?" Maria's grey eyes had widened again at this information.

"Why yes Mrs Weston, Maria. You don't think that we have finished do you? Especially after the mess that Mr Leonard here has made with his willingness to show his little powers to the general public. Look at the next screen, please."

Mick, Maria and Paul looked up at the third screen as it showed the insides of different buildings, all lit by candlelight and all with hundreds of people moving around in them, some being shepherded by men in grey suits and some people in white, doctors style jackets.

"As you can see," explained Burn, "where you were was just one of many places where our work is taking place. You were lucky enough to be in the original building, the place where myself and the Rector would call our base, but moving to different parts of the planet to oversee things isn't a problem for beings such as us. Just look at this room's entrance for example."

Looking around they noticed that the Rector was opening and shutting the door and waving to them. Mick knew that he had been standing by this man only a second ago so the fact that he was now on the other side of the room was mind boggling.

"You mean to say that only you two run the whole show?" Maria asked.

"My dear Maria," retorted Burn, "you flatter us! No, as much as I would love to be in two places at the same time I am afraid that even for someone as talented as me that would be nearly impossible! No, let me introduce you to *some* of my family."

A hissing noise filled the room and Paul knew immediately that it was coming from the containers that he had seen before. He offered advice to those around him.

"I'd pull your jackets over your noses if I were you. This doesn't smell good."

Mick counted five lids slowly opening with a red mist spilling out of the containers they belonged to. This smoke like substance crept towards them and its odour became stronger and sharper until Mick, Leonard and the Westons were all choking back tears, the backs of their throats feeling hot and sore as the vapour travelled up their nasal passages and down their trachea. Maria was hugging Emily to her, pressing her face into her stomach and covering her head with her jacket, but even this was not enough to stop the child from choking as well.

Paul knew it was only a matter of seconds before a red, ugly mass, just like the one that killed the lovely Becky would soon appear from the containers and he wondered how his companions would react when they saw it.

But Paul's response was to feel just as nauseated as the others as instead of a bubbling conglomeration of jelly like substance, figures slowly started to stand upright as the lids went further and further back against the walls.

Then as the red mists cleared a little it was obvious to the onlookers that these beings weren't human and Paul remembered Burn's appearance when he killed his friends and also of how Becky had tried to explain the way that Burn had looked in the hall when the front part of the crowd had been dissolved.

But this was worse.

Through stinging eyes, Maria realised that she was seeing what Burn had become before; but these creatures had changed further and were a blood red, taller, thinner and were absent of any form of clothing. Their heads were perfectly round with a dark, deep indentation about two inches from the top of the head and below were two white circular dots that must be an inch in diameter. These white dots were producing a white luminosity, almost like a mini torchlight, that swept the views before them as they straightened up. Steam was rising up from their hairless heads and was fizzing off their entire bodies. Their mouths opened to reveal fang like teeth and also an abyss full of needles that looked lethal.

Their arms were narrow and almost stick like with hands that were being raised to show wriggling eel like creatures that protruded from them. They had two legs that were also slim and weirdly straight; the only pointer that these obscenities weren't at all robotic was the bubbling, slithering flesh that covered all of them looking as if it was a life-force of its own.

"Jesus save us!" lamented Leonard, his face red from choking and yet full of sheer terror.

"Ah there's that name Jesus again," responded the Rector, "I have learned so much about religions since being here and how useful he would be to you now I am sure, but my dear Leonard you surprise me! Why, I was under the impression that you wanted to be like us? Isn't that so, oh great Leader! No, I am delighted to introduce you to some of my kin. We have kin in all of our other places, in your pathetic form of course, aiding and accelerating the work we have to do. Would you like to shake their . . . . hands?"

Leonard backed away, still covering his nose from the pungent stench, and without seeing a long bar of metal from the broken conditioning chair behind him, he stood on it, lost his footing and fell to the floor in a painful slump.

The Rector slid towards Leonard, moving in a motion that was silky and not giving any indication of using his legs in a walking action. He looked down at Leonard and thrust out his arms, the palms towards the sprawling man. With a twist of his wrists he moved his arms upwards and Leonard started to rise off the floor, his legs straightening under him as he began to hang in the air before them.

"No Rector! I don't want to go near them! Put me down. I only wanted to help the cause. Look, I'm sorry if I got too keen, I didn't mean to cause trouble. Please, *please* let me help you further."

"Ah well," acknowledged the Rector, "*that* is *exactly* what you are going to do, so you need have no worries there my little leader friend. Now, just let us *help* us to *help* you and you will have no more concerns."

Mick shuddered as the Rector's voice started to become deeper and wetter towards the end of his last sentence until it was very similar to the one that Burn was now using. It seemed that Leonard had become aware of this too as his face twisted in dread as the words reached his ears.

Then with another gentle sweeping motion of his arms, the Rector directed Leonard across the chamber and Mick noticed that he was being flown to one of those bigger containers that were spread sporadically around the walls. One of those tall, white boxes with a chrome like front. As Leonard got closer to it there was a loud click and the front of the container started to slide open from right to left reminding Mick of one of those connecting doors in Star Trek only moving more slowly.

Burn had moved to where this container was and as the door opened he gave his audience a little description of what was inside.

"Nowhere to sit I'm afraid Mr Leonard, no room as such, but you will notice that there are a couple of arm and leg clamps that will make you more . . . . comfortable and stop you from becoming too unattached from what needs to be done. Now, if my colleague here can just land you safely in front of this exciting apparatus and I think it would be lovely if one of our guests here could give us a hand. Ladies and Gentlemen, I give you Mr Mick Rogers!"

Mick looked around. What was he being asked to do? Paul gave him a venomous look and Maria stood open mouthed towards him. Burn was beckoning him towards the huge cabinet as Leonard was lowered onto the floor and pushed with ease by Burn inside it where he squirmed uneasily, his face now contorted with panic.

"Come Mr Rogers, for this is just the start for you. It's time for you to hit back at all the pain that you have suffered, all the things in this world that have irritated you for so long. For you Michael, if I may call you Michael, you *know* why this world is so intent on destroying itself and your anger will become so invaluable to us. Come and start your work for us."

"I said he was trouble." muttered Paul.

"Not at all Mr Weston," the Rector replied, still in that voice that was sodden with corruption. "Mr Rogers is quite the eyewitness when it comes to your people. You clearly don't know him at all do you?"

Paul had flinched as the Rector spoke, unaware that his muttering had been heard. Mick was staring at the cabinet and the flailing figure of Leonard as he looked despairingly at Burn who seemed to be daring him to leave the white box.

"What are you waiting for Michael? Come and help Mr Leonard complete his . . . transformation."

Leonard now looked between Mick and Burn after Burn's invitation to the graphic artist. He tried to speak but all that came from his lips was spittle and the beginnings of words. His efforts were ignored as Burn realised that Mick was still rooted to the ground, either not wanting or not able to move.

"Ok Michael, a little inspiration maybe? A little carrot to dangle in front of your indecision? Hmmm, let's see now . . . ."

Using a similar action that the Rector had used with Leonard, Thomas Burn directed his hand towards Emily who Maria was holding onto tightly. But even her secure grip was not enough to stop her sister from rising into the air where she hovered six feet from the ground, Maria reaching out to grab her legs and pull her down . . . an effort that was in vain.

Emily's face, for the first time since she had been in this ex tube station started to crease and she sobbed, tears streaming down her young cheeks as she spoke to Burn.

"Please Uncle Tom, please don't hurt me. I haven't done anything . . anything wrong . . . ."

For a second Mick thought he saw Burn waver at Emily's heartfelt cries, but if there had been a moment's pause it was passed over as soon as Paul shouted his response to this scene.

"Fucking move Rogers! If my sister gets hurt I swear I will fucking kill you! Anymore damage to my family and I'm gonna rip your fucking head off!"

Maria looked at her husband and despite her panic over Emily felt love rush into her heart. She knew that Paul was a good man, otherwise why would she have married him? He wasn't one for outbursts of love though, and this sincere protection of his loved ones had her realising that for all of his shortcomings, Paul really did love her and Emily. She reached out and grasped his hand and then coolly looked at her lover from many years ago. Her voice was so much calmer than she actually felt.

"Do whatever you need to do Mick. You *know* what you need to do."

Mick had seen the look of love that Maria had given to Paul and felt it squeeze his heart until it hurt. But then he looked up at the sobbing figure of Emily and nodding his head walked towards the cabinet that Leonard was now resident in.

Burn nodded towards the inside of the cabinet.

"If you'd be so kind as to just click those arm and leg restraints onto our . . . . leader, then if you look to the right you'll see a metal clamp type appendage hanging from the wall of the cabinet. This needs to be wrapped around and locked onto Mr Leonard's forearm. I wish I could be more graphic in my advice, but you see, this is actually the first time we have used this little . . . . invention of ours. Ha! *Relax* Mr Leonard! You really are letting yourself down you know!"

Mick did as he was bid. The arm restraints were circular clip looking items that were parallel to the leader's hands, looking like handcuffs that had had their chain removed and been imbedded into the back of the cabinet, their chrome material just adding to this illusion. The leg restraints were similar if slightly bigger and when Leonard had been secured he stood with arms and legs parted as if he were a standing sacrifice to an unknown deity.

The 'metal clamp type appendage' looked more like a chrome version of the black sleeve that you see connected to a blood pressure monitor; it was on a thick, black wire but it was malleable enough for

Mick to be able pull it straight and wrap it shut with a click around Leonard's left forearm.

"Beautifully done." rasped Thomas Burn.

Mick looked at the speaker, trying to ignore the fact that steam now seemed to be coming with increasing flows from the figure that was clearly finding this an enjoyable process.

"What are you going to do to him? What did you mean, the *first time* you have used this thing?"

"Just watch and learn Michael, as indeed will I and the . . . Rector! Ha, isn't this exciting! I think, if you don't mind me saying so, that this will be a resounding success, but as we have seen with your kind, Mr Mistake does like to make the odd appearance does he not? Now, we *had* planned to close the door before the process begins, but in matters of science and as we need to see if all goes well, obviously, I think we should leave it open so that you can enjoy the process too. Now, are you ready oh great and powerful leader?"

Leonard's panic was now such that his words resembled those of a child that has not got his or her own way.

"Nooo, I have only tried to please you! I did as you asked! I have done as I was told to! *You* encouraged me to be the leader, *you* told me that I was the one that could change people's ways! Why are you doing this to me? Why are you doing this to . . . ."

His words stopped abruptly as Burn held out his hand towards the cabinet and Leonard's body stiffened. His face was pale and emotionless and there was no movement from the leader or the cabinet. But there was a hum, that stopping and starting hum that Paul had noticed and it was getting louder.

Maria called to Emily to close her eyes and the child responded by shutting them so tightly that her little face creased up.

The acrid smell of before returned. It had lingered in the air since the creatures from the containers had appeared and stood their ground, but now it was more powerful again and was coming from Leonard.

His clothes started to singe. Not catching fire but seeming to turn brown, letting off puffs of black smoke and this odour of burning material mixed with that putrid smell that came naturally from these creatures.

Then bit by bit, clothing fell to the floor; Leonard's jacket, shirt and casual slacks. When eventually his plain, light blue boxer shorts browned and fell to blackened rags too, Maria noticed that the pubes around his wrinkled penis were starting to singe as well and then she looked up and saw that the hair on his head was smoking and falling away too. She wondered at noticing the burning pubes first and just put it down to generic female interest.

Leonard's body started to glow pink which in turn became a darker and darker red. His skin started to loosen and bubble. Despite no noise coming from the ex leader, his face suggested such agony that Mick felt his teeth go on edge and he started to feel nauseous as Leonard's head started to squeeze inwards, losing its oval shape and becoming more round. A tapping noise against the cabinet from halfway down and Mick noticed that Leonard's fingers had narrowed and become longer; they were moving as if they no longer had bone in them and it was their contact against the cabinet that had caused the sound that had alerted Mick.

"Oh my God! Oh my God!" Maria was screaming, but not at the change in Theobald Leonard. She was staring at the Rector who was standing naked, red, steaming, his eyes replaced with small, glowing white dots and that strange indentation, his mouth fanged and needled. He had become like one of the creatures from the containers.

Mick noticed that Paul was looking in the direction of Burn and he didn't need to turn his head to know that Burn had joined the Rector in changing too. The sharp smell from that mortal was enough to let him know what had happened.

The cabinet that held what used to be Theobald Leonard had lowered its humming noise and now returned to the level it had been before. Mick looked at the ex leader who had developed that indentation across his forehead and whose eyes were half open. Mick noticed that despite the changes that had taken place, Leonard's eyes were still in place, not the same as the likes of Burn and the Rector and yet when they suddenly blinked open he had still expected the white beam that came from those creatures. Instead, there were just red caverns looking to Mick as if Leonard had suffered the worst case of bloodshot on medical record.

Leonard's mouth opened. No fangs or needles in there but it was the sounds that made Mick shudder.

"*Betor mundi, betor mundo, ai friz a mundo, sssssss . . . . Betor mundi, betor mundo, ai friz a mundo, sssssssssssss . . . .*"

As if this wasn't enough to freak him out, this mantra started to be repeated around the chamber as Burn and Leonard's 'kin' joined in.

"Betor mundi, betor mundo, ai friz a mundo, ssssss . . . . Betor mundi, betor mundo, ai friz a mundo, sssssssssss . . . . Betor mundi, betor mundo, ai friz a mundo, ssssss . . . . Betor mundi, betor mundo, ai friz a mundo, sssssssssss . . . ."

Louder and louder these unearthly words became, Burn and the Rector now also taking part when suddenly Burn raised his arm and they ceased.

Now Burn spoke with more grating spite than previously heard.

"Not a total success, but not a total failure instead. Now, Mr Rogers, do you think that your people would take to such a change so readily? Once we have them so happy and calm and willing to do as we please, to join our *cause*, I feel that we will have a plentiful supply of future participants." He pointed to the screen that showed the 'brothers and sisters' in different candlelit buildings, wandering around with the guards and 'doctors'. "Just look at them all, wandering around so calmly, getting their friends to join in. Some of them even getting rid of those that offended them! Amazing! I am sure that you would approve of that Michael. Haven't you felt the need to offload those that irritate you?"

"You fucking freak Rogers!" Paul spat out.

"Ssshh!" returned Maria. "Let him speak!"

"Before I say anything," replied Mick, "let Emily down. She is innocent in all this, let her down."

Burn raised a hand and Emily floated back down. She ran to Maria and Paul and hugged them both.

"I don't know who you think I am," continued Mick, "I don't know why you speak of me as having such a problem with people. I am sure that a lot of people feel stressed with life in general."

"Ah but not like you, your feelings of *stress* are quite indicative of a person that knows how to change things for the better, but I fear that people who know you see you as a bit of a dreamer, am I right? As a bit of a *freak* as your friend over there says."

Mick, despite his abhorrence of this Burn creature, knew that he *was* right. Wasn't that why Maria had left him? Wasn't that why he was pretty much friendless and without a decent girl by his side? *Hmmm, he has you there Micky boy. So, what to do? Let's face it. Maria will always stay with Paul and you will always be fucked up by what you believe is wrong with the world. Maybe these sods have got a point after all?*

"I don't really care what Paul thinks of me. He wouldn't be the first person to slag me off anyway. Although, before he knew of my connection with his wife he seemed to like me, so work that one out!"

Paul said nothing and Maria looked at Mick with genuine fondness. What the fuck had he got himself into now?

"But you feel aggrieved don't you Michael?" suggested the Rector. "Help us with our work. You will find it so much more rewarding. We need your energies, your clear and honest opinions of what is wrong with this planet to help us. We have been aware of you for some time so what do you say?"

"But you still haven't told us what you *work* is!" exclaimed Mick. "For God's sake, what is your reason for being here?"

Burn raised one of his tentacled hands and flicked it towards the screens. All of them showed the fighting that had kicked off outside the station.

"Aggression." grated Burn. "Aggression in so much in your way of life. Wars against those of different cultures and religions. Wars against those who prefer a certain deity and the sinless that make themselves hypocrites with their hatred and bile towards those who think differently. Wars for the protection of fuels. Wars for the protection of pieces of land."

"People who kill for fun." joined in the Rector. "People who kill for sexual thrills. People who kill because their brains have malfunctioned and are telling them to kill. People who kill because it is their law. People who kill and maim because they think it will impress others and make them feel part of a crowd or even attractive to the opposite sex. People who kill because they are too drunk or high to know what they are doing."

"Countries run by people that lie. Countries that are led by those that refuse to listen to their people's views even if they know better. Countries that are so poor because their leaders take all the money that their countries have and leave their own to die hungry, painful deaths."

"Anger on the roads. Anger on the streets. Anger against those that are paid to nurse, heal and educate. Anger against different sporting teams! Anger, aggression and hatred." The Rector took in a wet breath before he continued. "Now, you may ask what this has to do with us? Well, with such a weak species before us we would be ignorant to ignore the opportunities to expand our own race. Knowing of the way that a lot of your people are attracted to religions and other such cults and knowing that there are a lot of people like Michael here who want a better way of life and despair with the world, it made perfect sense to get people together and condition their minds to a utopian vision. You see, aggression is negative and therefore is never going to offer any final answers but it is also dangerous; by removing aggression in people it would make our *cause*, our desire to eventually remove your type from this rock so much easier."

"Your species is on the path to self destruction anyway." agreed Burn. "We are only speeding up the process and probably saving your planet in the meantime. You morons don't deserve to live here and we are going to make sure that you no longer will."

Maria stepped forward. Her head was spinning at everything that was taking place but her sense of right was as strong as ever.

"What you bastards fail to understand is that yes, we have made mistakes, *huge* mistakes. We continue to make them and probably always will. And if they make us a 'weak species' then fine, we are weak. But surely by rushing in and taking over because you want somewhere else for your freaks to prosper is just as bad as all the wars that take place in this world? It's the same thing! How can *you* be so hypocritical?"

"No!" snapped Burn. "You have had your chance to lead fruitful lives, but generally you have made a mess of it all. Can you honestly say that there will ever be a time when your people will have no hatred in the world? None at all? No, I don't suppose you could."

"It's called human nature." suggested Mick.

"Ah," rejoined the Rector, "the blessed human nature. Well, *that* makes it all right then, doesn't it? I mean Michael, it has stood you in good stead hasn't it? You, who are so happy with your lot? I am surprised that you don't want to kill Paul right here and now. Well, let me help you with that. Let me help you get some relief from the pain that you feel in your heart. Let me give you a revenge that will never be revenged and that will surely help you see that we mean *you* no harm, only help. We can make you powerful Michael. Isn't recognition all that you have ever wanted?"

Paul was about to yell his feelings about this but felt himself being lifted up like Leonard and Emily had been before him.

He felt powerless as he drifted through the air. Maria, as with Emily before, tried to grab hold of him and stop his flight but was again unable to do so. Emily screamed for her Uncle Paul to get down, now letting her young emotions free which Mick felt strangely comforted by—she had seemed so distant ever since he met her and now she was acting like he felt a little child should.

The Rector was orchestrating Paul towards one of the containers which held the kin and as he got closer the being inside it reached out with its thin, red, bubbled arms in welcome to the air traveller. Paul fought this force as hard as he could but as he got closer to the ghastly creature, its powerful odour piercing his nostrils, he realised that it was hopeless. They would do to him whatever they wanted—he just hoped it would be quick. As that member of the kin laid its wriggling distensions on Paul, he gagged as he felt them hot and slimy even through the sleeves of his jacket.

Paul was slowly lowered to the floor and facing the others he felt the kinsman wrap his long arms around him as if to stop him from moving.

"Now," said Burn, "now Michael, here is a great opportunity for you. We have our own form of what you people call hypnosis to make others do our work, we used it on Emily ages ago as we knew that it would drag Maria into our plans and maybe you too, but I don't think you need that influence. I think your anger and bitterness will be enough to carry you through. Take this blade, and like little Emily, use it for good. Thrust it into this murdering man and use your constant animosity for something positive and worthwhile."

Burn had a six inch knife in his hands with a slim blade that curved slightly upwards; it was so sharp and serrated that Mick would normally have doubts about even picking it up. Its handle was black with two slim bands of blue tinged chrome about an inch apart wrapped around it. Burn held this murderous weapon gingerly by the blade and offered Mick the handle.

The artist looked at Paul's growling face and at the disgusting thing that was holding him. This creature seemed to be smiling as if what Mick had to do was a good joke.

Mick took the knife and held it momentarily, feeling that it was heavier than it looked. He turned to Paul and stepped towards him with the blade pointing towards him.

"Mick noooooo! You can't! You can't! Please, I'll do anything! Don't hurt him please!"

Mick had an instant where Maria's offer of 'doing anything' appealed to him. *All these years I have been gagging for her to come back to me and say that and all I had to was walk towards her husband with a vicious looking knife and surrounded by beings from another world. Blimey, if only I'd known that was the answer!*

Paul didn't move but as Mick and the knife approached him he saw the horror on the faces of Maria and Emily and realised that this wasn't just about dying quickly, this was about the hurt it was cause those he loved. And what would happen to them should he die? Would they persuade Mick to kill them too?

"You gonna kill me then Mick? Just do as they ask you to? What, do you think Maria will go back to you just because you get me out of the way? She loves me not you. Killing me won't solve your problems you know."

Hearing Paul say this didn't help Maria's husband's cause. Mick hadn't felt anger, he had felt a strange curiosity as he let the blade get closer to its intended victim, curious as to how Paul would react and if Maria would just let it happen. *Maybe she would eh? Maybe she actually loves you after all and would be quite happy for Paul to be out of the way?* But Maria's cries and Paul's insistence of her love for him did trigger resentment and now Mick Rogers pressed the end of the blade just above Paul's 'adam's apple', the very tip of it causing a small hole and a miniscule river of blood to seep out, and with eyes narrowed spoke to his opponent.

"It's better if you shut up Paul. I'm not gonna lie and say that I don't have feelings for Maria anymore, I do. I always have done and probably always will. She may treat me like shit for the rest of my life and you can threaten me as much as it makes you happy, but I can't stop the way I feel. Don't you think that I've tried? Christ knows I've tried! But I knew ages ago I was wasting my time. I don't need you and your fucking boasting to give me extra grief. I don't believe for a second that I could be just friends with her and I wouldn't even try because it would make things too complicated for all involved and believe it or not I don't want that. I'm sorry if you think that I'm responsible for you all being here, but do you *really* believe that I would put the life of someone that I still love at peril? Not only her but her little sister too? No Paul, you have me all wrong. I would *never* screw things up for you and Maria. The best man won I guess. You have a wonderful wife—you should always cherish her."

"That would be difficult Michael," responded Burn, "for you are to end his miserable existence here and now, right? No, I believe what you meant to say was that he should *have cherished* her. Clearly he didn't and he has lost. *You* are the better man Michael. There is nothing stupid about you at all—very wise I would suggest."

Maria's voice was choked with emotion as she pleaded with Mick to spare her husband.

"Mick nooo, I'm so sorry I hurt you. I know I hurt you but what could I do? Please don't take it out on Paul, he isn't to blame, *I* am! If you should kill anyone it should be me! I am the one that has messed up your life. Kill *me* not him!"

"No!" screamed Emily as she hugged Maria tightly around the waist, her little face now full of anguish.

"Why kill her Michael?" countered Burn, "when we could make her do whatever you want her to do? How about your own little sex slave, would you like that? Maria's body on tap whenever you needed it. Just imagine the fun, the *power* of it all! Why, we could do that now for you as a little gift, maybe get her to undress for you? Would you like that Michael? Or maybe you should kill her nasty little husband first, so that he doesn't feel anymore embarrassment? Make your decision but make it now."

Mick was so close to Paul and the creature that he could feel Paul's deepening breath on his face and the evil stench wafting from the kinsman. The light from the kinsman's eyes were on him, lighting and warming up his face like two small sun lamps and Mick felt himself push the blade into Paul slightly more, enough for more blood to dribble from the small wound. The artist whispered to his love's husband.

"I'm sorry Paul. So sorry."

"No Mick, no DON'T!"

Maria screamed at Paul's panicked plea and then fell silent as she stood and stared at the event that fell before her.

Mick had put himself in a stance that showed he was going to thrust the knife deep into Paul's throat.

Then at the last second he pulled back, the knife glinting in the bright lights of the chamber and showing beads of Paul's blood on its end. With a roar that came from somewhere deep inside him, Mick directed the knife at the face of the thing holding Paul and embedded it deep into the indentation across its forehead.

The creature screeched as the brutal weapon disappeared halfway up the blade. Mick instinctively wriggled it, feeling it rub against hard bone like substance and squelching in something like jelly. This caused the kinsman to screech even louder and let go of Paul who moved away from the deafening howl of the being that was swaying from left to right, not making any attempt to grab the artist's hand that was pushing the edges of the knife deeper into its red, steaming face.

The other kinsmen in the containers started to screech too, as if they were feeling the pain of their family member and soon the chamber was full of an intense howl that Paul realised was not unlike the alarm noise that had been triggered off in the HQ.

Burn and the Rector were howling too, their searchlight eyes beaming this way and that and their bodies moving back and forth, their skins bubbling even more ferociously. Leonard was howling and trying to break free of the restraints that still held him.

As these beings swayed, Mick saw an opportunity and called for Paul, Maria and Emily to get out. Paul grabbed the powerful torch that Leonard had left on the floor and as they went through the door and down the stairs onto the old platform, Mick saw that old vision of himself. *They may not be dragons breathing fire, but my God they have something in them that is dangerously hot.*

Paul turned to Mick on the platform as they quickly walked.

"What can I say? Thank you?"

"Let's not talk about it eh?" replied Mick. "It seems that hurting one of that lot hurts the others too. Quite sweet in a nasty sort of way."

"You could've made me do what you wanted. They said that. You had a chance to get your own back on me." stated Maria.

"I could never make *you* do what I wanted Mezza. What would be the point of them hypnotising you to strip off and be my lovely little 'sex slave'! After all, I know what you look like naked anyway!" He said this with a mischievous smile and Paul, after an initial scowl, quickly saw the funny side and laughed. Maria clapped her hands over Emily's ears but the little one just giggled. As Paul smiled he raised his arm in mock anger and Mick noticed that he had also picked up a length of chrome tubing that seemed to come from the broken conditioning chair. It was almost a metre in length and looked quite weighty.

"You come out armed then?"

"Well, I thought I might need it as a crutch to get up them bloody steps. Have you forgotten that we have to get up them bloody quickly to get out of this place?"

"Why this place though? Why a defunct tube station?" wondered Maria.

"Well, they scare me, don't they scare you?" asked the artist.

"Not really. Bloody dark and damp though, although not as dodgy as that passage me and Burny came through." answered Paul.

"Yes, you did make a surprising entrance."

"One minute we were in that HQ, all the brothers and sisters wandering around lost or screaming in pain, the next he was dragging me through this passage. God it was narrow. There were mouldy brick walls inches either side of us but he managed to pull me here as if I was light as a feather, I swear my feet didn't touch the ground. I couldn't see a bloody thing but he could and now I've seen their weird torch eyes I know why!"

"*All* screaming in pain?" queried Maria.

"It's a long story. I'll tell you when we get out of here."

"*When* you get out of here Mr Weston? Oh, trust me, you will *never* get out of here now. Not even you Mr Rogers. You have made the biggest error of your miserable life."

As they talked they had approached the opening that led to the link between the two old platforms but they turned around abruptly at the hate filled voice behind them. The creature that had been Thomas Burn was floating there, the redness of his skin glowing and pulsating in the darkness.

Mick looked through the small passage to the other platform and coming into view, blocking the entrance to that platform, appeared the Rector creature who was now mouthing that weird mantra from before, his fangs and needle teeth seeming to glow in the darkness.

"*Betor mundo, betor mundi, a friz a mundo, sssss. Betor mundo, Betor mundi, a friz a mundo, sssssssssssssssss.*"

"Oh God, oh God, oh God, oh God!" moaned Maria as she pointed behind Burn. There behind him were more of the creatures, the kinsmen of Burn and the Rector. They floated spitefully along with their thin beams of hot light directed at them.

Mick looked around and saw the entrance to the lift and shuddered. Even if they forced the rusted gate open, jumping down into the shaft wouldn't save them, even if he did actually find the guts to go down into it.

"So what now Micky boy?" asked a shaken Paul, "any answers? Cause I'm sorry mate but I think we're fucked."

Mick looked down at Emily who was clinging onto Maria's leg and sobbing. He felt like a rat trapped in the dead end of a sewer. He looked up at Burn and hoped that his words would at least give little Emily and her guardians a chance of getting out if not him.

"Look, wait Burn! Before you do anything . . . hasty. You said you wanted me to join you? Well, I can't say that the idea excites me but if you really want to use my mind, and God knows why you do, then I'll come quietly. You can even do to me what you did to Leonard. But please, please let these three go. Look at Emily, can you really say that you would want to hurt someone as gorgeous as her? You may not be human, but surely even you can understand that to do that would be just wrong."

As he spoke these words a warm breeze started to push itself through the link between the platforms. It was obvious that another train was making its way through the old station and as Mick concentrated he realised that it was coming from the southbound platform, the one that the Rector and Leonard had just appeared from.

"Why do you think we'd use you now you stupid man? You may give chances in your pathetic world but you have seriously wounded one of my kin and caused us all great pain. I suppose you have shown great courage though Michael, a courage which has surprised us. You see, you may be mentally suitable with all of your negative views of your world, but you have never had much courage to change anything have you? You really did surprise us, did he not . . . . Rector?"

Paul listened to Burn's increasingly wet and malignant tones and he felt he had to ask the question that the creature's words had prompted in him. As he asked it the breeze grew stronger and now there was that rumbling noise that was familiar to anyone who has ever waited for a tube train. He started to raise his voice more as the rumbling grew louder.

"Caused you *all* so much pain? Mentally or physically? Or both? You didn't look very healthy when Micky boy here stabbed your ugly kinperson with that knife! You mean to say that you felt that pain too?"

"Whatever pain we may have felt Mr Weston will be nothing to what I will put you and your family through, Emily included. She served her purpose and now we shall be revenged for your treatment of our younger kin. You see that is the problem with your species, when it comes to the crunch you just don't . . . ."

Burn didn't finish his sentence. As he had been speaking, raising his disgusting voice to combat the approaching train, Mick had become more and more incensed at the thought of little Emily and Maria being hurt and he had been staring, his brows furrowed, in the direction of the southbound platform. His frustrations finally spilling over, he spun around.

Before he knew what was happening, Paul felt Mick grab the tubing he was carrying and as if in slow motion saw him whip around and fling it in the direction of Burn. He only had seconds to think that this really wasn't going to save them when Mick gave a yell that sounded almost guttural and rushed head down towards the figure of the Rector that was still standing in the entrance to the platform. The breeze became harder, the rumbling louder and to their horror they saw Mick, his arms wrapped around the Rector's pulsating body and pushing him with all of his might towards what would have been the platform's edge.

As they neared it Mick gave one last heave and felt his feet leave the floor as he and the stunned looking Rector headed towards the track and the third rail.

Throughout this manoeuvre Mick saw himself standing at King's Cross station, the very station this train was heading towards, his toes over the platform as thoughts of a quick ending had genuinely flashed through his tired, numb mind.

The only thing that stopped me then was that nobody would've cared. Just another loony that chose a gruesome way to end it all. Completely pointless. At least I'm doing something positive for once and taking a dangerous freak with me.

He heard Maria scream his name and a small smile started on his lips. He could've thought of worse ways to go than one where his unrequited love was screaming for him.

Mick and the Rector landed on the track, the artist on top as the Rector's back pressed against the third rail.

There was a loud bang. Blue sparks and smoke flew from the area where they had landed and Mick momentarily felt power surging through the Rector before he was catapulted back towards the old platform's wall his head making contact with the old brickwork.

The Rector remained against the rail, stuck to it, as the voltage surged through his red, throbbing frame. His mouth was open but no sound came out. But Burn and their kin was now screeching once more but this time the noise hurt the ears of Paul, Maria and Emily so much that they fell to their knees, fingers pathetically trying to block the assaulting wail.

Through this excruciating outcry Paul noticed that its tone had started to change a little. From the one of similar anguish that they had heard in the room with the monitors, it was losing its edge and was becoming deeper and stronger and . . . . victorious. He didn't know why that adjective had occurred to him but there was a definite positive vibe now coming from Burn and his kin and as he looked up there was a sickening grin on the face of Burn as he looked alternately at Paul and then at the Rector.

The Rector was still pinned, shaking to the rail but he was growing. With each massive throb of electricity his body enhanced, became wider and taller, his skin bubbling more ferociously and glowing, if possible, even redder and now Paul saw that he was grinning a similar vile grin like that of Burn's. This creature was *enjoying* the electricity!

Now the rumbling was closer and as the dusty wind blew strongly in their faces, ruffling their hair and adding its heavy timbre to the horrendous noises coming from Burn and his kin, Paul noticed that these disgusting beasts, with the exception of Leonard, were expanding too and now they chanted their mantra with an ever stronger purpose.

"*Betor mundo, betor mundi, a friz a mundo, sssss. Betor mundo, Betor mundi, a friz a mundo, sssssssssssssssss. Betor mundo, betor mundi, a friz a mundo, sssss. BETOR MUNDO, BETOR MUNDI, A FRIZ A MUNDO SSSSSS.*"

The screams of his wife and sister in law. The sickening hymn of Burn's family. The crashing of the steel wheels on the track as the wind blew and the rumbling reached its apex . . . .

Paul flinched as the next Piccadilly line southbound tube rushed from the blackness of the tunnel and cringed as beneath the racket of the train he heard a deep bumping noise. He turned to look at the flashing lights of the carriages, vaguely seeing the blurred passengers as they commuted and thought the train was doing a slight jump as it journeyed on.

Then the back red lights of the train disappeared into the darkness, the rumbling subsided and the wind abated. Maria and Emily were whimpering and clutching onto each other, but apart from this there was silence.

Paul looked at the thing that had been Thomas Burn. It was swaying silently, and a red jelly like substance started to bubble from his mouth. Its eyes were no longer glowing and the skin, which had previously been a disgusting, palpitating material was starting to liquefy. Burn's head tilted upwards slowly towards Paul and he tried to raise one of his thin arms in order to make a final point to him, but with a wet, slushing outbreath, he collapsed to the ground where puddles of red, gooey liquid started to pool around his motionless body.

"It's happening to them all Paul. My God, what's happened to them?"

Maria was pointing at all of the kin and just like his wife had said, they were collapsing in a dissolved mess that increased the redness that was running over the dirt and the rocks of the old station floor.

Then they saw slumped against the lift gate the body of Leonard. His red eyes were staring at the opposite wall but apart from red liquid pouring from his mouth he didn't move.

Paul walked slowly towards the track and pointed the torch towards it. There, lying motionless, with deep lines across his chest and legs as if he had been set to with a circular saw, was the Rector. Electricity was clearly still entering his body but the reaction was a gentle jerking motion. There was more of the red jelly substance that had come from the rest now seeping from the Rector's open mouth and those clearly fatal deep lines.

"The train killed him and his death destroyed the others!" gasped Maria. "They really were connected to each other in more ways than one."

Paul looked at his wife as if he had remembered something really important.

"Dan and Becky! They had some sort of connection too. They had a career that involved caring, showing compassion for others, and they managed to free their minds somehow of the conditioning! Whatever it was that those machines were doing to people it seems that their ignorance of the empathy that humans *can* have was able to offer a release to their zombie like state. Becky said that seeing Burn in his proper form shocked her mind back but I think there was more to it than that."

"It seems," Maria added, "that they concentrated so much on the bad side of the human race that they didn't recognise the strength of the good side."

A moan from the old platform caused them to turn around abruptly, their hearts in their mouths. Mick. They had forgotten all about the man who had triggered off the creatures demise.

CHAPTER THIRTY THREE

"How you doing hero?"

Mick looked around the hospital ward, feeling the tightness of the bandages that had been placed around his chest and then smiled as Maria approached him and looked at the place where his head had smacked against the platform wall.

"Been better Mezza. Sorry, Maria!"

"You can call me Mezza. I don't mind you know."

"No, maybe I shouldn't. Too much history attached to it. Water under bridge etc." Maria smiled and Mick sighed. He knew her smile so well and still it made him feel light headed. "Have the police been to the old hotel yet?"

"Oh yes. And the tube station. Did you know that there's been talk of them opening it up again? Not sure I'd feel happy using it or going through it now though. Anyway, they have all kinds of people looking at those that were in there."

"And all that fighting?"

"It seems that it all calmed down. Maybe Burn and his kin being killed did for the influence they had on them all? As we saw, they were seriously connected to each other in quite a few ways. I think the conditioning hypnotised others in being a little bit like them. But, no Burn, no Rector, no influence! As for why a tube station. Well it seems that there was a lot of electricity still running through that old station and you saw what it was doing to the Rector before he got run over. They clearly took their strength from it."

Mick rubbed his chest and drew in a sharp breath.

"You still in pain?"

"Well, my head seems to hurt the most from where I whacked it, but I get the odd twinge every now and then yes. How is Emily?"

"She's fine. She has been so brave the poor little thing. She's with Paul. He's taken her to Hamley's in order to bring her back to some sort of normality."

Maria sat down on the plastic chair next to Mick's bed and holding his hand looked at him deep into his eyes.

"Paul's ok too. That's if you wanted to ask!"

"Of course! I was just going to. Just wanted to ask about Emily first though!"

"Mmm I bet you were Supermick!"

Mick looked down at the severe white cotton of his bed sheet and felt Maria squeeze his hand.

"Sorry Mick. But, you were really brave you know. I thought I knew you so well but . . well . . . you did surprise me. Sorry, but it's true. But one thing I want to know. You said to Paul that you could never be just friends with me. Is that true? After everything we've been through surely you no longer mean that?"

"Well, I did but . . . no maybe not. It would make sense to me in one way but in another it might help if I knew where you were and that you were ok, if that makes any sense? It was the not knowing what you were doing that made me think of you more so maybe if we did stay friends then it would help me get over you?"

Maria grinned, got up to give Mick a quick peck on the cheek and sat back down again.

"Spoken in the Mickish language that I know so well! And yes it does sort of make sense! Paul is ok with you now, just behave yourself ok?"

"As if I wouldn't! Anyway, it's better to have loved and lost . . ."

"Than never to have loved at all! You ok Mr Rogers? Anything I can get you?"

The saying had been finished by a slim, blonde nurse who had looked at the chart at the end of Mick's bed and who flashed him a bright, sunny smile. "Or is your own personal nurse giving you anything you need?"

"He's ok Rachel. I'm sure you'll be the first to know if he starts moaning though, ain't that right Mick?"

As Rachel moved away Maria laughed as Mick followed the departing nurse's movements.

"She's a lovely girl is Rachel. 24, split up with her boyfriend three months ago. Likes nights in, pubs, the cinema and an unerring devotion to David Beckham. Would Mr Rogers like me to get in contact with her for you?"

Mick blushed and turned quickly to his teasing ex.

"I look nothing like David Beckham!"

"No, this is true," responded Maria. "But your views of the world will obviously keep her riveted on a cosy night in! Now, is that a no or a yes?"

Mick laughed and then groaned as his beloved Maria winked and went to make for a pen.